LEAGUE OF THE STAR

by N.R. CRUSE

LEAGUE
OF THE
STAR

by N.R. CRUSE

Stonehouse Publishing
www.stonehousepublishing.ca
Alberta, Canada

Stonehouse Publishing Inc is an independent publishing house, incorporated in 2014.

Cover design and layout by Janet King
Cover illustration by Rachel Cruse
Printed in Canada

National Library of Canada Cataloguing in Publication Data
Cruse, N. R.
The League of the Star
Novel
ISBN: 978-0-9866494-6-2 (bound)
ISBN 978-0-9866494-2-4 (paperback)
First Edition

Marcel de la Croix to Henri Renault

England, December 16th, 1792

Dear Friend,

My passage to England could not have been more strange. I was utterly disgusted with the world, and I hardly need add, myself. I averted my eyes generally from the assortment of pathetic souls fleeing their own unfortunate country.

We were supposed to leave tomorrow, but there was a fright and the Captain feared the ship might be searched. The haste with which things were decided upon left many sad souls staring out at our vessel upon departure, and I, sorry creature I have become, felt only relieved to be one of those on board.

It is difficult to tell the high from low in our company, for no one wishes to broadcast his wealth if he has it, and every Count wears a shabby coat. Or at least that is the general rule, as you will hear.

I could have wished the entire boat to hell, so foul was my mood. I went below deck, where I found a quiet corner to bury myself. A few other miserable souls occupied my vicinity, but I paid them no attention at first.

My thoughts were occupied with the most painful reflections and memories, which I shall not mention here. Presently, I became aware of a little commotion around me. Directly across from me, two young noblewomen and an elder female companion were seated. The first young woman appeared about twenty. Her dress was not designed to conceal her condition, as everything announced her to be a woman of wealth and property. Property! What do I say? What noble retains their property in France during these times? Nevertheless, you understand me.

Her bearing was haughty, and I pitied her. Her future life will surely be miserable if she cannot be humble. But what happiness is in store for any unfortunate refugee? Beggars from our own land, reliant on the hospitality of a country that it has been our delight to scorn these last two hundred years.

Forgive me. As I was saying, beside her and leaning upon her shoulder asleep, was a younger girl, perhaps fifteen, more simply dressed. The fretful old woman beside the first girl had every appearance of the small-minded simpleton families often select to help illuminate the minds of their daughters.

What was surprising was that they seemed to have undertaken this perilous journey with no other guide, servant, or protector. The exchange that caught my attention seemed to have proceeded from the Captain's insistence that one of the trunks they had brought with them be unlocked, having attracted attention because of its heaviness.

"I must needs know what contraband is brought aboard my ship," he declared, causing the old attendant to comply in fear. Had they been able to rely on anyone who had practical knowledge of these matters, they might have been able to satisfy the Captain privately, but as it was, the small trunk was opened publicly, and its contents of gold and jewellery were revealed to anyone who happened to be nearby.

The Captain was modest enough in what he confiscated, under the pretence of recompensing himself for the additional risk he took allowing them to take French gold from France. Such a claim was preposterous, since it is illegal to transport emigres at all. Nevertheless, one may not quarrel with a Captain on his vessel. But who, I ask you, would send three women out on their own with a trunk full of treasure, without making any effort to disguise it or to protect them? Might they not have concealed some of it about them, or distributed it evenly throughout their other luggage?

Needless to say, it was difficult to ignore their plight, for the sight of the treasure had attracted the desperate and brutish, who no longer feared any civilized institution. What is there, after all, in nobility, government, religion, or even the intellectual class, which can claim an ounce of respect from the average Frenchman, who has spent the last five years or more witnessing the ruination of his country at the hands of each? The common man understands strength, and this power will be respected by him while it is wielded. Principles, in and of themselves, are reserved for those whose lot in life has granted them leisure to contemplate their deeper meanings. For whatever good that may do him!

"Well," cried a dirty-looking fellow, addressing everyone and no one, "my needs are not less than the Captain's. One hears enough about equality nowadays, and I swear I've not had my share!"

Two or three instantly echoed his sentiment, emboldening him to go further. He moved towards the ladies, and making a mock bow in their direction (the youngest was still asleep), he said, "Pardon me, ladies, but equality demands it. I shan't take more than I'm due, like the captain."

The elder lady seemed as though she would faint, but the younger one, who was evidently the owner of the chest, seemed not less outraged than frightened, wearing an expression of helpless contempt.

I intended to keep to myself the entire journey and disguised in a tattered pedlar's cloak, had attracted attention from no one. All the same, I could not witness these friendless women prayed upon by idle opportunists without doing something. As the first man stooped forward to meddle with the latch whose lock had been carelessly restored by the Captain, I stood up quickly and drew my sword.

"What is your business here, my good fellows? What right have you to these ladies' possessions? The Captain, to be sure, can please what he likes aboard his own ship, but he shall not mind if I kill one or two of you, since you have paid your fare in advance."

"If these are your relatives," replied the foremost, "I shall heed you, but otherwise, 'twould be better if you would see about your business."

"My business is mine to decide, and my protection is mine to accord as I like. I assure you, you shall not live to enjoy what you seek to possess."

The sort of scoundrels who would steal from defenceless women are not the sort who relish a contest, and therefore I was able to clear the room of the three or four fortune-seekers, relatively easily.

I sent a servant for the Captain and when he arrived I told him what had occurred, adding, "I am sure you will agree with me that these respectable women must be sheltered from the rabble for the remainder of the voyage."

"As you wish," said he, with a shrug, adding, "It is foolish for women to travel unprotected, but these are strange times. It is fortunate for them they have met you."

With that the four of us were left in silence. The old woman soon ventured to express her gratitude in the most exalted language.

"We shall be forever indebted to you for your kindness to us. Oh, how Providence has blessed us! How many terrors does one feel when travelling with such innocents. You have preserved Mademoiselle's dowry!"

Here she was interrupted by the elder girl, who said, "Thank you, Monsieur, you have laid us under heavy obligation."

Her manner belied her words, however, for it seemed clear she felt such debts amply discharged by the privilege of speaking to her.

I merely nodded and introduced myself as M. Gramont, a name I have used intermittently while travelling. The choice was arbitrary; the only Gramont I had ever known was a lawyer. The older woman identified herself as Gaspar, and the girl who had just spoken was Mlle de Courteline, while the younger was Mlle Vallon. I retook my seat, preparing to resume my contemplations. It was at this moment that Mlle Vallon opened her eyes and fixed them upon me, with an expression I could never describe. I tried at first to ignore her, under the assumption that she would look away, but she did not. She looked at me as if she could look at me her whole life without lessening her amazement. The smallest gesture or expression on my part caused her to jump, and her hands clung fiercely to her companion's arm, till the other complained that she hurt her.

One rarely meets with a girl of that age whose eyes are not lowered almost as soon as they are raised, and yet here was a young woman who seemed afraid to blink in my presence.

After several minutes, I could not prevent myself from inquiring after this strange phenomenon, saying to the elder girl, "Be so good as to tell me, Madam, why Mlle Vallon stares at me? Have I offended in some way?"

"No, Monsieur," returned she calmly. "She looks at you this way because she has never seen a man."

I paused for a long moment, unwilling to understand what she had said.

"That is not possible, surely?" I exclaimed, at last.

"Of course it is. She is my cousin, and she has been raised in a convent."

"Then there are Priests..." persisted I.

"Her mother donated her fortune on the condition that it was so. I assure you, till now she has never seen a man."

"Even if it were possible, she could not have boarded this ship without seeing a coachmen, a servant... Nay, I tell you, what you say is impossible."

"I have no great wish to convince you, Monsieur, but the truth is demonstrated easily enough. My cousin grew up in a convent, which she was not permitted to leave except by necessity, whereupon she wore a blindfold. A short time ago, my father felt it would be safer for me to reside there with her, since it was one of the last left unmolested in France. From early times, however, this convent has closely guarded the secret of a long tunnel to the sea. For this reason I was lodged there whilst my father awaited some political intelligence. Yesterday, he sent an urgent message instructing my cousin and I to find safe passage to England as soon as may be. As soon as a messenger brought word that the ship was preparing to depart, we made our own way here. The unusual excitement was more than my cousin's nerves could handle, and nearing the end of the tunnel, she collapsed. She was carried aboard the ship along with our baggage, and only just now she wakes."

"Ah!" cried I, in amazement. "How barbarous! I prefer not to believe that such a destructive, unnatural plan could ever have been conceived or carried out."

"You sound like a revolutionary, Monsieur, more concerned with 'nature' than civilization," she observed disdainfully, "And where have Rousseau and the other lovers of our natural state, led our country?"

"Dear Madam," I replied, "must the French bring this quarrel wherever they go? This system of depriving your cousin of knowledge of the other sex, can only have evil consequences. Lack of imagination alone could convince anyone otherwise."

"Oh, to be sure, it was well thought out," interjected the old woman. "Her intended, M. Savard, is much older than she, and what better way to reconcile her to her duty than to give her very little to compare her future husband to?"

All the while we conversed, the poor girl looked at me with the same expression, and I could do aught but pity her. I can scarce imagine what I might have felt had I arrived at the age of fifteen without having seen a woman! What an unnecessary experiment!

It would seem to me that of all the victims of the revolution I have known, this poor girl stands only to gain from a circumstance that weakens the control exercised over her by the most perverse relations.

The first young woman seemed about to respond, but then her eye fell upon the star branded unto my left hand, and she fell silent. A look of uncertainty and distrust newly occupied her face, and she was silent for the rest of the journey.

* * *

What a strange country is England! It is like nowhere I have ever been. It stands alone in Europe, or I believe, in the world at large. Englishmen themselves have a strange air of self-sufficiency which seems to say they are happy to set themselves at odds with the rest of Europe. No one is more enamoured with their own systems and traditions than the English, and it seems they are a most happily independent nation, especially in contrast to our own tortured homeland.

The weather has been poor since we arrived, but the English don't seem to notice. Our presence here is viewed with curiosity. I censure myself harshly for having never learnt the language, and now for the life of me I cannot make myself understood.

I will write later. My accommodations are bad, for our fellow countrymen are already housed in the best rooms in this inn.

I am told there is an inn a short ways away, well known for their accommodations of those fleeing from France, and so I will make my way there.

I wish it had been possible for you to join me on this trip, yet I understand why you chose to remain in Switzerland. I shall tell you what I can of England, as you requested, though so far I have seen but little. I realize that in your present seclusion you are more in need of entertainment than bitter reflections, and so I shall try to please you better in my next letters. The English air does me good already.

I shall send this to you today, and you may write me at that location, where I intend to be for a fortnight or so while I determine my course. Nevertheless, write, and if I leave this house before your letter arrives, I shall order it be sent after me. I have no reason to fear pursuit.

Yours ever,
MC

Marcel de la Croix to Henri Renault

December 19th, 1792

Dear Friend,

I arrived at Margate this afternoon, after a very short trip of less than twenty miles or so. When I arrived at the principal inn here, I noticed another carriage stopped at the door, and as I waited, I saw the unfortunate young lady from the boat, Mlle Vallon, being carried within. It seems she had become overwhelmed by all that is new to her, and the talk within the inn is that she is gravely ill with a fever. I have not yet seen any other in her party in the common area, and I suspect it is deemed beneath them to appear there.

The innkeeper speaks broken French, and can hardly communicate the simplest things. Nevertheless, in these parts he is thought a masterful linguist.

* * *

I have spent nearly all my time here speaking to a brutish fellow emigre, M. Tolouse, who has fled France for lack of employment, since he was so unhappy as to lose his leg fighting for the republicans. While the majority of Frenchmen feel horrified by the unnecessary bloodshed of the last few years, he has left it unwillingly. He has no loyalties, nor any sense of the political or philosophical underpinnings of the unrest, he only wishes to fight, and is bitter to be denied the opportunity. He feels that even with his injury, he can fight better than most other able-bodied men. From the look of him, I would hardly doubt it, for he is a hulking creature as one rarely sees in France.

Since we parted several months ago, I have felt I owe you an apology for my reticence to speak of my past. The truth is that I sought the peace of the monastery more as an asylum for my mind than my body. When we first met, I sensed the weight of guilt and grief upon you, but although I was greatly affected to hear the sad tale of loss which had brought you to the same place, I could not bring myself to follow your example. Perhaps it was not so much reluctance as inability, for while the revolution raged outside our temporary refuge and recent events were so fresh in my mind, I felt an absolute repugnance to speak of the past.

Several times I saw you were familiar with my name and once you alluded to the League of the Star in a manner which indicated you guessed I was proud of my association. At that time, I almost conquered my dislike of the subject to attempt to clarify; in truth, I feel neither pride nor shame, yet it is not quite ambivalence. As with rest of my tale, I fear explanations cannot be given piecemeal, and if you are still kind enough to wish to hear it, I propose to tell you my life from the start. Though I have been in England only a short while, the tumult of our country seems somehow far away, and what happened only two years ago seems like ten. Travel is slow at the moment, and it might be necessary to occupy my time in the free hours in-between stages.

The first thing you must know, which I think you may have guessed, is that I was reared far away from my home by a good gentleman doctor my father had hired to educate me. We lived for a while in Vienna, for a while in Geneva, visiting home only months at a time. My father desired I would become a distinguished intellectual, and he assumed that the position and wealth to which I was born would secure me to the conservative cause, which my education would allow me to defend eloquently.

My father had known Dr. Bourden in college, and he was extremely respected in our circles, though his principles were more difficult to decipher. His popularity within aristocratic circles caused my father to assume his views were with the Ancien Régime, but alas he deceived himself. It is not that I regret my education, which was decidedly liberal, but I often wonder how it might have been if my father and I could have seen eye-to-eye... Certain things could not have changed, however, but I digress.

My memories of my home and family, for the brief months I visited every so often as a boy, are happy and spirited. I remember running through the fields of flowers, fresh baked buns from the bakery in town. Hazy images of childhood games, fishing, stone throwing. One or two cloudy circumstances complete the picture. Acts of cruelty against some poor peasant who had annoyed the neighbour unintentionally, and a poor sickly child who seemed too tired to play, left me with a feeling of uncertainty but I was not there long enough to gain any true understanding of the situation which existed.

I did not return home again till the age of seventeen, when it was decided that I should live permanently in France. I still remember the feeling of pleasure and anticipation that marked my return to a country I still considered my own. How can I hope to describe how the eyes of a man now saw this country, his countrymen, and his peers? Poverty and want I had seen in other countries, but where does it take on the quality as in our land? Walking skeletons lacking even the strength to describe their pain, and even were they to attempt it, who would listen to them? What has happened to the hearts of our brethren that they have become so indifferent to the plight of their fellow man? Is there another country in Europe where the rich have tried to take as much from the common people? How wide a gulf does there need to be between those who have little and those who have plenty? Does the honour of the lord of the manor really require he squeeze the land and people of every last drop of life which might sustain them? How many babes had to die because their mothers were too malnourished to give them milk, merely that a useless trinket might be bought and then discarded by a person who had truly begun to believe his smallest whim was worth the greatest sacrifice by any other? The France I returned to had lost its soul. Mercy seemed foreign to its nature.

Now tell me, friend, does the young man I describe sound like the ideal person to maintain and continue the system he abhorred?

Yesterday, M. Tolouse came to let me know there was great 'concern' amongst some of the fellows at the inn, as to the safety of three unprotected women rumoured to be carrying a vast deal of money with them.

"Dangerous situation, I would think," observed he.

"For all around," replied I.

"How's that?"

"I am merely remarking that however unwise it is for ignorant women to be sent into the world with trunks of money and no type of security, it is more dangerous still for the would-be thieves. The ladies stand to lose only money, which can be replaced or done without, whereas the thief or thieves shall lose their lives, when I am forced to find and kill them. I flatter myself I have never yet failed at anything I set my mind to, and even were that not the case, an idiot with a trunkful of gold would not be difficult to find."

"You are a strange fellow." said he. "Before a man's mind has been warped by principles and education, he can see things clear as day, and he would choose ease, money and comfort over a thankless effort in a cause that does not concern him. Be that as it may, I should not like to oppose you. All the same, it seems likely you will be riding around the country plenty soon, and I have more than half a mind to join you. Riding and killing are two of my favourite things, it so happens. Don't suppose there will be money in it though?"

"None that a man would not be degraded by accepting."

"A fine philosophy! A toast to degradation, then!"

His certainty as to the likelihood of the theft was alarming, and I took no further notice of him, going immediately in search of the prospective victims.

I was admitted cordially by the elder woman, Mme. Gaspar. The haughty young woman, Mlle de Courteline, greeted me with the coldness peculiar to her kind, while the younger, Mlle Vallon, was still not well enough to leave her room.

"To what do we owe the honour of your visit, Monsieur?" Mlle de Courteline inquired presently, in a manner designed to communicate its unwelcomeness. I could see, at the same time, that she was disquieted, her thoughts preoccupied with unusual fears.

"You will recall that when we last spoke, I was surprised to find three ladies were not better attended. To put it bluntly, madam, there is both folly and danger associated with your present circumstance, and I feel compelled to offer my assistance."

"Your concern is unnecessary, Monsieur," replied she, though she seemed far from at ease. "I assure you my father never intended for us to be so long without assistance. He had instructed me to come here to await his arrival, and I expect him always. Even this moment, his carriage might draw up to this wretched house."

I could not help but evince surprise. "I am glad to hear it, madam. Is he indeed expected today?"

"Oh yes," cried the old woman, "he is expected every day!"

"Every day? Since when?"

"Since we arrived."

"You are troubled, Monsieur," said Mlle de Courteline, calmly, "he is simply delayed, for I assure you that nothing could prevent him from fulfilling his promise. Honour is indispensable to a man as my father."

"May I inquire his name, Madam?"

"Indeed, though it can be of little significance to you, my father is the Comte de Courteline."

I thought for a long moment before I posed the following question, almost fearing to hear the answer:

"Forgive me, madam, but has your father told you much about the unrest which grips our country?"

"Why should you ask that?" replied she, with an expression of discomfort. "Certainly there is something afoot, but not such as would prevent my father from following us. He assures me that he and his friends shall be able to right the heinous crimes committed by the masses, and the temporary madness which prevails is about to be overcome. 'Naughty children may well not see the need for their parents,' he is apt to say, 'but that shall not obviate the necessity.' I have no doubt he is right. He shall be able to tell you so in person, soon."

"I hope so, Madam," replied I, "and then I shall show him how the analogy is flawed. It has been a long time since the French aristocracy acted as the benevolent guardians of the people."

Mlle de Courteline quickly readopted her initial coldness.

"Thank you for your offer to aid us, Monsieur, but it would seem our conditions and principles are too divergent to make that practical."

"As you wish," said I with a sigh, "but I charge you to remember I have made it all the same."

This was a very unsatisfactory conference. I believe Mlle de Courteline is not at all aware of the danger faced by any aristocrat still in France, now more than ever.

I will wait at this inn till I receive the letter I hope to receive daily. In the meantime, I shall try to find out the latest news from France. It is possible, I believe, to procure a list of the most recent people to lose their heads, and I shall endeavour to do so.

Your loyal friend,
MC

Marcel de la Croix to Henri Renault

December 23rd, 1792

Dear Friend,

The letter I have been waiting for has not yet come and I am almost tempted to leave without it. I have been at this inn for several days, and have already traversed every path in the area. The party of ladies keeps largely to their rooms, and aside from the occasional company of M. Tolouse, I speak to almost no one. I have had more time than I should like for my own thoughts.

Shall I continue my history, while I wait? I will, if you can bear it.

Before I got carried away in my last letter by my various views and opinions, I was describing my feelings when first travelling through France, after a long absence. The happy fragmented memories of my youth had not prepared me for the sight of the faces, wasting and worn with the most cruel deprivation, or for the scandalous indifference of those who inflicted it.

My father had instructed Dr. Bourden to give me a substantial travelling purse, and the good doctor, knowing the condition of France and my own disposition, (better even than myself) added to it for reasons I did not understand at the time. He anticipated that my natural generosity could not refuse to help the suffering people who met my eyes every way I turned.

The trip was long, and my heart was broken at the end of it. I will not recount all I saw or did, since time does not allow for it. You have no doubt travelled our country in that time, and know what desperate creatures could be found there.

I was travelling from Switzerland at the time, carrying with me some of my most valued possessions. By the time I had reached Paris, I had no money left, and therefore I paused long enough to sell most of my books and trinkets, and even some of my clothes. I knew I could not stay long, however, for even I could not flatter myself that the little good I could do there would have any real effect. I stayed for three days, and each day the number of petitioners tripled at my door and by the last, I was forced to sneak away in the dead of night to avoid the crowds that assembled there from the early morning onwards.

I knew my father would be able to pay my fare when I arrived home, so I continued to stop and give relief wherever I saw necessity. I longed to see my father and to describe to him the horrors I had seen. I imagined myself conferring with him regarding a broader plan to reverse the injustice in our country, and I felt certain he would be only too happy to assist me in planning the most comprehensive measures to do so; at the very least in our own neighbourhood and area of influence.

I did not stop to consider at the time that the evil I saw while passing through had been a part of his daily experience for countless years, and had he truly felt like I did, he could not have allowed it to continue.

He was surprised, initially, to learn I needed him to pay for my carriage from Paris, but he said, quickly enough, 'Well, well, that is the fashion. Young men never have enough money, and you can afford to spend it better than any. Come, come now, your sister, your aunts and uncles are waiting for you.'

I told him I had the most pressing matter to speak to him upon, but that I should not hesitate to follow him immediately to greet them.

'No, no, do not dream of it. No one is in that much haste. I suppose it is unlikely that a learned man should teach you fashion, but never mind, everything has been anticipated. Go to your room and get changed out of your travelling clothes. You will find only the best ready for you.'

I did not truly understand what he meant, but I was eager to oblige...

I am sorry to have cut off my relation so abruptly, but I was forced to do so after receiving the letter I have been awaiting. Among his other communications, Dr. Bourden has included a list of the most recent persons executed by the Guillotine. I was extremely sorry to see that three men on the list bear the name of de Courteline, which I can only assume are the father, brother, or uncles of Mlle de Courteline.

Scarcely anyone could have expected otherwise, but it is all the more unfortunate that no one has attempted to prepare them for it. I have resolved to say nothing of it, in the assumption that some other kind friend will be able to inform them before long. It is doubtful I should be believed, in any case.

Screams raised the entire house last night. I put my clothes on as quickly as I could and ran out, fearing the worst. The landlord was already present in the room of the ladies, while Mlle de Courteline was screaming nearly incoherently, pointing at the unconscious body of M. Tolouse. It appears he mistook their room for his own, and using tremendous force to make his entry, he thereafter collapsed insensible to the floor.

Poor Mlle Vallon had fainted at this ghastly apparition. Unused to the sight of men, she could not withstand exposure to one of the most gruesome specimens of our kind; his brute strength, his size, and the smell and dirt which surrounded him were too much for her fragile senses to bear.

The landlord and two servants carried him to his own room, and everyone else retired at the same time. The incident was the only topic of conversation at the common room today, where none of the ladies in question have ever shown themselves. Mlle Vallon's fever has returned.

* * *

I received a summons today from Mlle de Courteline. It appears she has had no word from her father, but is discovering a great aversion to staying at this inn any longer.

"Monsieur," she said, as I entered her accommodations, "I begin to feel it will be necessary to retain your services."

"Perhaps you mean accept?"

"Certainly not," returned she. "It would be highly inappropriate for us to accept a favour from a stranger. There can be no discussion of it, so pray only ask for what you wish, and it shall be given you."

"I fear I would make a poor servant," said I, not staying to hear more. "Good-day, madam."

An hour or two later I was recalled by Mlle de Courteline, who said, "You can see plainly I am not in the position to make conditions, so let us say no more about it. Until my father arrives, there are certain things we may not do for ourselves, but seem to me of the most desperate and urgent nature."

"I should be happy to help."

"Why then, Monsieur," said she, with the utmost sincerity, "there are two matters which require your attention above all others. The first is the good man who owns this house. Though we do not speak the same language, it is impossible for me to ignore that he shows me the most scandalous disrespect, and I believe he must be forcibly corrected."

"My dear madam," replied I, "it is impossible for me to beat a man while I stay in his house; I feel you will find this true anywhere. Tell me first what he has done and I shall try to determine what is possible to rectify it."

"As you wish," replied she, calmly adopting an impartial manner, before continuing. "Every day, for breakfast, lunch and dinner, he brings us the most inedible swill. I thought at first that he was trying to poison us, but have become convinced thereafter that he wishes to extort money from us. Since that time I have given him more than the average servant makes in a year in France, and the food has become progressively worse. I have scarcely eaten since I have been in this country. Moreover, every day of my life till now has begun with drinking chocolate or jasmine tea, but since we have been here, we have been brought only milk or..."

"Madam," said I, fearing how long her list of grievances may continue, "however grievous these affronts may seem to you, I assure you that it is not intentional. More than once, since I have been here, I have heard the landlord boast about the exquisite quality of the things he has been able to order for you, about the skill of his cook, and how handsomely you have demonstrated your appreciation. I cannot help but guess that you have not been accustomed to anything but the best our country can offer, and therefore I advise you to temper your own expectations while expanding your tastes as much as possible. I recommend this for the sake of your own peace. Pray tell me, is there not a more concrete concern at present?"

Mlle de Courteline appeared truly horrified, and she was silent for a good while thereafter.

"It is hard to believe what you say, but I am not well travelled, and must try to accept it. But tell me, Monsieur, have the lower classes no deference, no respect for their superiors?"

"Not such as you may have found in France in times past. Such little marks of deference as you have observed are customary here."

"Ah, how I long to return to France! I am losing my own sense of what is proper. Placing that aside, however, we are in need of a servant who can speak both languages, and as I cannot traipse about looking for one, I ask that you engage one for me. Let them be clean and pleasing to look at, gentle, obedient, amusing, clever, quick and diligent. Let them come this evening and I shall be ready with orders."

"I do not doubt it, Madam, and I shall do my best. Perhaps in the meantime it would be best to contrast your customary meals at home and the meals here, with your expectations in a servant, and the qualities they are likely to possess. Is there any other matter before I depart?"

Mllde de Courteline still wore a look of horror from my previous statement (I hope to do better than I have promised, but having severely depressed her expectations, I hope to exceed them). After a moment or two, however, she said sadly, "Tomorrow is Christmas, M. Gramont. If possible, I should like to attend a Catholic Mass, and yet I expect that would be difficult, in this country."

"It would indeed, but perhaps there is a Chaplain hereabouts who might be brought here to say a few words. I shall inquire into the matter. Good-day, Madam."

I pity her, though a representative of what was reprehensible in the ancien régime, she is as innocent of malice as she is of knowledge. She no more understands the pain of hunger and deprivation than she understands mornings without jasmine tea. Dear Sir, I am ever,

Yours,
MC

Marcel de la Croix to Henri Renault

December 27th, 1792

Dear Friend,

Although I am as restless as ever to continue my journey up the coast, it is difficult to reconcile myself to doing so while the ladies remain in some danger. Mlle de Courteline provokes me repeatedly and many times I have resolved to leave them all to their fate. Again and again, however, I am brought to pity her in my reflection, for she is merely a product of her upbringing. What would I be, after all, if I had not been raised by my dear Dr. Bourden, but by my own parents? What then would have been my prejudices? Might I not have looked at the world, much as she does? And yet I confess it is not merely a sense of duty and honour which keep me here, for however strongly I feel an obligation to assist those who are ill-equipped to assist themselves, I have been far from successful in my own enquiries. The person I hope to find in England proves elusive, and all of my efforts thus far have been fruitless. This morning I had all but convinced myself to strike out in another direction, but as it was still rather early when I finished my breakfast, I decided to take a brief walk and then take leave of the ladies thereafter. By the time I returned, the gloomy skies had turned into heavy rain. I inquired of the innkeeper whether things might still be got ready for departure, and he advised me that unless I was in a great hurry, I should wait another day or two and spare myself the difficulty and expense of finding conveyance in a downpour.

I felt the decision had been taken out of my hands, in some respects, and so am now returned to my room. With nothing better to do, I propose to give you some more of my history, if I can but recall where I left off. I believe I had been telling you of my trip home to France as a young man, and the shock I sustained to witness the increasing depravation in the land.

The shock had not worn off upon my arrival to my family home, and for a while I allowed myself to be soothed, primped and pampered from the ordeal of travel, lying in exhausted contemplation. I could not long remain that way without being forced to note the contrast. The opulence of my chamber was extreme. Five servants undertook the duties of my toilette. I was drawn from the stupor I had fallen into by an unrequested cup of chocolate.

I was in horror! I felt at that moment that I caused the pain around me. It was for my sake the land was raped and left unfit to grow crops for the people around. It was to procure me luxuries that the whole world seemed to slave and die. I was brought drinking chocolate on the same night that children in every hovel within miles of me, went to sleep hungry and near starvation.

I suffered greatly in that moment, and could not stay to be dressed. I already found myself clothed in the finest silk, powdered, wigged and booted, as was the fashion. I ran downstairs in search of my father, with five anxious servants trailing behind me, protesting that they had not been permitted to finish my ensemble; touching and picking at me like so many wild crows.

I burst into the drawing room where I found my father entertaining a whole assortment of company. The young men looked like

I was meant to, only carrying themselves with better grace, and the ladies like painted statues. My sudden entrance, and the wildness of my expression, caused every one some consternation. My father too, seemed surprised, but diffused the oddity at once, declaring,

'Ah, it would seem my boy has been on the road so long, he is impatient to dine. Come, we only waited for you to begin, and there remains only the introductions before we do so.'

He performed all the introductions with incomparable grace and composure, allowing me to collect myself as he did so.

Immediately thereafter we entered the dining room, which was lit up with a thousand candles. Musicians stood by, ready to play, and forty servants brought out our various courses. I lost count of how many dishes there were, but I watched in horror as I saw them picked at and removed, destined to be discarded. The atmosphere was merriment, the occasion was my return, and in the midst of it all, I sat silent, horrified and largely unregarded.

I will leave off my story now, as there is an increasing sound of bustle in the inn, and it seems high time I put down my pen.

I have not yet left the inn, but much has happened since I last wrote. Two days ago, my brutish companion, M. Tolouse, hinted to me that we would soon have cause to chase about the country. I was alarmed to discover he had been unable to dissuade his associates to abandon their plan, questioning him closely to that point.

"Can it be that anyone would act so rashly, knowing full well the result? Do I err in thinking you have openly represented it to them?"

"Nay, I don't care to do them any favours. Besides, desperate men act strangely, and I shan't interfere."

"But if you mean to help me kill them, as you claim, should you not tell them so, while they confide their plans to you?"

"I didn't say they confided, exactly," replied he, "for they speak in code. All I can say, however, is that when poor men celebrate, and talk of 'birds' and 'nests' and whatnot, there is something afoot, and it ain't my duty to ferret out exactly what beforehand."

Hearing this, I went to speak to Mlle de Courteline, who received me again, seated, with the same haughty demeanour as one hears a petitioner. I was annoyed, not merely at her but at every occupant of the inn besides; but nevertheless, I held my purpose, saying:

"Mademoiselle, it is my unfortunate duty to inform you that it becomes increasingly unsafe for the three of you ladies to remain at this inn, lodged as you are at present. I must recommend that you take steps to remove from here at once, to an area where your circumstances seem less known, where I propose to accompany you. If Mlle Vallon's condition does not permit immediate travel, then I must strenuously recommend that you accept my offer to lodge with you, in a separate apartment, till such time as my first recommendation can be accomplished."

Mlle de Courteline's expression revealed her to be horrified by this suggestion, which she appeared to deem hardly worthy of a response.

"Your concern, Monsieur," she said coldly, "is extremely affecting. I thank you for your solicitude, but what you suggest is as impossible as it is inappropriate. Mlle Vallon remains too ill to be moved, and even should she recover, I believe I have already told you, I expect my father here daily..."

"Forgive me for interrupting, Madam, but you may easily leave direction for how you may be located. The objection may be overcome."

"I fear, Monsieur, that it is my own faulty behaviour that has encouraged the liberties you take, and for this I apologize. As for your other recommendation, I shall do you the favour of pretending it was not made."

"Madam, I see that you believe my offer is indelicate, but I cannot help attempting to cause you to see reason. The scruples arising from notions of propriety, while they do you credit, were not intended to be upheld when true inconvenience and danger shall be the result. I give you my word of honour that I have no other purpose in mind than what I have declared and would take no advantage whatsoever of the trust reposed in me."

Her manner was unchanged, and she made it clear she scorned any talk of honour unaccompanied by a family crest she had been taught to respect.

"I come to believe, Monsieur, that I have asked too much of you already."

What more could I say? I bowed and left in disgust.

That same afternoon an errand took me a few miles away. I had hoped it would prove to be worth my while, but alas it was far from it. The countryside was beautiful, and the weather had become quite fine, so I delayed my return until the evening. The concerns of Mlle de Courteline and her party had left my mind completely, as I was brought to contemplate certain other matters, nearer to my own life. Upon my return, however, I found the whole house in uproar. The common room was unusually bare and silent, while the sounds of dismay and heated conversation rang out from other parts of the house.

I guessed immediately what had occurred, and could not but fault myself for my absence, especially at such a time as I knew and had represented to be dangerous. I passed the Landlord on my way and asked him what occurred. I believe he guessed my question, but his answer was in English, followed by a shrug that said more plainly 'It is not my concern, and there is nothing to be done.'

For some reason I was reluctant to speak with Mlle de Courteline immediately and went to my own room to send a message summoning M. Tolouse.

Scarcely three minutes later he appeared, outfitted for the saddle and wearing a comical assortment of battle gear. Adding to this was his nearly festive demeanour. He greeted me by saying,

"So you've heard, have you? I am the very fortune teller, and before long I mean to be the fortune breaker."

"I have heard nothing. Pray indulge me."

"Why then I shall tell it as I heard it. This afternoon, as usual, Mademoiselle asks the servant to inquire for messages from her father, long expected. This time, word comes back that a message came telling them to go at once to a house down the way, where a foreign gentleman is ill. All three gentlewomen leave at once, taking none of their belongings in haste. They search for word of the foreigner (that is, the Frenchman) in vain, for nobody around here knows anything of the matter, and what's more, scarcely any of them can make themselves understood. So, several hours later they return, weary and despairing, only to find their door has been forced and all their belongings looted. The ladies have received precious little sympathy in their ordeal, and our innkeeper has made it his business to know whether he may be paid what they owe, and to that end he has 'accepted' a bracelet from one of them, to ensure against his expenditures."

"And you are ready to accompany me, Monsieur, I presume from your dress?"

"Indeed, I should have set out on my own before now had I not been stayed by your message."

"Wait for me, then, for I must speak to Mademoiselle before I go."

"Perhaps I might join you, if it's all the same to you?"

I made no objection. The two women were beside themselves. Mlle Vallon, who had apparently exerted herself so much as to join them on their outing, was once again confined to her bed.

I wasted no time in telling Mlle de Courteline that I was sorry to hear of what had befallen them and that I was preparing to depart immediately to go in search of their belongings.

"Ah, Monsieur," replied she, throwing herself all of a sudden at my feet, "do not now abandon us to these barbarians! Decency, rank, religion, mean nothing to them! Dear God in heaven, what will become of us in this accursed country?"

In vain did I assure her of my quick return and their relative safety, now that most of their valuables were lost. In vain did I represent the urgency of a quick pursuit. Mlle de Courteline had begun to fear they were surrounded by murderers, and when she said so, Mme. Gaspar declared, "Oh, to think I should live to see such dear girls murdered by rascals and highwaymen! Let me drown in their blood rather than live one more moment in such a world!"

At that moment, M. Tolouse offered to go on the errand himself so that I might stay and keep watch over the women. I was far from approving this plan, which I said directly, having no reason at all to assume he should return in the event he was successful.

"Pish," said he. "What sort of animal would I be if I could harm good ladies in need?"

Mlle de Courteline seemed to have no doubt she could inspire such fidelity and desire to serve, and gathering her strength and composure, she turned to me and said,

"Monsieur, you often indicated your desire to serve us, and I am certain you will not leave us now in our time of need."

Mlle de Courteline seems to possess an incredible determination to be opposed to anything of common sense, and to that end she ignores prudent warnings when there is real danger and invents danger when there is none.

I was beginning to restate my conviction, when to my surprise, Mlle Vallon suddenly appeared from the next room, and placed herself gently on the bench beside the door, as if she had not the strength to move further. Having done so, she looked up at me intently, wordlessly supplicant.

Everyone was silent temporarily in surprise. M. Tolouse, appearing more thoughtful than usual, said, "Doubtless, Mademoiselle is right, and you must remain here. I am happy to go on my own. I have, however, important documents I should like to leave in your hands: I brought with me a deed to my father's land, which, though modest, I hope the future political climate will allow me to reclaim, and in addition, I should like to leave with you this cross," (which I had previously seen him kiss, on occasion) "given me by my late mother. See no harm comes to it, mind."

At this offer of security, I could no longer resist the appeal to remain. M. Tolouse has not yet returned, but he has sent a short note saying he has caught a clear scent, and hoped to return immediately.

I have received no letter from you, though I realize your replies may be delayed somewhat. I had hoped that mail between Switzerland and England would be largely unaffected by the trouble in France, but I suppose that remains to be seen. I will write again soon. May God preserve you till we meet again.

Yours ever,
MC

Marcel de la Croix to Henri Renault

December 30th, 1792

Dear Friend,

I begin to wonder whether I may ever leave this inn! M. Tolouse has not yet returned, but I feel a strange confidence that he will do so. Nevertheless, until he does, I will be forced to remain. None of the ladies wish to venture out of doors at the moment, and as the theft occurred when I was gone yesterday, any hint of going anywhere is heard with horror. All three ladies are pensive, and there is little conversation to be had with any of them, (though Mlle de Courteline seems to wish for some distraction) so I am once more in my room. I will write you a little more of my history while I have the time:

Those who attended the celebration of my homecoming seemed to be oblivious to the contrast the excess and profusion made with the want which surrounded us on all sides. The great house was like an island, cut off from the rough seas, and the inhabitants were universally unmindful of the rising tide.

In these days of my youth, I still looked to others to find reflections of my own soul and feeling. Amidst this company, my soul had never been more alienated. All thoughts seemed to centre around outward appearances, self-interest and the all-consuming spectre of success or failure in their social endeavours.

Though my heart began to misgive me on the subject, I was more determined than ever to unburden myself to my father. Seizing the first opportunity, I said everything that I felt. I attempted to appeal to his humanity by every avenue available: pride, humour, family, justice, sympathy, religion!

He was silent as I spoke. I told him everything I had considered during my journey; the proposed economies of our family, the improvements to our land, suspension of rents, and the portion of our property which could be given to the people themselves.

My father was by temperament a quiet, stoical man. He was silent a long time after I was finished. At last he said, 'I had hoped, my son, that duty to your father's wishes would be foremost in your mind, but I find you are disposed to gratify only your own ideas, whatever the consequences to your family. Should you persist in these ideas, so long as you are my ward, you shall not have a penny to throw away in this irresponsible manner. I pray only that your principles are not ruined beyond repair.'

With that he left me, standing like stone, alone in the hall of our ancestors; the blood in my veins cold, and my heart still as if forever.

December 31st, 1792

Returning once more to England and my current progress, Mlle de Courteline has condescended to take my advice to remove from this inn. She had developed a horror of it since the time of her loss, and we await only the return of M. Tolouse to depart.

His absence has extended to three days, but I continue to have faith he shall return.

Mlle de Courteline insists upon my presence, and has become almost at ease. Since she had never come to the common room, I had assumed she was a woman of ample internal resources, but I find far otherwise is the case. She pines and languishes without conversation and amusement, and protests she has never been so long in her life without it. Since her earliest years, she has been accustomed to being the object of the attentions of not merely her family, but her entire neighbourhood. Her smallest whim was indulged, no matter the inconvenience.

Her pride alone prevented her from seeking out conversation with the other occupants of the inn, for she declares she cannot abide the degradation of conversing with common folk.

My dear friend, on this, the last day of 1792, I wish you a more peaceful 1793.

* * *

January 1st, 1793

Early this morning, M. Tolouse returned victoriously from his errand. It appears his objects fled when they discovered he was on their heels. He gave good chase, which delayed him somewhat, but it seems they scattered at that point, and the retrieved item was too heavy to make further pursuit practical.

Mlle de Courteline was fascinated by his account, causing him to recite it for her several times.

It seems he chased them from inn to inn travelling northwards, when finally he arrived at a house just after they had left it. He gave chase immediately, and easily made up the gap between himself and a well-laden wagon. The thieves were greatly frightened by his pursuit, and in their desperation, dropped the trunk and the majority of its contents on the dirt road.

This clever decision seems to have saved them in the end, for M. Tolouse was forced to stop and gather the contents, unwilling to leave money strewn all over the road, even for a short while. The fall of the trunk scattered the contents over a large area, some even amongst the grass. By his account he spent nearly four hours gathering its contents. If he has taken any, it is impossible to tell. The original thieves doubtless kept some, and some more shall become the property of some lucky peasant. Mlle de Courteline has rewarded him handsomely, and it would seem her fortune has suffered comparatively little as a result.

Her reserve has relaxed considerably, despite her best efforts to maintain it. She relapses from time to time into her former haughtiness, but it seems difficult for her to remember. Mlle Vallon is too ignorant and withdrawn to make much of a companion, and of course Mme. Gaspar is only barely rational. We shall set out tomorrow, and then at least we shall see new sights.

* * *

We have arrived at an inn in Gravesend, and I believe we are all relieved at the change of scenery. I succeeded in convincing Mlle de Courteline to join us in the common room on our first evening. She was in rare form, as you will see.

"This is why I do not like the English," said Mlle de Courteline, speaking French with the full freedom and confidence that no one else staying in the inn could understand her. "Look at that pitiful creature in the corner," said she, motioning at a young boy, seated pathetically a short ways away. "Look how he stares at us with no shame. Observe his countenance, how low, how sullen, how stupid. Such a heaviness about him; it is disgraceful! Can you imagine a Frenchman looking so? Why half of those headed to prison or worse, must have had more lightness and gaiety. Ah, I despise such wretchedness in temper!"

The boy looked about twelve or thirteen. He was very thin and pale, though by no means unkept.

"Do not speak so lightly of such things, mademoiselle," said Mme. Gaspar, "only think how many of our countrymen have perished that way!"

"But so morose!" persisted she, "Is he not the very picture of 'John Bull'?"

"At the risk of pointing out what seems obvious," said I, "it would seem the young fellow is overwhelmed by cares."

"And do I have less? What more can possibly be endured? Has he been chased from his native land, with scarcely any hope of returning? Has the money and property that were his birthright, been all but snatched by thieves and murderers on the street? And yet, do I not bear it well?"

"Excessively so, but as there are few other ways to distract oneself at present, I am tempted to prolong the argument by pointing out that the sorry young man in the corner is unlikely to have grown up in the very profusion and abundance which has characterized your life till now, and his disposition, if it may be called glum, is possibly the result of a life of privation and despair."

"Then perhaps by now he ought to be used to it. Do not you philosophers say that it is harder to be deprived riches than never to have tasted them?"

"I give up, madam, as I find you defend a bad argument better than most do a good."

"Believe me, Monsieur, I have as little taste for it as you, but look how he stares at us!"

I gazed at him a moment in thought, before saying, "Perhaps he speaks French?"

"'Twould be nice if someone at least could be of use to us. Did you not say you went to University, M. Gramont? May I ask how did it come to pass that you did not learn English?"

"I quite had my hands full with Italian, Greek and Latin. Had it been possible to foresee this day, I would certainly have done differently. But what about yourself? Was not your library at home well stocked with Goldsmith, Shakespeare and Richardson?"

"Aye, indeed, but show me the heroine who could read Sir Charles Grandison in English? 'Tis nearly two thousand pages!"

"Peace. Your reasons are as good as mine, no doubt, but it will do us no good to quarrel. Whatever else may be said of your friend, I feel it likely he understands us, and therefore I shall try to engage him as a translator. I have not yet found the servant you requested, after all."

"Oh, I am much obliged! To choose the very person I have singled out with dislike for my servant! Why stop there? Perhaps we may add several other dirty low fellows to our travelling party before we leave?"

"I see no way of securing us a more permanent lodging if we have no method of communication. Here is our landlord, who can ask for money in any language. I shall signal him to send the poor boy over."

A moment or two later, the boy approached reluctantly, and I addressed him as follows in French:

"Greetings, good lad. Our party has need of a translator. Do you speak French, by any chance?"

The boy did not answer and only continued to stare uncertainly.

"If he does not speak French," observed M. Tolouse, carelessly, "then perhaps I ought to kill him for his lovely ring."

The boy jumped, his eyes widening with fear.

"Come, boy," continued I, "it is plain you understand us and we are in need of your help. Your services will be fairly rewarded. I can see you are hungry, and I shall see you eat first. Ask what you like of the man of the house, then tell him we shall set out tomorrow. We are in search of a place to let. Be quick about it, and let no one say the English are not kind to travellers in their time of need."

I am in some hope that he may be of use to us. I hope you are well, and that I shall hear from you soon.

Yours ever,
MC

Marcel de la Croix to Henri Renault

January 4th, 1793

Dear Friend,

We are preparing to leave Gravesend tomorrow. We would travel today, but the preparations cannot all be made in time. The weather is grey again, and there is little amusement to be had. For all this, I have spent the better part of the day with the ladies, and am only just now able to return to my own room. In the time before supper, I will continue writing my story. When I last left off, it was at a crucial moment in my life, and the events which followed have been on my mind since then.

The tension between my father and I was great for those short weeks. On his side I could see he was profoundly disappointed by my views. Like many French aristocrats, he had sacrificed the basic needs of the poor to enlarge the means of his family. He expected gratitude and obedience and was incensed to an incomparable degree to find instead that I abhorred what had been done for my sake and wished nothing more than to reverse it by any possible means. I had described the past and present conduct of our family as immoral and he considered it an almost unforgivable betrayal.

Nevertheless I was his son, and he did not have another. Had he, I have no doubt he would have turned me out of doors immediately. As it was, he was determined to move forward with his plans for me, for which I was almost irrelevant.

I was to marry a wealthy neighbour with desirable connections. He informed me unceremoniously of this requirement (for so it was) and I did not object.

The cruelty of my fate had torn from me any wish to resist. There seemed to me few things worse than being alienated from your only surviving parent, and I sunk into a malaise of apathy and discontent from which no one took the trouble to rouse me.

Time was nearing when I was to come of age, and a large party was planned in celebration. I was not consulted, for it concerned me by name only.

Everyone in the area worth inviting was to come. Though I had professed myself indifferent, the profusion and excess of the preparations turned my stomach.

Curtains were replaced, furniture followed. A stage was built in our Courtyard, and actors hired to perform a tragedy. A huge tent was erected in case of poor weather, and warming stoves were placed around the perimeter to keep guests warm, for the same reason. Walls were built around the tent at the last moment for fear of wind.

On the week of the party, the weather became grey, calm and cool. Morose clouds seemed to hang around our hearts, and an eerie silence infected nature.

I had confined myself largely to my room. Two days before the date of the party, a mysterious note was slipped under my door.

The tiny slip of paper was wrapped in a roll and tied with a simple ribbon. Its appearance filled me with fear and excitement. I contemplated it at a distance for some while, reluctant to leave my window-seat to read it. After all, I thought, who has something to say to me? Was it my father? Had he broken his silence to heap me with curses? No, it was not his way, but yet I hesitated to pick it up.

At last I opened it. It read simply:

Be at the rock at Swallow's field tomorrow night at eleven, if you have a heart. A life depends upon you. Send no replacements.

All of my feelings changed at this juncture. I was excited as if my blood was on fire. I had the opportunity to do some good, and my presence would be useful to someone. I had no fear and no doubt. Death would be preferable to languishing any longer as I did. The true feelings of a man were indeed developing within me, and each day that I moped like a helpless calf was killing my spirit.

January 6th, 1793

Last night I stopped writing with some reluctance, and I am surprised to find it is almost cathartic to relive my own ordeal. I only hope it pleases you as well.

Today the ladies, M. Tolouse and I travelled nearly all day. It does not seem ideal to go from inn to inn, and we are travelling along the coast in the hope of finding a suitable place to settle for a short while, from where we can begin to determine our separate destinations. We are now arrived at an inn in Essex. The boy has accompanied us here, and so far he has proved helpful, though he hardly speaks a word. Mlle de Courteline has nicknamed him

'Mouchard,' because he is always sneaking around. As he has given us no other name, we have all taken to calling him thus.

When we arrived, I instructed him to inquire after a place which might be let, or preferably two separate lodgings on the same land. He came back a short time later, but he said not a word.

I imagined he had no success, but presently he prepared to go out again, and when I inquired the reason, he said,

"I go to call at the main house nearby, for I was told to come back after two."

"Is there something nearby?"

"Near Harwich, Monsieur, so it will be another days' travel, if you wish it. The owner lives a short way from here."

"Very well."

Mouchard returned a short while later to say he was told to come at the same time the next day, as the owner had not been at his leisure to see him. I relayed the news to the women, since I felt we would need to stay at least another day, at which Mlle de Courteline declared,

"Ah! I fear I shall perish from ennui before the day is out. At least little Mouchard may amuse himself scurrying about the country. In my father's house, I assure you, there was no servant who was not capable of amusing one. Summon him, I beg you, for I grow desperate for some distraction."

I summoned Mouchard, who came with his customary timidity. Mlle de Courteline placed herself on a chair before him and said,

"Come here, Mouchard. Tell me, child, have you any skill with which to amuse me? Do you play any instrument, recite any poetry? Know you any riddles?"

The poor child shook his head with embarrassment.

"Do you know any worthwhile tales? Can you perform any tricks, or feats of agility? Do not be shy."

He was silent but his look became more intense, as if he had something to say but was uncertain.

"There is something, I can see. Do not be afraid, you may tell me. If you amuse me, I shall be pleased, if you do not, you shall fare no worse than before. Come, speak."

"I only have one story, Madam," said he quietly, almost in a whisper.

"I suppose that is a miracle in itself, and we must not complain. Let it only be a French story, and I shall be happy."

"It begins in France," replied he, "but much of it takes place in this land."

"Ah, then I should rather die of boredom."

Mouchard bowed without surprise and returned to his room, while Mlle de Courteline, slightly vexed he had not attempted to convince her, amused herself with a variety of witticisms against the English, which I imagine you have heard before and will spare you. Her resolution against the scant entertainment available to our party was short-lived, however, for her temperament is not suited to calm or reflection.

"Let him be summoned again," declared she, after a short period of quiet had reigned amongst our weary party. "Perhaps the story he has proposed to tell us may be amusing, if only unintentionally so. Let him come in."

A few minutes later, the boy came in, bowing to Mlle de Courteline.

"I have decided your story may have merit after all, since you say it begins in France. Good origins matter to plants and people, as they might to stories. But why, if your story starts in France, does it not stay there? Must everything be chased out by revolutionaries?"

Her jest failed to please even herself, and after a moment or two of awkward hesitation, the boy replied, "In a manner of speaking." He paused again, stammering in a way that did not promise well for his narrative. He seemed to dislike speaking more than a word at a time, and therefore this was to be expected. I concluded quickly he would not be able to say more. He stumbled, once more, but then assuming a faraway look and averting his eyes from all of us, he began to speak in a calm, steady manner, as a man far beyond his years.

The tale begins in France in 1788, with one of the first victims of the revolution, a young Viscount, who was then a boy of six. His mother, the Viscountess, had raised him from infancy with the most tender maternal affection. Anything which might upset the child was banished from his presence. Guests who had the misfortune to displease him were rarely invited back. The first years of his life were spent entirely in his family home in the country, as his mother was convinced that any more populated area, especially Paris, would place him at a heightened risk of disease. As a result of the shelter and indulgence prescribed by his well-meaning mother, the child arrived at the age of six with a rather more delicate temperament and appearance than usual. This difference, which his mother could not help but notice, caused her to fret all the more for his health and safety. The very early rumblings of the revolution shattered her nerves, and her constitution faltered, confining her to bed at last.

Early unrest in the neighbourhood in which they lived culminated in a mob burning two of the chateaux nearby, causing panic in their family. It so happened, at that time, that an Englishman of remote acquaintance was passing through the area, charged with delivering a letter to the Viscountess. He called upon the family, and discovering the cause of their distress, he painted the coming destruction of the revolution in the most vivid colours, which he contrasted cleverly with the peace and calm of his own homeland. He wasted no time in proposing to take the little Viscount back with him on his return, and shelter him in some remote corner of England.

'Believe me, my dear Lady, nothing shall be more sacred to me than the care and protection of the dear child. Alas, I fear for him greatly if he was to remain here even a week longer!'

The poor Viscountess was more tender than she was discerning, especially when it came to character. Her dearest wish was to protect her son from harm, and although she could hardly bear to be parted with him, her fear for his welfare if he remained in France was greater. As her own feeble condition did not permit her to accompany him in his flight, she proposed joining him in England as quickly as may be. The child's protector, Mr. Grey, was given fifty thousand livres for the journey and expenses, and he promised that the child should receive every care and luxury he might expect at home.

The gentleman was not, in truth, a black-hearted villain. He was unquestionably unscrupulous in his honesty, and promises were not made to be remembered. Often times when he made them, he was as sincere as anyone could wish, but merely failed to take into account his own changing inconsistent personality, which made the thing he pledged today of absolutely no importance tomorrow. It is probable he meant to serve the Viscountess as he proposed, and merely enrich himself in the process.

For the two nights he remained on French soil, he behaved with relative restraint. The child, meanwhile, was stupefied by the sudden change in company and surroundings, and caused his keeper very little trouble.

Once they arrived on English shore, the child's stupor was only heightened by the predominance of English spoken around him, no longer understanding anything he heard.

Mr. Grey proposed to go directly to the home of a friend of his in Essex, from where they would make additional arrangements. His newfound wealth complicated his journey somewhat, as it seemed there were debts to be settled and new wagers to be made at every stop. He spared no expense in travel, for himself and the companions he made along the way, till at last he appeared to find himself in some difficulty regarding a disputed sum, and was forced to leave his lodgings with the boy in the middle of the night.

The details of what happened next are confused at best. They finally arrived at the home of Mr. Grey's friend, to whom he also seemed indebted. His own affairs required he continue moving, and therefore he proposed to leave the child with his friend for a few days, along with a small sum of money for his keep, promising to return within a week. It is doubtful he revealed any particulars about the boy at that point, for fear the other would seek to profit from the connection.

The second gentleman had no great wish to be encumbered with a tiny child of six, and merely a week and a half beyond the time Mr. Grey had promised to return, he deposited the boy at an orphanage. From there he was sent to the vicarage of a neighbouring family, and since the local vicar had no use for him, he was given into the care of some poor farmers, who were meagrely compensated for housing him.

What cruelty was in store for this child of privilege! No kind of abuse or deprivation was spared him. The brutal pair had taken on his maintenance solely in the hope that his labours might lessen their own. His weakness and frailty incensed them, but as they were ignorant and cruel, they sought to correct his deficiencies through increased punishment.

This treatment soon left the child fit for nothing. His mind and his soul could not withstand treatment that nothing in his entire life had taught him to expect. He became almost senseless, and lack of sleep and nourishment made him unequal to the smallest tasks.

He suffered this way from Winter till Summer, till at last his brutal keepers saw he would never be of any use to them. One beautiful morning, they loaded the poor sufferer onto a small cart and drove him a fair distance from their hut, where they left him on the side of the road like any unwanted baggage.

How much of this the child was aware of is impossible to know. Time does not always seem to exist in the same way. What is known for certain is that he was found several hours later in this very position, huddled up in preparation for death. His saviour (for so she was), was a young girl of thirteen.

The moment Miss Reckert laid eyes on the tiny shivering child, she entertained no doubt of what she must do. The child jumped when she touched him, and did not appear to hear her when she spoke. His clothes were tattered, his frame gaunt, and though fully seven years old, he might have been taken for half his age.

Without hesitation, she picked up the small child (who nevertheless was a great burden to a young girl) and carried him the entire way home.

In one short day, the fortunes of the poor child were entirely reversed. Miss Reckert tended to him faithfully, as a child does an injured bird. Under her watch, his wounds were healed and his health was restored. As his senses gradually began to return, he responded to her affectionate care, though like a wild animal, recoiled at the presence of any other.

Miss Reckert lived with her father since the early death of her mother. Her father loved her dearly and because he hated to oppose her in anything, her ascendancy within the household was complete.

When first she had brought the boy home, no thought had been given to anything else but nursing him back to health. After a week or so had passed, Mr. Reckert spoke to his daughter gently about what was to be done, saying, 'It would seem to me that the child has come from somewhere. Do you not think it is time, my dear, that we attempt to discover where?'

'Indeed,' replied she, without considering any other meaning than her own, 'for it is important that whoever is responsible be punished.'

'Ah, but what if they be his parents? Do not parents sometimes beat their children, but still retain them in law?'

'Beat them, maybe, but here is one as good as dead. If I had not found him, 'tis sure he would have perished, and therefore, whosoever it is he was, has claim to him no more.'

'And what if they came a-looking for him, my dear, what shall I say?'

'You may say only what is just, that you have expended certain monies saving him from death, and that if they may pay for his care and treatment, not to mention boarding, then show evidence he is their child, you will allow them to attempt to justify their shameful mistreatment. In that case they can have him back. Ah, poor thing, how he jumps! It is certain, I think, that he understands you. Dear Thomas,' continued she, 'mind not what I have said, for I swear, by all that is good, you shall never go back from where you have came from. You shall stay with me, as long as you will be satisfied to do so.'

'Dearest daughter, take care, for he is a boy, not a dog. There shall be more concerned with keeping him than you can imagine. I see you have given him a name. Can he talk? Will he give you no other?'

'No, dear Sir, he says not a word, but one might not wonder at it, when one sees how he has been treated for however long. We must keep him, father, of that I am certain. Fate has brought him to me, for I shall take care of him. If his board and keep are what concerns you, I shall give up my pocket money to make it easy.'"

"What a strange story!" declared Mlle de Courteline, when Mouchard stopped speaking. "I do not dislike it, though I had rather it was a romance."

"I fear it is an allegory," replied I. "The rank of this helpless boy is surely meant to stand for France, and the Heroine is England herself, come to save us. It is patriotic, to boot."

"Come, little Mouchard," said Mlle de Courteline to the boy. "You have done well today, far better than I had expected. You have eased my cares. Tomorrow you must come again and tell us more, but have a care not to dwell so long upon poor children mauled and left on the roadside. Tell us more of your story, by all means, but let there be love, I beg you, for the sake of my nerves."

I will close here at the end of Mouchard's tale. I have stayed up late trying to capture it as I heard it, for I fear by morning it would mostly be lost, or at least altered, and it was worthy of preserving.

Yours ever,

MC

M. Henri Renault to Marcel de la Croix

January 7th, 1773, Switzerland

Dear Marcel,

You cannot imagine how I happy I was to receive your letters, which arrived together only today. I suspect normally they would pass through France and take eight to ten days at the most, but the postmarks reveal they have travelled instead through Belgium and Germany, taking two weeks to arrive here in Switzerland. All mail in France is now being opened and inspected as the revolutionary government is determined to detect any possible plots to rescue nobles from the guillotine.

Your letters are all the more welcome just at this time, as we receive almost no news at all of late. Even the revolutionary propaganda has become somewhat precious through scarcity.

I am more grateful than I can express to find you have kept your promise to write and also that you have consented to give me your history, as I have often hinted I wished to know it. Your timing could not be more perfect, for I have become quite desperate in my boredom. Since you left, our friends Father Galois and Father Schelling have taken vows of silence, and there is now almost no conversation to be had. I have tried to reach out to some of the other monks in the hope of filling the void, but most of them are so used to solitude and deprivation, they hardly notice. As you may remember, the library here, though large, is almost entirely ecclesiastical (I suppose it is no wonder). There are no novels and only a smattering of verse, all of which I have read and reread. There are even fewer Roman and Greek authors, which have been objected to on Pagan grounds.

Your letters were like an oasis of amusement and information in this desert of both. Yet I cannot repay you in kind. You would not thank me if I wrote about my chores, my painful reflections, or my little experiments in the garden (these I should hardly mention, but

I confess they are my sole delight, of late.)

Pray write as you have, I beg you.
Your devoted and grateful friend,
Henri Renault

P.S. Both Father Galois and Father Schelling have hinted (albeit mutely) that reading your letters would not violate their vows. I told them I should ask for your permission, as I do not know if you would like your history known by more than myself. Pray write on that point.

Marcel de la Croix to Henri Renault

January 9th, 1793

Dear Friend,

It has become more difficult to find time to complete what I started, at least in terms of my history. Mlle de Courteline occupies much more time than I would have expected, if only because she is unable to occupy herself.

I had hoped to have given you more of my own tale by now, and I fear I am exhausting your patience with my slowness and detail. Yet I shall continue in the same vein, for want of any other approach.

Returning to where I was in my history:

I thought only of the note I had received. I went through the motions of my life, counting the hours and minutes till the time appointed.

I took no trouble to make any excuses for my absence. At quarter to eleven exactly, I mounted my horse, armed with my sword and rifle, and rode to Swallow's field. I rode fast, for my entire being was consumed by what I was doing.

At first I saw nothing when I arrived. I was early. The night was clear and the moon shone down, periodically covered by clouds.

An eerie artificial silence was in the air, but the night seemed pregnant with sinister possibilities.

The area I had been called to was a slight upraised hill, long and wide. On all sides at a distance, there were tree-lines, and on one side, hedgerows at a fair ways to the left. My horse was restless and I had great difficulty compelling him to be still.

Presently I saw a shadow approach from the opposite direction I had come, and before long I heard a voice cry:

'Hark, who stands there? Identify yourself at once!'

'I am Marcel de la Croix,' replied I, 'son of Marquis de la Croix.'

'I know of you.' said the voice. 'You are coming of age tomorrow, it seems. But what is all this business? If you needed my help, why did you not ask for it as a gentleman?'

'Hush,' I whispered, 'I was summoned here myself; someone approaches.'

I signalled for him to accompany me in moving to the side of the mound closer to the tree line.

As we did so, the moon was covered by a cloud. We began to hear quiet murmurs of conversation, and gentle commands whispered by a woman to a servant. But a moment later we heard a cough, and then the timid voice of a young man cried out, 'Is anyone there?'

'I have come, Sir, since you have summoned me,' replied she, 'but be warned, if you intend anything untoward, I have not come here alone.'

'Aye,' sounded a gruff voice beside her.

'Begging your pardon, madam,' returned the same timid voice, 'but I thought it was you who needed my help, or so the note said.'

A consternated silence followed. Suddenly a light appeared in the distance on the other side of the hedgerows. All attention was instantly focused there, as the light dipped ominously, and became two. This process was repeated on either side, and the light of torches silently spread from two to four, and then upwards, growing more numerous with each moment. The torchbearers seemed to be arranged in a circular pattern, and gradually we became aware that we were surrounded on all sides at a distance of perhaps thirty or forty paces. When all was said and done, their lights numbered perhaps one-hundred and fifty.

The faces of the torchbearers were largely obscured by the distance, but it was clear they were largely peasants, both men and women, with expressions as grim as death. My heart beat as it has never since, through all I have experienced. It was, after all, the beginning of everything.

My companion drew his sword, and I followed suit, in a dreamlike state. Our other three companions then became aware of us, though it was evident we were in no better position to defend ourselves than they.

Suddenly, out of the crowd came a man on horseback, bearing a torch like the others, and wearing a mask over the lower part of his face, in the style of an English highwayman.

'Greetings!' cried he, once he was close enough to be heard. 'It is good of you to join us on this momentous evening. Drop your weapons, gentleman, else you will be responsible for the deaths of the others. Otherwise, we mean to let you all live.'

'Good God!' cried my companion, addressing me rather than the man who spoke, 'How are we to be expected to believe such men as these?!'

'Why, if you like, I swear it upon the success of our cause (you will perceive we have one). Upon freedom and equality. That will be all; you may believe or not. I tell you again, discard your weapons. You have no hope otherwise. We have a message to be delivered to all of France.'

I threw down my weapons first, and my companion could not help but follow, with a look of misgiving to me.

'Come, bind their hands,' cried the man on horseback, and immediately seven men came forward to do so. The five of us were compelled to sit with our backs toward each other, in the shape of a five-pointed star.

All this was done roughly, formally and begrudgingly. When it was done, the man on horseback addressed us again, trotting round us in a circle while he spoke.

'You will be curious, no doubt, to know what has transpired and why you were called here this evening. You may be surprised to know that the same note sent to you was sent to every 'distinguished member' of every 'distinguished family' within five leagues of this spot. It seems that among the families hereabouts, there are but five, nay, four,' pondering the large servant who accompanied the young woman, 'decent people who thought it worth an hour of their time to save the life of another. Your mothers, fathers, sisters, brothers, all thought it too heavy a price to pay, and now they shall perish, if they have not already. How differently would they have acted had they only known that the life they were to save was their own! Except yourselves, the hereditary line you have sprung from is now as extinct as it is corrupt. A new order is dawning. The decency of your character alone has spared you, and after today, you shall have little else.'

We stared at him in horror, hardly comprehending what was meant.

As he was speaking, a rough, dirty-looking man, his eyes flashing anger nourished by a lifetime of hardship, approached us all. Without a word of warning, proceeded to brand each of us on the hand with a cattle-prod, rudely fashioned in the shape of a star.

'Think of this as a mark of favour,' continued the man on horseback, ignoring the screams of the young girl, which had not subsided. 'For thirty days at least, no one will harm anyone bearing that mark, but after that, if you choose to stay in the area, no one can guarantee your safety.'

He paused, looking at us all contemplatively. 'A short way from here there is a large oak tree in a field. By that tree there is a little fire, and if it burns still you may use it to free yourself from the ropes that bind you. Consider this as exquisite mercy, not often to be repeated.'

With this he turned his horse from the circle, and after he had gone, the torches moved slowly away from us, extinguishing gradually in different directions, slowly scattering into the night.

I will close my story here and feel relieved to have got this far. It has been the work of a better part of the morning. I have kept to my chamber since we all breakfasted together in the ladies' room, as is becoming customary.

Mouchard returned this afternoon with welcome news: namely that the house is available, but as we are French, the owner stipulates three months' rent in advance.

I sent him to return at once and complete the deal, and almost immediately that he had departed, Mlle de Courteline appeared in the room.

"Did I hear Mouchard?" inquired she, without ceremony.

"Yes, he has but just departed again."

"Well, but is he to be gone long? You must call him back, in that case, for I am bored, and I have a strange desire to hear more of his tale."

"He has but just gone to settle with our new landlord, for a house near Harwich."

"Ah, that is good news! I only hope it shall be a decent sort of place. Was there no money needed? Perhaps the man has heard of my family?"

"The English are practical people, Madam, and he required three months' security."

"Ah, barbarous! Well, perhaps we should give him four, to give him a right idea of our contempt. But stay, why did you not come to me if money was wanted?"

I was a little abashed at this, but I said, "I did not think to."

This answer seemed to cause her a good deal of consternation.

"Thank you for managing this matter," said she at last, feigning unconcern, "for perhaps it is not suitable for me to do so, and it would be more appropriate for Mlle Vallon's intended, M. Savard, to settle accounts with you when he arrives shortly. Nevertheless, I trust you will not allow yourself to be strained unnecessarily, as our trunk may be lightened without any inconvenience." She paused, for a moment or two, "Ordinarily, I would not accept such assistance, as it is not generally acceptable for women in our position to accept any generosity offered them by a person heretofore unknown to them, for fear of creating expectations or obligations such as might taint the character of respectable women."

She stopped again, seeming quite pleased with the dignity she assumed during her speech, and after taking a breath, she said, "However, I doubt many persons have been in a situation such as ours. You are now, I hope, too suitably familiar with my name and character to think that any obligations conferred would entitle you to any kind of indecent freedoms. Moreover, you are aware we are hardly in a position of want, and we may easily repay you at any time you should desire."

I hardly knew how to respond to this harangue, so I said nothing. Mlle de Courteline turned, perhaps expecting some sort of acknowledgement, but seeing that I was silent, she said, "And perhaps I should add, that although we have made your acquaintance under truly distressing and unusual circumstances, you have acted quite honourably."

I bowed, hardly overwhelmed by this scant acknowledgement. Before putting an end to this unnecessary and uncomfortable interview, I said, "You have mentioned M. Savard, who I believe you described as the intended husband of Mlle Vallon. Do I understand you expect him here in the next little while?"

"Yes, Sir. He wrote several days ago to inform us that my father is unfortunately prevented from coming here at present, but he sends M. Savard in his place to assist us."

"You mean your father has written to say he is sending M. Savard for your protection?"

"No," replied she, evidently displeased by the question, "my father must have some reason for sending his messages through M. Savard, but in any case, I am sure all will be cleared up upon that gentleman's arrival, which no doubt will be soon."

I merely nodded and bowed.

"In any event," added she, "I thank you again for your consideration. Pray let me know when little Mouchard has returned."

With that she returned to her room. Mouchard returned a short while later, bearing a note from Sir John Etheredge. It was written in English, but roughly translated by Mouchard, it said:

Dear Sir,

I am honoured to acknowledge such distinguished citizens of our neighbour country as my honoured tenants. Many apologies for the coarse formalities of this business, but things being as they are of late, we have had many recent occurrences where some of your countrymen are unable to meet their expenses (doubtless through no fault of their own, as these are treacherous times).

Nevertheless, I ask your apologies for anything that may have seemed excessively rigid in my precautions, and welcome you and your party heartily to Sorsten Manor. Your servant has described your need for separate accommodations, and I think Sorsten will suit you vastly well, as there is a Parsonage not thirty paces from the main house.

I have sent my man to Sorsten just minutes ago, to prepare for your arrival, and I shall answer it will be ready for you in a few days at most. I have given your boy directions, and if you travel leisurely, I am sure the timing will leave nothing to be desired.

Be so kind as to dine with me and my family tomorrow, before you set out, (if that is your intention.)

Your most obliged servant,
Sir John Etheredge

This letter, which I conveyed to the ladies (with the help of Mouchard's translation) was received quite favourably. Mlle de Courteline appeared to think it necessary to conceal some of the pleasure it gave her, and after a short time, she said,

"Pray, where is Mouchard?"

"I sent him out again to speak with the landlord, but I am sure he will be back at any minute."

"Summon him to our room immediately, and I will have him

continue his tale. You will come as well, I imagine, since I venture to guess you have discovered no secret source of amusement?"

This was an interesting choice of words, as it turned out, for she reflected immediately on what they might imply, and then she coloured, looked displeased and said, "As you please."

Though I had every intention to come, since I was intrigued by the seeming character change it caused in Mouchard as much as in the story he told, it seemed I was required to now, or else suffer the imputation she had inadvertently made.

I know not quite how to explain the situation I find myself in, for I am neither truly known or obligated, but yet I feel I cannot leave either, and have committed myself to continue functioning as either protector or nursemaid (I cannot tell which, myself) for some while longer.

M. Tolouse came in a short while later. He was happy to hear the news but declared that he would prefer to meet us in Harwich and take his own route. I expect he feels constrained in the presence of the ladies, and cannot rid himself of all his bad habits. He has elected to leave tonight and when I told him of the invitation from Sir Etheredge, he declared, "That sort of thing is not for me. Enjoy yourself, with the ladies, and we shall meet up again in a few days. Be so good as to convey that to the ladies in my absence."

Mouchard returned shortly thereafter, and not too long afterwards, we entered the ladies' room together. They all appeared quite happy to see us.

"Now, young man," said Mlle de Courteline, once she had seated herself ceremoniously, "you have pleased me greatly with your story, which I must warn you is not so easy to do. However, as I told you yesterday, I am quite worn from misfortune and do not wish to hear of it. Take your story in a cheery direction, pray, and tell us of love."

"My story only has one direction," said he stoically, looking as if he wished to tell it as much as he feared to.

"Well, indeed, then you must begin, that I may decide how well it goes."

The boy hesitated as before, but then placing himself as if apart from us in some respects, and gazing out a window, he said:

"*It will be* wise to give a short history of the family whose paths have now crossed with the unfortunate child's. Mr. Reckert, as I indicated before, was an indulgent father and a widow. His marriage had been short and happy, for Mrs. Reckert died when Miss Reckert was near five or six years old. In the grief of his wife's passing, Mr. Reckert threw himself wholly into the pursuit of his favourite passion: political calculation and manoeuvring. The rise and fall of adversaries, the success or failure of strategies, were to him the stuff of life. Though he loved his daughter dearly, like many parents, he did not know how to raise or guide her. He did not think to initiate her in his passions or interests, but to make up for his frequent absences, he refused her nothing. His absences and distraction, however, were a blessing of sorts, for they ensured he paid her too little attention to truly ruin her character through over-indulgence.

From the time of his rescue, little Thomas remained her constant companion. She spoke, and he listened, she taught and he learnt, coming gradually to understand her character better than he did his own. Though the loquaciousness of her youth lessened somewhat with time, Thomas had learnt to read her thoughts and feelings effortlessly, so important was she to his daily existence. When Mr. Reckert was home, Thomas would administer to his needs as well, often flitting about the house like a shadow, always ready with the thing desired even before it had been thought of.

Truth be told, in his complete innocence, Thomas had acquired almost the habits of a spy. He was timorous and unwilling to call attention to himself unless it was necessary. He hung near doors, listening to conversations, or following behind people as they walked, waiting and anticipating any need which might arise, upon which he would suddenly appear, ready to serve.

In the same year that Thomas joined the Reckert household, Miss Reckert's future tutor, Mr. Seymour was also introduced there by chance. Mr. Seymour was a most amiable, diligent, learned man, whose principal fault (it seems we all must have one) was a lack of curiosity regarding others. Though he was then well into his forties, he had retained the child-like habit of looking at everything chiefly with an eye to how it related to himself, and if a matter was outside of this scope, he listened only to be polite, and thought no more about it later. His two guiding passions were medieval archaeology and cartology in general. Though strictly an amateur in these fields, he was nevertheless very knowledgeable, and pursued study of them with single-minded enthusiasm.

It was his interest in old ruins which had first brought him to the home of the Reckerts. The ruins of an old fortress existed at the far edge of the current property, and the original acquaintance between them had begun when Mr. Seymour had called upon them to ask permission to explore them.

At that time the fort was inaccessible, due to the shallow muddy moat which surrounded it, and Mr. Reckert had invited him to stay with them for a short while till they might assemble the proper materials to cross it. To everyone's amusement, Mr. Seymour's impatience led him to surmount the moat, without aid, the very next day, sacrificing his coat and trousers to the mud in the process.

This spirit of adventure had greatly pleased the young Miss Reckert, who became his help-mate. Her father prohibited her from attempting to cross the moat herself, and therefore she contented herself with contriving a small catapult to convey Mr. Seymour supplies and nourishment during the day, to save him the trouble of going back and forth.

It was soon apparent to most that they were well paired with one another, for the young lady seemed slightly older than her age, and Mr. Seymour, though learned, often lacked the patience and restraint which suited his age.

The ruins provided Mr. Seymour with ample material for exploration, as they had been untouched for many years. His stay extended from days to weeks, during which time Miss Reckert happily assisted him with all he attempted. The eventual decision to engage him as her tutor was almost a formality to acknowledge the arrangement that already existed between them.

Throughout this time, Mr. Reckert continued to be wholly preoccupied with the considerations of public life. Always a wealthy man, he coveted influence, and found even the most minute details of strategy exhilarating.

Like many men in his position, he regretted never having a son, and it seems likely that this unfulfilled yearning contributed to the readiness with which he formed a bond with a young man of ambition, Mr. Harland. Mr. Harland was then nearing thirty years old, a member of the House of Parliament, he owned a country seat in Hertfordshire, though his primary residence was in London. The two men collaborated early on a project for which they shared a good deal of passion, and its eventual failure seemed only to strengthen their connection. Despite this early setback, the fortunes of both Mr. Reckert and Mr. Harland improved steadily from the time of their acquaintance, and they sustained a very cordial and profitable relationship."

"Pray, Mouchard," interrupted Mlle de Courteline, "you do not mean to turn this into a tale of political intrigue, surely? Why do the English think of nothing else but politics?"

"Indeed, Madam, I am sorry to have displeased you," said the boy, meekly.

"Pay no mind," I offered, gently, "if the story leads to political intrigue, I, at least shall not be bored."

"It does not, Sir," replied he, hesitantly, "but I know not how to tell it otherwise."

"Pray continue."

"In the happiest period of his youth, Mr. Reckert had been the cherished companion of the celebrated Earl of C, who had grown up in the same neighbourhood. The Earl of C had enjoyed a storied ascent to prominence. His military career seemed almost charmed, and his personal conduct in battle had been nothing short of heroic.

After one of his successful campaigns on behalf of the King, the Monarch had rewarded him with a sizeable bequest of land. It was in this same year the entire neighbourhood experienced a drought which resulted in poor harvest and increased suffering to the poorest labouring families in that area.

In a gesture of great magnanimity, the Earl pledged half of this gift of land he had received to the many hardworking farmers in the vicinity, to whom he also pledged the rights to the large quarry on his land, providing they would do the work to construct their future settlements. A new town was proposed in an area central to these modest plots, located where Mr. Reckert's property intersected with one of his neighbour's, Lord Ladderly, Southwest of the original town of Gibbons. In the spirit of the Earl's generosity, each gentleman pledged to allow the development, and hinted at their willingness to do more once the project was completed.

Alas the proposed development was not to be. The Earl of C perished, with all of his immediate family, upon an ill-fated sea voyage to Italy.

The property and title of the Earl accordingly went into abeyance till the King could choose among the Earl's many indirect heirs (among whom there were upwards of nine, each in varying circumstances). His Majesty was reluctant to choose between them immediately, and therefore the land of the Earl was suspended along with his title and possessions. Moreover, though the Earl's intentions were much known and celebrated, whoever inherited his property was by no legal means obligated to follow-through with the former Earl's plans, and the poor people of the neighbourhood (some of whom had already begun to build) had no claim beyond the late Earl's goodwill.

Mr. Reckert and Mr. Ladderly saw no reason to bequeath their land while the fate of the whole project was in jeopardy, and both declared they would wait upon the King's decision, which every year seemed less imminent.

Soon after the initial connection between Mr. Harland and Mr.

Reckert, Mr. Reckert discovered with pleasure that his friend was amongst the nine potential heirs of the Earl, though he was, by his own acknowledgement, one of the least likely to prevail in such a claim.

Nevertheless, early in their acquaintance, Mr. Reckert made a personal appeal to his Majesty, in favour of the succession of his friend, in the hope that his own historical connection with the heroic Earl, would weigh significantly in the favour of Mr. Harland.

The answer, given by a trusted surrogate of the King, was that although Mr. Harland was not presently favoured by the Monarch to succeed his famed ancestor, his Majesty was willing to delay his decision several years long, in which time Mr. Harland was advised to give careful thought to any decision which might significantly improve his eligibility in the eyes of his sovereign.

This answer was received joyously by the two friends, who perceived that much may happen in the course of a few years to improve Mr. Harland's standing. By then he was relatively wealthy, but his wealth had come without rank, and it was clear that a well-positioned marriage had the greatest chance of improving his standing.

Now such a plan would not be agreeable to every man, but we must understand that Mr. Harland's temperament and situation were eminently suited to it. By then he was around thirty-three years old, and had spent the first part of his life almost entirely focused on his own personal advancement, giving little thought to women. When he was younger he had one significant connection which had ended badly for reasons he had never understood. His high opinion of the lady prevented him from guessing that her insincerity itself was to blame, and the incident had retained more mystery than it ought to have.

Now, many years later, he was more than content to avoid any such perplexities in choosing to marry only as it may improve either his wealth or his standing. As his disposition was well known by Mr. Reckert, he approved of the plan most heartily. The potential advantages of a great many alliances were considered between them, but alas nothing was truly decided upon.

By this time, Miss Reckert was a young woman, and Mr. Seymour had ceased to be her tutor and had become Mr. Harland's steward. The task of proposing a suitable alliance was then given over to the province of Mr. Seymour."

"Well!" cried Mlle de Courteline, interrupting suddenly, "this is truly romantic, I do swear."

She appeared to forget, in her sarcasm, that Mlle Vallon's destiny was hardly more so, and at her remark, the young girl dropped her head in silent thought.

The boy likewise looked at the ground, seemingly unwilling to speak until commanded, and Mlle de Courteline at length begrudgingly bid him to continue, evidently preferring him to begin on his own.

"It is demonstrable," said he, after a moment, "that certain meetings between people have more significance than others, and such was the case for Mr. Harland and Miss Reckert."

"Indeed!" declared Mlle de Courteline, but this exclamation appeared to have been entirely spontaneous, as she resisted the temptation to say more, and waved for him to continue.

"By this time, Miss Reckert was a beautiful and charming maid of seventeen. Already she was beginning to acquire a number of admirers and had begun to feel pressure from her father to decide amongst them and to marry. The introduction between she and Mr. Harland was brief and very formal, as no-one thought it of much importance. Mr. Reckert himself was unaware an introduction had never been performed between the two, and Miss Reckert had entered her father's study that morning without realizing anyone else was present in the house. On Mr. Harland's side, he admired what could not be ignored, but with the detached manner of a man who surveys a raffle prize without a ticket.

Had one been able to question Miss Reckert on the subject, they would have found she felt very little about it. Mr. Harland was neither attractive nor unattractive, agreeable nor disagreeable. It was only several weeks after this brief encounter that she was forced to acknowledge to herself that she found him strangely compelling and thought of him more frequently than she knew how to understand.

From nearly the time of this seemingly insignificant meeting, a slow but undeniable change was wrought upon her. The admiration of her suitors was no longer found agreeable. The adoration she had once beheld with pleasure or indifference, now dismayed her.

Prior to this time, it had seemed only natural to her that admiration should give birth to love and love in turn should lead to marriage. Now, it seemed to her that compliments had metamorphosed into flattery, and flattery begot vanity, rather than true affection.

It should not be assumed that the lady herself made any connection between the event and its subsequent effects, but merely that they occurred, were remarked, and carefree gaiety seemed transformed into slight melancholy.

One might not wonder to hear that in a year's time all suits had been refused and a degree of concern had begun to be felt by her father. The lady was quizzed as to her feelings, but as she herself was yet to guess at them, nothing was learnt.

In that entire year she did not see Mr. Harland above twice. Once, unobserved from a window as he strolled up the lawn, and again when she had entered her father's library, once again unaware the two were in consultation. On this occasion he had nodded inexpressively, and she had excused herself for the unintended interruption.

Too often, after all, one thinks without examining ones' motive for doing so, and such was the case with Miss Reckert, who thought of that gentleman without any idea why she did so. The truth was not discovered even to herself until prompted by the questions and remarks of her cousin, Miss Graham, she discovered the nature of her own views.

Whenever her cousin praised a quality possessed by another gentleman, she felt her own internal voice cried out a preference, and by this means discovered that in every respect she believed Mr. Harland superior to all others of his sex.

Being conscious how absurdly her cousin should regard such a confession, she was silent, and inwardly resolved to examine her own feelings more closely when alone.

What strange revelations awaited a girl who had been taught that only superficial graces and abilities could inspire such a passion! In Mr. Harland, she fancied she had descried the far more worthwhile indications of character and strength, added to which was overall quality or appeal she could not explain. It seemed to her as if substance had vanquished superficiality, which was, after all, more in keeping with the nature of her education than with the general views of the world.

'But what of it?' she was forced to ask herself. What use was it to discover a partiality towards someone who showed no same partiality for her.

There was one more trifling connection between the two, of which she was only then to become fully aware; namely, that her friend and tutor Mr. Seymour was now Mr. Harland's steward. Though she had previously known of this circumstance, it had been before her acquaintance with Mr. Harland, and therefore had made no impression upon her until Mr. Seymour chanced to visit on an errand related to Mr. Harland.

He came on this occasion to speak with Mr. Harland and Mr. Reckert upon the matters that were in agitation between them. His chief duty, of late, was to search for a suitable alliance for that gentleman, and as he freely explained to Miss Reckert, it was largely a question of widows and neglected daughters.

'Mr. Harland,' he said, 'prides himself upon being indifferent to the matter, but this can never be as true as he wishes, and if I propose a match where the woman in the case is truly unappealing, but the situation is perfectly eligible, he will tell me that I need not go that far in 'that direction', by which he means less money or fewer connections would please him better than being repulsed by the person of his wife, and so it becomes a more difficult business than is admitted.'

'And is Mr. Harland so cynical, Sir?'

'Practical, rather, I should think. It would not do for him to be chasing after young things who have plenty of suitors more to their taste, and if a man's heart is not to be consulted, then many other things must be.'

'I should think temperament would be foremost.'

'Aye, it is important, for all the practical benefit in the world will not avail one much if they are being driven mad on a daily basis, or if ones' wife is carrying on in a manner..., nay, I should not like to go further, begging your pardon.'

Miss Reckert sighed. 'But if I understand the purpose of your current visit, you must think you have succeeded?'

'As to that, it seems rather doubtful, but I must see before I proceed further. As important as it is, I fear Mr. Harland does not relish the process. He is to take a short trip to Calais, and thus I must speak to him before he goes, but very little is like to come of it.'

'Do you stay long?'

'Nay, madam, now we come to it. From here I intend to pay a visit to the Devon area, where I hope to speak with a gentleman on the same matter, but only guess what is in the same vicinity, why, in the same park, almost?'

'I cannot, Sir.'

'A Benedictine nunnery, my dear. I can scarcely believe the luck. Do you recall the map I acquired in London?'

'Not at the moment, I fear.'

'Never mind, it is of no import. In any case, the map itself is in very poor shape, else I would have brought it to show you. I was told it was four-hundred years old, but now I am inclined to believe it is even older. Nay, I am getting ahead of myself. Let me start from the beginning. Several months ago, when I first thought it might be eligible to suggest an alliance with this family, I was naturally interested in the extent of the property in question, for the lady is an heiress. It shall not very much surprise you to learn I was curious to contrast the current map with the old one, and was surprised, nay, delighted, to see that there is a nunnery shown right by the Cathedral. I took the liberty of inquiring after it by letter, among my other communications with her father, and he informed me that the Cathedral was burnt and entirely demolished over the years, but the nunnery was generally spared, and most of its walls and cloister are still intact, though the roof is gone. I am anxious to go there as soon as may be, and I have studied the old map so carefully, I intend to follow it by heart to see what else might have changed in that time. I hope, when I return, I may be able to bring with me some memento of the place.'

'Do you intend to bring back a stone, Sir, or do you have some more ambitious hope?'

'Nothing but some sign of its former inhabitants shall satisfy me!'

'I fear that will be too much to expect, for it is likely the area has been much gone over.'

'Here I hope to prove you wrong. The gentleman mentioned the owner of the property has entirely neglected the spot in his life for fear any attempt to restore it would cause his neighbours to suspect him of popery, and therefore it is my hope he might not object to a more thorough search.'

Miss Reckert diplomatically said she hoped it would be so, and they parted shortly thereafter; their thoughts occupied in two entirely different ways.

The beginning of this conversation was all too informative to Miss Reckert, who understood all the more that there was nothing to expect from the gentleman she had the misfortune to admire.

Mr. Harland left the country for several months and then returned. She compelled herself not to seek any interaction with him if it were possible, and indeed very little was possible. Two more offers were tendered to her father by neighbouring gentleman, and refused by the lady. In both cases she had very little interaction with the gentlemen in question, and the offers were made merely owing to their eligibility. Her father could not bear to oppose her, but spoke despairingly of the whole matter to many. He was too fond of his daughter to cause her pain, but was yet convinced her behaviour was more fanciful than justified.

For her own part, Miss Reckert confined her social circle all the more. Most days she would walk out to call upon her cousin, Miss Graham, or one or two of the friends she had known since childhood, and then spend a majority of the day out of doors. Since this arrangement was more conducive to allowing her to avoid visitors who called on the house, she petitioned her father to allow her to have a little gazebo built next to the greenhouse where no one would look for her. For the next few months, much of her time was occupied observing its construction, till at last she was able to move a great part of her things into it; among them her books, writing desk, a table to entertain any visitors, and ample seats and sofas. During that time, Miss Graham was married and moved out of the county, and at her departure, Miss Reckert scarcely made any attempt to replace her companionship.

Though he had given permission for the gazebo to be built, Mr. Reckert was dismayed at the final product. Every detail of its comfort and arrangement spoke to the designer's desire to shun society. This prediction was fulfilled much as he feared, for Miss Reckert was desirous to avoid anything which was likely to give rise to further hope and inevitable disappointment in her father. Her ample fortune had begun to feel like a burden of sorts, since it ensured some offers would be made regardless, but at least she was determined not to suffer the visits made to this purpose.

This situation carried on for several months, and would doubtless for several more had not circumstances conspired to force a change. The first of these was a rather commonplace decision of Mr. Harland to commission work on his estate. Once begun, the work seemed to become more extensive and inconvenient than he had anticipated, and he observed to Mr. Reckert on one occasion that he was forced to track through nearly four inches of dust every day. Many of his servants had declined to bear the inconvenience with their master, and to add to this, he had developed an irritating cough as a result of the dust. Mr. Reckert immediately offered him the use of the house adjoining his own, a sizeable and respectable property left him by his younger brother, a bachelor.

Mr. Harland hesitated somewhat to accept and the matter was dropped for the time being. Nearly a month and a half later, the two gentlemen saw each other again when Mr. Reckert called upon his friend at his house on his way back from London. The condition of the house had only become less liveable in that time, and Mr. Harland was forced to entertain his guest in the garden in order to spare his clothes from the dust.

'Dear Mr. Harland,' said Mr. Reckert, 'I am upon the verge of being insulted you did not accept my offer, considering how things go here.'

'Forgive me, Sir, I do not mean to give offence. The truth of the matter is it is not merely myself you would be inviting, for my nephew is to come to me even next week, along with his aunt, my sister. I would not trespass so much on your kindness and generosity as to bring so many strangers into the immediate vicinity for so uncertain a period of time. There is, however, no question that we must all live elsewhere, for I cannot even keep the east wing free from dust. I intend to rent a place in the area as soon as may be.'

'Nay, do not even think of it or I shall be truly incensed. Surely you cannot have any objection to the place?'

'No, for I have never seen it, though I am sure it is eminently suitable. I could not bear to live there without renting it from you, however, for why should you lose money on my account?'

'Lose money, my dear Sir? There has been no question of that for the place is empty year-round. I do not let it, Sir, for as you say, it is a little too close for strangers, but I could hardly consider guests or family of your own as such. Indeed, I am sure their presence would enliven the area.'

'In that case, I believe it shall be ideal, but pray do not ask me to live there for nothing, for that should be against my very nature.'

'As you wish, though I do so only to carry the point. And you shall let me set the price myself, nor quibble with me about it, for I shall have you in some respects, my guest.'

This compromise was agreed to, and preparations were soon made to make the house ready and transfer his belongings."

It was here Mouchard stopped speaking, and gently bowed his head to indicate he was finished for the time being. Mlle de Courteline looked rather frustrated, but seemed unwilling to command him to do more, since it might reveal how interested she had become in his story. Mlle Vallon also looked quietly disappointed, but the old guardian, Mme. Gaspar simply looked up from her knitting to inquire, 'Is it supper time, already?'

I cannot deny that there is something quite pleasing and ingenious in the story he tells, and I do not know where it is he can have come across it. I will close my letter here.

Yours ever,
MC

Marcel de la Croix to Henri Renault

January 12th,1793

Dear Friend,

This morning while I was out walking, my thoughts drifted to where I had left off in my history, and as I have some time this morning before we set-out again, I will write while they are still fresh in my head.

If I recall rightly, I left off in the dark of 'Swallow's field.'

As the torch lights retreated and the darkness descended, complete silence reigned, but for the tiny sobs of the woman.

The gentleman I had first encountered rose to his feet, bringing us all up with him.

'Come,' he said grimly, 'we must see what this is all about.'

We stumbled awkwardly along, mistaking the direction twice, but eventually, with the help of the moon, we descried the tree and the little fire blazing nearby.

It seemed to me that I could smell this fire even before we saw it, for the misty air had a trace of smoke.

We positioned ourselves with difficulty, but at last the rope was burnt through, and we struggled apart. The recent burn of the brand on my hand was re-aggravated by the heat, and I sought to press it on the wet grass to relieve the pain.

The first gentleman disappeared immediately, but in a very short time, he reappeared on horseback, leading my own horse with him. After handing me the reins, he turned again to leave, and I called out,

'Wait! How shall we meet again, if all is as bad as I fear? How shall we leave the others in this condition, and a woman?'

'Let us meet here tomorrow night, if needs be. Escort the girl, I am obliged,' added he, already in mid-gallop.

Those of us who remained had no torch, and the way proved hard and uncertain. After a brief inquiry, I discovered that the young lady, Mme. Depuis, was staying with neighbours of mine, the Renees, while her husband was abroad.

Mme. Depuis was distraught, and she made a poor guide, but using what little knowledge I had of my surroundings, we were able at last to find the right path.

The little road we had stumbled upon was surrounded by bushes and trees, running along the top of a hill overlooking the gardens belonging to the Renee family. The air now had the unmistakable odour of smoke, and as we moved beyond the bushes to a point where we could see the house, we saw what we had all feared and expected.

The great house was visible at once in the distance, for it was entirely consumed by fire and smoke. Mme. Depuis screamed, while the rest of us stared in horror.

At that moment I thought only of the fate of my family, though in my heart I knew it already. In hindsight, I doubted my decision to accompany a strange woman, while my family was in peril, but it was in my nature to do as I did, for good or evil. It was soon clear, in any case, that by the time any of us had been released, it was too late for any of us to help anyone.

Looking back I know that it was at that moment, amidst tragedy, that I truly became a man. In such situations, one does not have a choice if one does not mean to perish.

As I watched the fire, I was possessed with a strength and determination that heretofore had not been part of my character. No longer doubting what needed to be done, I leapt upon my horse and turned to Mme. Depuis, saying,

'I am deeply sorry for your loss, Madam, and I fear that before the end of the night, you will not be alone in your grief. I leave you in the care of your protector, unless you desire otherwise, but at this instant I must discover what has become of my family. We are all bound to help each other now since our fate has been connected by the events of this evil night. My name is Marcel de la Croix, and hereafter any of you may find me at your service in the home of my ancestors, or whatever remains of it.'

I turned and rode away as soon as I had finished, not remembering to wait for a reply. I rode as fast as possible in the dark. Sometimes a sort of dizziness overtook me and I felt I might fall from my horse, but each time the feeling would gradually subside, and I remained upright.

Smoke was now heavy in the air and as I neared the Chateau, I could see nothing. It was not till I stood barely forty paces from it on the lawn, that I could see the flames devouring it through the smoke. The fumes were nearly overwhelming, but I could not move, transfixed by the sight, while hiding my face intermittently in my shirt.

The whole right portion of the house, which encompassed all the living quarters of my family, were entirely aflame. The smoke was black, curling in ominous clouds around it. The fire burnt in a slow, irresistible way, like a lion methodically devouring his prey, with no fear of interruption to cause him to hurry.

As I gazed at it, it seemed like a dream. Two hands grabbed me under the arms and pulled me backwards. I did not resist, as I was beyond doing so.

I was dragged, then carried, a short way, and then I found myself face to face with Philip, a loyal servant of my family and a rugged man of about fifty.

He looked at me grimly and said, 'That is better, young Monsieur. Best not get too close. Nothing can help now. The fire was set in too many places at once, I reckon. It was a deliberate act, of that you may be certain.'

Close by us, most of the servants of my family were gathered on the lawn, weeping or speaking quietly amongst themselves. I looked in that direction, and seeing me do so, Philip said,

'It was the family quarters which were set on fire, and the rest of the house was not touched.' He paused, and looked at me intently. 'The chaos and unrest hereabouts was not to be ignored. When men and women are desperate, there is no telling what they might be put to. What has started here will not end here.'

I must end here, I cannot write more. I did nothing to try to save my family; too easily persuaded nothing could be done. Although they were but strangers to me, I fear I have done more for true strangers since. I think perhaps I ought to have died in the attempt, rather than live with the consciousness for doing nothing.

We have but just returned from dinner with our new landlord, Sir John and his wife. I am not yet tired, so I will attempt to write the day before I go to sleep.

After breakfast today, the ladies closeted themselves away and the only evidence of their continued presence in the inn was the steady train of servants. Mouchard had not proven sufficient to perform the duties required and now served as an envoy to the maids of the inn who scurried back and forth with pins, hot water, and even flowers from the fields.

At last they emerged, dressed with elegance and finery one could little conceive possible in a country inn. Although they were both adorned with jewels, I was relieved to see the end result was not as excessive as it might have been. Mlle Vallon seemed entirely unaccustomed to her own finery, admiring herself with amazement, and beaming with joy to hear herself complimented.

The four of us rode together in a carriage. On the way it occurred to us that we had brought no one to translate, but as it was too late to return and fetch Mouchard, we kept on our way.

Sir John and Lady Beth received us as so many French curiosities, though the richness of the dress of the two young women, combined with the haughty demeanour of Mlle de Courteline, secured us the most gracious attentions.

Mlle de Courteline apologized immediately that none of us spoke sufficient English even to converse lightly, but Lady Beth replied in immaculate French, "Do not make yourselves uneasy on that score, for I believe I retain enough French to supply our needs for this evening. My husband, I fear, speaks no French at all."

"Oh!" cried Mlle de Courteline, with unexpected energy, "you speak French so perfectly, I am certain you have lived in France!"

"For a time before my marriage, when I was but a girl. What a tremendous pity it is that things have changed so much for the worse since then. But come, we shall not speak of that now."

Lady Beth led us quickly into the dining room. She was a small, genteel woman, whose expression and manners revealed she had spent more time travelling and in society than her husband. Nevertheless, she was rather cold-tempered by nature, and her smiles did not seem to come from the heart.

Sir John was much the opposite. He was simple and straightforward in his dress, manners and conversation. He said no more or less than he felt or he meant, and made no kind of pretence to elegance.

It would be difficult to find this breed of 'Country Gentleman' in France, for we have more trouble keeping them in the country, and their manners become more Parisienne. As Sir John spoke no French, Lady Beth translated his conversation, which she seemed to improve so much through translation, you could not be blamed for doubting he said anything like the final result.

On another occasion, Sir John spoke for several minutes, with great energy and enthusiasm. When at last he was done, he glanced at his wife that she might translate for us, while he set about his plate. She turned to us with great composure, and said in French, "Sir John has said something else about his dogs."

Sir John looked up presently, surprised that his meaning had been captured so succinctly in French, but as we all could not help but smile, he was satisfied, raising a general toast to 'wives.'

Sir John and Lady Beth have four children. The oldest girl and boy were above twenty, while the other two children were below fifteen. Sir John's brother, Mr. Etheredge, was also present that evening at dinner, seeming an average sort of man in his late fifties.

It became quickly apparent that Mlle Vallon had almost never been in any kind of society at all. She received any attentions from the eldest son, Mr. Thomas Etheredge, with the most open ingenuity, with no trace of artifice. If he complimented her in broken French, she would smile and blush, and on one occasion was brought to exclaim, "Oh, Sir, can you truly think so?"

The poor young man seemed quite beside himself to receive such friendly encouragement and approval from a young woman so richly dressed. Both Mlle de Courteline and her cousin are very handsome, though they each strike one quite in a different way, and each seem to possess a beauty that rather grows on you.

Lady Beth seemed to be somewhat less than charmed by the young lady's reception of her son, fearing lest she was a fortune hunter. The contrast between her behaviour and Mlle de Courteline's could not have been more stark than at that moment, for Mlle de Courteline appeared to wish to compensate for her cousin by adopting an attitude of extreme rigidity and severity.

Mlle Vallon was also quite diligent in her observation of the rest of the company. She seemed particularly taken with the contrast between one gentleman and another.

"I was hesitant to bring up the tumultuous happenings in your country," said Lady Beth to me presently, "but I must confess I have a great desire to know the latest news. Several of my cherished friends live in France, and I have been wracked with grief to hear nothing in several months."

"You must not assume the worst, my lady," replied I, "since the mail in France has been very unreliable for months. As to the situation in general, I fear the less said the better."

"Oh, indeed," declared Mlle de Courteline, "I fear the republicans have stopped the flow of mail almost completely, for I have not received any word from my father since we arrived several weeks ago."

"You must be terribly concerned," remarked her Ladyship.

"Concerned?" replied Mlle de Courteline, surprised, "why indeed I am, for it must have been more than a slight inconvenience to keep him from us so long. No matter, however, for he has sent his friend in his place, and we will soon learn all that has delayed him."

Lady Beth was evidently surprised by her assured manner of speaking, and looked at me inquiringly. I could only convey in response that I understood her surprise.

"When I was in France," continued Lady Beth, "I stayed near in Joigny in Burgundy, for the most part, and I believe the Gramonts lived in the area. Is that true, Monsieur?"

"The Gramonts are scattered all over, I believe," said I, to avoid being more exact.

"Of course," replied she, with a smile, "am I wrong to think there is a family connection between the de Courtelines and the Gramonts? It is quite a while since I thought of such things."

I was silent and Mlle de Courteline looked her amazement. Her feelings of family pride recoiled to have my supposed family tree mingled with hers.

I am not certain whether Lady Beth sincerely remembered a connection, but whatever the case, she convincingly pretended not to notice Mlle de Courteline's reaction (which was hardly possible), but then presently said, "Ah, forgive me, I had thought you were cousins, but no doubt there is another association between you."

Immediately Mlle de Courteline's thoughts seemed to turn upon how to explain the connection between us with propriety, and at last, with much perplexity and reluctance, she said, "The connection is distant indeed, my Lady."

The evening as a whole was very pleasant, but there was a strangeness in its very mundaneness. The English have been extremely insulated from the madness our country has endured and it is almost miraculous to see how little it has touched their lives, while it has all but destroyed ours.

The ride home in the carriage was extremely diverting.

"Dearest cousin," exclaimed Mlle de Courteline, immediately we were seated. 'What do you mean by looking that young gentleman full in the face that way? How strange in a young lady!"

"I am sorry to have done wrongly," replied the other, "but I know not how I have erred in doing so?"

"Why a young woman must not look so at a gentleman. One may look once, to be sure (as is only proper), but then one must look down, or elsewhere, and if a gentleman persists in looking at one again, and still, one must not look at him for anything. Really, I verily believe you looked at every man there as if the world had not enough of them! What must one think?"

"I am sure I should not have done it if I had known it was so wrong, but why is it that no one told me? Do inform me completely now, for I fear I do not yet comprehend. Tell me, I beg you, why was it so and what harm do you foresee?"

"Why only think of the expectations you might have raised with such imprudence?"

"You frighten me, cousin! What expectations, in whom?"

"Lord knows! Why, with everyone! What is the young man to think when a woman looks at him so? Pray, Monsieur, do assist me!"

"I do not know what to say," replied I, as gently as I could, "for it is plain that Mlle Vallon's upbringing has been to blame and she cannot be expected to conform to ideas she knows nothing about."

"Pray, M. Gramont," said Mlle Vallon, looking at me with the greatest sincerity, "do you agree with my cousin; have I done wrong?"

"I do not know that you have done wrong, exactly, but your cousin means only to spare you inconvenience, were you to unintentionally encourage unwanted attentions."

"Nay, I do not understand. Did I not look at the gentleman as you did, and as I did you?"

"'Tis true."

"But what expectations are these? Have you such?"

"No, but I might, were the circumstances different, and were I not aware of the specific details of your upbringing."

"Ah, then you must tell me what my cousin does not wish to!"

"I fear it would be inappropriate for me to do so."

"Your curiosity is unseemly, cousin," exclaimed Mlle de Courteline, in frustration. "But tell me, why did you look at that gentleman so?"

"Why, merely that there was such a difference between Mr. Thomas Etheredge and Mr. Etheredge. The first was rather pleasing to look at, while the other was just the opposite. The smiles of Mr. Thomas caused me a pleasant sort of agitation, while the smiles of Mr. Etheredge caused me to feel unsettled in an entirely different way."

"Oh, very well!" declared the other. "I guess we must merely be thankful you did not thank Mr. Thomas for these sensations. Have a care, however, that you do not develop too much inclination for the younger over the older, for your fate does not lie in that direction."

"What do you mean?"

"Why, M. Savard is a man of nearly sixty, and therefore you must not accustom yourself to preferring the smiles of young men over old."

"If M. Savard is like Mr. Etheredge, I believe I shall have no difficulty obeying your injunctions, for I should as soon not look at a man as that. But tell me, cousin, why must I only think of what is contrary to my liking? Would you instruct me to do likewise at the dinner-table, and eat only what repulses me? Were I to seek a friend, would you tell me to look only to those my nature repels?"

"M. Savard may not have youth or beauty on his side, but as he has been chosen for you by those who have your interest at heart, you may be sure he will be a better choice than you should make by mere ogling. Must you not, sometimes, have carrots over cake?"

"But then how must such a decision be made?"

"You need not be concerned with that, for they have already been made for you, and in the meantime, you must adhere to the principles of conduct which have been designed for your benefit. You must forebear exhibitions like this evening. You must refuse to speak with any gentleman you do not know, and avoid any circumstance which finds you alone with any person of the opposite sex, excepting only M. Savard or a member of your family."

"Oh no," cried Mlle Vallon, "I am sure you do not mean to include M. Gramont! Might I not speak with him alone, if he requested it, or help him if he required it? Surely you do not mean to include M. Gramont!"

"Oh, very fine!" cried her cousin, again. "And this you think to say in front of him?"

"Oh, indeed, for I am prodigiously fond of him, and I am sure you did not mean to include him."

"Did I not? He may be the worst of the bunch, for aught I know. Is he not a man as any other? Depend upon it, cousin, a man is all the more dangerous in a circumstance of familiarity, especially where there is no guardian to protect a young lady. And what if M. Gramont were to speak to you alone one day, and speak to you of some terrible disorder you might relieve, brought on by your beauty..."

"Oh, I should be more than happy to relieve it!"

"Good God! And is this what you have learnt in the convent?"

"Certainly, dearest cousin, and I should do as much for you and more, should you ask me. Do not the nuns relieve pain where they find it, and would it not be cruel to refuse the good gentleman anything, after he has assisted us so?"

"Cruel? I see you would supply the very language to be used to accomplish your own debauchery!"

"Forgive me, cousin, you are disturbed, and I am no less so. I see I do not understand what you say, or even the full meaning of the language I use. Can you mean to say that M. Gramont is less trustworthy than M. Savard, and I am to show him less respect? No, I am sure you do not mean it, though you are a woman of the world."

"I am no such thing!" snapped the other. "And you may be sure I have made no trial of the gentleman. But can you compare the two circumstances? Is not M. Savard the partner chosen for your life by those most dear to you? Though, no doubt, M. Gramont has acted well by us till now, and we all owe him gratitude, neither ourselves nor our families have any knowledge of him and his family. How then, might you in your ignorance, justify giving him a trust and deference that is sanctioned neither by your family or by your own length of acquaintance?"

Mlle de Courteline spoke heatedly, but I was too amused to take any offence, and she is unaccustomed to consider the possibility.

Mlle Vallon eyed me hesitantly for a short time, before saying quietly to her cousin, "But you do not mean less trustworthy than others, in this respect, which I fear I cannot guess?"

"Neither more or less so. All men are suspect in this regard."

"Why is it so?"

"It is like a sickness they are inflicted with, which leads them to evil."

"Ah! Then how I shall pity them!"

"Hush," replied the other, with sheer exhaustion, and I preferred to pretend I was asleep.

* * *

The next morning, according to Sir John's suggestion, we began our slow journey to Harwich and to Sorsten Manor. As Gravesend is near the water, we were obliged to cross the river Thames by ferry, before hiring a carriage on the other side. I rode on horseback alongside and about five hours after we had first set out, we reached the inn Sir John Etheredge had recommended. Sorsten is reportedly located between Colchester and Harwich and to our surprise we found it was estimated to be only another five or six hours journey from that point.

"Perhaps we should continue the rest of the way tomorrow," said Mlle de Courteline, "for I see no reason Sir John should mind if we occupy the house earlier?"

"It is likely a great amount of dust has been accumulating while it has been empty," replied I, "though I fear we will have to be somewhat early, regardless. No doubt there is much to see in this area by the sea, so perhaps we might be advised to stay here two days and explore."

Neither exploring the seaside and the cliffs or arriving at a dusty house seemed to have much appeal to Mlle de Courteline, but she submitted without complaint. The other two ladies walked out for a little while before dinner, while Mlle de Courteline stayed at the inn to write letters to her father and M. Savard, giving them the exact direction of Sorsten Manor.

Once she had done and the other two returned, we all supped together in the ladies' apartment.

"Now," said Mlle de Courteline, barely as the last spoon had been set down, "as we have nothing better to do, let us summon Mouchard and hear some more of his curious tale."

It was done, and Mouchard came in as before. Modest and unassuming, he nevertheless told a story like a master; increasingly he spoke as though none of us were in the room, and he addressed a larger audience.

"*When we last* left Miss Reckert, she had but just learnt that Mr. Harland and his relations would begin staying at the other house on their property. It shall be easy to guess Miss Reckert's consternation at this development. No part of her rejoiced at the news, from which she foresaw only awkwardness and pain. She was too proud to wish to attract someone who was neglectful of her in general, but unable to outwardly justify fully avoiding someone who had given her no other offence.

The whole party was to dine with them a week after their arrival. The behaviour of Miss Reckert on this occasion was quite subdued, exactly the reverse of young Mr. Whinston, Mr. Harland's nephew, to discover his charming neighbour. His uncle had made little mention of her, and so he had assumed there had been little to mention. His surprise seemed to heighten his delight, as he stationed himself near her and talked to her all evening.

Mr. Whinston's company was by no means disagreeable to Miss Reckert, since his volubility spared her much of the trouble of speaking. His presence also relieved her of some of the awkwardness she felt, being for the first time so long in the presence of Mr. Harland. Her gratitude and relief were so great that she went so far as to offer the temporary assistance of her cherished Thomas when she heard he had strained his right hand and could not write letters. It was common knowledge that Mr. Harland typically did not keep many servants about, even for his own needs.

This mark of favour was rare indeed, though she was careful to ensure Thomas would be treated well, confiding to the young gentleman that he was not strictly a servant. Mr. Whinston was delighted, assuring her that he would treat him with the greatest care.

Miss Reckert did not consider the conclusions which might be drawn from seeing the two so long contentedly in conversation with each other. Preoccupied with not betraying a hint of what no one would dream of guessing. On the point of retiring, she congratulated herself when she was, for having concealed all so well.

Not surprisingly, everyone present interpreted her complacence with other significance, including the young gentleman himself. Returning to their own house that evening, he expressed all his hopes and admiration to his uncle, who replied with cautious encouragement.

'I own I was myself surprised to observe Miss Reckert's demeanour today, for it is not quite like I remembered it, but I have only ever seen her briefly.'

'Ah, such sweet, expressive eyes were never seen–.'

'Allow me to interrupt, since I have looked at the Miss Reckert well enough this evening to imagine you could go on forever in this strain. Forgive me, dear nephew, but I feel it only right to caution you that the young lady in question has acquired a seemingly deserved reputation for changeability.'

'I will venture to think that is lucky for me, for otherwise it seems likely she would not be free.'

Finding how sanguine his nephew was inclined to be, Mr. Harland did not venture any further words of caution, but rather resolved to see how his friend, her father would view things. As it turned out, Mr. Reckert was nearly as sanguine as the young man himself.

'It bodes well, I think, for the future,' said he, speaking of Mr. Winston's reception when the two met the next morning, 'and indeed, I cannot think of anything more desirable. Yet I hesitate to judge prematurely, as I have no better idea what is to be expected than another.'

'I am in complete agreement, Sir,' replied Mr. Harland, 'as I can think of few more advantageous alliances, and I need not say that all the honour would be to my family. But as desirable as a match would be, I believe it is best we resist the temptation to interfere as much as possible.'

'You speak rightly, and though her father, I do not so much flatter myself as having the influence one might expect. One has only the influence one is prepared to command, and all too often women are immune from this. If it were possible to enforce happiness through filial authority, I would have done it long ago. Nevertheless I do not think it would hurt to facilitate meetings between them, wherever possible, for my daughter is apt to shun company of late.'

Mr. Harland felt this was a reasonable approach, but was far from encouraged to hear it was thought to be necessary. For the sake of his friend and nephew, he was still willing to hope for the best.

As they had but lately dined at the main house, it seemed only natural for the occupants of the other house to return the invitation. This action was taken by Miss Harland, without the instigation of her brother, since she deemed it only natural to do.

Thus it was that within the week, Miss Reckert had another ordeal to manage.

After dinner the entire company removed to the drawing room, whereupon the subject of the environs was raised, and Miss Harland inquired to know how far west the property extended.

'The original property was not as far west as it is now, Madam,' replied Mr. Reckert, 'for when I was a boy, my father purchased a smaller neighbouring property, which was vacant but for the ruins of an old fortress.'

'Indeed,' cried Mr. Whinston, 'I think we cannot have walked far enough, for we saw no signs of it on our way. I should most certainly have walked farther to see it, had I known one was there. May I ask what remains of it?'

'My daughter knows best, to be sure,' replied Mr. Reckert, 'for I am certain she goes to see it every week.' With this he looked in expectation at Miss Reckert, but as she made no remark, he said, 'You will be amazed to learn that it is only this past year we have been able to explore it at all, as from the time my father acquired it, it has been surrounded by a deep, wide moat, empty but for several feet of muddy water at the bottom. The drawbridge which must have been in use was no longer in existence, and we were forced to try to make other ways across it. Once or twice we frolicked around in the pit as boys, but we could never make it up the other side. Eventually we made do with logs and planks, but my dear mother could never abide the idea that we were crossing so, and ordered they be removed and no one be suffered to help us replace them. The fortress itself is mostly grass. It originally boasted two outer walls, portions of which are intact in some places, but on approach it looks like a large mound, with stones jutting up at various places, and a solid staircase in the foreground winding up to reach the top of its fallen walls. In some places the walls still stand near fifteen feet high, but the stair is near thirty, and was built into the side of a hill, where it remains so well preserved. In time I had nearly forgotten about it entirely, but my daughter has ever insisted some attempt be made to preserve or use it in some manner, and therefore we have but recently made a drawbridge of sorts to cross it (though it is not fit to be drawn).'

'I am more eager than ever to see it,' cried Mr. Whinston. 'Is it much further than the stream?'

''Tis as far as the stream again,' replied the other, 'but if you would like to see it, I should be glad if we all were to go together. I have not crossed to the fortress myself since I was child.' All voices were in favour of this excursion, save Miss Reckert, who was silent.

'Does the plank still hold, my dear?' inquired he, addressing her.

'Very well.'

'Then you must show us all what has been uncovered there, for I'll wager you might do it in your sleep.'

'I should be happy to.'

Of all possible excursions, this was the one she had no opportunity of declining to join. Her fondness for the area and the subject in general was so well-known that any reluctance would not go unmarked.

She was applied to several times during the evening to answer various questions about the place, but her replies were so short and laconic that no one could be blamed for thinking she knew little about it in truth.

Her taciturnity did not discourage the others, and many follow-up visits were made to plan and discuss the outing, which had naturally become a picnic of sorts.

'I hope you do not think me presumptuous, Miss Reckert,' said Miss Harland, upon one visit she made with Mr. Whinston, 'but I should very much like to be trusted to arrange the entire provisions, for that is just the sort of thing I like to do, though I would not like to infringe upon your privilege.'

'That is very kind of you, and I am very far from wishing to monopolize the preparations myself.'

'Why then it is settled, and I shall see to it all. But when shall we go?'

'As soon as possible, I should hope,' injected Mr. Whinston, 'in the next few days, at the very least, or I shall ask Miss Reckert to take me there by herself.'

'But would you have the rest of us stay home?' cried Miss Harland, who had no understanding of levity. 'I am sure I should be very disappointed, and it shall only take one or two days to see about the food.'

'Nay, aunt, I hope you did not think me in earnest.'

'I am glad to hear it indeed, but all the same I think we must make it soon, that you don't change your mind. Perhaps we should settle on Saturday? Would that be agreeable to Miss Reckert?'

'Yes, indeed,' replied Miss Reckert, in the hope that a fixed date would obviate the need for frequent conferences on the subject.

The following day she was distressed to find that Mr. Harland himself called upon them early in the morning.

'Forgive me for disturbing you,' said he, approaching her after paying his respects to her father, 'but my sister informs me that Saturday has been chosen for our outing, and I wished to tell you I fear I cannot join the party on that day, for there is a gentleman expected to visit me then from London. I wanted to give you my regrets in person.'

However straightforward this announcement, it caused Miss Reckert a multitude of perplexities. Her own preference was that he not attend, but as there was no particular reason they were to go on Saturday and not another day, she felt as the host it was incumbent upon her to change it. And yet, as he had professed a degree of complacency about it, she feared her own partiality might be suspected by sheer willingness to accommodate him.

All this ran through her mind in the short interval whilst the gentleman waited patiently for an answer. Consciousness of her hesitation added to the awkwardness she already felt in speaking to him alone for the first time. At last she said, 'Indeed, Sir, it will be just as well to do it another day, if Saturday does not suit you.'

'You are very good,' replied he, but then after another pause in which he expected she might name one, he said, 'Shall I tell my sister another day, Madam?'

'Yes, indeed,' said she, but as she was not entirely able to think clearly, and wished to end the conference as soon as possible, she had understood him to mean he would choose the day himself, and only realized her mistake upon finding he waited.

'You will greatly oblige me, Sir, if you will name any date,' ventured she, looking downwards in the hope of ending the interview.

'As you wish,' replied he, somewhat surprised, but nevertheless he bowed and took leave of her.

Such insignificant occurrences were truly trying for Miss Reckert, who found it impossible to manifest the calm unconcern with Mr. Harland she customarily adopted with most other gentlemen, including her previous suitors. She dreaded the trials in store for her in the future. The next morning she walked out early in order to avoid any further visits, and found upon her return that Miss Harland had sent her a short note, begging her to approve of one of several dates. In spite of herself, she chose the farthest one, but regretted her cowardice in not getting it over with as soon as possible.

Another week of planning and anticipation was sufficient punishment. Mr. Harland only accompanied his nephew and sister on one occasion, but any company was a source of aggravation to Miss Reckert at that time."

It was here, to the dismay of Mlle de Courteline, that Mme. Gaspar announced she was too fatigued to stay awake longer and Mouchard was obliged to stop. We are all quite taken with the story. It is as though a novel has been serialized merely for our benefit, (and your own, of course). I look forward to hearing your impression of it. I have tried to preserve it mostly as he delivers it, substituting my own words for his when my memory fails me.

I hope to hear from you soon.
I am ever your faithful friend,
M. C.

Marcel de la Croix to Henri Renault

January 15th,1793

Dear Friend,

Our travel progress is slow, intentionally so, as we would not arrive before our new lodgings are fully ready. We are staying two days at the inn we are stopped at now, though we may just as easily spend one. It is a better inn than most, however, so we are content to do so. I am grateful for a little extra time to write, that I may progress in my history before I forget my place. I am alone, at the moment, for the ladies have taken a walk.

It is difficult for me to clearly recall the events of the days which followed. Chateau de la Croix is an ancient fortress, equipped with a moat and many other defensive mechanisms, long since relegated to mere decoration. The drawbridge was wooden, and destroyed in the fire, but the metal gates were intact. When I woke up after sleeping the first night in the servant's wing, I found Philip had lowered them overnight as a precaution.

The two wings of the fortress are distinct; the main wing was entirely destroyed by the fire, save the rock walls themselves, while the opposing wing, separated in the middle by a courtyard, was as if untouched. A quick inspection of the smouldering mess of the main wing showed there was no way of exploring or finding remains; the way was blocked by masses of charcoal from the collapse of the storeys above. With the help of Philip and the few servants who remained, all openings to that side of the fortress were boarded up. I ordered for the wing to remain untouched till a time might come when more could be done to find those who had perished there. While securing the entry points, I noticed some evidence to indicate the house had been partially boarded at the time of the fire, to prevent anyone who awoke from escaping. It was a grim undertaking, and when we were finished I felt tired to my core, though I had no heart for sleeping.

The countryside was wild with rumours, and many who had not perished or been involved came by the Chateau to consult, exclaim or take leave, sometimes the three at once. The Priest who ministered my father's tenants, Father Matthew, was one. He had no intention of remaining in the area after the horror which had taken place, but I asked he consecrate the portion of the fortress which entombed my family, and he did so before leaving the area for good.

Although the apparent leader of the night before had appeared calm and ideologically driven, the majority of the peasants in the area seemed either senseless or frightened to desperation.

The object of their attack (aside from revenge) seems to have been to raid the grain stores and lay their hands on the feudal documents describing their rents and other obligations.

My father (God rest his soul) was a careful, covetous sort of man. I had never thought to inform myself where such documents and valuables were stored, and was still a child enough not to have considered the matter in the aftermath.

It was Philip who educated me on these points, taking me below the ruins to the cellar. Below a large stone lay a vault containing the entire fortune of my family, my father's will and personal belongings, as well as the deeds and records detailing the exact obligations of peasants and tenants. What a strange circumstance it is that the poor are thought in constant obligation to the rich? Let me say no more of that, however.

In my despair, I resolved at once to rid myself of the horrible contracts which had caused so much pain and inequality in the area, and led eventually to the murder of my family.

Seizing the collection of them, I instructed Philip to see them burnt in the large fountain in the garden. To that end, I said,

'Do your best to make sure it is known of in advance. I imagine anything which is done at this time will garner attention, but be not long in the production of it. Employ as many labourers as possible in gathering fuel for the fire and do not hide from them what is to be burnt.'

'Young Master,' replied he, gravely, 'be sure of what you are about. These records have been the basis of your families' livelihood for generations. They alone testify to the rights and nobility earned by the deeds of your forefathers and granted by the King. These must seem like desperate times, to be sure, but with the Estates General now becoming the National Assembly, who knows what will be decided tomorrow, or if our problems are to become better or worse? The peasants say the terms are unfair, and few would argue that, but is it therefore necessary to abolish them altogether? Be careful when you do whatever cannot be undone. Order may yet be restored.'

'You speak wisely, dear friend, but my family is no more, and these obligations no longer exist. I need them not.'

He bowed and said no more. My instructions were followed meticulously, and by nightfall there was a curious crowd, observing from a distance. A few furtive people attempted to get a closer look to ratify the identity of the papers. Guilt seemed to hang over most of them, but soon a kind of fever gripped the whole, after one or two had shouted with jubilation, waving papers in their hands.

Philip wisely retired at that point, seeing that his involvement would not be necessary to light the blaze. The sight of the fire sickened me.

January 17th, 1793

Your letter has finally arrived! I am amazed to find how slow the mail travels now. I confess I was relieved to finally read your reply. As to the unspoken request of Father Galois and Father Schelling, I am more than happy to have the letters read universally among all those who care to. I am sure you exaggerate the pleasure they have given you, but in any event, I am more than happy to continue as I have if you have the patience to read them. As I have some time to myself after supper, I shall continue my history:

Rather than watch the spectacle unfolding, I determined to keep the appointment from the night before, and perhaps discover the identity of my fellows in misfortune.

Sure enough, when I arrived at the tree we had parted from the night before, the gentleman I had spoken to was already there, pacing about impatiently. No other was present, but in truth, I did not expect there to be.

'So,' cried he, 'you have come. I fear that does not speak well for your affairs, which may be as poor as mine. It is the story I hear from all of our neighbours. What have you left in the world, may I inquire? Forgive me, perhaps I should introduce myself first. My name is Pierre Lafont, and my family hails from Eperney.'

'I am Marcel de la Croix and my father was the Marquis de la Croix. My family is dead, and half my house is burnt.'

'If it is only half your house, then you have been more fortunate than I. It is true I have an aunt and cousin who escaped the fire, but no part of my house or my fortune have survived it. I have what you see right now; my horse, my clothes and my will.'

'Then return with me now, for while I have half a house, you are welcome to it. There is little point to standing around in the cold.'

M. Lafont agreed immediately, and we returned the way I had come. The crowd which had assembled there was dispersing by the time we arrived, and M. Lafont quickly drew his sword at the sight of them.

'Come,' said I, immediately, 'there is no need for bloodshed right now.'

He put away his sword, looking at me with surprise, 'I will do as you suggest,' said he, 'but I do assure you that blood shall be shed for what has occurred,' surveying the scene very keenly as we passed.

Once we were indoors, he said, 'Pardon me, Monsieur le Marquis, as you must know your own business, but it seems to me highly strange to let the murderers of our families congregate around your house.'

'I cannot kill every peasant in the area,' replied I, quietly, 'even could I be convinced I should do so.'

He did not reply directly, but hardly looked in agreement. 'Tell me at least,' inquired he, 'Why so many have gathered here together without violence?'

I explained what I had instructed Philip to do, and he seemed both horrified and disgusted to hear it. He objected strenuously against my reasons for doing so, and we continued to dispute, calmly enough, till our supper was laid. Once the few servants I had retained withdrew, he said,

'Forgive the inquiry, but can this food be trusted? There is something afoot, to be sure, and I think we may no longer trust those beneath us without reason.'

'My loyal servant Philip selected those who remain, and I have no choice but to rely on them, since I cannot cook and shall not starve. I shall eat first, and if I fare badly, you may abstain.'

This resolution seemed to impress and amuse him, but he refused to let me take the risk alone, saying, 'We are brothers of the star now, and I believe we must live or die alone. To the former, however,' cried he, raising a toast, and so we toasted to life.

Needless to say, our meal was not poisoned, and we continued to speak in hushed tones of our separate plans. M. Lafont declared his intent to raise a counter-revolutionary force, and recruit whoever he could to help him. He intended to ride to the home of his uncle the next day, who lived in a nearby province, and from there he would plan his strategy.

'And what shall you do?' inquired he. 'Shall you stay in this house? Surely you must join the revolution or resist it, and I feel confident at least that you will not join it.'

'I shall stay here and do neither, if I can. Beyond that, I do not know. I owe it to my father to travel to Paris, pledge my service to the King and relay what has taken place here. My father was his vassal, and so it seems am I.'

'And yet I think this is not to your inclination?'

I made no response, but I fear it was obvious how little this course appealed to me. I liked neither his strategy nor mine, in truth, but what else was possible?

As dissimilar as we were, I could not help but be pleased with my new companion, who seemed to advocate a course I wished I could take, had my disposition been different. We spent the evening deep in conversation, comparing our various thoughts and impressions regarding what had happened, and what would happen. In the morning, we parted on the best of terms. As he mounted his horse, M. Lafont said,

'Adieu, Monsieur le Marquis. Misfortune has bonded and branded us, and however different our feelings, I shall pledge to aide you whenever it is in my power. Most of my family has perished, and from our brief meeting, I am disposed to think of you as such. I will send you word of my doings. Farewell.'

January 19th,1793

Here in England the weather has been rainy and cold, and we have not yet recommenced our journey. Mme. Gaspar and Mlle Vallon have come down with colds, and Mouchard's story has been in greater demand than usual. I have amused myself continuing to write his tale (somewhat imperfectly) and I will send the latest portion to you when I have finished. I have also had some time to practice my English, and I am pleased with my progress.

Amidst this company I almost forget my purpose here in England, though I fear it cannot be delayed much longer.

Tomorrow, we intend to finish our journey to Sorsten, from where I will write again. In the meantime, here is more of Mouchard's tale, roughly as we heard it after tea today:

"*A day before* the intended outing, Mr. Reckert fell ill and was confined to his bed. Miss Reckert's concern was evident to all, as she spent a most of her time by his bedside. Initially he refused to send for a doctor, and felt that time alone would see his recovery.

'One does not need to call the doctor for every complaint, my dear, and though I fear I must miss our outing tomorrow, I am certain it will do me a deal of good to hear of it from you.'

'You must not think of me going, father, while you are in this state. It is impossible.'

'Nonsense, dear, I am only out of sorts, and I do not see what good it will do to disappoint our new neighbours.'

'I wish most fervently to believe you, but I could not go through with our plans now, even if I wished to, for it would be better not to go at all than to go in this state of mind.'

Mr. Reckert, who in truth felt more poorly than he let on, had not the strength to oppose her any further, and word was sent to the other house of the unfortunate postponement.

In a few days' time a doctor was finally sent for. His opinion was somewhat less than straightforward, for Mr. Reckert was of an advanced age, his health was not perfect, and any little thing he contracted took on a more serious appearance. The waters at Bristol, he thought, were certain to be of some help ameliorating his overall condition.

This recommendation was made privately to the patient himself, who felt it very prudent to follow, and accordingly set his own course before communicating it to his daughter the following morning.

'I omitted to mention yesterday that the doctor has advised me to travel to Bristol, and I have decided it is best to heed his advice.'

'Certainly,' cried she, with surprise, 'we shall leave directly; tomorrow, if you are fit to travel.'

'Dearest daughter, I had no idea of you coming with me. There is no cause, you may be sure.'

'Do not dream it, father!' cried she, in shock. 'Why where else would I be? Do you think I would let you travel, or even live by yourself, in your present state?'

'Pray do not oppose me in this, for I am quite decided, and I should like in some matters to flatter myself I am the parent.'

'I can hardly believe you are in earnest. It hardly seems possible. Even could I suffer to be parted from you under such circumstances, I know not how to conceive of living here alone, just at this time-nay, it would be highly improper.'

'Your scruples are unnecessary, for we have no guests here at present, only neighbours. And even if we had, I should feel completely confident knowing Mr. Harland is so close-by; you may rely upon him as myself. Moreover, your aunt and cousin Gregory are expected to visit us in the next little while, and I would not have them cancel their journey.'

'Surely they may join us in Bristol.'

'And spend time with an invalid rather than where there is young people and merriment? Nay, I should not dream of proposing it. Come, my dear, you are now in your twentieth year, and as it seems you have no idea of leaving me to begin your own life...'

'Papa–'

'I think it is high time you begin to do the honours of the household, in preparation for a time when it will always be necessary.'

She sighed. 'You distress me greatly to speak this way. Do I not already perform this function? I am sure I need very little additional familiarity with it.'

'Nay, I believe you are wrong, for though you do it well enough when you are present, you have shunned company all too much lately to be truly proficient at it. Come, do not despair. I shall return in good health very quickly, and you may resume your old ways. Do not fret, my dear, and do not quarrel any further with a weary old man who *will* be indulged. You shall distress me more than I can say if you protest any further.'

Mr. Reckert was truly one of the most yielding and affectionate fathers, and his supplications were impossible to deny. Miss Reckert was obliged to submit to his wishes, unable to explain the true nature of her objection.

When she was preparing to leave the chamber to allow him to rest, he requested she send a message to Mr. Harland, with whom he wished to speak.

Mr. Harland arrived shortly thereafter, but as Mr. Reckert was resting, he decided to wait with Miss Reckert in the drawing room for him to awake. Miss Reckert seemed understandably out of spirits and he did not trouble her much for conversation, after a few brief inquiries as to her father.

Perhaps an hour or so later he was called to Mr. Reckert's bedchamber.

'You are good to come so quickly, dear friend' said Mr. Reckert.

'Say nothing of it. I had intended to come around this time before I received your daughter's message.'

'I thank you. You have perhaps heard that my physician, Dr. Whitley, has been here to consult with me, and he has seen fit to recommend I travel to Bristol as soon as I am able, for he believes my ill health requires it. I am loathe to leave you all at this juncture, but I fear it cannot be helped.'

'I hope you would not consider sacrificing your health merely to entertain us?'

'No, Sir, I do not flatter myself my company is of such great value. I grieve, however, that I am forced to ask you to look into my affairs while I am gone, for I know not how well I may do so myself. I did not invite you to live in the area to take undue advantage of your kindness, however, so I ask you to tell me frankly if it would inconvenience you too much, and in that case I shall make other arrangements.'

'It would be no trouble at all. Much of our business is already intertwined and it would hardly be any additional work to mind your affairs as well as my own.'

'I am happy you feel thus. I have, I fear, another charge to bestow upon you which I hope will prove equally easy. I have told my daughter that she is not to accompany me on this journey, as I do not wish to part the young people so soon. I ask only that while I am gone, you give occasional thought to her interests, and wherever possible, act so as to secure her happiness.'

'Of course, if you wish, dear Sir,' replied the other, caught somewhat off guard. 'But yet I am surprised to hear it. Would it not be of some comfort to have your daughter near, especially as you seem more particularly concerned for her welfare of late?'

'Do not be frightened, Sir, I do not believe there shall be all that much to it. Visit her periodically, and be so kind as to relay any marriage offers you receive to me. Under different circumstances perhaps I should agree with you, but there are several reasons I feel otherwise at present. The first, I have already expressed to you, that I am reluctant to separate her from your nephew just at this time. The second is that I fear I shall not return as speedily as I hope, and I know my daughter well enough to see that she will confine herself with me for months or more if need be, and thus put an end to my hopes of settling her in the near future. Alas, my last reason I shall admit to no one else, and that is simply that I suspect my illness is owing in part to the anxiety and distress I suffer on her account. Her fate is my primary concern, and more and more I have reason to fear. Her actions confound me, but who can understand the choices of a young woman?'

'Indeed, Sir, you could hardly select another person less capable of doing so.'

'All I can hope, and indeed, all I do hope, is that my health will improve when I am not daily plagued by apprehensions on her account, which I dare not show her. The advantage you have over me is that you lack paternal affection to cloud your judgment.'

Mr. Harland was unwilling to admit how little he relished this particular charge. The motives and behaviour of women were always a source of mystery to him, and although he had a genuine desire to serve his friend, he despaired of being able to do so. Moreover, he felt uneasy at the prospect of so close a connection to Miss Reckert, whose overall attractiveness had not escaped his notice. All the same, in a strange parallel to the situation Miss Reckert had found herself in several hours before, Mr. Harland had no choice but to submit to the request of his friend–"

Mouchard paused here, uncertain if he should continue. Mlle de Courteline signalled that he do so, and he silently complied.

"With the removal of her father, Miss Reckert likewise retreated into her own world. Visitors to the main house almost always discovered she was wandering in the garden or otherwise unavailable. Miss Reckert was scrupulous in returning visits paid her, but often it seemed as though she returned them at a time when her hosts were likely to be away or unable to receive her.

When the new neighbours did chance to see her, her demeanour seemed entirely different from on the first night of their meeting. Though she was amiable and obliging, as was part of her disposition, she was also withdrawn and slightly melancholy. She made no effort to begin particular topics of conversation, and did not contribute much to what was going forth.

'My goodness!' exclaimed Miss Harland, on one occasion, 'I really cannot understand what has happened! She seems almost another woman. Perhaps something has displeased her?'

'Doubtless, it must be concern for her father,' observed Mr. Whinston, though seeming himself uncertain.

'What do you think, brother?' inquired Miss Harland.

'Forgive me,' replied he, looking up from the table he had been seated at, examining some papers, 'I did not hear what was said.'

'Well, I fear you did not miss much in the presence of Miss Reckert.'

Just then Mrs. Churling, the wife of the vicar was announced. After some small preliminary pleasantries, Miss Harland said,

'You have but just missed Miss Reckert, I fear.'

'Indeed?' declared the other, 'Perhaps it is just as well, for I have all but given up hope on the girl, if one might speak plainly.'

'Indeed?' cried Miss Harland, with surprise.

''Twas nearly a year ago she was the most promising creature who ever lived, as light and gay as anything, and now she is as morose as an old statue. And what pains I have taken with her! Her dear father knows little of feminine refinement, and has left her to herself in nearly all respects. My own nephew paid court to her, you know, at the beginning of this year. Oh, he is a fine fellow, if I do say so myself, but he is in London now, and all that is at an end. And what was I to tell my sister, when matters had seemed so promising at first? What goes through her head, only the lord can guess!'

'This is most surprising!' declared Miss Harland.

'Aye, and there were few as surprised as me, seeing as I have known her since she was a girl. Not that I would say a bad word about her for the world, for I have loved her as a daughter, and taken a great deal of care of her. It is her own welfare I worry about, for never was there a girl so promising, all of a sudden determined to end a maid.'

'It would be a shame, indeed,' remarked Mr. Whinston, 'but surely young ladies are allowed to have their humour, or to prefer one suitor over another?'

'Would that was all it was. Believe me, I am not overly-biased in favour of my nephew, for I should have been equally happy to see her marry any of her admirers. Depend upon it, however, at present, she has no thoughts of leaving her father's house. And why should she, indeed, for where else could she be so well indulged? And there are so many other fine young men,' added she, as an afterthought, looking pointedly at Mr. Whinston, 'who would not be unworthy of her, though she is a prodigious heiress.'

'This is most distressing!' exclaimed Miss Harland, 'She is such a charming girl, or at least she seemed so. I do not understand why any young girl should seek to discourage eligible admirers. Since I am an old maid myself, nothing is more incomprehensible!'

'Well I am not prepared to give up,' declared Mr. Whinston, heedless of speaking before Mrs. Churling. 'A man who is easily discouraged is one unworthy of the prize.'

In the coming days and weeks, conferences like this became a mainstay of sorts, for Miss Reckert continued ever 'unaccountable,' and neither Miss Harland or Mrs. Churling ever tired of speaking of it. Little Thomas, meanwhile, was at home in both houses, for Miss Reckert was happy to share his little services while they were needed and welcome, and Mr. Whinston was unwilling to give up this little connection between them. He often made pretence of calling upon Miss Reckert to thank her for her consideration in that regard, though in truth, he asked Thomas to do very little.

Though Mr. Whinston was very sanguine by nature, even he had difficulty taking any encouragement from Miss Reckert's behaviour. Mr. Harland had privately become quite convinced that Miss Reckert was as unaccountable as she was considered by Mrs. Churling and his sister. After all, it was his general opinion that women were unaccountable, and if one was thought to be so by her own sex, it must be indisputable fact.

In keeping with the duty invested in him by his friend, Mr. Harland called upon Miss Reckert once a week, beginning one Thursday evening after dinner. This particular time, chosen unintentionally by himself, was the most difficult for Miss Reckert to evade callers, as it would seem unusual if she did not dine, or was out in the garden much in the evening.

Moreover, Mr. Harland was a man of habit, and before she had been able to settle an acceptable plan of avoidance, three weeks had passed during which he had called upon her promptly at seven o'clock. Though no agreement had been made between them, habit was like precedent, and had formed a compact. Had she been away from home at that very time sometime thereafter, it would have seemed intentional; a breach of contract.

During these meetings, which neither relished but each submitted to, Mr. Harland would typically inquire after her health, and ask if there was any way he could be of service to her. Miss Reckert would report that she was well, and thank him for his offer, but assure him she had no cares whatsoever with which to trouble him.

Mr. Harland was tempted at times to turn the conversation to his nephew, but as Miss Reckert seemed so generally reticent to discuss any matter whatsoever, he did not ever actually broach the subject.

After several weeks had passed in this manner, he and Mr. Whinston, trailed harmlessly by little Thomas, encountered Miss Reckert embarking on one of her solitary rambles in the garden. An enclosed area had prevented her from avoiding them in time, for she did not descry them until she emerged from a little thicket, and once she did so, there was no longer any choice but to meet them.

Mr. Whinston greeted her with undisguised joy.

'What a pleasant meeting! Truly, I have often wondered that we have never met before, for Miss Reckert is hailed by everyone as a prodigious walker, yet we have never encountered you till now!'

Miss Reckert thanked him, unsure what more to say.

'Why, where do you go this afternoon, if I may?'

Hoping to tailor her own answer to suit her purposes, she was perplexed at being unable to tell from their direction whether they meant to return home or continue elsewhere, and therefore she hesitated to reply.

'I hardly know,' she said at last, though it must have seemed odd that she did not.

'We walk in the direction of the Parsonage.' continued he. 'Perhaps you are heading in the same direction, and we may walk together for a time?'

'Indeed,' stammered she, 'I believe I meant to walk through the cornflower field.'

'Well then perhaps we might take a diversion and walk with you, if you would not mind the company?'

'Oh no,' cried she, with alarm she did not mean to show. 'I would not wish to deny Mrs. Churling her company, especially as I should make such a poor substitute. Forgive me; I wish you good-day.'

With this she hurried away, ashamed of her own incivility.

Once she had disappeared, Mr. Whinston sighed at this most incontrovertible proof that she was determined to avoid his company.

'I am sorry you are disheartened,' said Mr. Harland, 'but I can hardly pretend you have not reason to be so. However, it is best to have such confirmation sooner rather than later.'

This was small consolation to Mr. Whinston, who said nothing in response.

For her own part, Miss Reckert was becoming increasingly distressed by her predicament. While the specific nature of Mr. Whinston's intentions had not occurred to her, prolonged proximity to Mr. Harland, whose disinterest could not be more apparent, rendered her desirous of seeing no one connected to the adjoining manor.

Miss Reckert's aunt and cousin Gregory had lately arrived at

Kettich, where they meant to stay a few weeks before going to London. Mrs. Gregory was inactive and generally taciturn. Her daughter was a pleasant young woman, a year younger than Miss Reckert. She was simple, straightforward, uncurious, and in many ways the opposite of her cousin, but the affection between them was sincere.

After encountering Mr. Harland and Mr. Whinston that one afternoon, Miss Reckert began to take the precaution of fetching her cousin as a companion whenever possible. On one particular afternoon a few weeks after their arrival, the two young women were walking together in the direction of the house, when Miss Reckert thought she saw figures up ahead, and suggested they detour into the woods. The path through the forest was more uncertain and in her haste, Miss Reckert turned her ankle on a root concealed beneath some brush. She rested for a while on a stump till she was able to walk with the help of her cousin and a makeshift walking-stick. After a short ways, the exertion and heat obliged them to rest again, and Miss Gregory proposed she go fetch help while Miss Reckert waited in the shade.

Eventually the gardener approached, and Miss Gregory explained their predicament. Mr. Robson was of an advanced age, and could be of no greater use than Miss Gregory, but pledged to seek further assistance while the young lady returned to her cousin. He encountered Mr. Whinston shortly thereafter, being on his way to call at the parsonage. That gentleman was eager to be of service, telling Mr. Robson to proceed onwards and find his uncle, then going himself to find the young ladies.

Having easily done so, he determined Miss Reckert was in no condition to walk on her own and pronounced that she would need to be carried.

'I sent the gardener to my uncle, who shall certainly be here directly,' said he. He hesitated a moment or two more before adding, 'If Miss Reckert would not like to wait, I would be happy to supply his place.'

Alarmed at the thought of Mr. Harland carrying her, Miss Reckert accepted his offer after a small protest regarding the inconvenience to him, which he energetically dismissed. He could hardly conceal his delight at her acquiescence, and with no further ado it was agreed he would carry her a short way to the gazebo, where she would be more comfortable until another conveyance could take her the rest of the way to the house.

Mr. Harland arrived in a very short time, observing with some surprise that matters had been resolved in his absence. It was only afterwards he came to learn the full circumstances from his nephew, who had drawn the most favourable conclusions.

'It is remarkable,' remarked he. 'Especially if you had told her I should come at any minute. I should be surprised to find she had any great aversion to me, which is the only other thing which might satisfactorily explain her actions. Perhaps she was more disturbed by the heat than you imagined?'

'That will not do, I will not allow myself to be discouraged. Had I heeded such doubts this afternoon I should have failed to make the offer which procured me such exquisite happiness.'

'It was not my intent to discourage you, yet with a woman of such an unpredictable nature, I feel it is only wise to proceed cautiously.'

'Perhaps you advise well, nay, forgive me, 'tis more than likely you do, but I no longer feel able to restrain myself. If you give me your blessing, I will request to speak with her tomorrow, and at least we may put an end to suspense, which is the worst of all things to endure!'

'As to your general intention, you can have no doubt of my approval, if you are absolutely certain of yourself. But as to the rest of it, I fear it would not be entirely proper. Though I am your uncle, for the time being you must consider me foremost the temporary guardian of Miss Reckert, and should your offer fail to find favour with her, it would no longer be agreeable for you to live so close by. For this reason I recommend that you wait to declare yourself till before your stay here is almost at an end, or failing that, you make some other arrangements directly, and allow me to make your proposals for you once you are gone; to Mr. Reckert first and then to his daughter.'

Mr. Whinston was hardly pleased with the proposal of any plan which called for a removal from the object of his adoration and an unspecified delay till an offer could be made. But all this, he could not refute. Moreover, although he was of age, it would be unforgivable for him not to acquaint his parents, (his mother being the eldest sister of Mr. Harland) of his intention beforehand.

Accordingly it was decided that he would announce his intention to return home immediately on unexpected business, and leave at the end of the week.

Mr. Harland wrote immediately to Mr. Reckert, describing the incident which had given such encouragement to his nephew, and requesting his leave to place a formal offer before him, before it was made to Miss Reckert. He relayed the steps that had been taken to ensure Mr. Whinston would not return to the area unless his suit was successful.

In the meantime, Miss Reckert had little idea of any of this, and mostly congratulated herself from the escape the day before. Her ankle restricted her movement and therefore she was obliged to stay home and receive visits.

Her first visit was understandably from the two gentlemen, who came together the following morning to inquire after her health. Mr. Harland was content to make the most basic enquiries, before taking leave. In contrast, Mr. Whinston elected to stay longer, and his most earnest and pressing concern for her welfare caused her for the first time to fear she had behaved imprudently the day before.

This idea had scarce crossed her mind, when he said,

'Forgive me for taking up so much of your time this morning. I crave your pardon on the grounds that I have lately discovered I am to take leave of you in a short time, though I hope I shall be able to return before long.'

'Indeed, Sir,' replied she, 'I had thought you were to stay the next few months at least?'

'If I could believe Miss Reckert regretted my absence, it would make the necessity almost agreeable.'

'You are good to say so, Sir, but I am sure we shall all regret the loss of your company.'

Despite the flattering manner he had couched his departure, the news that it was to occur entirely calmed her rising fears, and with renewed complacency, she wished him a happy journey.

Her recent experiences, after all, had humbled her in her own perception, and she was all the more likely to ascribe any attention she received to common gallantry.

A week after Mr. Whinston's departure, Mr. Reckert wrote back to approve the steps Mr. Harland had taken, thanking his friend for his care. He begged him to put the entire matter before Miss Reckert, upon whom he said it would rest completely.

Although it was the answer he had expected, Mr. Harland would have been happy to have the duty eternally postponed. Nevertheless, that very evening he went to call upon Miss Reckert. He was quite surprised to discover she was not indoors, but rather had managed to convey herself a short way into the garden, despite her injury.

He found her but a short way from the house on a little rock terrace.

'Forgive me, Madam, I had hoped to speak with you and you were not to be found indoors.'

'Indeed, Sir, I was not aware anyone had been looking for me.'

'I hope you are well. Perhaps it is superfluous to ask, as I see your movement is no longer confined to the house.'

'I am better, Sir. I hope you have received no ill news from my father, for I confess I am somewhat surprised to see you?'

'No, I am happy to report he is improving somewhat, but no doubt he has told you the same in his last letter.' He paused for a moment, preparing himself for what he wished to say. 'Madam, I am not used to having this sort of conversation, so I ask your pardon in advance. I hope it will come as no surprise to you that an alliance between your family and my own is a most desirable event, and as it happens inclination is not at all wanting on one side, my intention in speaking to you is to discover your own sentiments, since your father assures me he will leave the matter entirely to you. I hope there is no need to speak plainer, and you will be so good as to speak to me freely.'

Miss Reckert looked all the amazement she felt. As her own thoughts had been so long centred upon himself, she assumed that he was speaking for himself, though his detached manner contradicted that hope, even as his words raised it. Even had he meant to declare himself, acceptance of such cold professions was impossible, and her face turned white and red with each passing thought.

'You have entirely perplexed me, Sir, and I must beg you to be more explicit.'

'If one can credit your mystery,' said he with surprise, 'I fear it does not bode well for my errand. Can it be that the admiration you have inspired in my nephew has gone unnoticed by you, and that you are truly surprised by what must seem only natural to any onlooker? Mr. Whinston had much rather make this declaration to you himself, and no doubt he might have done it more convincingly than myself, but I felt it best that your feelings be consulted more gently.'

Whatever the intention, such a declaration from this particular messenger was the most mortifying and aggravating imaginable. Had her own thoughts not been unavoidably distracted, she would have known better to expect it, but as it was, the full force of her foolishness was only now apparent to her.

Once she was able to restore a portion of her composure, she replied quietly, 'I thank you, Sir. I am sure you will all too easily believe me when I say I am unworthy of the honour Mr. Whinston intends me.'

'I must confess that however sorry I am to hear it, your answer does not surprise me. To his misfortune, I fear my nephew has interpreted your recent behaviour more favourably.'

'I am sorry for it.'

'It shall do no good to dwell on it, Madam. Tell me more precisely, what answer am I to return him?'

'I would be obliged if you would say that his regard places me under heavy obligation, and I am most sincerely sorry for my inability to return it.'

'Indeed, madam,' replied he, with evident surprise, 'if all your refusals are so gentle, I should not wonder you find it difficult to rid yourself of suitors. I fear you cannot hope to discourage him in this manner.'

'Then you must phrase it differently, Sir, only let it be understood it is unchangeable.'

'It may be easier to accomplish this if there was some objection you might arm me with,' pressed he, more for his own knowledge than the one he had stated.

'Indeed, Sir, I have no objection aside from what is dictated by taste and inclination.'

The very lack of energy in her refusal, caused him to wish to question her further, but her increasingly apparent sadness and withdrawal made it impossible to do so. Instead he merely apologized for detaining her so long on a subject she seemed to find disagreeable, and wished her a good night.

Unsurprisingly, he found her behaviour disingenuous and inconsistent, though he was reluctant to judge her too harshly, for there seemed to be an element of sincerity to her distress. Her faults, no doubt, were most likely ingrained in her nature, and her father was the most to blame for giving her discretion where she most seemed to want guidance.

Without hesitation he wrote two letters; the first to his nephew in which he wrote simply what had passed between he and Miss Reckert. Although she had instructed him to word her response however he felt would seem the most final, he opted instead to relay her words verbatim, and thus congratulated himself on interfering as little as possible. His affection for his nephew caused him to wish to avoid completely destroying his hopes, and the unintentional sweetness of Miss Reckert's refusal seemed preferable to anything else.

To Mr. Reckert he was more explicit, confessing how little he understood Miss Reckert, and how incomprehensible her apparent surprise seemed to him.

Less than two weeks later, he received this response from Mr. Reckert.

Dear Sir,

I cannot say how greatly I appreciate your attention to this matter, so much closer to my heart than the rest of the business you have been kind enough to see to for me.

I fear my health is not the better for your last letter. It is my own doing, since I had allowed myself to hope happier tidings might be forthcoming. Do not despair at your inability to comprehend her actions, for I scarcely know of anyone who could do better. I confess my mind is not at all at ease regarding her fate. I only wish I might live long enough to see her safely settled.

Allow me to hope that disappointment on behalf of your nephew, (which cannot be greater than my own) will not prevent you from continuing to look kindly upon my daughter. I am convinced that your guidance and influence will prove extremely beneficial to her in time.

I trust your judgment in all things. Dear Sir, I am,

Your most sincerely obliged,
Mr. Reckert

To this letter he wrote back:

Dear Sir,

Assure yourself I shall continue to have only Miss Reckert's best interest at heart. The decisions of young women in general seem to me to defy reason, but I shall endeavour to overcome my vast shortcomings in this area.

It is possible there is still room to hope, for my nephew has written me as much, though I believe there is no reason to persecute Miss Reckert on that score unless there is some evident change.

Of the very little I feel sure of, I am confident that no good can come of pressing her further at the moment, and I beg you not to be distressed if I am silent on this subject for a short while, as I do not expect to have much to relay to you in the near future.

Pray put your mind at ease, and I shall hope to hear a better account of your health soon.

Your servant, Sir,
Mr. Harland

Mouchard stopped here. For the second portion of his story, he spoke from just after dinner till nearly 11 o'clock; Mme. Gaspar was snoring 'ere he finished. I wrote what I could of it for the few hours after, but then sleep overtook me as well. I woke up early this morning and now I have finished writing it, yet it occurs to me that this package is overly large. I must send it to you now while I may. If I am to judge from your last letter, you may be waiting impatiently for it. I thank you for the latest news from France, though I shall not pretend to have found it encouraging.

I hope you are well and that your mind is more eased from care than when we last met.

Yours ever,
MC

Marcel de la Croix to Henri Renault

January 23rd,1793

Dear Friend,

We have at last arrived at Sorsten Manor and I find it a very convenient, respectable place. The ladies have set up house in the main house, and I am established comfortably by myself in the Parsonage. M. Tolouse should join me in a few days, but I am happy for the little peace afforded me. My reflections have helped me crystallize my purpose, the urgency of which I have permitted to lapse during these last few weeks. Soon I feel I shall arrive at an important crisis, which will certainly decide my fate.

* * *

January 25th, 1793

Only just today the news has reached us. I know not what to make of it, but nothing contradicts it.

The first word of it came from Lady Etheredge, in the form of condolences. I had called at the main house in the morning, as I do most days, when a letter arrived from her ladyship.

Mlle de Courteline no sooner read it than she went into a strange stupor, from which we were hard-pressed to rouse her. Our repeated inquiries finally caused her to weakly offer the letter to no one in particular, whereupon I took it and read the following aloud:

January 25th, 1793

Dear Mlle de Courteline,

We are all shocked and horrified by the news. What atrocious villains are now in control of that once noble country! Whatever else the revolutionaries could be guilty of, I little thought they would stoop to regicide.

Accept our sincerest condolences on the untimely death of Louis XVI. May God bless his soul and protect any other who still lives in the power of the dreadful revolutionaries.

On a lesser note, please accept the gift of the two servants I send along with this message. I well know you were in great need of a female servant, having only a manservant, so I have taken the liberty of sending you a gentle young maid, perfectly fluent in French. I have also sent a man who is the brother of one of our own most valued servants, whom you are free to retain or send back, as your convenience dictates.

With genuine sadness at our mutual loss, I am,

Your servant,
Lady Etheredge

If the King is indeed dead, I am at a loss for words. We nervously await necessary confirmation. The ladies are in a truly pitiable state, and until more is known, visiting them is awkward and unproductive.

I confess I find it difficult to think of anything else, but there seems no more news to be had tonight. Thoughts of France and of Louis returns my mind to the past, and as I have nothing else to do, I will take this interval to give you more of my history:

After my new friend, M. Lafont, departed, I wasted little time before leaving my dreary surroundings and heading for Paris. The countryside wore a strange appearance of unrest and everywhere I went people seemed newly unsure of behaviour and roles taken for granted till this time.

I saw no evidence of an organized revolution at this pass, but there was no doubt the peasants were as angry as they were hopeful; looking to freedom from oppression at the same time as they feared it would be snatched away from them.

At most inns on the road, travellers seemed both hesitant and eager to talk. Reliable news was hard to come by, and newspapers were scarce and out of date. Bizarre rumours regarding the Queen satisfied the curiosity of most. Needless to say, in most places sentiment was largely in favour of the Third Estate, along with the leaders of the emerging revolution.

The second inn I stayed at on my journey was in Corbeil. Royalist sentiment seemed to be stronger in that area, as many who lived thereabouts were devout Catholics who feared the radical ideas of the revolutionaries.

How strange it was to find that I felt at home in neither camp; royalist and revolutionary alike made me uneasy!

As I was preparing to set out on the morning following my arrival, I was made aware that a prominent minister of the King's, M. Montrond, was staying in the same house. It was thought he retained a reasonable degree of access to Louis XVI during this time, and I immediately desired to speak with him.

I sent in my name, along with the message that I was en route to Versailles and would be grateful for a brief word with him before I set out, having particular news to communicate.

M. Montrond graciously invited me to join him at his meal and I gladly accepted.

He was a slight-looking man of perhaps fifty years of age. He was tired and worn by cares, though as gracious and civil as a courtier.

He listened with great attention as I described my experience only days before, sighing as I concluded my narrative.

'I am sorry to say, Monsieur le Marquis, that this is not the first report I have heard of this sort. The degree of violence you have described is the only thing which separates your case from others that I have heard. In most other situations, real harm upon a lord's family does not seem to have been seriously meditated, and property damage and destruction have been the only result.'

His reply surprised me. I had little imagined such disturbances were happening all over the country, and were becoming almost a matter of course. As to the severity of the disturbance in our region, I could not help but suspect that the harshness of my father had contributed to this difference, though I did not share my reflections.

'May I ask what you intend to do now?' inquired he. His manner conveyed the impression that his inquiry was merely a matter of politeness, rather than a matter of any National significance.

'I mean to go to Versailles, where I hope to receive guidance and impart intelligence.'

He seemed to wince slightly at this answer, before sighing and waiving his hand in the air to denote helplessness.

'I fear it has gone beyond that,' said he, 'for the Estates General and now the National Assembly will decide what is to be done, and the King has his hands full as long as they are in session. He will see almost no one at the moment. No doubt all will be well, but I fear for the time being, we all must endure as best we may, and suffer as his Majesty himself suffers, for the sake of our country.'

This response, I confess, surprised me not a little.

'But is there no service,' I persisted, 'no commission, no instructions to be expected from his Majesty?'

'I think not,' replied he, looking around reflectively. 'Louis would have those who can, resist any attempts to undermine the systems and structures which have always been the foundation of our noble country, but this is little more than obvious. As to how one must do this, I fear I know not. Each man must best know how to secure his situation, his influence, and his dignity (not to mention his safety) while there is so much unrest, and he must hope to do so as long as necessary. Then perhaps at last he might expect some help from his Majesty.'

Merely surprised before, now I was completely astonished. M. Montrond appeared tired and disengaged, and through him I felt I could see the attitude of Louis XVI himself.

The ruthless rage of M. Lafont only the evening before seemed somehow refreshing in contrast, for he at least was fired by passion and drawn to action of some kind.

I remained in conversation with M. Montrond some while longer, but the more we spoke, the less I found was to be expected from either he or his master, in the way of leadership or inspiration. Accordingly, the more we spoke, the less inclined I felt to continue my journey.

After taking my leave of that gentleman, I needed only a few minutes of deliberation to decide to return the way I came. Once returned home, I resolved to reassess what I would do.

I travelled only a short way that night, stopping at an inn after dusk, intending to make the rest of my way home the following day.

Sure enough, I travelled a good distance on the second day and by the time night settled, I had only a few miles remaining. As I rode, I noticed that the countryside wore a different aspect in the dark. There was movement and activity far away in the shadows, in many directions. Single lights could be seen here and there, wavering in the dark. The darker the night, the thicker the mist became around me, till it was difficult for me to see several paces ahead.

I had ridden fast for the first little while, attempting to complete the whole of the journey that day, but by this time, my horse was tired and we had slowed to a nearly plodding pace. As I neared closer to home (or so I guessed, from what I could make out around me) I heard a commotion on the road ahead.

Several torch lights flickered. I could hear the sound of wheels on the rocks, accompanied by intermittent voices which betrayed a kind of excitement. As you may imagine, they were hardly welcome sounds in this particular climate.

I thought momentarily of slipping off the road to avoid them, if only to spare myself the inconvenience of delay, since I was tired and hungry. Even for those reasons, however, this course seemed cowardly to me. Instead I hailed them loudly, asking them to identify themselves.

All sound ceased at once, even the sound of the carriage wheels progressing.

'Who goes there?' cried a voice, and presently a man carrying a torch stepped out of the mist. He was wearing what I took to be mock military uniform, for it was like nothing I had ever seen before; perhaps self-constructed.

'I asked first,' replied I, 'but no matter. I am Marcel de la Croix. Kindly return the favour. Who are you, and what is this little procession?'

'That is not your concern,' replied he, attempting to conceal his surprise. 'I know who you are, but you no longer exercise authority in these parts.'

I was annoyed at this response, conscious that it associated me with what I despised, and therefore I said, 'On the contrary, my good man, for till recently, I have never had any authority to exercise. At present, I retain authority over my own person and judgment, and so it strikes me as right to ask you again what you do on the road at this time?'

The sound of my own voice surprised me, as it was steady and forceful. My words came out before I had opportunity to consider them, it seemed, (and I could not help but wonder), almost like I was a spectator to myself.

The first man was in the midst of giving me a second denial, when a larger, scruffier man stepped out from behind him, revealing a large grin.

'We are transporting a prisoner; a confessed enemy of the revolution. What business does a Marquis have with revolutionary justice? We have orders to let you pass, but you will regret any interference you attempt.'

By now I had moved close enough that I could see the entire party. Aside from the two men I have mentioned, there were seven more walking besides the carriage. Some were armed with swords and pistols, but many carried large sticks only, and were clothed much more raggedly.

'And who is it that you would imprison for these crimes of philosophy?' inquired I.

'Philosophy, do you call it?' cried the grinning man, 'and is treason any less so? 'Twill come a day when you yourself shall be carried to answer.'

Of the party, he alone seemed to relish this conversation, while the others appeared increasingly nervous. When I had asked the name of the prisoner, several of them had glanced furtively in the direction of the carriage, as if in fear that I could see inside it, and I began to feel quite certain it was in some way connected to me.

'If you have some better charge than you have told me,' I continued, after a moment's reflection, 'then perhaps I will not interfere, but until you tell me the name of your prisoner, I shall not let you pass.'

All were silent in consternation, save the grinning fellow, whose smile grew even larger. 'Bring out the prisoner, for it shall behove Monsieur le Marquis to see his future.'

The others were evidently reluctant to obey him, but after a little hesitation, the grinning man prevailed and the prisoner was brought forward.

Expecting somehow to see M. Lafont, I was amazed to see my servant, Philip. His face wore its customary expression, and he said not a word, either to me or to the two men who held him roughly by the arms.

I could see in his eyes a strange calm I wished very much to emulate within my own soul. For a moment I envisioned him being tossed around on a violent sea, looking ever thus; he was himself, and his conduct was delineated so precisely that it never allowed doubt or alteration. I knew too, as he looked at me, that my character and conduct seemed as certain to him as his own. This was all the more remarkable to me, as my own actions were an endless source of astonishment to me.

'By what right do you detain my servant?' cried I, after the brief moment during which these thoughts passed through my mind.

'Simply put,' answered the grinning man, 'he has disputed the authority of the revolution. We have reason to think you have concealed stores of grain which are now the rightful property of the people. You yourself have given up the antiquated rights of your family, supported by the blood of many, but in your absence, your servant has disputed our claim to retrieve them, and therefore will be tried for his crimes.'

'In other words,' returned I, 'In my absence, you and your fellows came to plunder my house for the second time, and have arrested this man using the questionable authority you claim, and accuse him of having the loyalty and courage to resist your cowardly plundering.'

The grinning man laughed at this, and drew his sword. 'In your words or mine, but all the same, he shall not go free. You may attend his trial, if you like.'

In response, I drew my own sword, and killed my jovial opponent. The other man who had spoken, as well as another grave-looking fellow who had been standing in the back, were the only others to engage me, and both fell at my hand. The others were mostly armed with sticks, and they fled quickly down the road, leaving both the carriage and their prisoner behind them.

I must ask you to judge by what you have read thus far, whether I was willingly drawn into this conflict?

January 26th, 1793

Returning to the present, the news of Louis XVI's death has been confirmed; all our spirits have been dampened. M. Tolouse has returned, and seems the least affected by it all. He hopes that it shall lead way to some political upheaval, though he cares not in which direction, so that he might be permitted to return and enlist in some cause or other. Mlle de Courteline prefers not to see him, now that she may exercise some discretion, but at the same time, any activity at all seems to be preferable to sitting alone.

M. Tolouse and I called at the main house together the last few days, but heard word only that the ladies were too unwell to receive our visit. Yesterday, M. Tolouse rode out somewhere by himself and I called at Sorsten alone. To my surprise, Mlle de Courteline came down by herself, conveying the excuses of the other two ladies, who were still too indisposed.

She said but little at first, appearing thoughtful. At last she said:

"Perhaps you are curious as to why I have availed myself of your conversation, despite the possible misconstructions I leave myself open to by this private discourse?"

She paused, undoubtedly waiting for some acknowledgment of her condescension, but I made none, preoccupied as I was in trying to determine what this prelude might lead to, and whether the misconstructions she feared were from myself or some unknown person. She seemed slightly chagrined to find it, but said,

"M. Gramont, you will agree that our acquaintance was made under slightly unusual circumstances. My father has often said that all things happen for a reason, and so I have begun to see for myself. Several weeks ago, Lady Beth alluded to a possible connection between our families, and however bizarre I found the suggestion at the time, I have now come to give it more credence than I did at first. Your uncommon care of us seems to show you have more than a common sense of the respect due the de Courteline name. Pondering this, I could not help but consider that a distant relation might be more aware of this than some. Is this not true? Speak to me honestly, for no doubt you know better than I, is there no connection between our families, no tie which perhaps you were reluctant to avow?"

I had not expected this suggestion, and struggled momentarily to see how to answer it. Mlle de Courteline beheld my hesitation with slight displeasure, before adding, "Indeed, Sir, to own the truth, it has long been known to me that the youngest brother of my father married in a way which displeased my grandfather, and indeed, my whole family. I was never told much more than this, but I think he was disinherited. Though I only heard the woman's maiden name once, I feel now certain that it was Gramont. In that case, Sir, we should be cousins, and the connection between us would be more than respectable. Do not fear to acknowledge it to me, Sir, for I shall be far from displeased. Though it has been through necessity alone, I have been grieved to be so much associated with, nay, perhaps even obligated to, a mere stranger."

"Though I am reluctant to contradict a notion which has soothed your scruples, I can in no way believe we are related to one another."

Mlle de Courteline was now silent in turn, evidently displeased with my response.

"It seems highly surprising to me," said she at length, "that after hearing me affirm I am all but certain a connection may exist, you dismiss it out of hand! Forgive me, Sir, but to my mind, it is all the more likely if one considers the workings of Providence, and how one's needs are naturally provided for."

I could not hide my own annoyance, and therefore interrupted her to say, "We ask far too much of Providence if we expect not merely assistance in our distress, but the smoothing of petty concerns relating to outward appearances."

I paused for a moment, pacing around somewhat, as Mlle de Courteline looked at me with wonder and anticipation.

"The truth is, Madam, I have no more connection to you than to the family of Gramont, since I have merely assumed this name for my passage to England."

Mlle de Courteline's expression betrayed all the horror at this revelation which one might expect. I saw immediately she concluded I was a fortune-hunter, an adventurer, or worse. I can acquit myself of the first charge, but as to the rest, the case is less straightforward.

When she recovered from the shock, she said, "Indeed, Sir, I hardly know how to address you. You have been kind to call here today, but I believe it shall no longer be necessary for you to do so. M. Savard is expected shortly, and no doubt he shall wish to thank you. Till then, I expect I will be unable to receive you."

This dismissal was what one could expect, being once familiar with her character and education. I shall look at it as a blessing of sorts.

* * *

Monsieur Savard has indeed arrived, and sooner than I had expected. He called upon us the second day of his arrival. He seems to be a practical, business-like man of perhaps sixty years of age. He was civil, but not particularly communicative. He thanked M. Tolouse and I for the services rendered the three ladies, explaining that Mlle de Courteline's father had never intended that they travel far alone.

"Does Mlle de Courteline's father expect to travel here soon, Sir?" inquired I, wishing to discover whether he had conveyed the news of his almost certain death to the ladies.

He looked up warily at this question, but then sighed and said, "I fear nothing like that is to be thought of at present."

"Mlle de Courteline no doubt expects him?" persisted I, attempting to draw out something further, but he only looked at me steadily in response.

"Mlle de Courteline," continued he, after a pause, "tells me there are numerous accounts to settle with you, and I wanted to assure you I am ready to do so whenever you are at leisure."

"It is not necessary," replied I.

"I will hear of nothing else," said he. "I have difficulty accepting obligation even from those I have obliged. There is, however, one thing I would ask you, though I am hesitant to do so."

"I shall try to oblige you," replied I.

"Why then, I understand that you have a servant named Mouchard, who amuses the ladies with a tale he tells? Their spirits are so low at present, I was hoping you would agree to give him to me, in exchange for one of my own, at least for the time being?"

"I would be happy to accommodate you in almost any other matter," replied I, "but I fear I have become quite attached to him, and I know not how to do without him at present."

"'Tis no matter, I am sorry to have mentioned it, yet if you should change your mind, I should be happy to recompense your inconvenience however you should wish."

Soon after he took his leave. I cannot help but suspect he is not eager to continue the connection, in view of the care taken to shelter Mlle Vallon heretofore.

* * *

Yesterday there came a letter from the main house, from M. Savard:

Dear M. Gramont,

Please do us the honour of dining with us this evening, along with M. Tolouse, if he is returned. Your servant is regarded to be a general source of amusement, and therefore you are quite welcome to bring him.

Your most obliged,
Pierre Savard

I was half-inclined to decline this invitation, knowing as I did that it was Mouchard alone whose company was desired. Having said that, I was not entirely without desire to hear more of his tale, though I was reluctant to ask him to recite it for my benefit alone.

I informed M. Tolouse of his share of the invitation, when he arrived home.

"I might as well come,' said he, with a shrug, "though I daresay it is the little whelp that is wanted. He weaves a yarn like a gypsy, but the food will be better than elsewhere, so I shan't refuse it."

As it turned out, but for the presence of Mouchard, we were a dismal party indeed. Mme. Gaspar was only partially recovered from the cold she had got after the shock of the news, and her strength was poor. Mlle Vallon was so little enlivened by the presence of her intended, that she hardly ever raised her head. Her cousin was quite full of her own dignity, and could hardly bring herself to say more than a word or two during dinner. M. Savard, despite being the author of the invitations, was far from pleased at being compelled to allow any other gentleman under the same roof with Mlle Vallon. M. Tolouse was generally absent, evidently more comfortable in a tavern or gaming house.

After dinner we retired to the drawing room, and it was an unquestionable relief to all when Mlle de Courteline sent for Mouchard, to request he continue his tale.

Mouchard alone seemed unaffected by the mood which infected us all. Before beginning to speak, however, he cast his eyes upon M. Savard with uncertainty and consideration, before saying,

"As there is a new auditor present, to whom all happenings are unknown, I fear I shall be compelled to start from the beginning."

"The beginning!" cried Mlle de Courteline, in horror. "Nay, I am sure there is no call for that. M. Savard does not require it, certainly."

"Not at all," declared that gentleman, somewhat surprised.

"I know not how to speak of things which will not be understood by all auditors," persisted Mouchard calmly.

"But truly," declared Mlle de Courteline, to no one in particular, "he cannot be permitted to start from the beginning, or I at least shall go mad."

M. Savard appeared somewhat exasperated, but declared, "It is of no matter, for in truth I have numerous letters to write, and should be quite content to attend to them in the other corner of the room. Pay me no mind, I beg you."

With that he retired at quite a distance. I was intrigued to perceive, or at least to fancy I did, that Mouchard anticipated he would do so, and had some wish not to speak before him. At any rate, once he was out of earshot, he began to speak as normal:

"*As I have* mentioned to you previously, the neighbourhood in which Miss Reckert lived had a singular history. The abeyance of the largest property in the area, the promise made to the townsfolk left unfulfilled, seemed to have imbued the area with a heavy restless feeling.

Events sometimes have strange consequences ranging outside of themselves. The report of what occurred at this time, so far as I understand, is as follows:

"One day a wealthy woman of advanced age, Mrs. Ladderly, was travelling by coach alongside the same field the Earl of C had once pledged to give the townsfolk. It was dusk, and as she looked out her window into the field, she saw, or thought she saw, the ghostly apparition of the Earl himself. When she turned to remark this to a female companion, both were frightened nearly to death by the same figure, which now appeared directly across from them in the carriage.

The fear and shock of the ordeal nearly killed the elderly woman, who was carried from her carriage in a pitiable state. The cause of her illness was circulated quite broadly, and very soon, nearly everybody had heard it.

After the death of her husband, Mrs. Ladderly was well known to oppose any step to begin the construction of the town the Earl had promised, and was evidently reluctant to fulfil her husband's portion of the pledge, declaring all had changed upon the Earl's death.

When news of her vision spread among the inhabitants of the area, there was one universal conclusion: The Earl of C wished his promise fulfilled, and could not rest while his will was unheeded, and his word given in vain.

The result of this extraordinary event was that upon the day following, every peasant and villager gave up what they were doing and marched together to the quarry, determined to access it. Ploughs were left idle, shops were unmanned, and everything else seemed to come to a standstill.

On this day of all days, Miss Reckert had received a short note from Mr. Harland, announcing his intention to call upon her that afternoon.

Apprehending that he wished to talk of his nephew, and fearing to meet him without preparations, Miss Reckert fled the house, walking in the direction of the town.

It was true that she had given the matter a great deal of thought in the preceding days, but two things yet eluded her: one, the composure to allow her to bear another interview with apparent unconcern, and two, the way to extricate herself from this disagreeable situation.

Thomas too, accompanied her, falling a ways behind at times, or pursuing some purpose of his own, but invariably nearby.

Choosing to walk on a path through the forest, rather than along the road, Miss Reckert saw ahead of her the two figures of Miss Harland and Mrs. Churling.

Their arms were linked in a familiar way and their heads were bowed as in deep conversation. Miss Reckert was in no hurry to interrupt them, so she followed at a discreet distance. Before she realized it, she had grown closer than she had imagined, and was close enough to be saluted by her own name, which had come up in their conversation:

'Aye, but Miss Reckert will not have it,' Mrs. Churling was in the midst of saying, 'and declared she would rather die than accept poor Mr. Whinston.'

'Die?!' exclaimed Miss Harland, who had a literal understanding, unmended by thirty-five years of exposure to common hyperbole. 'I wonder she should be so extreme!'

'As do we all, I assure you,' replied the other, 'if only Mr. Harland had heeded me, he might have saved himself the trouble of proposing it, for any young lady who could refuse my nephew could be pleased with no one. You can't conceive how many times I have told him so.'

Miss Reckert was by no means inclined to hear more, and rather than meet the two ladies, she turned in the other direction and walked out upon the road.

As a principle, Miss Reckert was not the type of person who had a great concern for what was said of her. Strong-willed and wealthy, she was sure at least of the appearance of approbation when she was in public. At present, however, she could not help but be dismayed to find herself the common topic of conversation, if only because she feared that the increased scrutiny of her motives might lead to the discovery of her secret.

When she was several years younger, she had paid a good deal of deference to Mrs. Churling, and that lady had been flattered by the influence she fancied she had gained over the young lady's mind. This mistaken impression had never occurred to Miss Reckert, who was as outwardly seemingly compliant as she was inwardly stubborn and inflexible. The discrepancy between appearance and reality was caused by her dislike of conflict, and her desire to have only pleasing interactions in society. By her easy and agreeable manner, she ensured herself light and easy exchanges, never troubling herself about the insincerity at the root of many of her connections, or of the mistaken impressions it might give rise to.

Mrs. Churling's nephew had paid court to her, along with two others, nearly two years before. He had few qualities to recommend him and she had never thought of him seriously. The influence that Mrs. Churling flattered herself she possessed seemed to put within her reach a most advantageous alliance for her family. She had all but guaranteed the prize to her sister, and Miss Reckert's refusal surprised as much as it mortified her. From that point, they had seen each other but little. Mrs. Churling was incensed, and Miss Reckert, guessing she might be, was unwilling to be exposed to awkwardness and resentment.

In the present circumstance therefore, as she was quite familiar with the disposition of Mrs. Churling, she was not surprised by her part in the conversations, though she could not help but be chagrined to discover Miss Harland was such a ductile pupil.

Occupied with these unpleasant ideas, she pursued her way into town. The main road which led to it crossed a little bridge, culminating into two main roads, along which ran the main part of the town. Crossing the bridge, Miss Reckert was nearly in town when she saw a large crowd heading towards her, both from one side of the fork and the other.

They were still some distance away but their evident haste and excitement seemed to present the very real threat of being trampled to death in their path. Her mental occupation and the sound of the brook had prevented her from seeing or hearing them sooner, and when she finally perceived them, she had no other choice but to hurriedly retrace her steps across the bridge before they could overtake her.

Ahead of her, she perceived another young lady who was likewise fleeing the crowd over the bridge. The young woman looked back presently, and calling to Miss Reckert to follow her, held out her hand to her. Miss Reckert gratefully accepted her assistance and together they safely exited the bridge, turning off onto a little pathway running out of the way of the approaching masses.

As soon as they were out of the way, Miss Reckert remembered Thomas, and looked wildly around, only to see him hastening after them a short way away. The other young woman did not seem surprised to see him, but merely led them onwards quickly towards a large house which was located a little off the main road. As they started up the lawn towards it, Miss Reckert noticed a tall man standing a little ways away, his eyes following the crowd with a strange almost reminiscent expression. He looked towards the little party as they approached, cooly scrutinizing them, but although they passed only a few paces from him, he made no acknowledgement and did not remove his hat.

Miss Reckert had not much time to contemplate this oddity, as her companion pulled her along at a hasty speed which scarcely abated till they entered the house, followed by Thomas.

'I am sure Miss Reckert will excuse my urgency,' said she, once the door was firmly closed, 'since she knows well the cause.'

Miss Reckert bowed, surprised to be addressed by name by a young woman she could not recollect meeting. Her companion, guessing perhaps the reason for her perplexity, said, 'I will alert my mother, Mrs. Lawrence, that you are here, and of the strange accident which has favoured us with your company.'

The two young ladies had seen each other rarely at social gatherings over the last few years, and as Miss Lawrence spent considerable time in Bath each year, Miss Reckert no longer recognized her. The Reckert's overall failure to cultivate a connection between the families had been construed as neglect by Mrs. Lawrence, who soothed her mortification by disapproving of the Reckerts whenever she could. The more the Reckerts were oblivious to the Lawrences', the more censorious Mrs. Lawrence became.

Of all this Miss Reckert was unaware, yet she was sorry to appear so ignorant where she was known, and resolved to make up for it as best she may.

In a short time she returned, saying, 'My mother is honoured by your visit, and is just now hearing details of what is probably the cause of this strange occurrence from a servant who has heard the account from her mother this morning. If you would be so kind as to walk into the sitting room, she will prevail upon the girl to tell it again.'

After a brief but somewhat strained greeting from Mrs. Lawrence, Miss Reckert seated herself and heard from the servant what I have already described regarding the circumstances which caused this sudden march.

'Thank you, Sarah,' said Mrs. Lawrence, when she had done, requesting she would bring in tea.

Once the servant departed, a very uncomfortable silence took place, seemingly almost intentionally encouraged by Mrs. Lawrence, whose demeanour was offended and severe. The surprise of Miss Reckert grew by the moment. Mrs. Lawrence seemed to regard her with a kind of haughty expectation, as one who waits for an apology. Miss Lawrence, in the meantime, said nothing but hung her head in apparent sympathy and embarrassment, darting looks of helpless apology to Miss Reckert, who looked to her for explanation.

Miss Reckert was upon the verge of rising to take her leave, when Mrs. Lawrence finally said, 'Well, Miss Reckert, this is an honour indeed which I did not think to expect. No doubt we shall have to be grateful for any disturbances which procures us such extreme favours.'

Not doubting but that this was meant as a sarcasm of sorts, Miss Reckert was at a loss to understand it. She was in the midst of making a haltering reply when Mrs. Lawrence added, 'Not indeed, that I would have you think I blame the people in general, for far otherwise is true. The Earl of C, indeed, might well be driven to walking the fields if he expected more to be done to fulfil his wishes, though your father and the late Mr. Ladderly doubtless know better than I.'

All this was said with an air of reproach and disdain so personally directed towards Miss Reckert, she was more surprised than she had been in her life.

'Does your little companion take tea, my dear?' cried she, modifying her tone slightly, and gesturing towards the door of the room where Thomas stood sheepishly, trying not to call attention to himself. In response, he shook his head and bowed faintly.

'Indeed, you are very kind,' replied Miss Reckert, 'but I fear we are imposing upon you to come so unannounced, and I think we must take our leave. Good-day.'

With this she stood up and began to depart, disconcerted and incensed by behaviour which seemed mysteriously calculated to insult. She stopped in the hall, hastily reclaiming her hat and cloak, but as she rushed out of the house, Miss Lawrence came running behind her, calling,

'Pray wait, Miss Reckert! Permit me to apologize for my family, for they are much in the wrong.'

'Perhaps as much as I am in the dark, Miss Lawrence, but excuse me, I think I must go,' replied she, slowing only slightly.

'Permit me to explain,' called out she again, 'though I hope not excuse.'

Miss Reckert stopped then, unwilling to appear discourteous herself, even with justification. She could not help but be truly curious and concerned as to the nature of the offence she had unknowingly given strangers.

All perplexity was put to an end quickly thereafter when Miss Lawrence said, 'Is it possible–, nay–, I can see it must be so, but allow me to say it anyway. Is it possible Miss Reckert does not recall the proposals of my brother, Mr. Lawrence, when he sued unsuccessfully for her favour last year?'

At this mention, Miss Reckert sighed, having a vague remembrance of this occurrence, which in truth, she had troubled herself little about, either at the time or since. In fleeing the road to escape one conversation of her romantic affairs, she stumbled into another. It seemed she could not escape the families of her jilted suitors.

'I do not dare excuse my mother,' continued Miss Lawrence, 'but I hope at least that her fondness for her son and disappointment on his account at least somewhat lessens your surprise.'

'Indeed,' replied Miss Reckert gently, more touched by Miss Lawrence's kind and open manner than by the excuses she had made for her mother, 'I believe I recollect now something of the matter, but I confess I had no memory of it hitherto.'

'Happy Miss Reckert!' exclaimed Miss Lawrence, 'to lay claim to so many admirers that she has not the luxury of remembering them all!'

'Ah,' replied Miss Reckert, with a weak smile, 'I fear I have little that way to boast of, for in truth your brother inquired so little into my personal accomplishments, that I am not certain I received more than a bow from him across a room before he tendered his proposals. My fortune seems often to hasten any approval my appearance may possibly excite.'

Miss Lawrence seemed quite pleased with this answer, and begged leave to know if it was possible Miss Reckert would allow her to return the visit, as she said she did not dare to solicit her to return, however much she wished to know her better. Miss Reckert said she would be very happy to see her, which was not less than the truth. Miss Lawrence then offered to walk her some of the way, and they continued their conversation till it was stopped short by the sight of the same man they had seen on their way in, pacing distractedly in a circle.

'Tell me, Miss Lawrence,' said she, struck with a sudden thought, 'is this the brother of whom we speak?'

Miss Lawrence laughed aloud at this question, saying, 'My brother must have made quite an effort to distinguish himself indeed if you do not know him upon sight. Even were I the most partial sister in the world, I could not blame you now. Nay, that is my uncle,' and lowering her voice, 'Pray do not mind him much. I stay out of his way wherever possible, as hardship and travel has given him strange tendencies, and to own the truth, I fear him somewhat.'

After receiving this caution, Miss Reckert parted from her, again assuring her that she would be happy to see her whenever she would be so kind as to visit her. Her walk home was filled with numerous reflections. The disturbance in the neighbourhood was something she had never expected, and Mrs. Lawrence's suggestion that her father had been less than honourable in his conduct towards the people at large was quite abhorrent, and she scarce thought it possible. Despite this, she could not help but reflect upon his temperament, which she well knew tended towards inaction rather than action, and where there was a real evil to be addressed, inaction was not therefore excusable.

It was Mr. Harland she thought of next, considering that it was to better position him to inherit the very property in discussion. What would he do were he in fact to be selected to succeed the Earl; how would he resolve the question which had so long hung over the inhabitants of that area, and what would be his thoughts as to the present disturbance?

From this consideration, she returned again to herself and the conversations she had overheard between Miss Harland and Mrs. Churling. The reception of the Lawrences convinced her that however little she thought about the world, her own affairs either offended or entertained the entire area. Up until this point, she had felt that by secluding herself from the world, she affected no one but herself, but now upon reflection, she saw that her behaviour and state of mind were not merely noticed, but much scrutinized.

'How foolish I have been,' cried she to herself 'in distancing myself from others, I have garnered more notice rather than less!'

She immediately resolved to take full advantage of the friendship which seemed to be offered her by the amiable Miss Lawrence. By attempting to bring her conduct more in line with others, she hoped to lessen the focus upon herself."

Mouchard stopped here, as the night was long. It is strange to hear a description of unrest in this country, even though it is fictional. Inequity and repression would have the same result in any part of the world, I suppose. I am eager to know how the story will resolve itself.

I will close here as well, having written till quite late. With any luck, this package shall get to you soon.

Your faithful friend,
Marcel de la Croix

M. Henri Renault to Marcel de la Croix

January 27th, 1773, Switzerland

Dear Marcel,

The permission to share your letters caused great joy amongst the brotherhood. All your letters up until January 15th have now arrived, and they have been read widely. In those who can speak, there is much approval of Mlle de Courteline (which no doubt shall amuse and surprise you), and also much sympathy for Mlle Vallon. There was much groaning and shaking of heads when that part of your account was read. It seems that our friends can easily sympathize with complications caused by sequestration from the opposite sex. I shall say no more on the subject.

By the time you receive this letter, you will no doubt have heard of the execution of Louis XVI, only four days ago. Word reached us the following day, January 22nd, which was remarkable in and of itself, for we had almost heard nothing till then. A servant who sometimes brings us the newspapers delivered the news by mouth that morning. We did not know whether to believe it at first, but the talk now is of nothing else. Who could have believed it would have gone this far?

I know not what more to say. I am at risk of becoming quite melancholy, and begin to regret my decision to stay here.

In closing, let me thank you again for the trouble you have taken on our account, and exhort you to continue as you have begun. We are enthralled.

Yours ever,
Henri Renault

Marcel de la Croix to Henri Renault

February 2nd,1793

Dear Friend,

Now that M. Tolouse and I are settled in the Parsonage and the ladies in the main house, I have an abundance of time on my hands. The news of the death of the King continues to weigh upon us all, and the English seem to have conceived a less favourable view of emigres than before. My accent and halting attempts at English meet with more suspicion and disgust than before the news arrived last week, yet still others pity us. For the most part I have been left to myself of late, and have become more than a little amazed at the situation I find myself in; connected, yet unconnected to a party of strangers, though countrymen.

At present, Tolouse is out upon some business, Mouchard cannot be found and I have no wish to call upon the ladies. Instead I am resolved to write and continue my relation, in the hope that you may have it in full before we are both old men:

By the time of the incident on the road, which I related in my last letter, the presence of an increasingly organized revolutionary movement was beginning to be evident in our area. Every day seemed to bring word of some new circumstance which indicated the strength and momentum of the revolution. Though but a few days before, I had travelled seeing nothing, by the time of my return, it was more and more routine for travellers to meet with some form of semi-official-looking men, who made free to question or detain them.

Philip and I spoke very little upon our way home. It was abhorrent to me to kill a man, and here I had killed three but moments before. I could not bear to leave them on the road, so I had paid some onlookers to take them to the officials in town, where their remains could be respectfully interred. I did not doubt that I had done right, or at least only what I could not help, but I was not happy for the necessity. Death was in the air over the whole countryside. However much my own philosophical inclinations opposed the side I was forced to take, my honour called upon me to defy the revolutionaries, and my experiences made them most definitely my enemies.

Our return to the Chateau interrupted a tiny group of pillagers. I was greatly angered to see it, and rode ahead of Philip, brandishing my weapon and calling upon any to come out and face me. At this sight and sound, a dozen peasants scattered into the woods, and I was at once ashamed and infuriated. Philip followed quietly behind me, giving orders to set everything to rights, secure the Chateau, and to open it to no one.

Neither he nor I slept that night, and instead together we explored every defensive aspect of the fortress, ensuring that everything made either to defend or withstand was in as good a state as possible. How little did I conceive that the relics of a bygone era which I used to marvel at as a boy would in my lifetime be revived not merely for show but usage! Most of what remained was in good order, though some parts had rusted together so firmly, it took more than four men to move them again.

At this point in time, with no direction from the King and no desire to seek out M. Lafont to join the counter-revolutionaries, I had no other purpose but to stand my ground as long as I could, and await the outcome of the revolution.

A man without connection to anything or anyone, as myself, is a rare thing indeed. My family was dead, the King declined to command or guide me, or even accept my service. No affections preoccupied my heart. Being raised elsewhere, I was almost indifferent to my native land, and for the same reason, I felt scarcely more connected to my family and its history. My own birthright seemed made for another. Surely I was not truly the Marquis de la Croix?

Prepared as I was to defend the fortress, to my surprise, and possibly even disappointment, no one gave me the opportunity. An edict was circulated in which I was branded a criminal by the new authorities. The events upon the road were therein detailed in such a way as to make me infamous. I was reported to have killed five unarmed men transporting a criminal. The paper bearing these assertions was brought to us by our cook, who had encountered it during her errands. I do not have it by me, but by memory, it said:

Let all free-people and lovers of liberty be informed that the Chateau Fort de la Croix continues to be a bastion of repression and inequity. On the - of - this day 1789, Marcel de la Croix did slaughter five unharmed men on the road, who were transporting a criminal, who though vile, was yet less despicable than himself. While this villain hides in the fortress which is in itself a symbol of the repression born by our long suffering people, he eludes the justice he deserves. Let it be known, therefore, that should any friend of the revolution encounter this cowardly rat outside of his hole, the principles of honour and goodness shall be served by his immediate destruction.

How strange was the unintended consequence of this publicized falsehood! The very day following this, three separate messages arrived from gentlemen of this area, each begging asylum for themselves or their families. I saw no reason to refuse them; I accepted all three without condition and instructed Philip to make ready to receive them with all the hospitality the Chateau yet retained.

The first who arrived was M. Mancette, who till recently had held the position of magistrate in the nearby town of Fiettre. Having served Louis XVI so faithfully for many years, he was greatly distrusted by those who had ousted him. Not having the means to travel directly, he had delayed departing immediately, and now was watched so closely that he daren't try to leave the area, for fear of being taken into custody if he attempted to do so. His request for new papers had first been approved, but then mysteriously denied.

'But two days ago,' said he, 'one of my colleagues, a gentleman of the first order, was taken into custody upon suspicion of this or that. I must confess that I have neither plans or means of escape this moment, but the account I read of you decided me. I believe I could do much worse than seek your protection, Monsieur le Marquis, for which I am extremely grateful.'

Dinner that evening was a most lively occasion, since few now assembled in places where they were free to speak their minds and compare their experiences. M. Mancette, of all of us was the most informed, and he revealed that the masked man I called the ringleader was called M. Hubert, and it was he who was now officially in charge of the district, which was in the hands of the revolutionaries. He further relayed that it was M. Hubert's deputies who had relieved him of his post.

'Word is that for the time being the revolutionaries have headquartered themselves a fair ways away, having taken possession of the old Verlaine place, when its owners took flight after the disturbance here. No doubt they were hoping to return to it someday, as we all must, but these revolutionaries are quite entrenched hereabouts. Let us only hope it is not as bad everywhere.'

I related what observations I had made on my brief journey, and there was a general relief to hear that not every place was as strongly under the control of the revolutionaries. But '*what would be the result of the new National Assembly?*' was the question on every man's lips.

Though M. Mancette was above forty, my other two guests, M. Egret and M. Calonne were approximately the same in years as myself.

M. Egret was perhaps slightly older than myself, but his deferential manners seemed to reverse the gap. M. Calonne was nearer to myself in age, wealth and temperament. He did not come from this area, but had encountered considerable difficulties passing through. He was the heir to a formerly great family in this area and had come to take possession of his property. Several months' delay arriving to claim it had made his trip for nought, and he found himself denied. Having unfortunately lost his papers three days ago, he had been unable to gain leave to pass. He had understood, moreover, that as the heir to his uncle, he was expected to answer for some of the late gentleman's offences. To his dismay, he found that although he could no longer inherit his uncle's property, he was at risk of being held accountable for his 'crimes'.

As he was struggling to find out how to extricate himself from a situation so insupportable, he happened to see the charges relating to myself, and considering that he was alone in an inhospitable environment, he thought it prudent to align himself with someone better situated to resist such injustice. From here, by my leave, he hoped to write to his family and friends, seek their advice and then plan his course, while heeding the progress of the revolution like we all must.

M. Egret, though he described his circumstances in less detail than the others, seemed to have almost equal reason to seek protection. One or two men with whom his family (most particularly his late father) had been frequently at odds with were now in a position to be revenged, courtesy of the shift in power brought by the revolution. Though of all three the most timid, he pledged, as did the others, to give his life in defence of the Chateau, should circumstances warrant it.

That night M. Egret begged to relieve Philip and I as sentry for the first portion of the overnight vigil, and M. Calonne offered to stand sentry for the second.

I retired late, blessing the circumstance which had allowed me two nights rest together. I lay awake for a while, thinking of all I had heard and wondering what would become of us all. I know not how long it was before I fell asleep, but scarcely had it reached four in the morning then we were all awakened by the sound of the old warning bell ringing.

Very quickly M. Mancette, M. Calonne, Philip and I were assembled along with M. Egret, who merely directed our eyes across a field. There we could see three torch lights approaching at a quick pace, indicating riding.

We watched in silence, waiting to see if they were indeed headed here. After a very short while, it became quite evident that there were perhaps nearly a dozen riders approaching at great speed.

Philip presently went to ensure that all of the fortifications were fast, while the rest of us merely watched to see what might unfold. There was truly little to fear from twelve men when inside a fortress, but that knowledge itself did not dampen the sense of alarm and expectation raised in every breast.

Suddenly I became aware that one or two lights were visible a ways behind the party we were watching. One or two minutes later, we could clearly see that there were two separate parties approaching, the second perhaps three times the size of the first.

At this discovery, we were unable to decide amongst us whether they were two parts of a whole, or whether one was in pursuit of the other.

A very short amount of time settled that, for immediately the first party arrived, its leader dismounted and cried out, 'Marcel de la Croix, it is Pierre Lafont who calls. Open the gate, I pray, for the enemy is at our heels!'

Without hesitation we scrambled to lower the makeshift bridge at once, and in the work of a few moments, they were well met within the inner courtyard.

'It is cowardly to flee, I know,' cried he, with no other preliminary, 'but they are better armed, dogs though they are!'

'Nay, surely there are thirty men following behind,' cried I.

'Well,' said he, taking no notice of my reply, but looking around at the three gentleman who were also there, 'I see you have done as I have and more shall come, no doubt. No one can remain neutral in a climate such as this.'

After a brief introduction all around, he said, 'Well, my dear Marquis, brother in misfortune, have you any arms? Swords and pistols would be most welcome.'

'What do you propose?' cried I, with visible surprise.

'Excuse me, Monsieur,' interjected M. Mancette, 'there is no call for concern, for we are well protected within these walls.'

''Tis only what has been said before,' said a man M. Lafont had introduced as his uncle, who was perhaps in his mid-forties, 'may your words be more successful than mine.'

'Forgive me, gentlemen, but I have something to communicate to the Marquis,' replied M. Lafont, drawing me aside.

'Who is it that pursues you?' asked I, not waiting for him to begin.

'Who should it be, but a pack of villains who have taken over our noble country?'

'There is but a moment, for I see you would do something about it. Tell me first how you encountered them.'

'If you are indeed of the same mind as I, then I shall tell you as quickly as I am able, lest they turn tail and run away. I went to my uncle's house, as I intended, and found the whole area beset by the same rascals which are everywhere. For a few days we visited and consulted with the other gentry about, to see what ought to be done. After a maddening deliberation the general consensus was that some of us should ride in a number to the town, of which my uncle was lately magistrate. For this we assembled any willing bodies, principally my uncle, his sons, and two or three more men from nearby. On our way, several other able gentlemen came to join us.

As soon as we reached the town where we had hoped to instil some order, we found them revelling over the murder of one or two good citizens who were accused of plotting against the revolution. My uncle attempted to calm the mob, but they were beyond all efforts. One of the bodies of the poor victims was raised, and as they prepared to do violence to it, I could contain myself no longer and fell upon every miserable person in the crowd with my sword. Seeing this, my companions had no choice but to take part as well. There was no resisting the sheer mass of them, for though there were few weapons amongst them, there were near a hundred miserable rats to contend with, and before long, my uncle called us off. I would feign have continued to fight, but I could not do so by myself, and unluckily I have lost my sword in the earlier skirmish. Feeling they had got the better of us, any poor fool with a horse made free to follow us, and they have been joined by more of their brethren on the way. I chanced to read of your exploits yesterday, and convinced my uncle to follow me here, which he was ready enough to do for fear of leading these rogues to his own house. Now I have done, what say you? Shall you join me in chasing them from your door, though the old men would tell us we are safe enough? Does safety appeal to you as it does to them?'

'In truth, it does not. Do you have another horse, for we do not keep any inside?'

'Aye, for one of us is a child, and he will be unseated well enough. Truth be told, all but four of them would easily give his place up to be lodged indoors.'

'As to the other gentlemen who came here for protection, I would neither have them shamed nor injured.'

'If they are cowards, why would you not have them be thought so?'

'Some men have more need of safety than revenge, and if I had anything at all which made my existence worthwhile, or any person who truly valued it, I would not be so ready to risk it as I am now.'

'As you wish,' said he, then turning to the rest, he said 'Monsieur le Marquis and I would like to have a word with the vagrants outside, so we shall go out the back when once we are readied. Our horses are limited and we shall not want all of you for this little business. Sort out amongst yourselves who will come, and we shall wait for you at the back gate.'

While he said so, I gave Philip some little instructions, and then returning to my three guests, I said, 'Take no notice of this, I beg you, as it pertains mostly to M. Lafont and myself.'

'But is it not madness to go out and face such a number, when you might better stay safely in your home?' said M. Mancette.

''Twould be safer surely, but I do not find my present style of life so worthy of protection, so I must either do what I can to change it, or end it all together. Adieu, Monsieur, God-willing, I shall see you again in a short while.'

From there I went immediately to find M. Lafont, who was waiting at the back outer wall. We conferred for a short while, for I wished to know if he had any plan. True to form he had no plan but to attack indiscriminately, and as far as I was concerned, no other plan was necessary.

Our collective anger and brashness seemed to have an emboldening affect, for as we prepared to set-out and looked behind us, I was surprised to see all ten horses manned. M. Calonne was among them, having replaced one of the initial riders.

Scarcely a month before, the very thought of such a circumstance would have filled me with fear and confusion, but at this moment, I welcomed any outcome at all. The merely sitting and waiting of the previous week had given me a fear of nothing so much as prolonged suspense and inaction.

Looking back at the men behind us, my eagerness received a sudden check, with the thought that their decision wholly rested upon ours. There was no time for much contemplation, however, and I calmed my conscience with the thought that the revolution was a force which confronted us all, and it seemed likely that sooner or later we would each of us need to stand against it. I inwardly resolved to ensure myself more than my share of whatever risk and fighting ensued.

As soon as we issued from the gate and began to round the defence wall in search of our enemies, M. Lafont began shouting loud threats and instructions, and truly I believe that the men gathered there in the faint light of dawn, thought us a much larger force than we were. By some considerations, had we not at least two dozen men, it would be foolish to leave our shelter, and therefore it was reasonable for our adversaries to assume we were more.

At the sound of our approach, several men were put to their heels. There are always some men who will join any enterprise when it seems sure of success, and flee when that is in doubt. To see it, M. Lafont seemed to grow even more outrageous, crying that we let no one who had dared to come here escape alive. This declaration put still more men on the run, but I had no longer leisure to contemplate it, for it was then I met my first opponent.

How strange is the memory for such events! I remember much, but I know not what I can rely upon. My heart beat loud and my ears seemed to hear sound in a muffled, slow way. Sight blurred, and it seemed as though I heard clank, clank, clank, with every clash of my sword, but in the midst of each seemed to come a stifled screaming, either near me or far. It was dark, but I recall that the first man I met was a large, grim fellow. There was perhaps seven blows before he fell, but I do not claim great skill in that exchange, for I merely swung wildly, determined not to disgrace myself. A strange calm enveloped me thereafter and I sought out the next opponent and the next with a kind of grim delight that I shudder now to think of. What they looked like or how they fought I do not directly recall, but I am certain that no other person I exchanged swords with had anything like the skill or strength of the first man. I did not kill all of those I met, and I do believe more than one of them managed to extricate themselves. I went riding after one man who did so, but by this point my eagerness was waning. Scarcely any of the men we fought seemed to present much of a challenge and even those with pistols shot wildly before running off into the woods.

Having charged out with the idea of revenge, my fury disappeared with the disparity of their numbers. As even more fled, I looked around for M. Lafont, intending to tell him it was no longer a fair fight.

I saw him a few paces away, in the midst of fighting a young man who seemed much less than him in years and stature.

'Hold, M. Lafont,' I cried, as he was about to get the better of him, "twould be a shame for us to fight any longer. Speak, lad,' said I, addressing the boy, 'how old are you?'

'Fourteen!' cried he, looking at myself and M. Lafont wildly, still in fear.

'Old enough to die, surely!' cried M. Lafont in disgust.

'Why have you come here?' persisted I. 'I am Marcel de la Croix, and this is my house. Should we not kill you?'

'Nay, if you shall put that question to every one of them, then we had better stop,' cried M. Lafont, but by that time the rest had scattered and only the twelve of us remained along with the boy.

The boy did not respond but merely looked at me in amazement, and I asked again why he had come, and what had given him the notion to assail my house. 'Are you an enemy of the King?' I demanded at the last

'No, I am an enemy of hunger,' cried he, at last, in desperation, 'since I am sure it will kill me and I was told we should have a part of what was inside.'

'By what right?

'Not right but need,' returned he. 'I have scarce touched a bite since my mother died a fortnight ago, and I thought this the surest way to get some food. Everyone says the great lords have locked away all the grain.'

'And so you would fight against the King to eat?'

'I should fight whatever one likes if I could but have some dry bread.'

'Why do you keep him talking?' cried M. Lafont, 'Half the bodies around might have told you the same story, though they speak no more, and some by your hand.'

'Swear you shall never again come to insult my house, and you shall go free,' said I, ignoring him.

'I swear it, yet know, good Sir, I swear it merely to go in the woods and die.'

'Here,' said I, throwing him a coin, 'you may eat, by all means, if it shall remind you how to behave.'

At this M. Lafont burst out in laughter, 'Why if you would pay him to attack us, perhaps we might have him to dinner? Come, lad, tell us how we shall make you comfortable?'

'Ah, Sir, if only you should feed me, I should be loyal to you for life!' said he, speaking to me rather than to M. Lafont, who all could see was in jest.

'Aye, and slit his throat while he sleeps,' rejoined that gentleman again.

'Come then,' said I, 'and you will eat, but meantime we must all set about burying your companions.'

'Nay, let them be burnt,' said M. Lafont, 'for we are all tired and hungry, and that shall be easier.'

'As we are Christians, we must bury them,' replied I, 'those too tired to dig will stand watch.'

No more argument was made, though M. Lafont did so begrudgingly, all the while directing his remarks towards the boy I had spared. His jests only came to an end once he asked how many cushions the boy should like within and the boy replied that he knew not what they were, but should like an infinite amount if they were edible. This response was made with so much earnestness, no one could doubt that it was sincere, and thereafter we were all of us silent.

In total eight graves were dug, and I being foremost in the work, no one hesitated to join in. Once all was done, we made our way inside, but the work of burial had made no one jovial. I explained to Philip what I had promised the boy, whose name was Joseph, and without question he undertook to give him some provisions and whatever else seemed reasonable.

I shall end my narration on this sober note. It is 10 o'clock in the evening and I have scarce been out of my room today; I have a slight cold and have not wished to leave the fire.

To return to the present, two rather curious things have occurred of late. Two days ago I became ill with a cold, and receiving an invitation to call on the other house with Mouchard, I determined to keep to my bed and not trouble myself with moving. At first I was determined to send a total rejection to the invitation, but at last I decided to send Mouchard alone, since I knew it was he who was wished for.

Mouchard returned home a little while later, but he said nothing of his visit and merely helped me get dressed. I went downstairs for dinner, but I was a little out of sorts. I often write letters in the parlour, and so I was writing to you when M. Tolouse came in. I greeted him as usual, but presently I forgot he was there. My head began to ache again and I grew warm with fever. I was resting my forehead upon my hand for a moment or two, but when I opened my eyes again, I perceived M. Tolouse looking at me with wonder, his eyes fixed upon the scar on my hand.

I am usually in the habit of taking some care to conceal it from an excess of caution. I wear longer sleeves, and gloves whenever I can, though I confess I am not as consistent as I should be. It is impossible to hide it from Mouchard though to him it can have little significance. I fear it was not so with M. Tolouse.

"I hope nothing ails you, Monsieur?" said I.

"No," said he, with a little start, "but I am sure the same cannot be said for you at present. Be best to sleep."

"I fear you are right," replied I, "be so good as to help me to my bed, and perhaps we will speak more tomorrow."

That night I slept a good many hours without interruption, and when I awoke, I was almost as new. Near noon, Mlle de Courteline was announced.

To my surprise, she was evidently out of humour, and had come to inquire whether M. Tolouse or myself wished to join herself, M. Savard and Mlle Vallon upon their little ramble around the area. I hesitated at first, slightly chagrined to find even my good offices were resented or ignored, yet I determined to join them merely from curiosity, rightly guessing that Mlle de Courteline was quite ready to enlighten me as to my crimes.

Both Mlle de Courteline and myself looked at M. Tolouse to know his pleasure, but instead of replying, he said he would know in a moment, but first begged to speak with me. Mlle de Courteline declared she would wait for one or both of us outside with the others.

"I merely wished to know whether you would have me go or not, Sir, since you might have something in view, for all I know."

This way of speaking was little to my liking and I told him to feel free to come or go depending on his own pleasure, but if he decided to join us, I should look for an opportunity to speak with him.

Hearing this he opted to join us, but as I walked with Mlle de Courteline, and M. Savard walked with Mlle Vallon ahead, he chose to hang back and walk by himself.

"You are much better today, I hope, Sir?" inquired Mlle de Courteline, with more accusation than concern.

"I am. I had hoped to have obliged you and Mlle Vallon by sending Mouchard without me, but I see I have failed, at least where you are concerned."

"I daresay Mlle Vallon has no greater reason to be pleased than I, for there was no purpose to send Mouchard at all, when first you forbid him to entertain us."

"Forbid him?" cried I, in astonishment, "Nay, that was the very purpose of my sending him. And did he say I did so?"

"There was no need for him to say so, for otherwise he would certainly have given way to our entreaties. Perhaps the thought of our dismay repaid you for the trouble you took."

"You are truly kind to suspect me. But what did he give as his reason?"

"He said very little, but merely declared he could not continue whilst you were not present. Poor Mlle Vallon even fell to tears, but the little vagrant was unmoved."

I little expected to hear such an account, and am resolved to think on the meaning of it when I have leisure. "He is certainly not without his singularities," said I, mostly to myself. "But who among us are?"

"Singularities are merely defects," replied she, peevishly "and good birth and breeding often remove them."

"Would that it were so! They are but more likely to instil them, else we would not have a revolution to contend with at all."

"Ah, scandalous! And would you blame the lords for the crimes of the common men? Nay, do not answer. We shall never agree on this subject. How I wish my father was here to explain it to you!"

"There at least we can agree. Is there not any news of him?"

"There is not," replied she, becoming more grave.

"But M. Savard surely brought some news of him?"

"I know not what to..." hesitating whether to continue. "I know not what to make of this situation at all." For a while she did not speak, and we walked on in silence. Eventually she slowed a bit, her annoyance seeming to fade the more she thought of weightier matters.

"M. Savard says very little," she declared. "He says we will see, and such, and we must pray all works out, and so forth. M. Gramont, you are a man of the world; let me ask you, in my place, what would you think? Nay, what would you do?"

"Since you invite me to tell you, I must say I think M. Savard is doing you a disservice. If he can give you good tidings of your family, he ought to do so, but otherwise he ought to acknowledge it frankly, and tell you to prepare yourself."

"Prepare myself?" cried she, in a loud voice, eliciting some curious looks from the others, who were nevertheless too far to hear our discourse. "Prepare myself for what? What do you imply?"

"You cannot be ignorant of what I mean," said I in a lower voice than she, "I am certain you have given the matter all too much thought. Prepare yourself, I say, to think and to act for yourself and Mlle Vallon as if you had only your own wit to rely upon. You may hope, and who should deny you that comfort, but M. Savard does you a disservice not to advise you as I have done, and his failure to do so is in itself a cause for concern."

Mlle de Courteline looked at me with an expression truly to be pitied. Anger and outrage struggled with fear, and without deigning to reply to what I had said, she stalked on to join M. Savard and Mlle Vallon.

As soon as she was at a fair distance, M. Tolouse approached, bearing the newly deferential aspect he had adopted.

"I am sorry to disturb you, Sir," said he, with a little bow, "for I see all has not gone well. She is hard to please. No doubt she will come around to whatever you propose."

I was in no humour to see this change in his behaviour, and therefore I said,

"M. Tolouse, I am glad you have come, and I should be happy to speak with you for a moment.' He assented readily and as soon as we were walking together, I said, 'I see you have seen my little scar and it means something to you. What I want to say on the subject is this: Spare yourself any effort you would make for my benefit. You are a well enough companion and I have no complaint with you, nor hope to have. No doubt you realize there is money to be made from the little discovery, but as to that, I hope for your indulgence in one little matter, which I shall speak as plainly as possible: if you intend to collect a reward for knowledge of my whereabouts, be so good as to kill me first. I have no desire to return to France, and as far as I am aware, the reward would be the same either alive or dead."

Having said as much I walked on.

"You wrong me extremely," cried he, running along side of me. "I am no school boy snitch, and I shouldn't want to kill you, whatever may be the reward. Nay, even if I should try to, how do I know but you might kill me instead, for seems likely you are more than able."

"That is no great obstacle," replied I, "for you may kill me in my sleep. Say no more of it, whatever sort of man you are, I feel certain you will oblige me in that at least, and so I will have done."

M. Tolouse continued his tiresome protestations during the rest of the short way home, into which he intermixed newly discovered exclamations in favour of the royalist cause.

Mlle de Courteline had stalked far ahead of all of us, and when we were near our lodgings, M. Savard took a distant leave of us, while Mlle Vallon only looked at us sadly.

We had been home but a short time, when we received a short note from M. Savard, requesting our presence to dine that evening, hoping my health would permit, etc. Mouchard was not mentioned, but there was no longer any need to do so. I accepted, but inwardly determined that as soon as he had finished his tale, however many days it would take him to do so, I would instantly take my leave of them all.

Mouchard seemed completely unconcerned by the news he would accompany us again. I shall not describe our dinner, as it was nearly exactly as before. Mlle de Courteline spoke to no one. Immediately after dinner, M. Savard excused himself to write a letter in an adjoining room, while the gentle Mlle Vallon applied to Mouchard to begin his tale again without delay.

Mouchard did not need any further prompting, and after giving a short description of where he had been when he last left off, he said:

"*The following day* brought word that the townspeople had successfully breached the quarry and were now by all accounts peacefully organizing to begin building cottages on the land the Earl had intended for them, along with several new buildings where the town was to be. Few now seemed to question their authority to do so, as there could be no higher authority on the matter than the disembodied spirit of the Earl of C.

The next day was designated for the departure of Mrs. and Miss Gregory, to whom Miss Reckert bid adieu with true regret, mostly on account of the latter. In the late morning, Mr. Harland sent a short message saying he was obliged to attend other matters and would postpone his visit until at least the next day or two, when he expected he would have opportunity to call upon her.

She could neither rejoice or repine at this news, finding the interview was still to take place. She resolved instead to fortify herself to bear it with steadiness, and thereafter turn her whole attention to how she might make her situation more bearable to herself. Mr. Harland, she knew, did not so much as consider the possibility of a connection between them, nor could she believe that any extraordinary inclination existed, for how then to explain that it did not occur to him? Her father seemed to wish to settle her with a kind of urgency that threatened his very health; but how to oblige him without paining herself beyond tolerance?

Such matters she had often pondered, as she did again with no better result. The following morning dawned, and upon hearing the bell, she prepared to meet Mr. Harland, but lo, Miss Lawrence instead was announced.

Miss Reckert was a moment recovering from her surprise, and struggled briefly to recover her normal demeanour, having adopted the rather constrained manner she almost always adopted in anticipation of Mr. Harland

Miss Lawrence easily perceived her embarrassment, though she knew not the cause, saying kindly, 'I hope, Miss Reckert, I have not come at an inopportune moment?'

'No, indeed,' cried Miss Reckert, 'but I rather thought you were someone else.'

'I am sorry to disappoint you,' replied she, though she raised her eyebrow in saying so to indicate she did not truly think this was the case. 'I had meant to come sooner, but yesterday was quite taken up with visits from our other neighbours, who are concerned about the disturbance which has taken place. They all wonder what, if anything, ought to be done about it?'

'And what is your opinion?' inquired Miss Reckert, her mind wandering to the allusion Mrs. Lawrence had made about her father.

'I see no use in having an opinion where I have no means of enforcing it,' replied she with a smile.

'Opinions and feelings are often involuntary,' said Miss Reckert thoughtfully, 'whether we would have them or no.'

'In any case, I suspect there is nothing to be done by anyone.

In your father's absence, Mr. Harland seems the proper person to decide how this matter must be handled. By report, he has ridden down yesterday to observe the activity, and finding everything organized and peaceable, he has declared that nothing shall be done at the moment. This, I believe, is the general opinion, with only one or two dissenting voices. But doubtless these are things you already know.'

Miss Reckert confessed she did not know anything of the matter, and looking up at Miss Lawrence, whose face betrayed curiosity and surprise, she said with a slight smile. 'Why should you be surprised? You have no doubt heard from the general report that I am a self-involved conceited sort of person.'

'I have heard many things,' cried Miss Lawrence, laughing, 'all of which are becoming harder to credit with each moment I stay with you. I am certain Miss Reckert does not much wonder or repine at the attention she receives, since one cannot expect to have everything their way. When Providence doles out wealth and beauty so abundantly, it cannot be without some balancing circumstance. No doubt the price you pay for your good fortune is to be the general talk of idle minds.'

Miss Reckert was preparing to reply when the sound of the door distracted her thoughts, and instead she sat in pensive anticipation till Mr. Harland was announced.

They both rose to receive him. He seemed momentarily surprised to find someone else with her, considering that of late she had seen little company.

Miss Reckert thought at first that the two were acquainted, as Miss Lawrence had spoken of him so confidently only a moment before, but when she discovered an introduction was actually necessary, she was flustered at her mistake.

'I had thought–,' looking to Miss Lawrence, 'since you mentioned–,' but then blushing to recall they had spoken of him, she then blamed herself for seeming ashamed at something so commonplace, and then with the greatest composure she could muster, performed the necessary introduction.

His presence invariably inspired Miss Reckert with a variety of emotions. Fondness and partiality were quickly repressed, and pride and pique at his general neglect invariably generally followed. Her own internal acknowledgment that she had no natural entitlement to more attention led her to sadness and shame. These conflicting thoughts and emotions caused her such awkwardness and confusion that she was forced to say very little, and often hesitated or misspoke. Her mistakes only added to her mortification, for she feared that their cause might be guessed.

Mr. Harland awaited the end of her hesitation with the air of someone who is content not to understand what they believe cannot be understood. However unusual, her behaviour was consistent, and he had ceased to wonder at it at all.

'Excuse me,' ventured he, 'I meant not to interrupt your visit. It was a pleasure to make your acquaintance, Miss Lawrence, and I shall presume to call upon you another day, Miss Reckert. Good day to you both.'

With that he took his leave, giving the exchange no more thought than it seemed to merit. Miss Reckert, however, was cruelly distressed by her inability to master her emotions, and sat for a while in pensive silence, discontentedly reviewing her conduct.

For a while she forgot the presence of Miss Lawrence, who observed her with surprise and interest, not venturing to interrupt her reverie. Though it was apparent her distress related somehow to Mr. Harland, Miss Lawrence thought it perhaps more likely to relate to the purpose of his visit, rather than the visitor himself.

When Miss Reckert finally brought her attention back to the present moment, she experienced another unpleasant shock to realize how her behaviour had exposed her.

'Forgive me,' said she, 'you must think me strange indeed.'

'I see something makes you unhappy, and I am sorry for it, but pardon me for saying that dissatisfaction is such a universal affliction, it would make you more strange if you were entirely contented.'

Miss Reckert appreciated this sally, in which Miss Lawrence

chose to forbear either inquiry or implication. The remainder of their visit was equally pleasant, and after Miss Lawrence departed, Miss Reckert congratulated herself on the prospect of a friendship with a young lady who seemed far more suited to her taste than any she had known heretofore.

Her missteps also convinced her that what her father had often told her was justified, and the more she shunned society, the more she forgot how to conduct herself. Accordingly she resolved to do all in her power to encourage this connection.

Despite the reception she had previously received from Mrs. Lawrence, the next day Miss Reckert prepared herself to return her friend's visit. She was upon the verge of going out when Mr. Harland was announced and seen into the parlour, where she was assembling her hat and cloak.

He apologized for causing her any delay, but wondered if she had a moment or two to spare before she departed. In the interest of putting the unavoidable behind her, she easily agreed, and seated herself to hear what he wished to say.

'I mentioned, I believe, my intention to speak to you once more upon the subject of my nephew, but once you have heard me, you may be assured I intend to mention it no more.'

Miss Reckert appeared pensive, but said nothing, and so he continued.

'I have relayed your answer to Mr. Whinston, and although he is evidently disappointed, his disposition is remarkably sanguine, and not easily discouraged.'

Miss Reckert remained silent, but looked downwards with an air of dejection.

'Have you any new commands to honour me with, in regard to that gentleman?' asked he, uncertain in exactly which manner to press the subject.

'No, not any new, but perhaps you would be so good as to enforce what I have already said, whenever possible, as I am certain it will not change.'

'I shall be pleased even to disoblige my nephew, if it would oblige Miss Reckert, but perhaps you might arm me with something which might enable me to discourage him more successfully? Tell me in confidence the source of your disapprobation, and I will endeavour to better convince him of it.'

In contemplating her motivation, Miss Reckert was prey to a quick succession of emotions, but considering that her indifference to Mr. Whinston would exist even in absence of her feelings for Mr. Harland, she said at last,

'I am sensible of Mr. Whinston's merit, but when thinking of a husband–,' she blushed and stopped for a moment. Beginning again, she said, 'That is to say, I should like to distinguish someone with a particular... I mean, not someone, but in the case of Mr. Whinston, I do not–' she sighed deeply, tiring of her own perpetual embarrassment, and managing at last to say. 'I do not feel for Mr. Whinston as I should like to feel for a husband, though this might easily be my deficiency as well as his.'

Mr. Harland looked his general confusion, but attributing her discomfort to the subject (and her sex in general), little remarked it. As to the substance itself, when at last he understood it, it seemed of all possible objections the least material.

Nevertheless, it was clear to him that to express this would be little to the point, and there was something in her manner and expression which conveyed a finality that her meaning did not. Nor was he, in truth, much more at ease than herself. He considered himself uniquely unsuited to conversations which required a great degree of delicacy. Miss Reckert's overall reluctance to speak on the subject convinced him there was an obstacle he could not fathom, but how to discover it, he was completely at a loss. This being the case, he saw no reason to pain her unnecessarily, and so took leave.

For the next few weeks, Mr. Harland continued to call upon her every Thursday evening. If Miss Reckert could devise no reasonable expedient to be unavailable, he merely inquired if there was any way he could serve her, and she invariably replied that there was not.

On one occasion only he brought with him the proposals of a nobleman from a neighbouring county, but as Miss Reckert had not even the opportunity of meeting the gentleman, so far as she could remember, she had no great matter in refusing them by proxy.

Although she could not completely rid her manner of awkwardness, pride and practise enabled her to retain her composure when saying very little. Still, her preference by far was to avoid these brief conferences altogether. Her increasing intimacy with Miss Lawrence gave her more plausible reasons to do so. All the same, Miss Reckert's first visits to the Lawrence home were made with trepidation, and received with a great deal of surprise by the lady of the house. As time passed, however, Miss Reckert was relieved to find her host appeared gratified, rather than incensed, by the additional attention.

As for Mr. Harland, he all but completely gave up any hope of truly serving his old friend by settling his daughter, though he ever continued his efforts to do so.

This unproductive pattern was eventually interrupted by a visit from Mr. Seymour, who arrived one morning around that time. He had come ostensibly to update Mr. Harland on various aspects of his affairs, among them the state of his home and the progress or lack thereof, of his own marital negotiations.

The two gentlemen conferred together for several hours, breaking for lunch around two o'clock. It had become customary for Miss Harland to invite the Churlings to lunch with them once or twice a week, enabling the ladies to discuss the latest gossip in the area. With the addition of a new person around the table, the perennial subject became once again new, and immediately that they sat down to soup, Mrs. Churling said,

'Did you hear, Mr. Seymour, a match between Miss Reckert and Mr. Whinston is now truly despaired of?'

'I was not fully aware there was one in the offering...'

'And what a glorious match it might have been. Two such houses, such fortunes and even such a pretty couple, to be sure and no one could find a thing wrong with it, unless they be the lady herself. Is it not a sad case?'

'Oh well. She has a mind of her own; we must not make too

much of it.'

'You of all people would say so, Sir. I suppose you are partially to blame. I told Mr. Reckert when he went about educating her, that he must not do too much, or else she will seek to control her own affairs,' turning to Miss Harland. 'Mr. Seymour had the charge of her education and I'll warrant he has made her more fit to be a country squire than a young lady. No offence to you, Sir, but a little French and a dancing master was all that was needed, and 'twould have saved his pocket as well to heed my advice.'

'I am glad he did not,' replied Mr. Seymour, unperturbed, 'for I should have been deprived a comfortable living and the most amiable pupil.'

'But do you find her sensible, Sir?' begged Miss Harland, in all sincerity, having been used to hearing Miss Reckert described as the most unaccountable kind of person.

'Sensible, Madam?' repeated he, with a good deal of laughter. 'I should hope so.'

Miss Harland was unwilling to confess she had not understood the cause for amusement, and Mr. Seymour did not enlighten her on his own accord.

In all truth the question could just as easily have come from Mr. Harland, who till then had all but forgotten that such a connection existed between them. Recollecting it now, he felt that Mr. Seymour might possibly have some insight regarding the lady which would help him, and resolved to speak to him on the subject as soon as he might do so more privately.

The conversation continued in the same strain, meanwhile, no restraint found necessary owing to the company of Mr. Seymour, who listened with the most absentminded attention.

Once the topic of Miss Reckert seemed to be exhausted, Mr. Churling addressed Mr. Harland particularly about his plans to build onto the rock wall by the Parsonage, in the section nearing the road. He quickly proceeded to enter more into his reasons and intentions, 'For,' he said, 'while neither Mrs. Churling or myself truly object to the lower height near the garden, it has become inconvenient near the road. Our sitting room, you know, is in that very corner of the property, and all who come around the corner come face to face with us directly–.'

'Not that I would have Mr. Harland think we wish to avoid anyone,' interjected Mrs. Churling, 'but it is disagreeable to be forced to look at every passer-by, by foot or carriage, whether we know them or no.'

'Precisely,' continued he, 'but as relates to the chickens–.'

Here he was interrupted by the action of Mr. Seymour, who, feeling his usual impatience in regard to matters that did not relate to himself, rose apologetically from his chair to say, 'Forgive me, I do not mean to interrupt, but I have brought several things for Miss Reckert and I do not want to risk missing her. Pray, excuse me.'

'Do you mean to say you have brought her gifts?' inquired Mr. Harland, with as much surprise as if he had said he meant to dance circles in the grass.

'I do not much see why I should bring her gifts?' replied Mr. Seymour, showing the lack of understanding was mutual. 'At any rate, you must forgive me, for I am afraid I have left it too long. Good-day.'

Though Mr. Churling continued to speak following Mr. Seymour's departure, he could no longer hope to retain much of Mr. Harland's attention. His mind was now completely preoccupied with trying to fathom what Mr. Seymour could have meant and trying to imagine what sort of exchange could take place between the two. So ingrained in his mind was the impossibility of reasonable conversation with the young lady in question, (or indeed any young lady) that the thought entirely baffled him.

As lunch was soon to be cleared away, he proposed to walk down in an hour or so to see exactly what Mr. Churling described. This suggestion was warmly received, and husband and wife quickly became anxious to return home and set things to order, and accordingly the whole company soon parted for one reason or another.

Though he scarcely realized it, Mr. Harland himself was motivated to suggest it by an irrepressible wish to observe for himself the strange phenomenon Mr. Seymour had hinted at. It was natural enough, in this case, that his footsteps followed the lead of his thoughts, and in several minutes he found himself outside in the garden, where he happened to see Mr. Seymour in the distance approaching the open arbour where Miss Reckert was reading, clutching a small package in his hands.

Mr. Harland stopped hesitatingly, not wishing to interrupt exactly, unsure of what he might say in any case, but tempted to overhear what was not intended for him. Nevertheless, his curiosity was strong, and the sincerity of his wish to better fathom the disposition and character of the young lady caused him to pause temporarily, until some favourable moment might arise for him to join the conversation without utterly diverting it.

'Do I intrude, dearest Miss Reckert?' began Mr. Seymour. 'I am sorry to find you look rather more pensive than I expected.'

'No indeed, Mr. Seymour, I should always be glad of your company. Say only you do not mean to speak on matrimonial prospects, and I shall be content.'

'Have no fear of that, for I had no intention of doing so, though I had gathered here and there that there was not much to be said in that direction, at any rate.'

'Many, no doubt, feel there is ample cause to complain of me for that very reason,' replied she, with a weak smile.

'If you refer to Mr. Harland, I assure you he has said nothing to me of the matter, but you must not think too poorly of those who wish to marry away a beautiful young lady, for it seems only natural to do so.'

'And perhaps all the more perverse in me to object?'

'As to that, it is your business to be as difficult as you please, and indeed, if it will do you good to know it, I cannot conceive of your being more impossible to please than Mr. Harland in the same regard. You may perhaps have guessed I have come here in part to forward some new possibilities, and to own the truth I hoped I had hit upon one which might please him, but to my dismay, he has happened to have met the lady, and I begin to despair of it.'

'You shock me deeply, Sir. Surely you have not chosen so badly?'

'I hardly know. 'Tis merely one possibility of many. Do you know Lady Mortely of Bath? Nay, look how large your eyes. Perhaps you might explain to me the objection, for I have never seen her?'

'I am sorry indeed that we have begun to speak of this,' said she, looking downwards, 'for I should not wish to do so without Mr. Harland's knowledge, or indeed, at all. Since you have mentioned Lady Mortely, however, I can assure you that the objection is not physical, for she is very well-looking, as things go, but her manner betrays a disposition even more difficult to please than that of your humble servant.'

'Nay, madam, the comparison is ridiculous, for you are not as stubborn as some imagine and...'

'In any case, certain defects of temperament are unconcealable.'

'I am indebted to you for this information. Perhaps you would care to give me your thoughts on another whom I..'

'No, Sir, not for the world! I beg you not to name another.'

'As you wish, madam. But here we have been diverted from what I wished to speak to you upon. When I last saw you you will remember we were of differing opinions on a little matter, and it vexed me greatly my entire journey to think you might be right.'

'Forgive me, Sir, I had not thought we were at odds?' replied she with concern.

'My expressions are too strong, but only look at what I have brought with me.'

With that he unfurled a little cloth, revealing a beaten metal cross, scarcely a third the size of a finger.

'What do you make of this?' continued he. 'Now where do you think I found it?'

'Now I understand you. I shall confess to being quite surprised if you have found this in the nunnery.'

'That is not all, not all,' cried he, jubilantly. 'Look at this.' With that he unwrapped a small shaped piece of lead, which he gave her to examine.

''Tis almost like a seal, nay, that is surely what it is. But is it the seal of the order? It is hard to make out. Ah, but you must think me a simpleton, for there is no coat of arms, and there I do see a ring of flowers and a cross. How deep did you dig, Sir?'

'I asked the gentleman, and he said I could dig myself to a better climate if I liked, so I did what I could under the sun (I only had three days). This, madam, is the surest piece of dirt, to the eye, though it had a different bounce to it as it hit the ground, and I was compelled to examine it.'

'How mistaken I was, Sir!'

'Ah,' cried he, almost skipping into the air, 'I thought you might say that, but you have not seen all.' So saying he removed a small ring from his little finger. 'This is the most amazing find, I am sure you will agree. Try it, for the bronze is hardly worse for several hundred years. Your father, I think, will not thank me for outfitting you as a nun. Mark the initials.'

'I.C.M. It is a little small, but lo, it shall fit well on my ring finger, I believe. Here, take it back; I am afraid every second I might lose it.'

'No, madam, I have decided that you shall have it. Indeed, Mr. Harland has put me in mind of it, for it is quite heedless of me to bring you no gifts, and simply require you to admire my acquisitions.'

'I assure you no gifts are necessary, Sir, nor could I justify depriving you of your best treasure, knowing as I do how well you enjoy showing them to others.'

Mr. Seymour hesitated only for a moment before saying, 'No, I have quite made up my mind about it. No one pays nearly so much attention to my finds in the first place, and I enjoy this feeling of self-commendation far too much to give it up. It is not so great an act of generosity, after all, for whenever you look at it, you will be forced to recall your scepticism regarding my plan.'

'If it is indeed a gift of spite, I shall have no compunction in accepting it.'

He bowed in response.

At this point Mr. Harland realized he had listened far longer than he had meant to, having been suitably surprised by the first part of the conversation, and then intrigued by the second. He no longer had any intention of joining them, and went at once to meet with the Churlings.

Accustomed as he was to having short, uncomfortable exchanges with Miss Reckert, he was surprised to discover that she was capable of much more, and seemed far more intelligent and reasonable than he had taught himself to expect. Mr. Seymour had treated her as an equal, capable of rational thought, and she had justified his belief. It seemed to Mr. Harland, upon hindsight, that his own approach had been responsible for the awkward, unproductive encounters they had till this point.

As soon as Mr. Seymour had returned to the house, Mr. Harland requested to speak with him, and began thus,

'I fear I owe you apology, Sir, and Miss Reckert as well, as I must confess to having overheard a good part of the conversation between you this afternoon.'

'Indeed,' said Mr. Seymour, visibly surprised. 'I am sorry for it, as not all of it was suitable for your hearing.'

'As to that, I have got no more than I deserved for listening to what I had no right to. I was surprised, indeed, to find you do not scruple to discuss such things with the young lady, but as I am forced to interest myself in her nearest concerns, it does not seem entirely inappropriate that she hear about mine. No matter, for in truth that is not why I desired to speak to you on the matter.'

Mr. Seymour appeared still more surprised, but said nothing, and Mr. Harland continued.

'No doubt owing to your previous connection to the young lady, which, though I do recall now, I had never happened to mark before, it is apparent you have a far better understanding of her disposition than myself, and I wish to ask your advice. As you know, it is my unhappy duty to carry out the wishes of her father, though I am truly very ill-equipped to do so. You heard of the affair regarding my nephew at lunch today, but additionally in other cases it has been very difficult to understand her conduct, and till now I made the mistake of believing it could not be understood. Pray tell me, in your own opinion (without reserve), how I might go about discovering what holds her back from making an eligible match, according to the wishes of her father, who has given her much freedom to do so?'

'I confess I understand very little of all this. If her actions seem incomprehensible, why do you not ask her to explain them?'

'Truly, I had never thought to. I can scarcely conceive of it being to any purpose to do so, but I see I have erred much in my thinking.'

'I really do think some things are complicated beyond all necessity. I should not expect her to divulge her most private thoughts to casual inquiry, but it seems to me that a sincere effort is not likely to be repulsed. At the very least she will not deceive you.'

'I confess if I had not been privy to the conversation between you just now, I should not have thought it possible, but now I shall not hesitate to try it. I am most obliged to you.'

That very same evening after supper, Mr. Harland went in search of Miss Reckert at the main residence, from where he was directed out of doors. He found her engaged with a book a ways from the house, on a little upraised stone patio which her father had built for her mother, and which provided a good prospect of the area around.

His unexpected appearance was quite alarming to Miss Reckert.

'Forgive the intrusion, Madam, I would not wish to disturb you.'

'You do not, Sir,' replied she, not without apprehension.

'I have come here as I feel it is incumbent upon me to offer you not one, but two apologies. In the first place, I must confess to overhearing a large part of your conversation with Mr. Seymour this afternoon, for which I most earnestly beg your pardon. And yet, Madam,' continued he, 'however wrong it was of me to do so, I am happy at least to say it has allowed me to see another more serious error I am guilty of in relation to you, which I hope you will allow me to correct.'

At first hearing he had been privy to her conversation, Miss Reckert blushed irrepressibly to recall what concerned himself, but his next statement seemed so cryptic, her curiosity somewhat bolstered her composure. As she did not speak, he continued.

'Before I do so, however, I must confess that I am ill at ease with the accusation of hypocrisy made against me by Mr. Seymour, the more so as I cannot entirely refute it. Perhaps you would be so good to think only that I may easily empathize with hesitancy in marital considerations, and for my part, I shall attempt to practice the same haste and decisiveness I must recommend to you.'

He paused for a short time, regarding her thoughtfully. Miss Reckert was silent, attempting to conceal her astonishment and dismay. Eventually he continued.

'You cannot fault me too much for heretofore avoiding long conferences with a woman whose company seems dangerous to the peace of so many. Regardless of this, I am called on by your father to take a greater interest in your fate than some, and so I must risk the exposure. Up until this point, I fear I have fallen short of truly fulfilling his instructions, and I am certain it will not surprise you to learn I consider myself highly unsuited to such tasks.'

'I am sorry you have been burdened so.'

'Indeed, I meant not to imply that I consider the charge burdensome, Madam, but to apologize for my failings, which have been many and unintentional. The conversation which I happened to overhear between you and Mr. Seymour has convinced me forcibly of my mistakes. I have omitted, heretofore, to ask for your confidence in this matter, that I might seek to serve you thereafter with greater diligence. As I do so now, allow me to hope your candour shall testify to your belief in my sincerity.'

Miss Reckert seemed relieved by the knowledge she had acquitted herself well, if only because she had not known she was overheard. Being proud by nature, her inability to master herself under such circumstances had long been a primary source of dismay. Increasingly pride had come to her assistance, of late, for the picture of herself as a stumbling fool was not one she could easily brook. On this occasion, she looked down, and said:

'If belief in your sincerity alone could secure the openness you request, you should always have had it.'

'Nay, madam, this cannot be allowed to suffice. What else can I presume but that you lack confidence in me, for you do not deny there is something you conceal?'

'I did not affirm it, either. Indeed, Sir– I spoke without thinking.'

'I am happy for it. But now that you have done so, will you not continue? Are you so certain I can be of no use to you, that I can perform no service on your behalf?'

'I fear it would be a very singular service indeed, and an even stranger request on my part.'

A short silence reigned. As it seemed there was indeed some kind of impediment, Mr. Harland took a moment to try to fathom what it might possibly be, and after considering for some while, he said:

'Tell me frankly, madam, is it possible you can have conceived an affection for one who is not among your suitors?'

Miss Reckert was silent, oppressed by her feelings.

'Indeed, I confess I am surprised and distressed to consider it. But surely such a thing must be impossible, for you have seen close to no one for upwards of a year now? An infatuation of such length seems more than incredible.'

'It is getting dark, Sir, I think perhaps we should go in.'

'Tell me at least: you have seen this man, and he has seen you?'

'I believe it is possible he exists only in your imagination.'

'Give me but your word that it is so, and I shall cease inquiry at once.'

A silence reigned again.

'Why then, be so good as to set aside any undue modesty, for I am not so new to the world to be unfit to hear answers to the questions I ask. However unsuitable you or I might think I am to serve in this role, your father has appointed me your advisor, and I beg you to treat me as such.'

Unable to refute his argument, Miss Reckert gave her silent assent, feeling she had no other alternative.

'Suffer me to ask again,' said he, 'you have seen this man and he has seen you?

'Indeed,' replied she, quietly.

'And have you ever occasion to speak with him?'

'Indeed, Sir, but let me ask you not draw too much from what little preference I am reluctant to avow–.'

'And is there anything which might prevent him from making an offer of his hand?'

A sigh served for a 'no.'

'I scarce believed it was possible! And yet, if such an offer was made, you feel you would accept it?'

'Unfortunately, Sir.'

'How unaccountable! Your father, indeed, would be happy to know at least one man has accomplished this feat. Forgive me, I do not mean to try your patience, only allow me one or two questions more.'

'I will allow all you like, but I do not know that I can answer them.'

'Tell me only if you have ever detected any partiality in him?'

Miss Reckert was reluctant to answer. Eventually– 'In truth– I think, I cannot hope to know.'

'And has he had opportunity to declare himself, if there was anything to declare?'

But too many! thought she, but only sighed in answer.

Again Mr. Harland lapsed into thought, at last breaking his silence to say, 'I am beginning to suspect this gentleman of yours is a rare manner of idiot, madam.'

'Why, here at least we can agree,' replied she with a sad smile.

'Forgive me, Miss Reckert,' said he, softened by her response. 'Can it be that this gentleman possesses your regard against your will?'

'What else could you think? Surely you do not imagine I should relish a situation both destructive to my happiness and painful to my vanity?'

'Ah, how wrong was I not to have spoken with you thus beforehand!'

'Allow me to be of the opposite opinion.'

'I hope to prove to you there is no need to be so. But I must confess I rejoice in finding your views so similar to my own. Therefore, I feel I must earnestly recommend you endeavour to repress any tenderness for a man so utterly unworthy of it.'

'And this is truly your advice, Sir?' said she, looking up with an expression it was impossible not to be moved by. 'I would wish you to believe your opinion holds more than ordinary weight in this matter, and therefore I will undertake to follow it to the best of my ability.'

Mr. Harland was again silent for a short time. 'Pray wait,' said he at last, 'it is possible I have spoken too hastily in my heat to learn of the stupidity of the person in question. But yet it occurs to me, in looking at you now, that it is nearly impossible he might be indifferent, and it would be wrong to deny him the happiness of knowing it is within his power to become the most fortunate of men, if also the most undeserving.'

'You amaze me, Sir! Surely you do not counsel me to declare myself, and thereby cast aside any remaining shreds of female dignity?'

'In all honesty, madam, I feel it is but a useless convention which tells us that only men have the right to acknowledge sentiments which form the basis for our culture, and even our species. Who among us does not believe that women are sometimes first to love, and even without encouragement? But as to the matter at hand, I had not so much forgotten myself as to propose something I am sure you would never agree to. Nor do I believe such a thing to be necessary. All I ask is to be trusted with the identity of this fool, that I may go to him as an emissary of your father, and gently probe his sentiments. In this, however, I must warn you, I shall have little patience. If he seems insensible of the honour conferred by the mere possibility of an alliance, or asks too pointedly about the settlement, or even asks at all, or looks at his watch, or speaks upon any other subject, I will invent some obstacle and declare the whole thing impossible. In that case, as improbable as it may be, I shall be forced instead to recommend my first advice.'

'It would not be necessary to do so, for I assure you I would not accept any other terms. I hope my pride has not so diminished as to make it possible. In that case I believe it would not be very difficult to return to my senses.'

'May I infer, Miss Reckert, that you mean to entrust me with this commission? As you know, I am obliged to leave England briefly in a few days time, but you may be certain that upon my return, perhaps a fortnight later, I should attend to this matter immediately.'

'I fear what you ask is impossible.'

'I am far from insisting upon it myself,' said he, with an exasperated sigh, 'but I fear your father will never be able to call himself happy till this matter is resolved. Unfortunate as it is, the (often idealized) merit of one member of the opposite sex can prevent us from seeing the very material merit of those who are before us. If I believed you were capable of thinking of it no more, I should not advise this course, but as it is, your father, who does not dream of such an impediment, would suffer for it. Nor can I entirely forebear advocating on the side of the poor idiot who may be deprived happiness merely from an extreme diffidence or some little confusion on his part, and the very strength of female modesty (and even vanity) in these matters.'

'The entire circumstance gives me very little cause for vanity, so I hope you will acquit me of that charge at least.'

'Forgive me, I had not meant–, indeed, I am very far from finding fault with you. I think you a miracle of your sex for even considering it. You surprise me beyond all expectation.'

'Nay, Sir, I see beyond your flattery. You mean to say you are aghast to see the state I have been reduced to.'

'Far from it, madam, for in truth I am not much prone to flattery, yet in your presence, I find I am forced to say much less in your favour than I feel, rather than more.'

Miss Reckert started, then blushing, but as he merely waited for her to reply, she finally said, 'I fear your words belie you, for they reveal you to be more courtier or diplomat than the plain-speaking man you would have me believe you to be.'

'Say rather that to my misfortune, Miss Reckert can turn all men into lovers. You sigh, madam. Surely you would say, 'All but whom you mean to.'"

'I sigh for a multitude of reasons, Sir, the foremost being the evil influence of this evening, not the least of which being yourself, which inclines me towards a step I should surely have all too many reasons to repent taking. Your words have had greater weight with me than I should like to admit.'

'Then pray, madam, give me the name directly, before you lose your courage, and I shall hazard to answer that you shall have no cause to regret it.'

A deep blush over-set her face at this suggestion. After some time, she said, 'Even if I were to agree to what you propose, do not imagine I could bring myself to utter it. No, what I had contemplated was merely giving you, upon your departure, what information you would need to discover it. And yet, I feel that before I could even contemplate bringing myself to do so, I must extract a promise from you that you will judge to be largely superfluous, but upon which I must insist all the same. Nor is it possible to overemphasize its importance to me, though I have no doubt you will oblige me.'

'I am glad to hear it.'

'I ask only, Sir, that if I can bring myself to follow your advice, you do not seek to discover it until you have left England. I confess that if I thought it was otherwise, I do not believe I could sleep.'

'I know not how to convince you these scruples are unnecessary. My admiration for you has only been increased as a result of your candour, though it does give me some concern to know your own opinion of the man in question is such that you tremble to think of what my own will be. But no matter, you have my word.'

'I thank you, Sir, and must venture to say that if I ever had reason to think you had not kept it, I could not be prevailed to trust you again.'

At this he was forced to smile. 'I should hope Miss Reckert herself would think such exhortations unnecessary, for I should not give my word unless I was certain I could keep it.'

'Forgive me, Sir, but words can sometimes have more form than meaning attached to them.'

Mr. Harland merely bowed his agreement.

A small movement in the corner caught his eye, for until that time he had not noticed the presence of Miss Reckert's constant companion. Thomas was at that time huddled a short way away on the grass with a book in his hand, his eyes widening nervously at the sudden attention he had drawn upon himself.

'Does the boy understand all that is said?'

'Yes.'

'Can he speak? I do not recall ever hearing him do so?'

'Aye, though he says but little.'

'Has he any useful skill; I understand he can write?'

'It is hard to tell, but he anticipates my wishes so clearly sometimes that I am certain he can read lips. I have taught him to read and write both French and English.'

'May I ask why you have taken the trouble to teach him French? Have you some profession in mind for him?'

'I am ashamed to say I have not considered it much. I have taught him to read French simply because he brought me a book written in French and seemed anxious to learn it.'

'How does he occupy himself, if you will forgive my sudden interest?'

'I fear he does very little. He prefers mostly to keep my company and read or pursue some other quiet occupation. I have always permitted him to do as he likes, for I see he has been deeply wounded in life, and I cannot bear to pain him.'

Mr. Harland smiled. 'Few men would not aspire to be 'deeply wounded' if it would enable them to remain quietly in the company of a beautiful woman. Though I admire your compassion, I fear he is not likely to learn how to be a man by lurking behind your skirts. I will take him to Belgium, if you have no objection. I could use a messenger who can write in both languages, and he shall profit from seeing more of the world than he has of late.'

Miss Reckert was evidently startled by this suggestion, but after a moment or two, she said, 'I cannot help but tremble for him at the thought, for it seems to me still that he is only a child. It is not a dangerous voyage, however?'

'No indeed, for we shall cross at the shortest point, and I have no intention of taking any risks. How old is the boy?'

'It is impossible to say for certain. I believe he has at least thirteen Summers this year.'

'He is undersized for that age, and his habits have given him a kind of delicacy which shall not serve him as a man, considering his condition in life. I assure you that no harm shall come to him in my protection, but I am certain he will be much better for the experience. I do not expect it to be a long trip.'

'Then he shall go, and I thank you. Spare him any rough duties, for my sake, for I have never treated him as a servant, and I fear the change would harm his constitution. Come, Thomas,' said she, turning to the boy, 'you have heard what has been said, and I believe you will do for my sake what I do for yours. When Mr. Harland departs, you shall go with him. Serve him well. He has shown himself a better friend to you than I have been myself, undesignedly. If you please him, you shall please me tenfold in doing so.'"

Mouchard paused here.

"What an extraordinary tale!" cried Mlle de Courteline, "I should hope you would not ask us to believe that any woman of decency would truly consider exposing herself so. I should rather forfeit my life than do so. Miss Reckert is much to blame if she contemplates it any further."

"No indeed," cried the soft Mlle Vallon, "if she is to blame then it is for not telling him in the garden, for he seemed inclined to like her, and in doing so she should please herself, her father, and I daresay, Mr. Harland!"

"Perhaps," replied her cousin, "but what man would prize so easy a conquest for long? Any woman's love worth having is worth much striving and toiling for! What obstacle has Mr. Harland overcome, what pain endured, what conflict fought?"

Mlle Vallon seemed part horrified, part mystified, and Mlle de Courteline applied to Mme. Gaspar next.

"Truth be told," replied that woman, "I know as much about such scruples as Mr. Harland, one might say, for if she must be settled, 'twould be a whole lot better for her to be settled than miserable, but sure it is that young ladies would like a whole battle to be fought before they can bring themselves to be prevailed upon, as they say. He seems an easy, agreeable gentleman, and if she be as well-looking as is told, then I am inclined to agree with Mlle Vallon, even though it can be thought a bit forward."

"Good God!" cried Mlle de Courteline, "Is there no one who would agree with me?" As she was still out of humour with myself, she applied to M. Tolouse for his opinion. "What say you, Monsieur? I suppose I cannot expect much delicacy of thought from these quarters?"

He seemed startled, not entirely understanding the debate, but he said, "I am in favour of fighting, madam, for any cause whatsoever, even love. Nay, I misspoke, for what I meant to say is that I should like to fight for any cause but the revolutionaries. Aye, and the child's story itself brings me in mind of an exploit some of my fellows and I, when I was in service of the his Majesty. But it is not fit for ladies' hearing, but to put it short, a whole number of them were sent to their maker."

"The less said about that sort of thing, the better," said Mme. Gaspar, not looking up from her knitting, "but I can't say I am the sorrier for it."

"Nor I," said Mlle de Courteline.

"But will you not also give your opinion, M. Gramont,' said Mlle Vallon, turning her eyes earnestly upon me, 'Do you think Miss Reckert would be wrong to do so?"

"In my own way of thinking, Mademoiselle, truth should always win over punctilio, and in this circumstance, it seems to me that the potential benefit far outweighs the risk. If Mr. Harland is as modest and unassuming in relation to women as we are to believe, it is unlikely he shall ever think to offer himself to Miss Reckert, and in that case, to spare only her vanity, both she and her father shall be unhappy. I do not mean to undervalue the homage I should pay to such a character, if indeed she does what the author implies she will, for I realize that women value themselves not a little upon their ability to attract the admirers they desire the most."

Mlle de Courteline was preparing to say something in response to this, but she was prevented by the approach of M. Savard, who having long since finished his letters, observed our general conversation. "I hope the little fellow has concluded his story now?" said he.

"Far from it," replied Mlle de Courteline, "and I am more eager than ever to have it continued!"

M. Savard was evidently displeased at this discovery. After a short consideration, he said, "And of course, if M. Gramont continues to be so gracious as to bring him, I am more than pleased he come again soon, but perhaps, to save him the trouble, we might ask if the little fellow has the original around somewhere that he could lend us?"

This suggestion was received with only a small amount of enthusiasm, but nevertheless all eyes turned towards Mouchard. In return he looked at us all blankly enough. As I had never known him to have any possessions beyond the clothes on his back, I declared that I had never seen any such, and so the subject was dropped.

"But I hope he will come again very soon," said Mlle de Courteline, looking at M. Savard with emphasis.

"As do I," said he, "but I will not be so guilty of trespassing upon M. Gramont's time and good nature to ask him hither every night, and it seems the little one does not like to tell it without him. There is not much help for it, I am afraid, but we shall see him again, by and by."

All three ladies seemed distressed, but M. Savard pretended not to notice. A short while after this, the evening ended.

It has taken nearly three hours to write you this account; I apologize for writing in so much detail. Now I must now go to bed. I shall send this with the next post. Dear friend, I am ever,

Your Servant,
Marcel de la Croix

M. Henri Renault to Marcel de la Croix

February 7th, 1793, Switzerland

Dear Marcel,

You cannot imagine what a stir your letters have created. The monks are divided in wishing to hear more of your own history, or at marvelling at Mouchard's yarn. I myself am captivated by your present doings in England, thinking all the more how much I should have liked being with you, rather than reading of your doings from afar. Through your words, I can easily imagine myself on the east coast of England, rather than in this increasingly prison-like atmosphere. Strange that I did not notice how stifling it was while I still had a companion in exile.

I am tempted to leave now, but as I am nearly fifty and not very skilled at combat, I feel less able to do so now than when you invited me yourself. I am still resolved not to return to France, but I might possibly consider going through Germany, which has not yet been overrun.

When writing your history, do not fail to include where you left the monastery, though do not rush to that part, I beg you.

I feel confident you will not fail to write as you have done, knowing how many poor souls depend upon you for amusement, not the least of which being,

Your friend and servant,
Henri Renault

PS, Father Galois has undertaken to transcribe your letters so far, and he intends to preserve them in the Monastery's library. He indicates he wishes to transcribe this letter too, and I believe he would be happy if he could include the first three I sent you (though he hardly guesses how brief and full with self-pity they were). Yet I said I would pass along the request I believe he would make if writing were not a violation of the vow. I am sure he shall return the originals to you, though I know they are not such as one might prize. In any case, I am happy that your letters shall be kept and honoured in this manner. Mouchard's tale is as close to a novel as has ever been near the library, which must make the collection all the more prized for 'novelty.'

Marcel de la Croix to Henri Renault

February 8th,1793

Dear Friend,

This morning I woke early quite full of energy, and after breakfast and a brisk walk, I have a mind to continue writing my history, with the encouraging thought that it will very soon be concluded.

After the violent evening I described in my last letter, events and circumstances seemed to pursue a path of their own. Word of our success travelled, increasing in proportion as it did so. Before long it seemed that whoever was at odds with the movement which swept across our lands arrived at my door. In the report of that night which circulated, we were said to be a hundred strong and very quickly thereafter we were.

The next day a small group of us escorted M. Lafont's uncle returning to his house. After a brief canvass of his neighbours, M. Lafont senior determined it was no longer safe for his family to stay there. As it was still thought to be safer in the Northern parts, he decided to immediately send his family in that direction, where they could be housed with his wife's relatives for the time being. As it would be necessary to escort them safely out of the region, M. Lafont took the majority of the men along with him, while I returned to the Chateau with the others. In his absence, which was perhaps a week, nearly a score of men arrived at the Chateau, proposing to join us. I turned no one away, but all the same I had no true idea of how we were to house or manage so many men.

M. Lafont returned without his uncle but with seven more men to take his place. He was delighted to discover more had come and still more seemed likely to. Between M. Lafont, Philip and myself we devised a bare plan as to how things could be managed on the short term, but not one of us felt able to consider more than a month at a time.

Amongst the new arrivals, precedence seemed to be given in a rather arbitrary way. Those who arrived earliest seemed to have the advantage of belonging over those who were more recent; those who were trained to fight held obvious ascendence over those who were not, while those who were formerly wealthy and well-bred generally seemed to retain these advantages amongst us.

Of them all, M. Lafont and I were regarded as the leaders. M. Lafont was large and fierce, brave and uneven-tempered, qualities which gave credence to the exaggerated reports of his deeds thus far. For myself, as the owner of the Chateau, I had a natural right to decide what was done within it. My unhappiness gave a grim taciturnity to my manner; I spoke little and observed much. My own deeds had been enlarged upon along with M. Lafont. Nor did it go without observation that both he and I bore the same brand on our hands. Though the circumstances under which we had both received the mark were hidden from no one, the character each of us seemed to bear soon transformed it into a badge of honour of sorts.

As to our over-riding purpose, as far as M. Lafont was concerned, all of our energies ought to be dedicated towards revenge. Accordingly, he bent all his efforts to finding and killing M. Hubert, who he held responsible for everything short of the revolution itself. For myself, I parted with him somewhat on these grounds. Though I shared his wish to see the murderers of my family destroyed, I could not entirely call it justice and I looked at the predicament of the masses and scarce knew how to condemn them.

Before I had time to settle my own mind as to how I thought we should achieve our ends, or what, indeed, our ends should be, events decided me in one particular direction. Less than a fortnight after that first altercation, which I described in my last letter, a man arrived by horseback in all haste. He was admitted on similar terms to most newcomers (by now a regular occurrence) but after introducing himself, he desired particularly to speak with me.

M. Gravel was his name, and he was a slight man of just over forty years.

'Forgive me for forcing myself into your acquaintance in this manner, M. Le Marquis, but these are strange times.'

'You say well, Monsieur. Pray do not be afraid to tell me why you have come here, for I perceive you do not mean to join us for long.'

'My frame prevents me from that particular privilege, I fear. As to my purpose, I come to beg your help, stranger that I am, for I know not where else to turn. If you permit me to do so, I will simply tell you my dilemma, and rely on your wisdom and kindness to inform me whether there is any help you are able or willing to vouchsafe me.'

With this he proceeded to tell me that he was in a particularly vulnerable political position, and feared to remain in Paris under the present circumstances. He wished to move his whole family out of the country, and therefore they were travelling in two carriages perhaps a day away. Yesterday he had received information from travellers on the road that impediments were likely to be encountered if they proceeded as they intended. At a nearby inn, he was privy to some part of the gossip in the area, and in short, hearing of the existence of a good many men here who opposed the revolution, he resolved to hazard travelling here himself by horse to seek any advice or assistance possible.

His own recitation of these circumstances was far longer in all detail, including various impressions, fears and motives which I did not choose to remember. I was very far from needing persuasion myself, for defence of the innocent was far more appealing to me then revenge upon the guilty. Before M. Gravel had even uttered his petition, I sent for M. Lafont, and began to deliberate upon how to secure him and his family safe passage. Hearing what was required, M. Lafont was equally in favour of assisting him. Between us we agreed that he should take his family along the nearest road around noon the following day, and that whether visible or covert, we should accompany him to ensure their safety. The last detail we agreed upon was that each carriage should bear a blue flag, in order to ensure we might be certain of it from a distance.

Rather than ride alongside the carriage en masse, I decided that only I would accompany them, while a number of men would travel in the woods nearby, ready to assist us if the situation warranted. Having decided this much, the next day all those who wished were invited to join us. In the end, we were a party of thirty of more. Once we neared Quereign, I took five men and proceeded into the town to meet M. Gravel, while M. Lafont remained behind with the others.

M. Gravel was prompt and his carriage was departing even as we approached.

'I am glad to see you, Marquis de la Croix. I hardly know how to express my gratitude and surprise that you have condescended not only to arrange our safety, but ensure it in person.'

He introduced me to his wife, who was a beautiful woman of around thirty years old, clutching two small children to her in the carriage. I told them both I thought there would be no resistance to their passing, and that I accompanied them merely as a courtesy and a precaution. As to the truth of this, I was internally undecided.

We did not stay long in conversation and I rode in front of the carriage to make further conversation impossible. We easily gained the distance to the Chateau, meeting no one but a farmer or two. Around this time some commotion seemed to call away the others. Looking back the way we came, I saw a man I guessed to be Lafont leading a group of riders in the direction we had just come. I was unsure whether we were in fact being followed or whether M. Lafont was merely going to intercept some other traveller, but I took no notice of it other than to reflect upon the likelihood that we were no longer very well attended.

I presumed that they would soon rejoin us and continued on without any change. We passed through the next village, Aubrey, which is the sister town to La Croix. Revolutionary flags and posters were to be seen everywhere, but it was so small a village that it hardly mattered. I had promised to see M. Gravel as far as Hierne, where there was still reason to believe the revolution had gained little foothold.

The next town we came to was Fiettre. It was a larger town, and wore a more organized appearance. Our arrival was greeted by many grim faces. Four officials came out to meet us as we made our way through.

It was clear that they knew or guessed my name before they asked it. I stood somewhat aloof from the proceedings. Many papers were demanded and examined, and many questions were asked and re-asked. In the end we were not quite permitted to pass, but not hindered either. A great many onlookers assembled in the meantime, and by the time we were able to depart, we were very happy to do so. There was still no sign of Lafont.

Scarcely half a mile beyond the town walls, we heard the furious hoof-beats of a lone rider, and turning discovered we were being pursued by a messenger. The messenger was a young man, and scarce catching his breath when he met us, he said 'Monsieur le Marquis de la Croix, the prefect, M. Rozier, left his dinner to have you called back. He would have you return to speak with him at once.'

'Does he wish to see me alone?'

'Yes, Marquis, the others may pass.'

'Then tell M. Rozier that he may go back to his meal, and I shall return to speak with him in a few hours.'

'He asked you to return at once, Monsieur,' replied the messenger, somewhat affrighted, but steadfast in his message.

'Then I can only hope you may remember my message to him as faithfully.'

With this we continued our journey, seeing or encountering

nothing more of note. In Hierne, though there had been disturbances as with everywhere else, official control of the town had not changed, and the surrounding inhabitants by and large still retained their support for his Majesty's representatives. During these times, every traveller was treated with a good deal of suspicion, but as soon as that was overcome, all travellers were harassed for any news from other areas.

Having settled M. Gravel and his family at an inn, I took leave with all imaginable haste. Nearly four hours later, I arrived back in Fiettre, where I was determined to keep the appointment I had made as a point of honour.

The town wore a vastly different aspect when I arrived. It was dark, and I discovered to my surprise that M. Lafont had brought all the men with him into the streets of it. Despite this, an unsteady peace seemed to exist. I was about to salute him, but a messenger intervened and bid me to follow him at once to M. Rozier, who had awaited my return. M. Lafont was watching us keenly from his position, appearing generally displeased, but he waved his hand in a gesture for me to proceed as I wished, and so I followed the messenger.

He led me into the home of the prefect, where I was seen into a small drawing room where M. Rozier was in conference with three other men.

'M. le Marquis,' said he, 'you are kind to return at my request, but you need not have summoned all your friends. A little talk was all I had in mind.'

'I did not realize they would be here when I arrived. But come, it is late and I am tired, forgive my precipitance, but what is it you would say to me?'

'I merely desired to serve you notice of a sorts. Though your earlier companions were allowed to pass, you may by no means be assured it shall happen again. Though their answers were satisfactory, I judge by several factors that they were by no means lovers of liberty, and so in the next instance, I might be forced to detain them.'

I laughed at this strange remark, and said that I guessed few would be so generally opposed to liberty as to welcome their own detention.

'I hope, M. le Marquis, that you do not intend to accompany very many more persons through Fiettre?'

'I equally hope there is not the necessity of doing so, though as long as it seems likely anyone might need assistance passing through, I shall pledge to provide it.'

He sighed, and thought for a minute before indicating to his companions that he wished to speak to me alone.

'Monsieur,' said he, 'I perceive you are a reasonable man, perhaps more reasonable than some of your friends. I have no great wish to restrain or incommode travellers, but in these times, I would not retain my new post long if I refused to do so. The revolution has been good to me, and it has my allegiance. This circumstance, however, will not prevent me from telling you there is a fairly decent road to be found a short way to the south of here, and if you or your friends should need to pass along it, I shall not see it as my duty to interfere.'

I sighed then bowed and thanked him for the information. He invited me most cordially to stay and have a drink with him, but I declined in favour of returning to the others. We parted on good terms, and the hint he gave me proved useful in the times to come. Outside all were still waiting.

'And what of your knight-errantry?' said M. Lafont, as we met, and turned together preparing to depart.

'M. Gravel and his family arrived without incident in Hierne, and I wish them a good journey from there.'

'As do I, though I dare-say Louis will not owe much thanks to cowards like him who flee when there is the most need for his friends to stay by.'

'A man such as M. Gravel can do very little for the King, I fear. And how did you fare?'

'Cowards and rascals on all sides,' was his reply. 'We could find no one who would face us. If I am ever persuaded to go on such a fool's errand again, I shall take no more than six men, and then I think we shall have greater business.'

''Tis no matter for sport,' said I, annoyed almost to amusement with his appetite for fighting.

M. Bretal, who had but lately come to the Chateau, and who was then riding a few paces behind said, 'M. Lafont has killed no one today, Marquis, and so it is a bad day.'

This jest was received well all around, though M. Lafont was evidently in no humour to hear it and merely rode ahead. M. Bretal along with several other men present that day, were more honourable than bloodthirsty, and I had the sense that it was owing to their presence that the day had proved so uneventful.

The following days, M. Lafont's mood was entirely restored by the discovery of a pamphlet in circulation, which read thus:

Let the freedom-loving inhabitants be aware that on the - - 1791, the numerous criminal aristocrats hiding from justice at the bastion of inequity called Chateau Fort de la Croix, have committed a savage and heinous atrocity, for which they shall be punished in this world and the next.

Ten honourable deputies of the revolution were slaughtered while they were performing a necessary patrol of the area. Three-hundred rabid criminals overtook them near the village of La Croix. Though slightly armed, these brave men are credited with the deaths of sixty men, before they at last succumbed to an inequity of numbers not to be withstood.

The most infamous of these criminals bear the brand of infamy placed upon them by the renowned M. Hubert, whose great generosity spared their lives. Any person who can show evidence of having killed a man wearing the identifiable brand on his hand, shall be handsomely rewarded for his service.

This billet was copied and circulated throughout the area for six weeks. Each person who copied it took the liberty of altering several details, and I read versions claiming far less or far more on either side were either concerned in the fight, or killed in it. M. Lafont was exceedingly delighted by this recitation, and after he had drunk a fair amount of wine, he amused us all by dictating several mock missives to the 'lovers of liberty' wherein he warned that the 'League of the Star,' which was comprised of half a million giants, poised to take sweetmeats from all the little children in the province.

I shall not tell you of every event which followed, for I feel time would not allow it. Instead I shall describe our progress in a more general way. For the next weeks and months, men continued to arrive and depart from Chateau Fort de la Croix. Some came merely for a short period whilst they plotted their own individual course, while others had no other refuge. The latter were more likely to devote themselves to the protection and defence of our fortress, and who gradually became known as 'The League of the Star.' Still others came in order to work to overthrow the revolution itself, though as time wore on, that goal appeared increasingly unattainable.

In the months to come, many of those who joined us chose to brand themselves voluntarily with the symbol. M. Lafont encouraged them to do so, but forbid any one to place a brand on their hands, an honour he reserved for he and myself. Brands were to be inconspicuous, and as identifiers, messengers often wore them on the soles of their feet to allow them to prove their associations when necessary.

While almost all of our efforts were crowned with success, our progress was not reflected in the rest of the country. The National Assembly deliberated on in Paris and each passing week seemed to bring word of some new loss or concession on the part of the King, who seemed to make almost no effort to resist the trend which daily lessened his power.

As to the League of the Star, we had gained control over the land five miles or so in all directions. This land was secured to us largely by virtue of M. Lafont's almost daily excursions in the area, ostensibly in search of any encounter which might forward his search for M. Hubert. The pressure his relentless hunt seemed to have on the particular faction of the revolution lead by M. Hubert was apparent in his practice of frequently changing his habitation, which was usually no sooner known than changed.

In this effort M. Lafont engaged the services of those amongst us who were most like himself, along with the many others who stood in admiration of his tireless determination. For myself, I had numerous reservations about his actions, mostly as I feared his conduct was not always what I would have liked to be associated with, and his sometimes brutal example encouraged others to follow suit. Despite these hesitations, I turned a blind eye to all I saw or suspected. I felt that whatever extremes he might be driven to by passion, drink, or temper, M. Lafont was a man of honour, and could be forgiven the occasional outrages. They were after all, I reasoned, no doubt a result of the unusual experience we had shared.

In daily affairs I gravitated more towards assisting those who were unfairly persecuted. Usually at least once a week I found myself escorting a passerby through the area. Although letters of request periodically arrived at the Chateau, more often I would police the road from the woods along with several other men. In many instances, our assistance was not required, and the travellers would depart the area themselves unaware of the security we had provided them.

M. Lafont would accompany us if nothing more exciting seemed to offer itself. If he had some involvement in arranging our escort, the service was most certainly to be paid for by the traveller. I had and continue to have, a complete repugnance to accepting money for any honourable action, but even Philip frequently hinted to me that it would be desirable for me to do so, in order to help defray the expenses of housing so many men.

Despite the difference in dispositions and proclivities which existed between M. Lafont and myself, our experiences had strongly bonded us to each other. M. Lafont was a violent, uncontrollable drunk, but on most other occasions when he was sober, he was intelligent and clear-sighted. The greatest area of difference between us was in regard to his nearly all-consuming desire for revenge. Though I shared his wish for justice or revenge, I saw it as an unpleasant necessity, rather than an end for which all others were sacrificed.

Towards that end we undoubtedly made progress. Several small skirmishes were fought and gradually supporters of the revolution were forced to pull back even further from our location. Overall, however, the momentum did not favour us, and our gains were diminished, and blood was needlessly spent on both sides.

Returning from one of these campaigns, exhausted and dirty, I could not help but contemplate the futility of it all. We were by then perhaps two-hundred strong, but there would always be more emboldened poor than there would be rich, and so we should always be outnumbered. It was late in the afternoon that day and M. Lafont and I walked together at the rear. Various among us made camp at different times, and so I proposed we sit down to eat before we continued any further. M. Lafont was in a good mood, but he did not make much conversation. Several others had stopped some ways before us and an old woman who lived nearby was slowly making her way from fire to fire, begging for something to eat and attempting to sell some little trinkets.

No one had repaid her for her trouble and by the time she reached M. Lafont and I, I invited her to come amongst us and take her meal and her rest.

She accepted quickly and ate heartily, eyeing us both quite keenly while she did so. M. Lafont looked at her briefly, having evinced neither surprise nor delight at my invitation, so long had he known me.

'Good friends,' observed she at last, partly to herself.

'What of it, my venerable old crone?' said M. Lafont.

'Shall you hear your fortune, young Sir?'

'Oh surely. And how much shall it cost us?'

'The bread is ample payment, my good lord, and I only ask for money if I am certain I bring good news. A strange fate awaits you both, I fear.'

'Then pray do not tell us,' said I.

She fell silent, but M. Lafont could not contain his curiosity, saying, 'Nay, I should like to hear it.'

'Not of the same mind, it would seem.'

'We have no need of a fortune-teller to tell us this,' returned he.

'Good friends make good foes.'

'And meat goes rotten on the fourth day,' cried he, his expression changing. 'Do you mean to give us a parable or a fortune?'

'What is written in blood is written in wine; what does not happen today, may happen in time.'

'An admirable couplet,' declared he, in disdain, 'and worth all the money that was paid for it.'

Wary of allowing this conversation to continue much further, I stood and began to prepare to depart. To my surprise, M. Lafont made no immediate sign of following me, declaring he would catch up to me in a short time. I saw that he meant to hear whatever the old woman would say, but seeing no help for it, I continued my preparations and departed.

Perhaps an hour later he joined me again. He had drunk a fair amount of wine, and his mood was one of forced levity. Observing this, I said,

'And so I see some dire fate awaits us?'

'You fare better than I. I suppose I ought to have invited the old witch to our repast, that I might have got the better of the two of us.'

'And do you not mean to tell me?'

''Tis a small matter,' said he, 'but it seems I am fated to die at your hand. I give you my pardon at once.'

I could not help but laugh to hear it. 'Then I am sorry you have pressed her to tell it, for foolish thoughts have a way of crowding out the more rational ones. I should not wonder if she was sent to us by design, to plant discord between us.'

This suggestion appealed to him immediately, and he no sooner considered it than he laughed at himself for his own folly.

Here I shall leave off writing as I have nearly lost track of time and missed my supper. Meals are not as regular in the Parsonage as they are in Sorsten, no doubt.

I have not written in a day or two, as I overexerted my pen the previous day.

We did not hear from the main house for two days after Mouchard's last recital. On the morning of the day following, I came down to breakfast to find M. Tolouse in a fine mood. It is customary for Mouchard, M. Tolouse and myself to eat together at the table. The boy does not appear to have the strongest constitution, so I am happy to oblige him to eat under the pretence of practising English together.

When Mouchard withdrew, as he usually does after little more than a bite or two, M. Tolouse said to me,

"I am glad to see you in good spirits, and I hope you have forgotten any of the nonsense that passed between us the other day," said he, referring to the conversation we had after he discovered my scar.

"I am confident that I need say no more, at least," replied I.

"Nor needed to say as much, I daresay, for how you could imagine that a man as myself should–, nay, begging your pardon, I did not intend to bring it up again."

I did not reply and we ate in silence for a little while.

"I would have you know, however," continued he, after a good deal of thought, "that I am another sort of man altogether. Though I say it myself, one could not ask for a surer fellow in any kind of combat."

I remained silent, and a short while later, he said, "Nor am I the sort who can't be trusted with a secret, and if I might make so bold as to hint it, I am perfectly ready to accompany you on any mission whatsoever."

I did not doubt this for a moment, and rather feared he would attempt to create a mission of some sort rather than let me be. Like Lafont, M. Tolouse was eager to fight, and welcomed any cause which might rescue him from the sidelines, as it were.

"I hope you will not take it amiss when I say that I would rather we were finished with the subject altogether. I assure you there is no mission to join."

His face revealed his disappointment, and in a moment he said,

"Have it your way, Sir, for I should not like to force my help upon anyone. Most people should think the same as you, mayhap, of a man who's lost his leg, but what I say is, let any man best me who has still what God gave him and I will be satisfied to leave off fighting. Forgive a man's boast about himself, but I used to formerly give out that I was as good as ten men, and now on account of my leg, I would put it perhaps at eight or nine."

I could not help but smile at this boast, but nevertheless I said, "I am obliged to you for this information, but the fact remains that I need no such services."

I excused myself shortly thereafter to avoid hearing anything further he might have to say or hint. Since then he has adopted the demeanour of a petulant infant.

In the afternoon of the same day, I received this billet from M. Savard:

Dear Sir,

In the next week or so I intend to take a trip into Suffolk, upon which all three ladies will accompany me. It is no great secret that the roads in these parts, (and in truth in this entire country) are infested with outlaws and unsafe for travellers. Having the need to bring some of our valuables with us, I feel it would be unwise to travel without additional arms and men, and so I do here invite you and M. Tolouse to accompany us. I am sorry for the inconvenience this might occasion you, and am prepared to offer you ample return.

If this proposal meets with your approval, I should prefer to set out in two days' time,

Your Servant,
Gerard Savard

You will not wonder to hear I was greatly incensed by this letter, and without any hesitation at all, I wrote him the following answer:

Dear Sir,

I hope you will not be too much surprised to learn that I should scorn to do for money what I would easily allow to friendship or even general courtesy. As I see M. Savard is in need of a hired servant, I am not very gratified to find your letter addressed to, your most obliged,

M. Gramont

My letter might not have been so harsh had I not taken a particular dislike to the sender. A short time later, I received another note from him, which read:

Dear Sir,

I crave your pardon for the error I have been guilty of. Be assured that my fault has stemmed from the utter dislike of obligation which marks my character, rather than any lack of respect for you. I should be sorry if this offence should lead to any lasting discord between us. Permit me to do what I ought to have done before, and rely upon the native generosity of your character for my forgiveness. In order to obviate my original fault, I now ask if it would be convenient for your party to accompany us on a short trip to Suffolk? If you deign to accept this second request, I shall truly be convinced that a pardon has been granted to,

Your most obliged,
Gerard Savard

I was largely indifferent to the whole matter, though not averse to a change of scenery. I put the question to M. Tolouse, determined to adhere to his decision. To my chagrin, he refused to make any decision at all, and merely begged to know my preference.

You may think me aimless that I do not embark on my own, even when M. Savard has arrived and the ladies no longer need protection (though sometimes I am inclined to think Mlle Vallon at least may need protection from him). The truth is that I am still uncertain which way to take and seem to lack the will to correct my deficiency. The letter I so anxiously awaited came a short while ago, but the agent I hired sent no useful information at all. I have not yet decided whether to hire an Englishman for the task, or attempt to do it myself.

I intimated often to you in Switzerland how burdensome my wealth seemed to be, and the heavy guilt which weighed upon me from a different cause. No doubt you recall that my hope in travelling to England was to locate a person who might help me with both encumbrances. The remainder of my history shall illuminate this further, but it shall suffice for now to say that finding a person lately travelled from France is quite difficult in the present climate, for so many of our countrymen have come here, that they no longer stand out. Philip would not have had this difficulty, yet I may no longer rely upon him, nor even know where he lives.

But returning to the present, and M. Savard's request, in the end I sent Mouchard to convey our verbal acceptance.

I hope you continue well and that the ravages of the revolution continue to leave you untouched.

Your sincere friend,
M. C.

Marcel de la Croix to Henri Renault

February 12th,1793

Dear Friend,

Yesterday was the day appointed for our trip into Suffolk. I confess that when I left France I thought I left behind all necessity for securing travellers from molestation, but it seems that in England, highwaymen are like proliferating insects, and the authorities have yet to find a way to combat them. Though I hesitate to confess my peevishness, I was exceedingly opposed to rising early this morning, and kept the whole party in waiting.

When I was at last dressed and ready, I emerged and prepared to mount my horse. I was arrested midway by the sight of M. Tolouse.

He turned away at the sight of my amazement, giving me full leisure to contemplate the sheer number of weapons he brought with him. I was tempted to laugh at the comical figure he made, but checked myself with the recollection that it was never wise to laugh at a well-armed fool. It also did not escape me that he adorned himself so to impress upon me his great prowess in fighting, never guessing that I had seen enough violence the last two years to last my whole life, and would be quite happy to never see a weapon again.

M. Savard, Mme. Gaspar, Mlle de Courteline, Mlle Vallon and Mouchard were already in the carriage and after a few brief inclinations of the head had passed between us all, I rode ahead with M. Tolouse.

M. Tolouse was not of the temperament which can hold a grudge, and before long he was chatting to me most happily. About midway there, however, his mood began to sour. He began to peer suspiciously at passing carriages, and exclaim that there were not more people around. Eventually he was no longer content to ride beside me, preferring to go ahead and investigate the travellers coming towards us. When I caught up with him a short time later, I found him quizzing an old farmer pulling a cart.

The farmer could not understand M. Tolouse's many improvements upon the English language. It was plain he took offence at being questioned so imperiously by a foreigner, but as he did not like to try his pitchfork against my friend's collection of weapons, he was answering him politely enough. As I approached, the farmer appealed to me to interfere and as my English has the virtue of at least being better than M. Tolouse's, I did my best to oblige him.

As soon as I had extricated the farmer from his importunities, M. Tolouse informed me that he had frequently gestured in the direction we came when M. Tolouse asked about highwaymen, and so he was determined to return that way. With that he raced off, passing the coach and proceeding at the highest speed back the way we had come.

"What is it, dear M. Gramont?" cried Mme. Gaspar, from her window. "What has M. Tolouse seen, for we are all affrighted?"

"He has seen nothing, Madam, have no fear," said I. I was upon the verge of adding that few would be foolish enough to try to rob us whilst a madman like M. Tolouse chased around in search of an adversary, but I thought better of it.

The next few miles were quiet and peaceful. I rode by myself and enjoyed the beauty of the view of the shore. The calm pragmatism of the English is a welcome relief to the tortured Frenchman, and I rode and pondered in silence.

Eventually my reverie was interrupted by shrieks. I had allowed myself to outpace the carriage by a fair way, and when I turned around I saw the carriage had paused, and a short distance behind it, M. Tolouse was emerging from the forest on the other side, pulling a helpless man by his hair. The shrieks were coming from inside the carriage, whose occupants had stopped at the commotion and were justifiably alarmed to witness this spectacle.

"Look!" cried M. Tolouse, dragging his victim behind him. "I have captured a villain who has been following us the last five miles. I have seen him sneaking in and out of the woods as I followed from a distance."

By then M. Savard was out of the coach and as I was drawing nearer, he began questioning the man held by M. Tolouse.

"Who are you, Sir, and why do you follow us?" demanded he, speaking English with a heavy French accent.

The captive looked towards me as I reached them, and I gasped with astonishment to see my faithful Philip.

"My name is Philip Renard, and I am the servant of Marquis de la Croix," replied he calmly, in French.

"The Marquis de la Croix?" repeated Mlle de Courteline, who by now had also left the carriage. 'If he has come from a Marquis, perhaps he brings a message from my father?"

"Release him at once," cried I, in almost the same moment, "as you value your life."

M. Tolouse did so at once, seeming somewhat dismayed that his triumph had ended thus, and then before I could say more, M. Savard said, "Speak then, if you will be believed. Do you carry any message for Mlle de Courteline, or any other of us?"

"I have no business with any but M. Gramont," replied Philip, hardly troubling himself to look at his questioner.

"Continue on your journey, M. Savard, ladies," said I, "for I have business with this man and I shall follow behind you."

"I shall attend you in an instant," said Philip, once they were gone, "but this man has taken me from my horse, and I must be in haste to retrieve it."

With that he dashed back into the forest and disappeared among the trees.

"Begging your pardon, Marquis de la Croix," said M. Tolouse, while he was gone, "but I hope you will acknowledge that I could not have known. If one could presume to beg a little confidence, I should hope to be told in the future if you mean to have us dodged the whole way. I am a sharp dog, if I do say so myself, and it is best to let me in on the secret, for it is ten to one I discover it regardless."

Having satisfied his wounded pride with this little piece of self-aggrandizement, he thought it best to catch up to the carriage, and therefore left me to await Philip alone.

Philip returned shortly thereafter, leading his horse.

"I am sorry to come upon you all of a sudden, dear Monsieur. I have been seeking you for some days and weeks. A few days ago I heard that of a man of your description called Gramont, was living nearby with a party of emigres. No sooner did I locate the place you were staying, than you set out again. I thought it prudent to follow you a while and wait the proper time to speak with you alone. I never dreamt that the big fellow would be on the lookout."

"I am more than happy to see you, even though I find you persist in my service, despite all my efforts to dissuade you. Have you in truth any message from anyone, or dare I hope you came to receive the portion I owe you but knew not where to send?"

"Neither. You owe me no portion as the money you gave me several months ago is plenty enough to meet my needs. As I am my own master, I choose to follow you and be of any service that I can to you. As the servant of your family, I do likewise."

"This will not do at all," declared I, "for in this country I have resolved never to bear that name or condition, and M. Gramont has by no means the dignity of a Marquis to support. You are welcome to stay with me as my friend, but as my servant, you cannot appear."

"Then I shall not stay long and shall do as you ask. I have obeyed your commands in at least one respect, of which I shall inform you presently."

Saying no more he went on ahead of me, causing me to wonder if I was ever truly master of such an original man.

When I arrived at the inn where we were to be staying, I discovered everyone waiting for me but Philip, who had rather unaccountably departed soon after he had arrived there.

I could see questions concerning him on everyone's lips, but none were raised. We proceeded to order dinner to be eaten in the ladies' chambers. When we had eaten our meal, Mme. Gaspar gently requested Mouchard continue with his story, upon which M. Savard begged to be excused, seeming extremely fatigued by the days' journey and excitement.

Mouchard readily agreed, and he began as follows:

"*In the days* following their singular conversation, Mr. Harland and Miss Reckert, seemed to avoid each other as if by mutual agreement.

Several weeks beforehand, Mr. Harland had written to Mr. Reckert of his intended absence, and now only waited for his instructions in order to depart. His reply arrived three days later. Mr. Reckert wrote to beg that his daughter would join him in Bristol, from where he meant to return home in several weeks, providing he felt well enough. Mr. Harland immediately offered to escort her there, but she declined, saying that it was too far out of the way and quite unnecessary. The gentleman was rather more relieved than disappointed, for he had begun to see the danger of spending too much time in her company.

Despite the apparent alacrity with which Miss Reckert had relinquished her little companion, she was by no means easy on Thomas' account. She recalled Thomas several times for preparations and instructions. On the day prior to their departure, she summoned him to receive a little parcel filled with every possible convenience not in itself burdensome to carry.

'Do not trouble yourself to write to me, my dear friend,' said she, 'but do not doubt that I shall think of you always while you are gone. You have been my companion for so long, I hardly know how I shall manage without my dear little shadow. If it was my convenience alone consulted, I should keep you by me ever, but this will not do for your future. I was blind not to realize this at first, but now that I do, I shall conduct myself better. Mr. Harland intends a very short trip, and then we shall be together again. While you are gone, I shall consult regarding how best to settle you in your future life. Do not look so forlorn, dear friend. You may be sure of my love, and I promise nothing shall be considered which will make you miserable.'

With that she embraced him affectionately and he returned to the other house. The following day, Mr. Harland called at the main house to take leave.

No mention was made immediately of the agreement they had reached the previous night. He began to suspect Miss Reckert had changed her mind, till in the very last moments as he was taking leave, she presented him with a small packet, encased in a velvet pouch.

He bowed, feeling compelled to thank her once again for the trust she had placed in him, whereupon she blushed, saying quietly, 'I do not think I could have entrusted another, Sir.'"

Here Mouchard paused temporarily.

"At the parting of Miss Reckert and Mr. Harland, we must take the fork in the story which follows the gentleman. After taking leave of Miss Reckert, Mr. Harland departed in his carriage to begin his journey to Belgium. He was surprised to discover how great was his curiosity and how strong his temptation to disregard the seemingly meaningless scruples which had prompted Miss Reckert to extract a promise not to inspect it till he had left English soil. It is circumstances such as these, which separate the truly honourable from the conveniently so, for as unnecessary as he felt the caution to be, he was nevertheless unwilling to break on oath for the sake of curiosity.

His departure from England took longer than he had anticipated, as weather and difficulty coming to arrangements with the ship's captain extended the time by more than a week.

During this time he was compelled to drive all thought of the package from his mind, being still very much upon English soil. Once he departed England, it was not till the second or third day of his voyage that it occurred to him to inspect the package stored securely in his waistcoat pocket. This operation was interrupted by the entrance of another person, and the packet was returned to its place until a more convenient opportunity could arise.

Travel soon gave way to business, and when they arrived in Belgium, introductions and deliberations seemed to occupy almost every moment for several days thereafter. When at last Mr. Harland found a moment to look into the matter, he felt strangely reluctant to avail himself of it. After all, he reasoned to himself, whatever the package revealed, he was very far from being able to act upon it, and any distraction from his present purpose would be unproductive. Moreover, any symptom of undue interest in this matter disturbed him and he felt it was wise to discourage in himself. Added to this was a certain sense of trepidation as to its contents, and eventually he was quite happy to delay acquiring that knowledge as long as possible.

As chance would have it, the trip that was to take a fortnight at most, was gradually extended week by week, till it had outlasted three months. The return trip was accomplished more swiftly, and nearly a hundred days after he had left, Mr. Harland returned to England, making land at Brighton.

His last letter from Mr. Seymour had indicated he would likely be in Brighton around that time, and therefore he sent to him immediately.

Mr. Seymour came at once and they spent several hours together discussing various matters. At last Mr. Seymour declared he was obliged to depart, adding:

'Your timing is quite fortuitous, for Mr. and Miss Reckert are also in Brighton, and they plan to return home in just a few days. Perhaps we may all travel together? I have promised to meet them at the Pump room at 4 o'clock. You are welcome to join me if you like, for I am sure Mr. Reckert would have extended the invitation himself if he had known you were to be here.'

Mr. Harland agreed to the proposal at once, but not without some embarrassment. Although he told himself that Miss Reckert was unlikely to be very dismayed with a delay in matters she had long delayed herself, he was conscious that his trip had taken far longer than he had intended, during which time he had failed to do anything at all. Upon the verge of seeing her he began to feel some need of apologizing for neglecting her affairs, lest she had taken his apparent silence ill. He felt for the package which was still in his pocket, but realizing he had no time to act upon it, regardless of what it contained, he resolved merely to look for a moment to speak with her privately and assure her he meant to correct his failings as soon as could be.

Such were his thoughts as he and Mr. Seymour travelled to the Pump room. The outer rooms were crowded, but after a minute or two they spied Mr. and Miss Reckert seated in one of the inner chambers. Mr. Reckert was reclining in a chair, supported slightly by his daughter.

Attracting Mr. Reckert's notice upon approach, Mr. Harland began his customary address. His appearance was greeted with pleasure by his old friend who had seen him first, but he was forced to stop midway when he beheld that Miss Reckert had turned pale at the sight of him. Such a reception greatly unsettled him, and forced him to begin to say he hoped she was not displeased with him, for 'although there may be cause for complaint, he believed he might be forgiven on the grounds that...'

'Indeed, Sir, you take too much trouble,' was the hasty response. With this Miss Reckert stood and hastened away, failing to notice either Mr. Seymour or Thomas who had remained behind waiting to be observed. Her figure was immediately obscured in the crowds who were continually moving from one room to the next.

Such a precipitant retreat was the last thing he had expected, and his consternation was extreme to encounter it. He found it difficult to maintain his share of the conversation with Mr. Reckert, all the more so as he found any further exchange or clarification with Miss Reckert would be impossible.

Mr. Reckert, meanwhile, was unsuspicious that anything had occurred to distress either party. His own weariness occupied most of his thoughts and after a short interval in which only he and Mr. Seymour spoke, he kindly begged Mr. Harland to call upon them where they were staying as soon as possible, as he himself intended to go home and rest.

Mr. Harland was glad, in spite of himself, to be relieved of his friend's company, as it would better enable him to contemplate what could be behind so strange a reception. He did not think it likely a mere delay on his part could have provoked such displeasure, and was at first inclined to think some misunderstanding must have occurred between them. It was not long before it occurred to him that something might have happened in the interim to make his errand meaningless, and he began to fear that the man in question had become engaged or married in the time he was away.

As soon as the possibility entered his mind, he became all the more convinced it was so, and hurried home to confirm his suspicion. Alighting from his carriage, he sent one of his servants in search of any papers containing recent marriage announcements. He then gave instructions not to be disturbed, and cloistered himself in his study in order to prepare himself to come to some terrible realization.

Following an irrepressible hesitation, he drew the packet from his pocket and began to unwrap it. Inside he found a little envelope, containing what appeared at first to be a kind of locket, covered by green embroidered fabric.

He opened it immediately, expecting to find some scrap of paper, but lo it was empty, being in actuality no more than a little pocket mirror.

It is difficult to say exactly how long it was before the truth dawned upon him, for even in a circumstance where it must have been self-evident, it was so foreign and impossible to his ideas that a part of him refused to understand it directly.

His first thought was, 'there is nothing,' but scarcely had he thought so, then the blood rushed to his face, almost without his knowing why. The dawning thought was dismissed before it could truly take shape, only to rise again as soon as it was silenced. The meaning was as obvious as it was impossible. He thought back at once to their conversation where she had said she meant to 'provide him the means to discover' rather than the name he had always expected it to contain.

The truth of the matter, thus revealed to him, struck him all but dumb.

What a strange and new light did it place the entire conversation between them on the subject; nay, their entire acquaintance! There was scarcely a word or action or meeting between them that could not be newly understood. How many soft looks or accents or sighs, avoidances, awkwardness now crowded to mind.

On the heels of these incredible revelations, the progression of his own sentiments was equally rapid. When he had first known her, she was but a child and he had admired her only reluctantly and sought to avoid her generally. As she matured and nearer proximity had been forced upon him, he had been only to happy to believe the worst in relation to her temperament and character, in order to lessen the effect of any contact with her, and lastly he had impressed upon himself so firmly the in-utility of such admiration, that he had been able to repress it almost completely.

All this was swept away in the face of this most unimaginable revelation. The ground kept forcibly barren was all the more fertile, and the respectful admiration which might earlier have grown there was superseded by a love as ardent as it was urgent; all the more urgent, perhaps, but the knowledge it had quite possibly arrived too late."

Mouchard paused here, and we were all well pleased with the direction of the story. There is something strange and wonderful in this tale of Mouchard's. I cannot help pitying both Mr. Harland and Miss Reckert. It is natural, I think, for Mr. Harland to have safeguarded his own peace of mind so as to avoid falling in love where there seems very little chance of success. And likewise, Miss Reckert, who is scarecely less modest than Mr. Harland, with apparently less reason to be so. Yet it is Miss Reckert who swallows her pride and hazards the risk in the end, and it is she I most feel for at the moment. Mouchard would give us no indication which way the story would go from here, no matter what we asked him.

Although in your last letter, you gave equal thanks and praise to my history and Mouchard's story, I should not blame you for preferring the latter, as I am sure must be the case.

* * *

I just received your letter dated February 7th. I am gratified that my long letters have still not tired out your patience, or the patience of our friends. I am delighted that Father Galois has chosen to preserve them for posterity, for Mouchard's story strikes me as quite uncommon, and it would seem a shame if it were entirely lost. I will return your first two letters with this packet, but I fear I did not receive a third (this letter is itself the third, by my reckoning). If another letter arrives, I will return it once I have read it, though I shall be happy to have it back, of course.

I do not think you need fear travelling through any country but France. A man may still travel with safety and convenience through most parts of Europe, excepting there. Do not forget your promise to visit me, if you decide to leave your seclusion.

Today we rose fairly early, and have travelled a fair distance. It is only two o'clock in the afternoon, but we are already settled in the inn where we are staying tonight; the ladies were reluctant to travel further. We had refreshments when we first arrived, and now I am without business or obligation for the next few hours, so shall write you some more of my history till supper is announced:

For the next few months, outside the walls of the Chateau, the revolution raged on. Though Louis XVI outwardly praised the work of the National Assembly, it became increasingly apparent that he was losing his freedom to do otherwise. The angry mobs in Paris, and indeed over the whole country, kept the National Assembly in session, and forced the King to seem supportive. Week after week I expected to read something decisive in the papers which reached us, but aside from the transformation of the Estates General into the National Assembly, whose mandate seemed perpetually expanding, the list of problems and grievances to be addressed only became longer.

Soon I became so desperate for any kind of progress that I rejoiced at any change, no matter how small it was. Still the National Assembly plodded on creating more work than they resolved. Though doubtless in our immediate vicinity, the League of the Star remained ascendant, nearly every week seemed to bring new life and strength to those who opposed us, so that for every foe we bettered, another emerged to try his hand.

While this endless challenge seemed to fire Lafont, it only wearied me. Our occupations became even more segregated as weeks passed, and I withdrew still more from knowledge or involvement in his activities.

One particular afternoon around that time, I went out as I often did, taking only Joseph as my companion, (Joseph being the name of the boy I had spared by my intervention several months before). Since that time even M. Lafont himself was forced to admit that he had become a most worthwhile addition to our number. Every day Joseph accompanied either M. Lafont or myself on whatever mission we embarked upon. He was intelligent, quick-witted and a quick study, reliable in almost any capacity. Though a natural soldier, he had a philosophical temperament which wanted only basic instruction to nourish. Philip and I alternately took it upon ourselves to tutor him in reading, and his passion was so fired by the enjoyment of books, that in a short time he was rarely to be found in any other chamber but the library.

It was customary for us to traverse a well-worn path in the forest which ran parallel to the road, though out of sight from it. By this time word had spread that this road was protected, but for the whole of the previous week I had seen no one at all upon it. I began to suspect that travellers were being stopped before they could reach it, and on this particular day, set out to investigate.

Bypassing the town of Quereign, I traversed the forest on the farther side. The road was situated a fair way from it and in order to take a better view of what was passing on it one needed to leave the cover of the forest. I rode a short distance further out in the open when I espied a makeshift blockade of sorts, made up of a few small buildings constructed near a small house. At a distance of some hundred or so metres, I could not properly judge the size of strength of it. I quickly determined that it was sizeable enough at least to make it unwise to approach without some reinforcement. I sent Joseph back to the Chateau to summon any men who were available, adding, 'I shall ride further along this path and keep watch for any travellers. With luck you shall return before I have need of you.'

I had travelled perhaps five more miles when I saw a carriage approaching the way I had come. After watching it pass, I left the shelter of the trees once more, crossed the expanse of field and began to follow behind at a slow pace. My intention was to watch from a distance and determine if the progress of the carriage was stopped. If it was permitted to pass, I planned to leave the road again for the forest, but if it was stopped, I meant to look more closely into the case and intervene when necessary.

Coming round the bend I saw that the carriage had indeed paused more than half a mile ahead of me. I slowed my pace, hoping all the while that it would continue again. As I drew closer I could see that the carriage had moved slightly to the side and its occupant had descended. I continued to approach, seeing five slightly armed men standing in discussion, and as I drew close enough to see their countenances, I could see the revolutionaries were in good spirits, laughing with one another. I looked again to see if I could see the passenger of the carriage, and to my surprise, I recognized M. Montrond, the minister of the King, who seemed decidedly more grave. What I found still more surprising was that he looked in my direction with recognition but not surprise, making no other acknowledgement.

'Halt, Monsieur,' said one of the unmounted guards, 'you must wait while we finish examining the man ahead of you.'

'Do you detain him?' inquired I.

'Seems likely, but what is that to you?'

'I am only curious what crime he might have committed?'

'Clean hands and an elegant accent are no great recommendations nowadays, Monsieur. Come this way and consult your own interest, for 'tis likely you shall not fare much better.'

I did not move, but rather continued to eye M. Montrond, who likewise glanced frequently in my direction.

The man who had laid commands upon me turned around presently and seeing that they were ignored, he said, 'You must dismount, Monsieur, for I can see you are lacking the proper respect for revolutionary authority.'

'I have reason to speak with the gentleman you have detained,' said I, again ignoring his instructions.

'Perhaps we shall house the two of you together,' said he, looking to the others, who seemed to share his jest. Here he gestured to another guard, who was on horseback nearby.

'This gentleman will be housed near the other,' said he, 'but first he must be unseated, as he has refused my commands.'

I shall never forget the look of the man who approached. He

was a grave, thoughtful man, and under any other circumstances, I should have been quite happy to meet with him. He seemed to understand the nature of the situation better than the man who summoned him. He looked at me silently for a long moment, and then said, 'You must dismount, Monsieur.'

'I desire merely to speak with that gentleman,' said I, 'and I have no intention of dismounting.'

'Revolutionary authority demands you do,' said he, drawing his sword. I drew mine in defence and we fought. We were each of us reluctant to begin, but there was no help for it and we exchanged blows with determination. After what seemed like an eternity, my sword came down upon his left shoulder and he fell. To my last day I shall remember that scene with pain and regret. I feel certain that if his fate had been my own, he would have felt likewise.

Those who had witnessed this most unfortunate exchange seemed quite unprepared for it. The makeshift outpost where we stood consisted of a small cottage built near the road, an old inn recently commandeered for revolutionary usage. Beside the inn there was another habitation towards which two men had begun leading M. Montrond when all this came about.

Two other guards mounted their horses at this point, while the first group I had met merely stared and waited to see what would unfold. By this time I could see over their shoulders several horsemen approaching fast across the field, and in a very short time, Joseph and eight or so other men came into view.

It was at this time that another man appeared, issuing from the main door of the former inn. He was a slender man, near five and forty, dressed in black from head to foot.

He seemed to take the whole situation in a single glance. He looked sharply in the direction of the man I had first spoken with, who instantly approached and spoke in his ear. When he had finished, the austere looking man turned in the direction of M. Montrond, addressing him audibly.

'Though your papers are by no means satisfactory, we do not find it necessary to detain you here, Monsieur.' With that he addressed the man holding him, 'Allow M. Guere to return to his carriage.'

As he spoke, everyone else remained frozen. I had signalled to the rest of the men that they were not to act but merely to wait.

With a look of surprise and relief, M. Montrond re-entered his carriage, which was permitted to pass without further ado.

'Now, Monsieur' said he to me, 'unless you have some other business here, I must beg you depart likewise.'

With this he made a curt bow. Without uttering word or waiting for more, we did exactly that.

After a signal to the others, I rode after M. Montrond, who opened his window in anticipation of my approach, and cried out, 'I am most extraordinarily grateful to find you here, my dear Marquis de la Croix. Would you do me the honour of coming with me into the carriage, for I beg a word or two in private.'

I replied that I should be happy to do so, but first would escort him safely through Quereign, and the surrounding region, which would be several more miles still.

'Do you do so alone, Monsieur?'

'Outwardly it shall appear so, but be assured that many more men are nearby if necessary.'

I advised him to drive straight through without stopping for any reason, and he assured me he should have his driver do exactly as I directed.

Once we were again on the road leading past the village of La Croix, I approached the carriage and desired to know if M. Montrond wished to take his rest at the Chateau.

'I am very grateful for the invitation, for there is nothing I should like better. I hope you will not wonder too much if I express a wish to keep my name and particular connection to the royal family secret from all but you, at least for the time being. I am travelling under my mother's surname, Guere, by which I beg you will introduce me to your friends.'

I made no objection and we proceeded to the Chateau. As there were at the time a great deal of comings and goings, the arrival of one more face was hardly much remarked. At dinner that evening I saw M. Montrond was more than a casual observer of all that went on. M. Lafont was in unusually high spirits during dinner, having drunk only as much as would make him gay, not yet enough to make him foul. M. Montrond's eyes were often turned in his direction, and he seemed to watch him with particular interest. Towards the end of the meal, he turned to me and said,

'I hope I do not impose too much upon your hospitality, M. le Marquis, but I confess I would like very much to see more of your majestic Chateau.'

I guessed he made this request in order that we might speak alone, and so I suggested we walk together above the battlements.

'I am glad for the opportunity of speaking to you alone, for there are many things I would tell you that I would not wish overheard.'

I invited him to go on.

'You may be surprised to hear that when you encountered and assisted me so heroically on the road, I was in fact on my way to see you. You may recall when we met several months ago, you pledged your service and assistance to the King. Are you still of the mindset you were then?'

Though somewhat surprised at the question, I replied in the affirmative.

'I felt certain this was the case, and so I have a most particular favour to ask you. Before I do, however, permit me to inquire somewhat as to your partner in this enterprise, M. Lafont. Not much is known about him in Versailles, but it is fair to say he has acquired a reputation of ferocity. My experience tells me that ferocity and discretion are rarely found in the same person. Having said this much, I leave entirely to your own judgement how far he may be trusted with what I am about to reveal. I hope the gravity of what I propose shall prevent you from feeling any offence on M. Lafont's behalf, where certainly none is intended. The fewer people who know what I am about to tell you, the better.'

I nodded in agreement, and was far from taking offence on behalf of M. Lafont. If he was sober, I felt confidence in his conduct, but increasingly I remarked that he was more often drunk than sober, and under such circumstances, I would vouch for him to no one.

The night was dark and clear, and for a while we walked along the battlements in silence, looking up at the stars.

'Your ancestors, Monsieur la Croix, have always been honourable servants of their sovereigns. What would they think if they could see this day? A King's very right to rule his people called into question, nay, removed!'

After this he fell silent for a short while, staring out at the sky and the tops of trees surrounding the Chateau, many of which were tall and ancient enough to obscure the surroundings.

'In three days time,' began he again at last, 'his Majesty craves your protection for two carriages which will be travelling along a route a short ways to the Southeast of here. Though to outward appearances the travellers may not seem to be of much note, their safe passage is of the greatest importance to his Majesty. If they fail to reach their destination unobstructed, I fear the event shall have disastrous consequences for the entire country.'

My wonder increased as the possibility occurred to me that it was the Royal family itself he spoke of. However poorly I had imagined things to be at Versailles, I had not then any idea they would reach this extreme.

'Does his Majesty choose that I should know who it is whose passage is deemed of such great importance?'

M. Montrond shook his head helplessly. 'I have been instructed only to say they are friends of his Majesty's, and to convey his great sense of urgency and obligation.'

I lapsed into serious contemplation for a short while, before finally saying, 'And is it certain, finally decided, I mean?'

'Irrevocably. But tell me, Marquis, are you disposed to serve your King in his time of need?'

'His Majesty may rely implicitly upon me, M. Montrond, but it is a long way from here to Versailles. If this voyage is so vital to his Majesty, I question why he does not take more effective means of ensuring it. Might he not make use of the army? Are there no longer some in Paris who are still loyal to the crown?'

'In such a climate as this, Monsieur, it is not easy to keep an army in the fields without sewing fear and confusion among the populace. I have advised against it, as I fear it shall be too difficult to fix the time. In concordance with my advice, I have made certain recommendations and in the hope that my advice shall prevail, I have set out to you to put in place the strategy I recommend. I feel that the least amount of attention drawn to the passage of the carriages, the better. From what I have seen of your proceedings firsthand, I believe you are perfectly suited to assisting his Majesty. Perhaps it shall not be necessary, and an army shall provide the escort in the end. I am not the only person who advises his Majesty, you see. A very short time will tell.'

We were silent again.

'I shall tell M. Lafont of his Majesty's desire, but I do not see any need to tell him very much in advance, as I shall be able to handle the preparations by myself. In all probability he shall not remark it much, for the request itself is not out of the ordinary, however eminent is the requester in this case.'

'That is just as I had hoped. I fear there will be a little travel, as the area in question is nearly half a days' travel from here. And then I think your men must find a way to blend with the countryside, to avoid rousing bands of armed peasants which are gathering everywhere on the smallest provocation. Tomorrow I shall show you the area on a map and we shall discuss it in more detail. By your leave I intend to stay here till then, for you may well imagine that my own affairs rest on the success and failure of this effort.'

I nodded in concurrence, deep in thought.

'Goodnight, Monsieur. God bless you, and God bless Louis XVI.'

I am being called to supper now.

Mouchard was not asked to give us any entertainment tonight, for M. Savard declared rest was more important for the ladies, and they reluctantly acquiesced. That gentleman is in a peculiar humour at present.

As I am once more in my room, I shall continue where I left off two hours ago:

I did not sleep at all that night. Whatever pressure I had imagined Louis to suffer while the National Assembly was in session, I had not ever believed him to be prisoner of the opposing forces. What chance, thought I, of returning to power had a monarch who fled subjects who had held him captive? Whatever his intention once he escaped, I could think of no outcome which promised peace and stability to our beleaguered country.

In these hours of sleepless contemplation, the face of the man I had killed that day reappeared to me constantly, amidst the intermittent visions of Louis XVI, (as he appears in his official portraits, for I have never seen him). How much nobler a soul seemed the other man, whose fortunes had been sacrificed, along with many others, to this cursed revolution. And who could deny that the revolution could not have taken place but for the wretched excess and mismanagement of the King and those like my father?

I had given my word to M. Montrond, and was in no way tempted to break it. Despite this I was filled with remorse for the action I had committed that day, and when I considered it along with the deeds of the last few months, I was quite dissatisfied with myself.

The next day I had opportunity to speak again with M. Montrond, who further described the area the carriages were to be met.

'I assume you are familiar with the Meuse region, which is perhaps a little over a days' travel from here. I have told, nay, I have urged his Majesty to take my council in this affair, and I believe he has heard me. In this case two carriages (I daren't hope that only one shall come, though I have begged and implored that it be so) –but stay, where was I?'

'In Meuse, with two carriages.'

'Aye, and so they shall need a change of horses, but it will not do for them to be staying long in any town. I have told his Majesty that horses shall be provided on the open road, halfway between Varennes and Dun. In such practical matters, a Sovereign must be carefully instructed, for they understand them no more than a child. It is those who can do for themselves who are the most free, for the grandest lord shall die the quickest in the forest, for he has never gathered his own wood, nor lit his own fire, and knows not how to warm himself or get his own food. At least the peasant knows what to do with grain when he has got it. But I have rambled again, where was I?'

'Changing horses, I believe.'

'Aye, yes, fifty good men and a change of horses is all that is needed. I intend to accompany the party, and shall myself approach the carriage, and ride alongside it. I am not the stoutest of men, but I should be happy to die in its defence.'

He paused again, looking off into the distance. When it seemed like his reflections were at an end, I said, 'You have not said where his majesties' friends are headed, and how long we are to accompany them?'

'To Montmédy, my dear Marquis, which will be but a few hours further, and it is until we arrive there I ask your protection.'

Montmédy is a fortified town near the border of the Austrian-Netherlands, and it was from there Louis obviously meant to oppose the revolutionaries, and attempt to regain control with the help of the Queen's relations.

I could not help but sigh to know it. On the one hand, it seemed like the most likely expedient to halt the revolution I had heard in months. On the other hand, a King who can only govern his people with the help of foreign armies is a failed monarch indeed.

The following day I sought out M. Lafont and told him we had received an important commission from the king, brought to us by M. Montrond.

'The King?' cried he, in surprise. 'Well that is out of the ordinary at least. And what does our beleaguered liege request? I dare not hope he has discovered the strength of monarchs of old, and intends to drive these rats into the Sienne?'

'I know not. M. Montrond only asks our protection for friends of the King, who travel through the area to the Southeast of here tomorrow.'

'And would he then aid the many cowards who have abandoned him in his time of need, rather than aid in his defence? I do not wonder that Louis is all alone if he vouchsafes his friends so much consideration that he aids them in their flight!' said he, with undisguised contempt.

'Do you intend to make one among us?' said I, with unconcern. 'M. Montrond asks for fifty strong men in the area of Meuse. We shall be required to wait from dawn to dusk, for now that he has left Paris, M. Montrond is privy to no more precise information.'

'Perhaps it is the Queen?' mused Lafont, thoughtfully. 'Perhaps the King no longer thinks it is safe for her to remain in Paris. If that is so it shall be welcome news indeed. M. Montrond has told you no more?'

I shook my head. The possibility that Louis should send Marie Antoinette and the children alone, while he himself stayed in Versailles, was far more pleasing than the idea that the King as well meant to flee. The more I considered it, the more I felt it was likely, and very soon I was entirely of M. Lafont's opinion.

To be the escort of the royal family without the King was a far more palatable charge, and the honour and importance of it all was not lost on M. Lafont or myself. With quiet deliberation we gathered together those we meant to take with us, tasking Philip with ordering our provisions.

M. Lafont and I rode most of the way, talking together like old companions. We were both of us in high spirits. M. Montrond, who rode nearby, was anxious and fretful.

Along the stretch of road where we were to wait, we positioned one or two men every hundred metres or so, instructing them to prepare for a long wait. M. Montrond elected to remain at the first station, that he might have the first view of all traffic which approached.

'Adieu, Marquis,' said he, as we left him, 'I hope we shall not have to wait long, but I ask that we wait till dusk at least, if need be.'

'Have no fear, we shall do at least as much.'

'If only they come, then all shall be well.'

M. Lafont and I were nearly the last to settle ourselves along the way. We chose a hill which afforded a broad view of the road and fields beneath. We drank and speculated and the hours passed quickly. We had arrived in the region in the morning and M. Montrond's information had indicated the carriages were to pass through the afternoon, barring any unforeseen delay.

Near four o'clock M. Lafont, and I were still in high spirits. We spoke of the events which had brought us together, a subject we had rarely touched upon those last months.

'Only think,' said he, 'how long ago it seems was the day we first met, and in so short a time, how formidable we have become! Even the King condescends to ask for our help.'

''Tis a short time in months, yet it seems an eternity in events. No doubt M. Hubert did not foresee the results of the introduction he orchestrated, in his attempts to spare the righteous from the revenge he carried out.'

'A dog and a fool!' cried he, his mood becoming darker at the mere thought of M. Hubert.

'I have often wondered that no more joined us that evening,' said I, 'for if he claimed to have sent the same appeal to every person in the area, there ought to have been scores of people assembled there that night. Doubtless he did not distribute it as widely as he claimed.'

'I see no reason to suppose so. I should not have been there myself, did I not think the message was from a maid I had a mind to. The other sex is fond of mystery and intrigue, and it seemed I had a good chance of being rewarded for my trouble if I extricated her from some scrape.'

He continued to speak but I hardly heard what followed. However commonplace this admission seemed, it had a profound effect upon me. Until that point, whatever else M. Lafont did or seemed capable of, his answer to the anonymous plea of that night had served to vouch for the basic goodness of his character.

To know by his own admission that he had only answered it in the hopes of taking advantage of a young maid staggered all my calculations. Try as I might to think of another memory of virtue which might re-establish his character in my mind, no such instance of goodness befriended me. I sat in silence while M. Lafont rambled on heedlessly, needing no encouragement but drink.

After a while he called my attention away to a cloud of dust which seemed to be rising far south in the distance.

'Something has gathered there,' said he, 'whether it is an army or a mob, I cannot tell.'

We looked long, straining against the fading light, but could make out nothing further. At last it was too dark to see more than a short way before us. We fell silent, growing more guarded in the enveloping darkness. We let our fire die down and waited. No carriage came.

We had agreed that as soon as darkness fell, the men stationed at the farthest point should make their way back to the spot where they had left the person before them. In a short time we saw a torch and heard the signal. We returned the signal and lit our own torch, and soon we turned back as four. No one said much, and as no one but us had any inkling of the possible significance of this foray, few evidenced much disappointment

We walked within a short distance from the road, though it could no longer be seen. I half expected the carriage to be heard as we walked in the directions of the first position where we had left M. Montrond.

Just before reaching him, we were nearly fifty men again, though we were loosely spaced. M. Montrond was silent when first we met, but at last he looked at me and said faintly, 'All is lost, Monsieur le Marquis!' The tension and dejection visible in his whole frame and bearing caused me to revert at least partially to my first surmise regarding the intended travellers.

By the time we returned to the Chateau, several hours later and an hour or two before the sun rose, rumours of what had transpired were already reaching the Chateau.

'The King has fled! He has been captured in Varrenes!'

I know not who uttered these words, or precisely how I heard it the first time, but the full impact was clear to me at once. Details of what had occurred changed with the wind those first few days. Who had accompanied Louis, where and under what circumstances they had been captured varied greatly, but there was no doubt as to the principal point: The King had fled.

At last we learned that Louis and Marie-Antoinette had fled with their household, expecting General Bouille's army to meet them at Pont De Sommervelle. General Bouille was said to have left prematurely, or else the carriage was late; I did not hear concretely. In any case, it seems the carriages had no escort at all. They might have made it through did they not have to change horses in Varrenes, where horses were scarce and there was time enough to betray themselves. I know no more than that, and it is probable you have heard much the same, or possibly more than I.

Almost immediately that the first few reports arrived, M. Montrond shut himself away from us all to collect himself. It was best that he did for as soon as M. Lafont realized the truth, he was outrageous in his execrations of Louis XVI. His exclamations lasted for several hours, finally to be halted by the simple question of a young man in our company, who said, 'Surely, M. Lafont, no one can deny that Louis deserves not the loyalty we have pledged him, but if not for the King, for whom do we fight?'

This question had no instant answer. M. Lafont dropped into a dark silence, and we all separated to rest, most of us having had none in a good long while.

Here I will pause and send this to you. May fortune follow you,

Your friend,

M.C.

M. Henri Renault to Marcel de la Croix

February 14th, 1773, Switzerland

Dear Marcel,

Your letters continue to inspire great gratitude and applause; not to mention, whet the appetite for more of the same. Although they comprise our sole amusement in this solitary place, I have no doubt they could stand their ground in any environment whatsoever.

As for myself, I am no longer satisfied to remain here. Your words have reanimated my thirst for adventure. I fear this safety is killing me.

When I announced my intention to leave, the brotherhood was more aghast than surprised, in fear that they should receive no more letters from you in my absence. We have come to an accommodation of sorts, which I hope will be agreeable to you too. If you will be so kind as to continue to direct your letters here, Father Galois shall copy them then add them to his prized collection. I shall send to retrieve them every two weeks or so, from wherever I am, since I do not know what other address to give you. I do not have a very clear idea where I shall be from week to week, as I am merely hoping to find my cousin in Germany. I have not entirely given up the idea of coming to England to visit you, if you determine to settle there.

When your letters reach me, they will be somewhat more delayed than now, and I will reply to you directly. Father Galois regrets these future notes shall be missing from his collection, but I believe it will improve it on the whole.

With fondness and gratitude, I am,
Your faithful friend and servant,
Henri Renault

Marcel de la Croix to Henri Renault

February 15th,1793

Dear Friend,

We are now arrived in Suffolk. M. Savard continues to be silent as to the purpose of our little trip, maintaining that it is purely a matter of business which calls him here. We are staying at an inn called The Thrush, not far from the coast. Yesterday, I spent much of the day walking along the cliffs by the sea. On my return I met M. Tolouse, who approached me with an air at once triumphant and deferential.

"Thought you might like to know, Sir," said he with a bow, "that I have spotted another man dogging us. I heard him questioning the Landlord about our party for several minutes, but when I thought to approach him to know why, he high-tailed it before one could get in a word. Thinking prudence might be called for, I made as if I hadn't heard a thing, but all the same have tracked him to an inn not too far up the road. So that is how the matter stands, and I hope you won't mind if one asks you if you know anything of it? Are there any more servants of yours about? Any games afoot? I put the boy to watching the inn, and he's to let us know if the gentleman stirs."

"Mouchard?" said I, with surprise. "I hardly think he is fit for such things. He has looked almost sickly of late. However, to answer your question, I have no knowledge of any person who's been lurking about, but all the same, perhaps it is best if we go to inquire together."

He appeared delighted at this answer, and we proceeded together. It was a typically English inn, called The Fox and the Hound, and the master of the house was a pleasant fellow who seemed to understand us better than we understood him. I would not have you think so ill of me as to imagine I have made no progress with English, but believe me when I assure you there are so many variations of the native dialect, one can easily lose one's bearing from town to town.

I told M. Tolouse that I preferred to handle the matter myself, and therefore taking from him the description of the man we sought, I drew the innkeeper aside and said,

"My friend and I have been staying a short ways away at The Thrush, though I now see we had better have continued along the road a short ways–"

"You are very kind, Sir," interrupted he, well pleased with the compliment, which was no more than the truth.

"At any rate, there may yet be some time to correct our error if you have room in your house, but before I forget the business that brought me here, I believe I have found the riding gloves of a young gentleman who is staying here. He wears a green riding coat, and I believe has come only today."

"Ah, I expect you mean young Mr. Etheredge," replied he. "Fine young man, to be sure, but they will all be heedless about their things."

He made a few more observations which I did not quite understand, and so I shall not attempt to do them justice.

At the name 'Etheredge,' I realized it must be the son of our landlord, Sir John Etheredge, whom we had met only a few weeks before.

His interest in our party was now placed in a much less sinister light, and I determined at once to inform M. Tolouse. I was delayed by the innkeeper, who asked whether I wished first to speak to Mr. Etheredge, or take possession of my room?

Speaking to Mr. Etheredge now seemed more a courtesy rather than a matter of any urgency, but having bespoke a room, I decided to follow through. I instructed him to make ready the room, and I would speak with Mr. Etheredge some time thereafter. In the meantime I ordered a good dinner for M. Tolouse and myself, which I meant to eat in the common room.

While I had been speaking to the innkeeper, M. Tolouse had disappeared. I presumed he was merely outside, but when I went to look, I could find no trace of him in or out.

Once back inside, I sat down to await our meal, which was brought with an almost alarming alacrity. When I remarked upon it, he assured me that it was merely owing to the fact that he and his wife had ordered nearly the same thing from the cook. It proved to be the best meal I had eaten in England, and I enjoyed it thoroughly, notwithstanding my growing unease to find M. Tolouse remained absent. When I had finished, I called for a pen and paper and wrote a brief note to M. Savard, informing him that we would return the next day.

Still there was no sight of M. Tolouse and I repaired to my room determined to wait there for him. A short time later he knocked at the door, having seemingly come of his own accord and without the knowledge of the innkeeper.

He seemed quite pleased with himself, and his whole face was flushed with excitement. I was inevitably concerned to see it, and said, 'M. Tolouse, I hope you have not done anything rash, for I have something of consequence to communicate.'

"Nay, nay," replied he, "you'll see, I have done less than nothing and shall leave the matter quite up to you. Pray follow me and I will show you. Quietly now."

His words at once concerned and appeased me, and I did as he suggested. He led me to Mr. Etheredge's room, entering it without knocking. To my dismay I saw within poor Mr. Etheredge seated in a chair, and bound head to foot; a bandage covering his mouth to keep him from speaking. Fear was depicted in his whole face. He seemed to recognize me at once, but was unsure whether to be frightened or relieved to do so.

I sighed deeply.

"'Tis as I said, Sir, for I haven't asked him a word, and shall leave that entirely to you. Not like a Frenchman, I think, but a little womanly all the same."

"M. Tolouse, I am certain you have done enough for the time being, so pray return to the room where you found me and do not stir from it till I return."

He seemed largely unaffected by my displeasure, as his self-approbation of his own actions was so high in this case, that my displeasure alone was not enough to dislodge it.

"My dear Mr. Etheredge," said I, the moment he had left, beginning to free him from his bonds, starting with his legs. "Please forgive M. Tolouse, for that is the name of the man who has rendered you thus. I have heard that a military man is the most difficult to restore into polite company, and there was never a finer example than M. Tolouse. He has overheard you asking about our party earlier today, and has immediately concluded you were a spy or villain. I had not time to convince him of his mistake when I discovered it. Accept my apologies on his behalf, I pray."

By then he was completely free, and able to speak.

"M. Gramont, is it not?" said he, breathing hard from his ordeal. "I must say, this is rather extraordinary treatment indeed... I say, most extraordinary!" He paused for a moment, then looked at me again. "I did indeed make some inquires of your party, but they were of a most polite, most innocent nature, I assure you!"

"I have no doubt of it, and I am terribly sorry for how they have been misinterpreted."

He paced around the room for a short while as if he had something else to communicate. Finally he said, 'Pardon the blunt nature of this question, but under the circumstances, I believe it can be forgiven. Has M. Savard sent you here?'

"M. Savard?" repeated I, with surprise. "I had not realized you were acquainted with that gentleman? However, in answer to your question, you may be assured no. Though we travel with M. Savard, I should scorn to be his errand boy. I have told you the circumstance which has led to the outrage you have endured, and while I am sincerely sorry to discover the usage you have suffered, I must warn you that my temperament is not mild enough to brook repeated doubts of my veracity."

Young Mr. Etheredge sighed. "The inquiries M. Tolouse heard earlier were merely to discover whether M. Savard was present with the ladies. I have tried in vain to renew my acquaintance with them, and of course yourself, but M. Savard has rebuffed my every attempt. I do not know if that gentleman is a friend of yours or no, but I cannot help confessing that I am little obliged to him."

"Indeed, Sir," replied I, still further surprised. "Have you called at Sorsten Manor?"

"Four times, Monsieur. The more I see of M. Savard, the more I cannot help pitying poor Mlle Vallon. For such a gentle creature to be shackled to an aged misanthropist, "'tis surely a crime!"

He was still pacing about, and his shock and emotion was beginning to get the better of him.

"Mr. Etheredge, pardon me for staying so long, as you clearly shall want peace and repose after the excitement of the evening. M. Tolouse and I shall be staying at this house tonight, and if you can bring yourself to be in his presence, I should be happy to introduce you tomorrow, that you might be on better terms. Perhaps we might have opportunity then to speak more of Mlle Vallon."

He hardly appeared eager to meet with M. Tolouse again, but at the hint regarding Mlle Vallon, he repressed his unwillingness and accepted with a bow.

M. Tolouse was not half as repentant as I expected, to hear he had used such means to detain the son of our landlord.

"The young gentleman ought not to have been snooping about if he wanted to be left alone. Don't meddle with others if you wouldn't be meddled with, there's a motto for you! Hah! In love with Mlle Vallon, perhaps. Who's to wonder, I suppose. M. Savard will not let her go. A bird in its cage has got a better hope of getting free than she."

The following morning, Mr. Etheredge was announced at my chamber nearly at the end of breakfast.

He and M. Tolouse exchanged cold civilities. M. Tolouse readily undertook to apologize for the misunderstanding which had led to Mr. Etheredge's confinement. He declared he had meant no harm by it, but was willing to offer the gentleman satisfaction, if he felt it necessary. Mr. Etheredge seemed far from thinking further bouts with M. Tolouse were necessary, and declared he was happy never to think of the matter again. Despite this, it was plain that they remained ill at ease with one-another and M. Tolouse was quick to make an excuse to depart.

When he was gone, Mr. Etheredge said, "I am sorry for the lateness of my arrival, but I was obliged to write a quick note to my parents, as my trip was rather in haste and I fear they may be wondering where I have got to."

"Indeed," said I. "You must have had a very particular purpose to have left so precipitantly?"

He did not reply directly, seeming to wish some internal consideration. At last he said, "M. Gramont, your manner and generous behaviour, joined to overall deportment, bespeak you a man who can be trusted with rather sensitive information. These circumstances, joined with my desperation, tempt me to ask for your confidence in a matter. If you are willing to hear me, I need only know whether you are a friend to M. Savard. If you are a friend of his, I fear it shall be impossible for you to be one to me."

"I am neither friend nor enemy to that gentleman," replied I. "There are those in life for whom we have neither great affection nor obligation, who we nevertheless would not willingly harm. Such is my relationship to M. Savard, and you may choose whether you wish to confide in me or no. If you decide to, you may assure yourself I am quite ready to hear you, and help you if I may."

"I thank you, Sir. *Harm* is a relatively broad term," replied the young man. "I feel I have no choice but to take the risk. Though it may not appear so, M. Gramont, I have a greater right to be concerned with the affairs of Mlle Vallon than you might guess. I make no idle boast, nor such a one intended to tarnish the reputation of that lady, which is as dear to me as– ah, I do not know. Suffice to say, it is quite dear to me, and I would not damage it for the world. I admire Mlle Vallon, as you no doubt have guessed, and have cause to think that were she at liberty, she would return my sentiments willingly."

"Have you conversed with Mlle Vallon since we dined with you several weeks ago?"

"Not exactly. As I said, I have called at Sorsten but was not permitted to speak with her. I contrived to send her a note via a servant, and though I do not write French half as well as I ought to, we have managed to say enough to make me confident that she does not wish to marry M. Savard, but fears that he, her cousin and the other lady, will insist."

I thought for a short moment. "I assume your intentions are honourable, Sir, or else you would not have disclosed them to me?"

He nodded.

"Well then, if you are sincere, then you have only to make her an offer. If Mlle Vallon's feelings are as you suspect them to be, then doubtless she will agree to elope with you. Is it in this you would ask for my help? If so then I assure you it is well that you do so, for if you attempted to steal her away without proper verification of upright proceedings, I fear M. Tolouse and I would be forced to apprehend you."

"I assure you there is no reason for any of that," said he with a shudder, "but all the same, it is not so simple. My mother, Sir, you met, and you may perhaps easily understand that she has sworn never to permit me to connect myself with a girl who has less than ten thousand pounds. If I disobey her, she has sworn to disinherit me in favour of my younger brother. All this I have explained to Mlle Vallon, and in turn she has informed me that while her dowry itself is all one might wish, it is no longer in her possession, but instead, entirely in the hands of M. Savard. In view of this, there is little chance he will voluntary consign it to me, once I have deprived him of his bride-to-be. His conduct, heretofore, has not impressed me with the greatest opinion of his rectitude, and the situation in France makes any kind of legal redress seem rather hopeless. You see the predicament I am in!"

"I do, and I am sorry for it, but pray tell me what you ask of me?"

"I hardly know! You seem a man of the world, and as you are a Frenchman I hoped you might have a better idea than I of the possible legal recourse available to me? Is there any hope, in your opinion, that France will soon be at peace, and I might sue to compel M. Savard to restore Mlle Vallon's fortune once she is my wife?"

"As to that, I am certain there is no hope at all. The very foundations of my country are in shambles, and neither wealth nor property are guaranteed to anyone. Each day seems to increase the confusion and uncertainty which prevail there, and any man who does not have gold in his pockets has nothing to hope from the government, or any future one."

"Then it is as I feared! But tell me, dear Sir, as you are the only one who is likely to know, is there nothing which may not have escaped the clutches of M. Savard?"

"Perhaps," replied I, thoughtfully. "It is difficult to say. If you wish, I can look into it further, but I hardly see what consequence it shall be. Even were it possible that Mlle Vallon has a thousand pounds in jewellery and valuables about her, it is all but certain she shall not have ten thousand. What's more, however low your opinion of M. Savard's probity, he may yet surprise you and return her fortune thereafter."

"But if he did not, how would we live? It is not for myself alone that I must settle these questions. I fear, however, that there is little time, for a few days ago I followed a messenger from M. Savard who lead me only a short way from here to a Catholic priest, a Frenchman who has settled in England to escape the revolution. It was this information which prompted my errand, for I called again at Sorsten Manor, only to find you had all recently decamped."

We spoke together for sometime longer, but I do not remember exactly what was said. Mr. Etheredge was too disordered to eat. He was concerned M. Savard intended to marry Mlle Vallon precipitously, and therefore he begged me to return to the Thrush. I told him that little could be done, in any case, unless Mlle Vallon herself refused. Nevertheless I intended to return there anyway, and I told him so. I pledged at that time I would also try to discover what I could regarding Mlle Vallon's fortune.

"I am no great friend to concealment, however," I added, in parting, "and I shall make no secret of your presence in the area. You are free to visit me at the Thrush, and in doing so you might meet with Mlle Vallon."

He thanked me eagerly for what small hope I had given him, and promised to take advantage of the opportunity as soon as may be.

Shortly thereafter I departed the Fox and the Hound to return to the Thrush; though not, I fear without some regret.

I saw none of our party when I returned. Once I was reinstated in my room, I had a short leisure to contemplate the situation of Mlle Vallon and Mr. Etheredge. I did not doubt that she preferred him to M. Savard, and would doubtless be happier with him than the other. But yet I could not help but find Mr. Etheredge's attachment more convenient than unequivocal, and it bothered me somewhat. At last I resolved to make no inquiries of Mlle Vallon at all, and merely inform Mr. Etheredge that he could count on her having two thousand pounds upon marriage. This amount, along with nominal support from his family and whatever she possesses, would allow he and Mlle Vallon to live quite comfortably. If he accepted, I intended to provide the dowry myself and to assist him in any other way possible. If he refused, I would trouble myself no more about it.

Having settled my own conduct, I began to take some notice of my surroundings. I discovered that in my absence my clothes had been mended and arranged, and a new supply of ready money had been placed in my purse. As I was marvelling at these circumstances, I was summoned to the common room for supper.

"Ah M. Gramont," said Mme. Gaspar, at the sight of me, "I am glad to see you. After you and M. Tolouse disappeared yesterday, we had no entertainment from Mouchard in the evening!"

"Then perhaps you meant to say more that you are glad to see Mouchard?"

Mme. Gaspar laughed. "I daresay I should be glad enough to see anybody, as I am so fond of company."

"Then you deny everyone the privilege of particular preference."

"Nay, Monsieur, I see you are in an uncharacteristic mood, but I am sure you know I mean nothing by it."

"Forgive me, dear Madam."

"There is nothing to forgive. M. Savard is none too pleased himself," she continued, in a quieter tone, as he stood near the fireplace a short ways away, "for the innkeeper has insisted on serving us in the main room, as he says it is too inconvenient to accommodate so many in there. M. Savard is distressed to be forced to be eating amongst the common folk, as it were, but for myself I do not mind at all."

All of us sat down together shortly after, save only Mouchard who was somewhere out of sight. Midway though our meal, I said, "I sense that Mouchard is coming to the end of his tale and perhaps we might hear the conclusion of it in a week's time. I have delayed my own departure for several weeks in order that we might hear it together, but alas I fear I can no longer delay my journey. If he has not yet finished in a week, I shall seek to accommodate him with you till he is done, at which time I request that you send him after me. I have become quite attached to him these last weeks, and as M. Savard uses his own servants for translation, I hope this will not cause any inconvenience. I will send my direction when it is established. Perhaps in that case he shall be able to tell me the rest of it someday as we travel, and I shall be called back to these weeks I have spent with my fellow emigres, united by our misfortune."

This announcement was received with general surprise, though relief was evident in more than a few faces when I indicated I meant to leave Mouchard for the time being. Of all, M. Tolouse seemed the most affected and I guessed that he was displeased I had not informed him beforehand, or invited him to accompany me. M. Savard seemed both pleased and relieved, and for the remainder of the evening he treated me with less suspicion and more grace.

Mme. Gaspar seemed genuinely sorry to learn of my departure and expressed herself so. The two young ladies seemed likewise affected by the news, to the degree you might expect.

"While M. Tolouse and I were exploring the area yesterday," continued I, "we encountered Mr. Etheredge, the son of Sir John Etheredge. He was pleased to learn we were nearby, and I invited him to call upon us here if he has the opportunity."

This news likewise had a different affect on its auditors. Mr. Savard's expression showed extreme annoyance, while Mlle Vallon was too much of a noviciate in the world to conceal her pleasure, and the dawn of hope bloomed over her countenance. I took pains to appear to notice none of it, and the remainder of our meal passed in relative silence.

After we finished, our party retired to the ladies' room to hear Mouchard. M. Savard retreated to the other side of the room, his patience likely growing thin with this particular form of entertainment. Mouchard began as follows:

"*After the most* restless night, Mr. Harland awoke and set out for the house at which Mr. and Miss Reckert were staying. His visit was ostensibly for the purpose of restoring Thomas to Miss Reckert, and he was anxious to formulate a method of doing so which would enable him to explain himself to Miss Reckert if it proved impossible to speak to her alone.

He was seen into the study, where he found Mr. Reckert in partial undress, gathering some of his papers.

'Ah, forgive me for receiving you thus, old friend, but I confess to being in a bit of a flutter. Miss Reckert wishes to return home immediately, and I begin to be quite concerned. The change of air does not seem to have agreed with her, and I have always thought sea air to be the least salubrious. I am myself quite responsible, for she has hardly been herself these last few months. I have pressed her to agree to see a physician but she has refused, and only last night she confessed she feels that country air will set her to rights. We are prepared to leave as soon as possible. You must forgive our haste in rushing off, but I am sure you will not wonder to find my apprehension, knowing as you do what a fond old doting fool your friend is. Oh, Thomas, I have scarcely seen you there! Miss Reckert has had much disquiet on your account. Pray, go to her at once, it will do her a world of good. She sees no one at present, but I am sure she will welcome you under any circumstance.'

Thomas went at once, leaving Mr. Harland to search his mind for an exigent which might permit him to explain what apparently seemed to Miss Reckert as unpardonable indifference and neglect.

Miss Reckert's situation was not much more to be envied. She was tired and worn, and most importantly, disappointed in love. She condemned her own folly and repented above all the step which had exposed her partiality to its undeserving object. Under duress, she admitted her feelings and now suffered all the humiliation she had feared. She felt as though she would give almost anything to have her admission undone. She saw herself in Mr. Harland's eyes alternately as an object of pity or derision, and she had sworn to avoid him at all costs. Her disappointment had been of the worst kind; not short or sudden, but prolonged, and inexplicable. And so it was that at a time when she had sustained the greatest disappointment of her life, she was deprived by the same person of the company of her dearest friend, Thomas.

The suspense and misery of the last three months had taken a great toll upon her. At times she feared they had both perished, indeed it often seemed like the most likely explanation for the prolonged uncertainty she endured. This fear was allayed by a word dropped here and there from her father, who corresponded with Mr. Seymour, who had in turn been in touch with Mr. Harland. This reassurance only played new havoc with her emotions; her fears were quieted, but her heart was broken and her pride was mortified.

Her reunion with Thomas was joyful on both sides. Even with her young friend, however, Miss Reckert found it necessary to disguise and dissemble her feelings. After compelling herself to speak calmly about his absence, though with much difficulty, she embraced him fondly again and again, before finally excusing herself to lie down.

An hour or so later, Mr. Reckert sent up word that the carriages were in waiting, and a short time later they were on their way home together; Mr. Harland had reluctantly been obliged to depart the house sometime beforehand, to allow Mr. Reckert to prepare for his departure.

Mr. Reckert was no longer of an age which made travelling convenient, and so it was necessary for them to take three days to complete a journey which might otherwise have taken two.

When they arrived on the third afternoon, they were informed that Mr. Harland had already called upon the night before.

'Ah,' said Mr. Reckert, 'that gentleman is a true friend! I fear he was distressed we were obliged to depart so suddenly. I shall be heartily glad to see him as soon as we are settled. Perhaps we ought to invite him tonight to supper?'

'Not tonight, my dear Papa, I beg you,' replied Miss Reckert, quickly. 'I was hoping to have just a little time amongst ourselves, and I do not feel at all well enough to entertain anyone.'

'As you wish, of course, my dear, though I daresay Mr. Harland is as much like family as one might have. I do believe he was quite distressed to hear of your indisposition. No doubt he has become nearly as fond of you as I am myself. I will write and invite him for tomorrow evening.'

Miss Reckert could think of no adequate excuse to prevent him from doing so, and instead hurried to her room. News of his earlier arrival unavoidably shocked and dismayed her. After a period of three months, during which he had availed himself of no opportunity to contact her, directly or indirectly, following a revelation of the most sensitive nature. For him to pursue her now seemed inconceivable! The most blatant neglect succeeded by unreasonable pursuit like insult piled upon insult. The reason behind it she could hardly conceive. Did he wish suddenly to trifle with her? Was his purpose in coming to reconcile her to his indifference; to belatedly offer to soften the pain of her disappointment? The idea was unbearable.

Gradually a still more disturbing possibility began to take shape in her mind. It occurred to her that Mr. Harland had seen Mr. Seymour in Brighton. As one of their subjects was most certainly marital considerations, the possibility that Mr. Harland had himself been disappointed in his first choice now occurred to her. In this circumstance, his current pursuit might now be explained if she were herself considered a consolation or an afterthought. The mere thought was a torment to one whose heart was as tender as it was proud.

The more she considered this tortuous question, the more she felt that no other possibility could so adequately explain how silence and neglect could so suddenly give way to pursuit and persecution. How she wept with sheer anger and vexation! Her torment was extreme to think that Mr. Harland might have so much mistaken her character as to think she would mildly suffer the indignity, the humiliation of pity and resignation in place of true regard. She thought back to his words that fateful night and her certainty wavered. Almost as quickly she recalled the duties of Mr. Seymour.

'How could I have been so foolish,' she cried, 'to expose myself to a man who is so mercenary, so ambitious, that his sole reason for marriage is wealth and connection. And now I see why he has returned! My love he scorns, but my wealth he shall accept, as long as there is no better offer. Ah, heartless man! Upon what a worthless object have I bestowed my foolish heart; and to what has its deluded longings reduced me!'

It was at this very juncture that a letter arrived from Mr. Harland. Miss Reckert had no sooner received it than she screamed and dropped it. For nearly an hour she sat weeping and staring at it from a distance, as if it held all that was at once dear and repulsive to her in the world.

At last she said in a weak voice, 'Take it, dear Thomas, take it whence it comes, and tell him I scorn to read a line of it–. Wait, stay, do not. From anger one might read affection, and that I can never again suffer him to suspect. Tell him, nay, tell him nothing but return it to him. Promise you shall relate nothing of this? Have I not still your loyalty, however debased an object I might seem at present? But perhaps you do not understand all. It is my hope.'

Thomas kissed her hand, and signalled he would do as she wished. He slipped into the other house with no difficulty at all, being easily admitted into either house, where all were used to his comings and goings. He made his way immediately to the gentleman's study, where he contrived to leave the returned letter on the desk in plain view, and evade potential interrogation. In order to ensure it was properly received, he concealed himself in a corner thereafter to await Mr. Harland's entrance. Not long afterwards that gentleman appeared. At the sight of the letter, he sighed deeply, placing his hand upon his head, remaining for a long time lost in the most unsatisfactory contemplations.

The next evening Miss Reckert did not appear at supper, sending word she was indisposed and would dine in her room. Mr. Reckert was genuinely concerned at this news, and acknowledged it openly to his friend. Mr. Harland, who knew all too well the cause of her absence, experienced great uneasiness on every possible account, and hardly knew how to conduct himself.

For the next few days he attempted in vain to avail himself of some opportunity to speak to Miss Reckert. Her pride, anger and sensibility combined most powerfully against him. The study of her existence became to avoid the pain and embarrassment which would certainly be occasioned by even the sight of him. However weak she had shown herself to be in her admiration, she was determined to demonstrate by her future conduct that her fault was more than corrected.

On the second day of her return, she called upon Miss Lawrence. They had only a short visit, as Miss Lawrence was going out, but two days later, Miss Lawrence returned her visit, and the two ladies set out upon a walk.

During Miss Reckert's absence, construction had continued at full pace on the unlicensed site of the future town. Miss Lawrence suggested they walk in that direction to see how the work got on. Much has been accomplished in those short months, and there were now more than a dozen cottages finished or nearly so, alongside several larger and smaller buildings, perhaps destined to be shops and the like.

The workers did not take too much notice of them, but it was evident all the same that they did not welcome observation. Miss Reckert and Miss Lawrence passed by quickly. Upon their return, they espied Mr. Harland walking towards them in the distance. Miss Reckert had purposely guided their path along the woods to enable them to avoid such an encounter should it be necessary, and now with an urgency she scarcely bothered to conceal, she urged Miss Lawrence that they take another way.

'Perhaps you would like to return with me?' said Miss Lawrence, 'It has been so long since we have spoken, and I should greatly welcome the chance to visit longer with you.'

Miss Reckert agreed at once and hardly lessened her pace until she was safely lodged in Miss Lawrence's chamber.

'Dearest Miss Reckert,' said Miss Lawrence, with a kind smile, 'since the beginning of our friendship, I cannot help but notice that the presence of that gentleman has always caused you extreme distress. May I be so bold as to bespeak a wish to someday learn what it is about Mr. Harland that so distresses you?'

Miss Reckert only sighed and Miss Lawrence continued.

'It has been my observation that one only avoids those who inspire them with strong emotions. Though Miss Reckert has so many admirers, if I may judge by the exchange I witnessed on one occasion, I did not believe Mr. Harland is one of her slaves–.'

Miss Reckert sighed again, unavoidably.

'But I confess,' continued Miss Lawrence, 'that if he is an object of your antipathy, I cannot guess the reason. Forgive me, I do not mean to pry, and I will try to suppress my curiosity. But tell me if you would avoid Mr. Harland, how is it you hope to do so while he is so intimately connected with your household?'

Miss Reckert raised her eyes and hands to heaven to indicate her desperation, but yet only shook her head in answer.

Miss Lawrence thought for a short while before saying, 'How much I wish it was within my power to afford you some respite! I would be overjoyed to have you stay here with us, but considering how strangely both my mother and uncle can behave, it would be hard for you to accept, I fear. Still less, if my brother were to return home–.'

'Dearest Miss Lawrence?' cried Miss Reckert, 'if you are in earnest, I should accept the offer with joy!'

'Indeed!' replied Miss Lawrence, raising her eyebrows with surprise. 'Of course you may rely upon my sincerity, for I should never have spoken otherwise, but you astonish me extremely. Can you so quickly resign yourself to bearing my mother's capriciousness, and the ominous and eccentric behaviour of my uncle?'

'Miss Lawrence's company shall make up for all,' replied Miss Reckert, not at all dissuaded. 'In any case, your mother has been almost welcoming to me these last weeks. Tell me only when it is convenient for me to come, and I shall be more than happy to stay as long as you will have me.'

Miss Lawrence laughed again. 'I suppose I have Mr. Harland to thank for my good fortune, and so I find I am more obliged to him than some. Is tomorrow too soon?'

'I am indebted to you,' returned the other.

As soon as matters were settled, Miss Reckert departed in order to speak to her father and pack her things once more to leave. She and Thomas walked home together.

'Come, my dear friend,' said she, 'do not trail so far behind me today, as I would like to speak to you. Certainly you heard what passed between Miss Lawrence and I, and know better than any the reason for it. I do not like to part from you so soon after we have been reunited, but it cannot be helped. Moreover, I cannot help but reflect that very soon you will be a man and it will not be so permissible for you and I to always be together in the same way we have till now. Over the last few weeks, I have had much time to contemplate these things. It is now high time some provision should be made for your future life. I have spoken to my father and he has promised you shall have whatever support required to establish you in comfort, but first you must be settled somehow. The army is out of the question, and though you are certainly suited to the church by disposition, I feel it would be difficult for you to develop the oratorical skills needed for a Pastor. For a trade, I fear you are unequal to the bodily exertion required, and I could hardly bear to see you toiling away after how I have raised you. And so by the process of elimination, I have arrived at several possible areas. But before I go any further, my dearest friend, tell me if you have ever given the subject much thought? Certainly you are apt to know your predilections better than I?'

Thomas was reluctant to speak, as his heart was heavy on the occasion, having long had a foreboding of their impending separation.

'If I am to leave you, dearest Miss Reckert, I would wish you to choose for me. You have ever been as a mother to me, and so I would have you continue.'

It was perhaps the longest speech he had ever made to her, and Miss Reckert stopped in sheer amazement. Tears started in her eyes as she embraced him. 'Ah, I am not wrong. You would make yourself a boy forever to stay with me, but inside you are becoming a man. We shall say no more about it at present, but I shall think upon the matter carefully, as there is nothing more vital to my happiness than your establishment.'

The rest of the way was travelled together in a sad silence.

Mr. Reckert had no objection to his daughter's plan to stay with the Lawrences, but was exceedingly surprised to hear it proposed so soon, being as he was in such general uneasiness for her health.

Early the next morning, Mrs. Lawrence sent a formal invitation along with a wish that she join them that morning for breakfast, and by ten o'clock, Miss Reckert was officially established with that family.

Mr. Harland heard the news of her retreat when he paid his daily visit that afternoon. His despair at hearing it was great. His acquaintance with the Lawrences was slight at best, and as he had been unable to speak even so much as a word to Miss Reckert while she had lived at a house in which he was intimate and always welcome, he was completely at a loss to fathom how he would begin to attempt it.

'Forgive me, Sir,' said he to Mr. Reckert, 'I am not quite myself. There is a matter I should like to discuss with you, but I fear I am in need of some time to put my thoughts in order before doing so. May I hope to call upon you again in a few hours?'

'My doors are ever open to you, dear friend,' said Mr. Reckert. 'I am sorry to see something is weighing upon your mind, and shall look forward to the opportunity of assisting you.'

After an interval of two or three hours, Mr. Harland returned. Once the two friends sat down together, he said, 'Forgive me, dear Sir. This is not the easiest subject to broach, for it is a matter of some delicacy. In essence, I wish to know how you should like me for a son-in-law, if I could dare aspire to that honour?'

'Good Heavens!' cried Mr. Reckert. 'As a son I have always thought of you, but as a son-in-law is impossible!'

'Because you should wish it so?' said Mr. Harland.

'I? Heavens, no! Were it my choice alone, I could think of no better match, regardless of any effect it should have upon our pursuit of the Abeyance. I say 'our,' as it is a liberty I allow myself on account of the many years I have wished it.'

'I needed no such explanation, for you have been equally concerned in the matter as Mr. Seymour or I.'

'Then as I was saying, the father in me would trump the politician, and nothing would make me happier than the thought that my daughter was cared for after my death by my dearest friend in life. However this might be, you of all people know I would never compel her to marry anyone, and I do not know how to imagine she would select to do such a thing herself, if you forgive me for saying so directly.'

'But you would not prohibit the attempt?'

'The attempt? Of course I would not, but come my dear Sir, think better of it. What good does it come for you or I to dwell upon something which is a remote possibility at best? Think only of the men she has refused, and do not waste your time pursuing the chimera of an idea. Though she is my daughter, I can think of no woman more whimsical in such matters! I did not always anticipate the difficulty in settling her, but such days are passed, and now I must advise you to give up all idea of it.'

'When was that, if I may ask?'

'Why these two or three years, I think. I do not know if you knew her much then, but never did a girl seem more likely to be easily settled. I thought at the time that I had only to speak and compel her to choose. 'She is still so young, now,' thought I, when I was tempted to do so, 'there shall be plenty of time!' But who could have foreseen the change wrought upon her?'

'Impossible!' declared Mr. Harland, who spoke more to himself than Mr. Reckert.

'Yes, indeed, but now as matters stand, how can you consider something so futile? Forgive my directness.'

'I hardly know!' cried Mr. Harland, 'but I cannot think of giving it up.'

'How little I expected this!' returned the other. 'And yet I ought to have foreseen it. I ought to have remembered you are not an old man like me, nor her father. As I have said, I should never fault the attempt, but I cannot help but counsel against it. Your experience these last months ought to have convinced you it was so. But perhaps you have gained some insight into her character which even her father lacks? Did you not write that you meant to make one last attempt to speak with her before you went to Belgium? Did something occur which you have not told me? I trust you would not have pressed your suit then?'

'I had no thought of it. Whatever insight I may have gained has been squandered. Our conversation then has led to a misunderstanding between us, and at present I do not believe Miss Reckert will speak to me.'

'Not speak to you?!' Mr. Reckert exclaimed, 'My dear Sir, and with this encouragement you hope to begin your suit?'

'I cannot explain myself better.'

'Then I suppose I must be satisfied. I have known you too long to doubt your honour. In the meantime, attempt to take my advice and think no more of this.'

'I cannot, but I have at least satisfied my conscience in speaking openly to you.'

With this he bowed and took leave, leaving Mr. Reckert to mull over such a strange and unexpected development.

The following day, Mr. Seymour arrived in the area to stay with Mr. Harland. He had reportedly been surprised by the abruptness of that gentleman's departure from Brighton, and followed to discuss some little details relating to what he had hitherto considered a most promising marital treatise begun while Mr. Harland was in Belgium.

He had scarcely been in the area for three days when he came to say good-bye to Mr. Reckert. His host invited him to take tea with him before he set off, and the other accepted without scruple.

'I am sorry to see you are leaving so soon,' said Mr. Reckert, when they had sat down, 'for I had promised myself the pleasure of your company for several weeks to come.'

'To own the truth I had intended to stay much longer myself, but I no longer know how I should occupy myself here for so long. Mr. Harland has lost his mind, and is intent upon squandering all of my toil so far. I have told him I do not mean to take up knitting, and so I shall depart since there is nothing else for me to do.'

'Do you mean to say you have resigned your duties, Sir?'

'It is better to say that Mr. Harland himself has obviated the better part of them, and who can stand to be so used?'

'But surely you do not mean to depart forever?'

'Of that I cannot speak properly now, for a man should not say 'never' when he is hot, but at the moment I can hardly say yes. I will not say more, in consideration to yourself, but it will suffice to say I will ask you to convey my regards to Miss Reckert. I will not risk conveying them myself, for fear I too will take leave of my senses!'

Although this last remark was sheer hyperbole, Mr. Reckert thought it was highly prudent.

'And where do you intend to go at present?'

'Of that, I do not rightly know, but there is much that I have wished to do. For the time being, at least, I consider myself very much the master of my own time, with no pupil to instruct and no other affairs to manage. Let us only hope my pocketbook will withstand my freedom!'

'Have you settled your accounts with Mr. Harland, Sir?'

'I had not the patience to do so, Sir, but no matter.'

'I hope you have not quarrelled much?'

'No indeed, but I daresay he was happy enough to see me depart.

A fool in love wants no advice from those who can see clearly, and I wash my hands of it all.'

A short time later, Mr. Seymour departed."

By this time it was quite late, and Mouchard halted. For the first time I thought Mouchard himself seemed anxious to continue, but M. Savard had begun to put his head in every few minutes or so, compelling him to stop. Thereafter we all repaired to bed, reluctantly enough!

This packet is large enough to be sent by itself. I pray you read it with pleasure, dear friend. I have tried to faithfully retell Mouchard's story, as much as possible, and I trust it has afforded you and our friends some entertainment.

Yours,
M.C.

Marcel de la Croix to Henri Renault

February 17th, 1793

Dear Friend,

This morning when we awoke, we found that M. Savard had taken the ladies somewhere quite early. M. Tolouse and I could not help wondering at it, but no doubt we shall find out presently.

While we wait, I am at my leisure and shall give you some more of my history, which is fast coming to a close:

Our whole enterprise wore a new face on the day following the revelation of the flight and capture of Louis. The King was not worthy of service and was presumably being kept prisoner in Paris.

M. Montrond emerged again among us the following day as M. Lafont and I, along with some of the more prominent members of the league sat down to a midday meal. He looked hardly more rested than before.

'What news, dear Marquis, I beg you?'

'The King and Queen are returned to Paris, and everyone assumes they will be imprisoned there.'

'But what of the events which led up to this capture? Had they no escort at all?'

'General Bouille's armies were said to be in the region around that time, and the countryside is wild with reports. Even some say that the King and Queen escaped, but that is certainly not the truth.'

'General Bouille?' repeated he with surprise. 'Why then I see that if only he had met them, we should not have been needed.'

He lapsed into silence. He had been silent but a minute or two when M. Lafont said,

'What is next, M. Montrond, for there can be no reason now to conceal your name. What is to be done?'

'I fear there is nothing to be done. All is lost.'

'May I ask what you intend to do yourself,' said I. 'Do you intend to stay here or return to Paris?'

'Neither,' replied he, 'I can do nothing either here or in Paris. There is no avenue open to me, or if I may say, to any of us, but to flee the Country as fast as we may.'

'I suppose nothing better ought to be expected from the King's Minister,' said Lafont, 'if even the King flees like a coward.'

M. Montrond managed a weak smile, 'Whatever you please to call it, M. Lafont, it was the last chance to resist this revolution. Surrounded and threatened by the mobs in Paris, his Majesty had no recourse but to attempt to launch a true counter-strike from elsewhere.'

'What can be done for the Royal Family? Are they to be left to the mercy of the crowds?' inquired M. Bretal.

'Perhaps Marie-Antoinette's family might manage something,' said M. Montrond with a sigh. 'I fear their fate is sealed. Monsieur le Marquis,' said he, turning to me, 'I owe you the most profound gratitude for the service you have rendered me, which I cannot help but wish to repay. Let me do so now with the only currency of any value in my possession, poor as it may seem: unsolicited advice. It was from the leaders of the Third Estate that I first heard of 'The League of the Star,' as it seems you have come to be called, by virtue of the scars given you by M. Hubert. Your name and the name of M. Lafont are well-known amongst those who shall be the most to be feared in times to come. The bounty on your heads is quite large, and shall perhaps grow larger if you remain. You may be safe in this fortress for several more months, but you have here but two-hundred men, and in a country gone mad, where armies of one-hundred and fifty-thousand men or more shall be at your enemies' disposal, I advise you to look to a time in the near future when another course might become necessary.'

'For myself,' declared M. Lafont, 'I shall neither stir, nor rest till I have killed M. Hubert. King and revolution alike be damned!'

'As to M. Hubert,' said M. Montrond, turning from M. Lafont again to me, 'I confess that he remains somewhat of an enigma. In the hopes of obliging you I attempted to gather whatever information upon him was available from my sources, but I regret to confess there was very little to be had.'

M. Montrond left the Chateau the next day with little more than some travelling money and the clothes on his back. I offered to escort him as far as he wished, but he said that as he was merely one rider, he was confident he could avoid any trouble. He intended to travel to the border of the Austrian-Netherlands by the shortest route possible. There he intended to seek an audience with Marie-Antoinette's brother, Leopold II, before making any further plans. He repeated his thanks and his warnings upon taking leave.

M. Montrond's open warnings and subsequent departure, combined with the desperate situation of the King, had an immediate effect on the members of the League who then lived at the Chateau. Till that time most of us, myself included, had cherished the hope of outlasting and even helping to defeat the revolutionaries. No one now entertained this hope, and the victory of our enemies was all but assured.

After the King's flight, any man among us who had connections or house of refuge in other Countries, prepared to depart. Even those who knew no one outside France chose to take their chances alone and friendless in other lands. I would not be surprised if some of those who left joined the ranks of those we fought, nor would I have judged them harshly for doing so.

The week following M. Montrond's departure, more than one-hundred of our men left together, intending to pursue the same path. Either in sizeable groups or one or two at a time, all but fifty or so of our men departed the Chateau in the short weeks following Louis' disastrous attempt to escape Paris.

This reversal in fortune had a substantial effect on M. Lafont's temperament and disposition. No longer did he possess the light-hearted humour which had endeared him to many. He rarely smiled, endlessly brooding and meditating on the destruction of M. Hubert, which never ceased to be in his thoughts.

From the time of Louis' flight, my disillusionment had been complete. The thought of the quiet dignity evinced by the revolutionary guard I had reluctantly fought and killed in defence of M. Montrond haunted me when I was alone. In the same situation again, I should act the same, yet regret was inevitable. The general exodus which followed had been a relief to me. I no longer wished to know M. Lafont, or be complaisant in his violence. I saw how greatly I had erred and despised the inherent weakness in my character.

The thought of making some kind of atonement for my sins first occurred to me here. I instructed Philip to make any discreet inquiries he could into the name of the guard I had killed, and any family he had left behind. At the same time I instructed him to make good any money which remained to me, by any means necessary. To my surprise I found that he had done so already, and many months back when travel and mail were less restricted, he had sent the bulk of my fortune to England in small increments, to be converted into English currency and stored with different banking houses. In livres, I had enough ready money to last some more months and added to this I had a collection of stones and jewels which might enable me to travel.

For the first time since the fire, I rejoiced to think my wealth had been preserved and might somehow enable me to make partial amends to those I had wronged. I expressed to Philip some part of what I meant to do, in my enthusiasm, and he merely shrugged and sighed.

Several days following this, I heard a knock on my chamber door in the late morning. When I opened it, I found it was Joseph, who begged to have a word with me. I let him in readily and with very little preamble, he said,

'I have never considered myself a rat or a spy, but the Lord knows I owe you much more than I owe Lafont, and I should consider myself ungrateful if I could keep from you anything I thought you had a particular right to know. I shall leave it up to you, for 'tis sure that you know best. 'Twill suffice to say I overheard somewhat last night I did not think right to keep to myself.'

'If you mean to tell me something of Lafont you think I ought to hear, I am ready to do so.'

He bowed and began as follows. 'Last evening I fell asleep as usual in the main hall by the fire. Sometime later I awoke at the unusual sound of hushed voices in conversation. If the voices had remained at the usual pitch, no doubt I should have slept on, but as it was, I heard Lafont say:

'La Croix has not the stomach for such enterprises, and would oppose even the death of M. Hubert if it was not to be done neatly. We have no time for pretty measures, however, and we have no longer anywhere near the men needed to take him by force. Mark my words, this dog shall die, and if I have my way, he shall die in flame, along with anyone who knows or befriends him.'

In short, Joseph revealed that M. Lafont had outlined the following plan: He had learnt that some representatives of the Third Estate intended to visit M. Hubert two days hence. To receive them, M. Hubert and others were to take possession of an old estate in Troyes, where they and their families would meet. To avoid calling any attention to their activities, the meeting was to be described as a merely social event. By all indications, the purpose of the meeting was to attempt to align the conduct of rural leaders of the movement with the aims of those who sat upon the National Assembly, and represented the revolutionary movement in Paris.

The intended location was a fortified mansion thirty miles from the Chateau. It had only two entrances and was constructed of old close stone, with batailler instead of windows for the first two floors. Lafont maintained it was well known the League had substantially diminished in numbers, and was no longer considered the threat it once was. He believed there were unlikely to be many men guarding the house, known as Gironde. His information indicated their main forces would be stationed about half a league away, ready to be summoned if needs be. For this reason, M. Lafont proposed a simple brutal strategy for killing the guards, blocking the doors and lighting the fire within by a volley of ignited arrows.

It shall not be difficult to imagine my horror and dismay to hear of such a plan. I demanded to know how his plan was received by the men he spoke to and he replied that they seemed neither to welcome nor abhor it, but were willing to accede to it in the understanding they would be rewarded.

I shuddered inwardly to hear it. I thanked him for this intelligence, and assured him I was very happy to have been informed. By this time I was no longer surprised to find that Lafont considered the death of untold numbers, including the families who would be present, immaterial when they ensured him the revenge he sought.

It was morning of the day before this plot was slated for. I sat by myself for an hour or more, considering every possible method of averting this act, and pondering the varying consequences of success or failure. I will not describe to you now all the various exigencies which occurred to me, but in the end I could decide on nothing but action itself, whatever the consequences.

I went immediately in search of Philip, to whom I gave hasty instructions regarding my general wishes, should I not return. Taking no company with me and no counsel at all, I packed a small bag of provisions and weapons, and headed in the direction of Gironde on horseback. It was then the middle of the afternoon.

I was in a frenzy, a type of madness. I felt no anger, but a species of unguided determination wherein prudence has no part. Gironde was three hours away by horse.

As I rode, I attempted to create a plan of sorts, but nothing came to me and still I went on. I had travelled by field for the most part, but now joined the main road. After several minutes, I beheld a horseman coming towards me, and presently I could see it was a messenger. I saw no reason to avoid him, and he hailed me as he approached.

'Forgive me, Sir, but I am a messenger from Gironde,' he said. 'Permit me to ask if you are Mr. Joivanity, for if so, you will save me the trouble of travelling to the next inn.'

I answered him in the negative, and he continued on with apparent disappointment. It was raining lightly and I travelled a good ways without pausing till at last I emerged from behind a tree-line and beheld the house in the distance. I stopped for several minutes, attempting to formulate a plan of conduct. Try as I might, I could not think clearly and the longer I waited, the more I risked doing nothing.

I moved a little further along the road, but presently I could see torch lights shining in the dusk, and realized there was a guard station a short way ahead of me.

After a brief deliberation I left the road and crossed the little expanse of field, presently reaching the small lane which led to the house, on the other side of the post. As I drew closer I could see that the old fortress had been altered into almost a delicate home, surrounded by fountains, gardens and hedges.

About thirty yards from the house, there was a second post where two guards were stationed on horseback. They were the same age as myself, which is to say they were still rather young by most standards. I had no torch with me, so I was rather close before they saw me.

'What is your business?' cried the first man.

'Your name and purpose,' called out the other.

Though they were wary, they seemed neither surprised nor alarmed to see me approach.

'I wish to speak to M. Hubert,' said I, ignoring the second request.

'You must give us your name and papers, Sir,' said the second man again. He was preparing to say something else, but at that moment a man issued from the front door of the house and hastened towards us.

'M. Siecle,' said the second of the two guards, 'this gentleman wishes to speak to M. Hubert, but has not given his name.'

'I have no business with any but M. Hubert,' repeated I, 'and I must speak to him this moment.'

'Patience, dear Sir,' said M. Siecle, 'For that may be easily arranged, yet you of all people must appreciate the need for caution in such matters,' looked at me knowingly. 'Pray give us your name, good Sir?'

I stared at him a long moment, but recalling the name used by the messenger I had passed, I said at last:

'I understand you have been expecting M. Joivanity, Sir,' not concealing the disdain I felt, but unwilling to claim the name myself. 'Am I mistaken?'

'No, no, Monsieur, believe me,' replied M. Siecle, beginning to appear seriously concerned at my displeasure. 'We expected you here even yesterday, and have sent a messenger to inquire after you only this afternoon. And yet I understand there is much for you to do in Paris.'

'I wish to speak to M. Hubert,' said I, once more.

'Yes, indeed,' replied he, motioning for me to follow him to the house. 'I am far from wishing to prevent you, and have no desire to know any affairs of state, yet there is a small circumstance I must acquaint you with before you speak to him.'

Saying this he motioned for me to follow him and led me into a small disordered parlour which had been hastily converted into a study of sorts.

'It may seem ostentatious to have placed guards at the gate and then again near the house,' said he, 'but we have reason for our precautions. I assure you the intent was neither to annoy or offend you, as we are extremely pleased that you and others have desired to meet with us.'

I did not reply but merely continued surveying the mess of books and papers scattered over the floor and surfaces.

'You are anxious to speak with M. Hubert, I know, but I beg leave to speak with you for a moment beforehand, that I might prepare you for any oddities you might encounter.'

At this I turned again to look at him, struck by the word 'oddities' and the entire deportment of that gentleman, which bespoke fear and nervousness.

'Oddities,' repeated I. 'What do you mean by this? Explain yourself.'

'I assure you it was what I meant to do from the start, if you will only be patient for a moment or two. First let me say that aside from yourself and the other esteemed patriots in Paris, there are few heroes of the revolution who may compare with M. Hubert. I have no doubt that our children will sing songs of him. In word and deed, he is like–.'

'I want no eulogies for the man unless he is dead,' said I, growing impatient again and fearing he meant to go on like this forever.

'Quite right, quite right, forgive me. As I was saying, it is an unfortunate truth that as great a hero as M. Hubert is, his heroism to the cause has not come entirely without a price. Like so many of our people, M. Hubert has suffered at the hands of the tyrant lords, who have preyed upon our people.'

'Speak clearly and to be understood,' replied I.

'Forgive me, Sir, for it is a secret I have guarded well and one does not speak such with the greatest ease and fluency. M. Hubert is at times prone to strange fits and humours, of which I would first warn you ere you speak to him. In such times he might seem somewhat incomprehensible, or despairing, but most often they pass quickly. I assure you that in all other respects, M. Hubert is the most capable leader imaginable, whose very deportment wins the loyalty of the many patriots who follow him.'

For several moments, surprise deprived me of all power of utterance. Mistaking the reason for my silence, M. Siecle said, 'I shall try your patience no further, Sir, and if you should wish, I shall take you to M. Hubert this minute. He is now collecting his thoughts in the garden.'

'Stay a moment,' said I, raising my hand to prevent him from proceeding. 'You have alluded to the cause of the distemper you describe, but you have said nothing of the exact circumstances.'

'I did not wish to tire you, Monsieur, but if you will wait but a minute or two more, I shall satisfy you as best I may. Even to myself, M. Hubert's exact history and extraction are a mystery. I have gleaned at least that his mother was English and his father French–.' and with that he told me the following story, which I no longer remember in his words.

At home in either country, M. Hubert at last settled in England and decided to marry an English woman like his mother. The rank and wealth of his bride were inferior to his own and it became necessary for him to return to France and reside upon his paternal estate. Fearing how his mother's family might receive the news, he sent his new bride ahead of him to France, proposing to join her in a very short time. For whatever reason and under what circumstances I do not know, the young woman fell ill upon her journey. By some mismanagement or other, she was taken to a small cottage in her illness. She was travelling by coach, which was dismissed for want of use. The servant who attended her could not be accommodated within the cottage, and so left in the carriage, with her mistress' money and belongings. It is not known how long Mme. Hubert suffered or under what circumstances she stayed there. M. Hubert searched for her in vain, but having no knowledge of her illness nor what misfortune had befallen her, he could discover nothing of her. At last, after a tireless search up and down the route she was to take, he heard of an unknown woman who had died in a cottage nearby after suffering an illness of several weeks. In despair he sought out the cottagers to hear an account of her. The remains of her clothing served to confirm her identity, while her body had been laid to rest in a simple grave nearby. M. Hubert's rage and despair were extreme. He loaded the poor cottagers with curses and blamed them for allowing her to perish without proper care and assistance. The cottagers protested that they had not money enough to pay any physician who came, but that they had sent messages begging for help to all of the noble houses in the area. Not one of them replied or offered help. The cottagers themselves hardly had enough to live upon, and what poor care they could give to the young Mme. Hubert was insufficient.

'Few minds could withstand such an ordeal entirely unaffected,' said M. Siecle, 'and knowing of his history, I trust you will know how to excuse any eccentricities he betrays. Perhaps it is unnecessary to add that it is for this reason he orchestrated such inspired revenge upon the families in that area. I am certain you join with me in admiring the brilliance of this first strike, however it might be said that his benign mercy to a few has caused some inconvenience hereabouts. And now, Monsieur, pray follow me.'

With that I was taken into the garden. We walked a short ways till presently I could see a figure I took for M. Hubert passing about in a small arbour, sometimes talking, sometimes singing to himself.

As we drew nearer he seemed to fall silent. I thought at first that it was owing to our approach, but I discovered presently that he had fallen into a trance-like state and was staring ahead of himself, deep in thought.

M. Siecle stopped before one of the entryways and bowed.

'Forgive me, M. Hubert, but there is someone here who has travelled a long way to speak with you.'

M. Hubert did not move or look in our direction. He was a man of approximately five and thirty, perhaps even as much as forty. His hair was raven black, and hung around his face, unkempt. I looked hard at him in the fading light, trying to be sure I had found the man I sought. I was not long in suspense, for his very presence seemed to cause a knot in my stomach.

M. Siecle repeated his request, but again it went unheeded. At last, after a minute or two more in silence, M. Hubert turned his head to look at me. The act itself was unnerving, for his way of moving was so fluid and precise, that it was alarming even when anticipated. He made no acknowledgement of M. Siecle, but looked at me with the long cold stare of a wild animal. Then slowly and even more unexpectedly, he smiled.

'M. Hubert, I have brought M. Joivanity to speak with you.'

I did not bow. Even were he not the murderer of my entire family, I would as soon bow my head to a lion or a wolf.

M. Hubert smiled slightly more, yet it was a mirthless, unnatural smile. M. Siecle shrugged his shoulders and took his leave with a slight bow, seeming to say to me that he had given me fair warning, and was now content to leave us to ourselves.

Once he had gone, M. Hubert continued to regard me calmly with the same expression. I did not choose to be the one to break the silence, for however intelligent he seemed at the moment, his air spoke of unpredictability. I had hardly expected to have come this far without effort and I was still forming in my mind the most basic outline of a plan.

After what seemed like an eternity, M. Hubert turned and said, 'Tell me, Monsieur, will you join me in a drink?'

I shook my head slightly as he poured himself a drink. 'You must help me with a mystery. I have heard it is M. Lafont who follows my every move and is bent upon destroying me. And yet by description and memory, it is Marcel de La Croix who calls upon me, is it not?'

I did not speak, struck dumb by his words.

'La Croix, La Croix,' said he, lightly to himself, 'a cross not a rose, a rose not a star, alas, alas...'

I remained silent in shock, but after a moment or two, I recovered to say, 'If you know who I am, you have no doubt guessed my purpose, and therefore I cannot help wonder you did not reveal it to M. Siecle?'

He turned away with an expression of scorn. 'And do you think I should flee you, a mere boy in years? He has no doubt warned you that I am growing mad, but I assume he has not given me out to be a coward, needing the protection of an old man? You are obtuse, while I am only insane. The irony is not lost upon me.'

He started humming, pacing around, his neck craned up at the evening sky.

'Well then,' said he, after an unnerving interval wherein I was completely at a loss what to do. 'Do you intend to kill me, or shall I return to my fatal deliberations?' He sighed a heavy sigh, then drank from one of the glasses he had been alternating absent-mindedly, as in a game of chance. Wine, apparently, for it had no effect. 'Really, Monsieur de la Croix, I pity you, for you have come to kill me, just when I want it most. A lunatic is not long in charge of the fate of men, and I do not need an untouched mind to see the inevitable. A man who has committed many sins, Monsieur, nevertheless shrinks from self-dispatch. One does not like to commit the sin which will take him at once to his judge. Three nights in a row I have come here with this intent, and now today I find God has sent me an assistant. But come, let us have no more talk. If you mean to kill me, be not long about it, or perhaps we shall both be disappointed.'

'Kill you I must,' said I, after a long moment, 'but I should rather do so when I could be sure you are in your right mind.'

'That I shall never be again. But come, let us waste no time.'

'If you are willing to face me like a gentleman,' proceeded I, 'I shall take my chances with fate, and can ask nothing more. I have two pistols with me. I also wear a sword, if you would prefer.'

'Your pistols shall suit me,' replied M. Hubert, and scarcely waiting a moment, he stalked out across the field. He walked swiftly, and I was forced to sprint to catch up with him. He remained several paces ahead as we walked, and light rain continued to fall as we made our way through fields and ditches.

At last he stopped and turned around wearily.

'Let us rest for a moment under this tree, and then we shall see how fate shall treat with me,' said he, sitting down on a stump. I followed his lead, and we rested for a time, during which he lapsed into insensibility.

After some minutes he sighed and looked around. After a moment or two, he turned to me with a more apologetic look and said, 'Tell me, comrade, why are we encamped here, and with so little equipment? Are we ahead or behind our fellows, for I hear no sounds of activity in any direction?'

He paused and looked at me but I did not respond, struggling to think what I ought to do under the circumstances. My dismay was heightened by the knowledge that M. Hubert would very soon be missed, and sought for. At last I said, 'Neither.'

Rather than pursuing his inquiry, he seemed to forget that he had made it, and sat down again on a stump nearby.

'I cannot recall when we last served together,' said he, presently, 'and I fear I can no longer remember the name of every man I have fought alongside. You are a young man,' continued he, 'yet you have already the bearing of a true soldier. Tell me, friend, are you not like me, a voluntary member of the Third Estate? Your gilded sword and tarnished buttons announce you for a Nobleman, though your deportment makes their testimony unnecessary. And do you believe so deeply in fraternity, liberty and equality that you would hazard your life and give up your own native privileges to raise up your fellow man?'

I was sullen in silence. His question very nearly framed what my sentiments might have been, had not his own actions interfered to change my destiny. I sighed and he seemed to interpret my silence favourably.

'Forgive my loquacity,' said he, 'but I feel somehow akin with you, and time draws near where I may no longer have the opportunity to pass along the wisdom I have gained. Give your heart to the revolution, young man, and be ready to give your life, but do not be persuaded to give your soul. Conscience is a delicate guide, and without it all men are debased.'

He was silent and I felt the truth of his words. The image of the man I had reluctantly destroyed appeared before my eyes.

'What is your name, Monsieur?' said he, a moment later.

'Marcel de La Croix,' replied I, without hesitation.

At the sound of my name, he brought his hand to his brow and a shadow passed over his face. He breathed a deep sigh and mumbled to himself. 'La Croix, La Croix, a cross, not a rose, alas, alas...'

'I am myself again,' said he, after a long interval. 'Give me the weapon and let us measure the distance.'

I did not move or reply, lost in thought.

'Come, be quick!' said he, 'There is no time to waste.'

Still I did not move, reluctant to do what my whole being repelled at and kill a man who was no longer possessed of his senses.

Reading my thoughts, his eyes flashed with anger as he cried, 'I spit on thy pity, Monsieur le Marquis. Do not forget that I have killed thy family, and were you to fail to avenge them, they would load curses upon you from heaven.'

Still I hesitated. The acts I had committed or enabled M. Lafont to commit, weighed heavily upon me. While I deliberated, M. Hubert took possession of the leather case containing the pistols. Beginning to load one, he cried, 'I defy your pity, and if you refuse to fight me, I will give you reason to repent it.'

He loaded both pistols methodically then offered me choice.

I received one from him reluctantly, but as he prepared to count the paces I said, 'M. Hubert, I have never killed a man who had not his whole wits about him.'

'Fifteen paces. By rights you have the first shot. If you give up that right, I shall not hesitate to take advantage of the opportunity. Walk!'

I could not refuse and having walked fifteen paces, I turned around to face him. His figure was vaguely visible in the darkness and I stood for a moment trying to make him out.

'Fire!' cried he, his voice loud and empty in the darkness.

'Wait but a moment,' said I. 'Hear me first. If I do not prevail, you must never return to Gironde, for M. Lafont means to burn both house and inhabitants.'

There was an audible groan from his vicinity, but no other sound. The clouds obscured the moon and I squinted to aim at the distant shape ahead of me. I fired, and after a short moment, I heard him call, 'Once more!' his voice more faint than before.

I fired again and this time there was no sound. I strained to hear or to see, but could do neither.

'M. Hubert,' cried I, 'do you live? Shall I prepare for you to return fire?'

All was silent. I could no longer see his figure in the distance. I walked towards him and slowly I made out a shape on the ground. At first I assumed my shot had found its destination but when I drew closer I could see that he was sitting not laying. His legs were crossed and he sat in gloomy meditation, his weapon still clutched in his hand.

'Why did you not fire?' said I. 'Get up at once if you are not hurt. I shall return to my spot.'

M. Hubert did not speak or move. I demanded again that he return to the field, but he only said, 'Fire, fire. Fires burn. M. Lafont knows not what he does. A fire in the soul is like a dry spruce ablaze. It cannot be controlled. Fire consumes all. Fires burn.'

The last remark was made more to himself and after saying this he fell into a profound reverie. I watched him for several minutes while his countenance and more particularly his eyes revealed the most acute sufferings.

From that time I lost all will to avenge myself. I took a rope from my bag and tied the miserable man to a tree, almost without his being aware of what I did. I left him to go in search of some horses. I did not search for long, as there were several grazing in a field nearby. As they had neither bit nor saddle, I mounted the first horse to herd the other, and after a great degree of difficulty, I returned with both to the spot I had left M. Hubert.

To my surprise he had fallen asleep in my absence. I roused him and told him to mount the horse. He complied without a word, hardly noticing the horse was bare. From there he followed wearily wherever I led, no longer seeming to care with whom or to where he went.

Having made my decision, my purpose was to escort M. Hubert as far from that region as was in my power, while still allowing me to return as quickly as possible to speak to M. Lafont. The disappearance of M. Hubert would soon rouse his followers in a manner so as to completely nullify M. Lafont's plan, but honour demanded I come to an understanding with him as soon as I was able.

During our travels, M. Hubert said very little but talked and rambled to himself periodically in a kind of dark and whimsically poetic style. At times he seemed to come to himself, whereupon he would look at me and at our surroundings, but refrain from either comment or question.

Near dawn we encountered a cottage which had a neat and inviting appearance from a distance. We had travelled perhaps sixty or seventy miles in that time and I resolved to rid myself of M. Hubert at the next opportunity.

I turned to M. Hubert intending to tell him to wait my return, but he was looking in the other direction, lost in contemplation.

I left him to himself and knocked on the door. The man and his wife were just waking up, but nevertheless they invited me inside and begged me to state my business. I briefly described the mental state of M. Hubert, and asked if they would give him shelter for a few nights. I offered to recompense them for their trouble and they readily agreed. I gave them more than enough to house him for several days and after that I would leave him to make his own way in the world.

Not exactly understanding my motives, the cottagers were determined to assure me that M. Hubert would receive the very best care. Their many pledges and assurances frequently delayed me as I was on the point of departure, and when I finally returned to M. Hubert, I discovered that he was nowhere to be found.

The cottagers were far more distressed at this discovery than I, for fear I meant to take back the money I had given them for his keeping. They vowed to search the entire area for him and enlist the help of all of their neighbours. I professed myself perfectly satisfied with their intentions and with scarcely another thought, turned my horse and departed for the Chateau.

My return journey was long and I was forced to stop repeatedly for both my own sake and for my horse. No change of horse could be got in the first town I stepped in and the sight of a man of my appearance, both wild and well-dressed, riding a bare field horse, roused suspicions wherever I went. I was well-armed, however, and no one attempted to obstruct me.

Many hours later I arrived at the Chateau, parched, worn, and famished. M. Lafont was one of the first to greet me and he expressed much surprise at my sudden disappearance. I told him that I wished to speak with him but required food and a few hours sleep to recruit myself.

'Then I will attempt to repress my curiosity till then,' said he, but his look expressed impatience and uneasiness.

I hardly spoke to anyone else but asked Philip to attend me at once. I told him all that had occurred since I had left, while he helped me bathe and dress. I ate and drank as quickly as I could, then said, 'It is almost certain that I shall fight M. Lafont, but I would not do so without at least a little sleep. Do not let me sleep more than eight hours, I beg you, and wake me immediately if M. Lafont readies himself to go out.'

Philip did as I asked and about five hours later, I heard a knock on my door. When I answered it, Philip told me that he had informed Lafont that I wished to speak with him before he departed.

'We shall ride out together. I shall be there in a moment. If I do not return, let my earlier instructions stand. If M. Lafont returns alone, it would be best if you can contrive some way of refusing his entrance. In that case, I shall be dead and it may be a risky experiment to either deny or admit him. In case you attempt to deny him, we must hope I may receive greater loyalty in death from those who remain, than M. Lafont may when yet living and breathing. It is not a certainty, by any means, I fear.'

I gave him some additional parting instructions and commended him for his unwavering loyalty to my family, to which he replied.

'You are a better marksman than Lafont. Only take care to load your weapon well, and I am sure to see you again.'

I thanked him for his confidence and went out in search of Lafont. At my suggestion that we ride out, he evinced some surprise, but nevertheless agreed immediately.

I proposed we ride to an unusual outcropping of stone on high ground nearby, which we called the lookout point. Not waiting to discuss my intentions, I jumped upon my horse and galloped in that direction. M. Lafont was still preparing to do so and I was able to maintain a significant lead, both to discourage conversation and permit me a short time to think.

When we reached our destination, M. Lafont had become increasingly expectant.

'M. Lafont,' said I, wasting no time, 'I have reason to believe that you have some plan in motion of which you do not mean to inform me?'

'If that is all,' replied he, with a dismissive air which almost seemed relieved, 'then you need not worry yourself. The little plan I had made was not such as would have suited you, so I spared you from hearing it. It was all for nothing, at any rate, for our enemies have begun running around like ants on an invading stick. I hope you do not intend to take much offence at the omission?'

His expression was not as cheerful as his words.

'I have seen M. Hubert,' said I.

At these words his whole frame seemed to spasm. He stared at me fiercely, waiting for me to explain words which were clearly beyond any expectation.

'I went to kill him to prevent the atrocious massacre you have planned. I have seen him but I have let him go. He is a victim of his own barbarity, and perhaps some of others. The state of his mind and his senses place him beyond the reach of any honourable revenge or redress.'

'Honourable revenge?!' cried M. Lafont, in anger and amazement at my words. 'The man who shirks from destroying the murderer of his family has no right to preach honour to others. If you did not have the stomach to do what must be done, why did you not bring him to me, that I might make up for your weakness?'

The question was almost rhetorical, but nevertheless I replied. 'I am willing to make you the amends you require. I shall give you the choice of weapons.'

M. Lafont glared at me, full of rage.

'And do you not tremble to meet me?' he sneered. 'Seeing that you are scarcely better than the boy I found shivering in a field but months ago?'

'I await your choice,' said I, still calm and resolute. I no longer respected M. Lafont as I once had, and his insulting taunts were of little significance.

'The prattling of the old witch has given you courage you would not otherwise have,' cried he, 'or else you could not face me so calmly!'

He paced up and down. Fury seemed to fight with superstition in his mind.

'It is a trick!' said he at last, with a kind of frenzy verging on madness. 'There is some sorcery at work here. Though I believed you my friend, I see you have ever been my enemy. It matters little. I have but one purpose in life and not all the hounds in hell or wretched old crones shall keep me from it. You have given M. Hubert a reprieve, but there is no power on earth which can prevent me from pursuing him, and doing what ought to have been done.'

With that he spurred his horse and galloped in the other direction.

Whilst I was writing my history, I was interrupted by the announcement of Mr. Etheredge. He was disappointed to learn that the other party was not within, but I reminded him it would allow us all the better opportunity to speak to one another unheeded.

"I hardly expected you could have discovered anything of that sort already," said he, with a cautious tone of hope.

"It was easier than I expected myself, but nevertheless, if you marry Mlle Vallon, you may rely upon the sum of two thousand pounds."

"Two-thousand pounds, Monsieur, that is more than I hoped!"

"Very well, Sir, and how does the matter stand now?"

"As you have said before, she was not likely to have what my mother required lying by, and yet I do not care!"

"Then you are decided? You are reconciled to your mother's threat, were she to follow through upon it?"

"It is not a little thing, Monsieur," replied he, "to resign one's fortune, one's birthright, but yet, I do believe I am."

At this time our conversation was interrupted by the loud sound of a door slamming. Mr. Etheredge and I froze temporarily to see what else could be heard. Hushed voices and tears were only barely audible, and a moment or two later, a knock was heard at my chamber door. I called out to enter, and Mr. Savard leaned in his head.

"We depart in half an hour, M. Gramont. You may come or wait, as you please, but we cannot be delayed."

With this he departed, darting a look of loathing at Mr. Etheredge as his only acknowledgement.

"What can have happened?" cried Mr. Etheredge. "What ought to be done?"

"You must leave that to me. Go home, and think some more of what we have said. I would not have Mlle Vallon marry a man who resents the sacrifice he makes for her sake. Go home and choose, and when you have, do not ever suffer yourself to look back."

Mr. Etheredge did as I suggested, though he hardly knew which way to look.

I went out to the common room and ordered some refreshments, intent upon seeing the party as they set out. Eventually their carriage was announced, and the two ladies came out, followed quickly by M. Savard. He cast a suspicious look upon me before ushering them along. Their hoods were drawn, but it was plain they were both distressed. Mme. Gaspar came behind, and by this time M. Savard was at the carriage.

"It is a sad business," said she, holding out her hand to me. "M. Savard has tried to compel Mlle Vallon to marry, but with no warning to anyone! The poor girl could do nothing but cry and the pastor said he could not do it in all conscience. Now they are all in a state, and so am I, I daresay, to see my dear girls so distressed. Do not be too long, Sir, if it is convenient, for all we should need is a highwayman behind us to compound our misery."

I pledged to follow behind before too long. I could not help but shake my head in wonder to learn the purpose of our trip was in fact as Mr. Etheredge suspected. M. Tolouse was quickly found and readied, and as we made good pace, we were soon in sight of the carriage. I had no wish to ride nearer though, and whilst we followed at a distance, I related to M. Tolouse the words of Mme. Gaspar.

The rest of our journey was uneventful. I called the next day at Sorsten, but no one was able to receive me.

The next day I woke up after a particularly long and restful sleep.

M. Tolouse was at breakfast when I came down. After a minute or two he said, "Far be it from me to pry into your affairs, M. Gramont, but I hardly think it is right for you to keep the little one up writing all night, while you sleep like a baby."

I had difficulty understanding him at first. "Do you mean Mouchard?" said I, at last.

"Who else should I mean, begging your pardon?"

"And he was up writing, you say?"

"Didn't sleep a wink, I am sure. Candle's burnt to the end. Thought it must have to do with your mysterious departure, and whatever else you've kept to yourself; meaning nothing by it, that is."

"Nothing indeed! And where is he now?"

"No sign of him. I figured you had sent him on an errand."

"You have attributed much to me while I slept."

"I hardly know whether to do less now, for heaven knows there is no one better at keeping things to themselves. Truth be told, I am a close dog myself. I have decided to leave in a day or two, seeing as there is no reason for me to have stayed even this long, minding maids and matrons, and amorous old men."

"Which way do you go, Monsieur?"

"I am not of one mind of it, yet."

"I am heading North, and if you were to end up going in that direction as well, I should be glad of the company while our roads converge."

"Shouldn't mind it much myself," replied he, with surprise, "and so shall make up my mind to do it at once."

Following breakfast, I proposed we call at the main house and take unofficial leave of its occupants, in the event that we were unable to do so in the next two days. M. Tolouse agreed, and we proceeded there directly.

When we arrived, we were seen into the parlour where the three ladies and M. Savard were taking tea. M. Savard invited us to join them, and learning that we were leaving in the next few days, he became slightly more cordial. The two young ladies were silent for the most part, and Mme. Gaspar upheld most of the conversation by herself. Part-way through, a servant announced the presence of a Mr. Seymour.

The name 'Seymour' seemed to excite a special interest in at least the two ladies and myself, and we beheld his entrance with slightly elevated curiosity.

"See him in," said M. Savard, "we have room for one more in any case." When the servant left he explained that a gentleman had called the evening before about exploring the grounds for some silly reason. "He seems harmless enough."

M. Savard introduced him rather carelessly, and invited him to join us to tea. They spoke French, and Mr. Seymour revealed that he had spent a year in France when he was a young man. In response to M. Savard's invitation, he said, "Thank you very kindly, I should like nothing better! I dismissed the carriage a few miles down the lane in order to take a closer look at the area, and now that I come to myself, I find I am in great need of refreshment."

"You are very welcome, Sir," said Mme. Gaspar, looking up for a moment from her needle. "M. Savard tells us you have expressed an interest in something hereabouts?"

"Why yes, Madam, I have long been friends with Sir John Etheredge, and the other day when I called upon him by chance, we began to speak about smuggler's caves. Such things have a particular interest to me, you see. Now Sir John happened to mention a series of interesting caves on this land, especially nearing the coast, which might have belonged to smugglers or pirates or the like. This piqued my curiosity extremely, and as just at this time I am quite at my leisure, he suggested I come take a look. By your leave, of course."

"Of course, my dear Sir," replied Mme. Gaspar, apparently drawing no connection between the man before her and the character in Mouchard's story. "My uncle was an explorer of sorts. He was fond of birds and would track and observe them relentlessly. As a child I began to think that all men climbed trees like apes. Used to bring us little eggs from time to time, and nests too. He was the greatest mimic in the whole world, and you'd sooner guess there was a bird coming up the lane than a man! Ah, how I miss such days. I don't suppose I shall see that old house again, or France itself, I daresay, which is now as lost to me as my late uncle!" With that she brought a handkerchief to her eye.

Mr. Seymour had been listening to her with the most distracted complaisance, and when she paused, he seemed to compel himself back to attention.

"Yes, 'tis a shame indeed about France," declared he, "and who knows when it will all be sorted out. There are some lovely churches there I should like to visit, but then there are plenty enough for my purposes on my native soil."

By this time, the interest excited by his entrance had been succeeded by a feeling nothing short of wonder to discover him the very picture of the gentleman in Mouchard's tale.

By this time he had finished his tea, and having eaten one or two bites, he seemed to be readying himself to depart. At this sight, Mlle de Courteline, Mlle Vallon and myself glanced at each other urgently, and feeling the need for one of us to say something, I said:

"Forgive me, Sir, but did you say you were from around here?"

"Perhaps forty or fifty miles to the North, Monsieur, near Colchester, in Crestham, but perhaps I shall settle elsewhere soon."

"Indeed," said I, inwardly grasping for some way to introduce the question upon our minds, "and do you know if there is a gentleman called Harland living in that part of the country?"

"Indeed, Monsieur," cried he with surprise, "there are few who know it better, for I am his steward. Do you know him, Monsieur?"

"Not directly. In fact, quite indirectly, I fear. I had heard he was married?"

"Married?" repeated he. "There is not a gentleman in England less likely to be so. I see your information is quite indirect!"

"I see," replied I, again at a loss for words.

"I beg your pardon, M. Gramont, for you have unknowingly touched upon quite a sore spot with me. For several years it has been my near concern to see him so, but now all of that is at an end. In truth, I am far happier rambling about pursuing my own designs than being prey to the whims and inconsistencies of others. Even were that gentleman to return to his senses, I question whether I could be bothered to resume such thankless business. At least my little jaunts make one person happy; namely myself. Forgive me, Monsieur, I am a little too prone to speaking my mind. It is a habit more suited to a man who boasts a larger purse than my own. If a man be wealthy, his directness is almost always forgiven. And now, to prevent myself from saying anything further, I shall present my compliments for your hospitality, and begin my exploring!"

With this he bowed and departed, leaving Mlle de Courteline, Mlle Vallon and myself in the most extreme consternation.

"Imagine those two names should be found together," cried Mme. Gaspar, again looking up briefly from her work. "They must be very common names in England, I think, or else it could not be," and with that she went back to her work.

Even M. Tolouse raised an eyebrow at this statement, while the ladies and I merely looked at each other in amazement.

"What can this mean?" said Mlle de Courteline at last, to no one in particular.

"'Tis very strange!" declared Mlle Vallon.

"It cannot be what it seems," added Mlle de Courteline.

I was about to reply myself when M. Savard said, "The gentleman was a little eccentric, perhaps, but I see nothing so very extraordinary about him."

At this remark, we all fell silent again.

I have written much and so I shall stop here and send it to you. There is much more to relate, and I shall return to my pen again as soon as there is opportunity. Dear Sir, I am ever,

Yours,
MC

Marcel de la Croix to Henri Renault

February 22nd,1793

Dear Friend,

I will begin where I left off and try to relate all which has occurred since I last wrote. I shall try not to hurry my pen too much, for fear of omitting something essential.

Shortly after Mr. Seymour's departure, M. Savard made it quite evident he anticipated M. Tolouse and I would soon do so as well. All conversation had stopped completely, for each of us were lost in our thoughts, unable to express our mutual amazement in the presence of M. Savard. Shortly thereafter we took leave.

"That was an unusual business," M. Tolouse declared, as we walked across the lawn. 'What do you make of it? What can Mouchard be about, winding tales about people who actually exist? And do you suppose much of it is true?"

I did not reply, intent upon discovering whether Mouchard had returned. The only other servants who live with us are our cook, and her son and daughter, and in response to my inquiry, the cook told me she had not seen him that day.

"Your other servant, Philip, was here a short time ago. He claims he has been with you for some time, but as I had never seen him before, I wouldn't let him amongst your things without me present.

He did not stay long, but I'll warrant he'll return soon."

I looked around somewhat myself, knowing how easily Mouchard snuck in and out unnoticed. He was nowhere to be found, but on my desk there was a large packet I hadn't seen before. It was addressed to me, and I did not know whether to expect it was from Philip or Mouchard. I broke the seal impatiently and read:

Dear Sir,

Forgive me for leaving so abruptly but I could not stay. I know not whether you will have actually seen Mr. Seymour by now, but I could not risk remaining once I caught sight of him yesterday. He is a good man, but I shudder to think if through him my disclosures were revealed to Miss Reckert. I do not regret his presence, however, for it prompts me to hasten my relation, and tell you by letter what I always meant to.

No doubt you must wonder to find that under the guise of fiction I have committed a violation of confidence which must seem like the grossest kind of betrayal. Nothing less than the safety of she who is dearest to me could have prompted me to take such a step. Whatever your opinion in the end, I hope at least to convince you of my motive for doing so.

When first I noticed you bore the same scar as the man I had seen, I felt certain you knew him, and knew why he sought M. Hubert. Although I know Gramont is not your true name, I know very little of Marcel de la Croix. Yet whatever your name, nearly from the moment I met you, I felt certain from you possessed strength, generosity and intelligence to help my benefactress, if only you could be persuaded to do so. I shall say no more by way of preface, for I fear I only explain myself poorly. But only first let me implore you, Monsieur, if my tale has touched you at all, do not fail to read it complete, and do not fail to act upon it, as I am certain only you can. I place all my hope upon it.

Yours ever,
Thomas

I glanced at the letter which accompanied it, and reading the first line or two, I found he continued the story much as he had left off. I was interrupted at that moment by M. Tolouse who gave me a small note. I opened it and it read:

Monsieur Gramont from Mlle de Courteline

Dear Sir,

I am certain you are far too aware of these extraordinary circumstances to draw any improper interpretation from my decision to write to you. I cannot help think it is imperative to speak to Mouchard at once, and discover the meaning of all this! Mlle Vallon and I shall contrive to be in the garden as quickly as possible. Come with Mouchard to the far wall, near the statues. I trust no other excuse or explanation shall be necessary,

Yours,
Mlle de Courteline

I was slightly annoyed to be hastened away so precipitously, but nevertheless I returned the rest of Mouchard's letter to its enclosure, and took it with me to the garden.

The place Mlle de Courteline appointed to meet was a fair distance from the house and as I walked, more than a few times I was tempted to take out the letter and begin to read it. I resisted, however, and located the ladies a few minutes later in a small alcove of sorts, which was adorned by three Romanesque statues, along with two benches set perpendicular near the garden wall.

Mlle Vallon was seated while Mlle de Courteline was pacing up and down.

"M. Gramont," said she, at the sight of me, "I see you have received my letter, but why did you not bring Mouchard?"

I bowed, saying, "When your letter arrived, I was in the process of determining his whereabouts. It seems he has disappeared early this morning, having caught sight of Mr. Seymour on his first visit to Sorsten last night."

"Disappeared!" cried Mlle de Courteline, collapsing upon the seat, "Impossible! But how can you know, Monsieur?"

"He has sent me a letter, or perhaps left it for me last night, I cannot be sure."

"Why, what does it say?" cried she, reviving a little.

"I have not had a chance to read it, Madam, or at least all of it. He claims he meant to divulge the whole, and I believe he has taken the trouble to write the remainder of his story down."

"Has he indeed? Do you have it here? You do not think little Mouchard could truly be a Viscount? I expect he has not told us strictly the truth, for I do not see how he could have known all he related. What is your own opinion?"

"I do not know. I have not had much time to think about it. I suppose a child may develop some kind of heightened perception as a result of trauma?"

"But M. Gramont," said the gentle Mlle Vallon, "if Mouchard or Thomas or whoever, if he has written the rest of the history, and we suspect it to be at least partly true, is it right that we should read it?"

Mlle de Courteline seemed horrified at the suggestion, but unable to answer it herself, looked instead at me as if in the hope I could.

"I cannot answer for the two of you gentlewomen," said I, "for you may very well have some scruple to doing so. For myself, Mouchard has begged, nay implored me to read it, and to refuse to do so without knowing his reasons seems to risk greater harm through inaction than by learning some other private detail regarding Mr. Harland and Miss Reckert, if indeed there prove to be two such people."

At this there was a long silence, during which Mlle Vallon stared downwards in thought. At last she looked up and said, "Perhaps my curiosity is greater than my consideration, Monsieur, but I would have you read the letter to us, if Mlle de Courteline does not object."

Mlle de Courteline seemed very far from doing so, and so with no further ado, I began as follows:

By now, you must know my role in this story. When I had last seen Miss Reckert, she had requested I come to visit her in two days' time. My visit was received as a formal one in that house, and I was shown to a far parlour to await her. To my surprise and slight trepidation, I discovered I was not alone there, as Miss Lawrence's uncle stood near the mantle, his back turned from me. The servant who had led me there seemed slightly surprised to see him, but motioned for me to remain. He had not moved at the sound of the door and stayed as he was, in rapt concentration, rhythmically stirring the ashes with the poker.

A moment or two later, Miss Reckert appeared, greeting me happily before she noticed the presence of a third party. At the sound of her entrance, Mr. Hubert turned and stared in our direction. He did not speak, but his black eyes flashed with a kind of animal intensity.'

I was forced to stop here for a moment, at the full realization of what was meant by this passage, and that the mysterious and eccentric character of Miss Lawrence's uncle was M. Hubert, but newly returned to England. It was a full minute or two till I could continue, at the urgent prompting of the two ladies, who did not understand my delay.

'Miss Reckert seemed unsettled and generally unsure what to do, for she told me later that Miss Lawrence had advised her not to speak with him if possible. Under the weight of his stare, however, prolonged silence seemed insupportable, and therefore she said, 'Excuse me, Sir, I hope we have not disturbed you. I did not realize you were present.'

The gentleman did not reply, but instead reached for his cane and walked slowly in our direction. When he was close enough, he looked us both directly in the eyes for an unnerving interval, before stalking out of the room without a word.

A moment or so later, Miss Lawrence herself entered, and as soon as Miss Reckert recovered from her fright, she described the strange behaviour we had witnessed.

'I apologize, Miss Reckert,' said she, 'but I cannot say I am completely surprised. My uncle has suffered much in his life, and my mother thinks it increasingly unlikely he shall ever return to himself. My mother has allowed him to stay here from compassion. The life he has led abroad has made him unpredictable and at times uncivil, but I do not believe he is dangerous.'

After this the subject was dropped, and soon after a walk was proposed. We walked into town where Miss Lawrence stopped at the milliner to fetch something her mother had ordered. Miss Reckert and I waited out of doors, and while Miss Lawrence was inside the store, Miss Reckert said, 'As we have a few moments, I hoped to speak to you again of your future prospects. It has often been remarked that you have a most elegant hand for letter writing, and therefore when the matter first occurred to me, I meant to ask you how you would like the work of copying and engraving? Indeed, there is much demand for a person who can write and draw with your precision, and for this reason I have written to Mr. Seymour for his advice and assistance. He has a great acquaintance amongst those who trade in the production of maps or other documents, and thus I think he is the best person to apply to. I had hoped to speak to him on the subject after his arrival here, but although he has already departed, I think it is likely I shall receive his reply directly. Does this possibility appeal to you, my dear child?'

I nodded silently. I had no desire to leave Miss Reckert, but if it was necessary, all places were alike to me. Upon reflection, however, I have realized that is not truly the case, and her choice was certainly the most wise and eligible.

A few moments later, Miss Lawrence issued from the shop, presently followed by a man of around thirty, slightly comical in his appearance.

'Indeed, Sir,' said she, to him, 'there is no occasion for you to inconvenience yourself, for if there is too much for us to manage, it may certainly be brought at any time.'

'I would not hear of it, Madam,' replied he, hastily securing several items to his horse, 'and I never miss an opportunity to do a service to a lady, if I do say so myself.'

'You are very kind, Sir,' said she, but nevertheless she did not seem desirous of waiting for him, and motioned for Miss Reckert and I to do likewise.

Seeing that we meant to go on ahead, the messenger began to scramble furiously to stow his packages in the saddle bags. We had gone only a short distance when he caught up to us.

'If I may make so bold, Miss Lawrence,' said he, 'I should propose to escort you home. Ever since the disturbance, these roads are hardly safe for one to travel on alone as before. Just yesterday a band of vagabonds over-turned a cart and sent a farmer scurrying into the fields. Two such handsome women ought to be protected wherever they roam, if you will pardon me for observing, and it should be my very great pleasure to do so at present.'

Neither of the two ladies objected to his plan, though it was apparent they would have preferred being left to themselves.

Mr. Richards, as was his name, continued to talk merrily of any subject which occurred to him, never omitting an opportunity for a compliment to either lady, and soon we had gone nearly half the way home.

Near this point the road was intersected by a wide path cut through the corn, and shortly after we passed by it, a group of around a dozen men issued from it. They ranged somewhat in age, but were generally young and evidently in high spirits.

Mr. Richards gave quite a start to see them, and stood up straight in his stirrups to get a better look at them. By contrast the young ladies themselves affected to take no notice at all and continued walking. Finding he had been slightly outpaced while he stopped, Mr. Richards raced after them at a furious pace, crying, 'There are nearly two dozen of them! I pray, ladies, stay near me and let us hasten away!' With that he raced ahead, eliciting a general laugh from the party behind.

Once Mr. Richards had got a short way in front, he raced back and cried, 'Sweet ladies, hasten, I beg you!' before racing once more in the direction he recommended.

Both women began to be seriously concerned at the spectacle he was making, and on one of his returns, Miss Lawrence seriously implored him to calm himself, lest he should create the mischief he hoped to avert.

Unfortunately by then it was too late, for the party behind had quickened their pace at the sign of some sport, and the foremost of the men now cried out, 'Sweet ladies, you have certainly misjudged your champion. See how he runs? Had you not better stay with us?'

Neither answered, but merely continued to walk as we were gradually encompassed by these incorrigible field workers.

'Is that not the Milliner's shophand?'

'Aye,' said another.

After a wide laugh, another man cried, 'Why these are fine ladies indeed, to be entrusted to such a fellow. Perhaps we ought to take on his charges?'

''Tis a boy here as well, perhaps he is the champion?'

Several more witticisms passed before one said, 'I dare-say they shan't mind if we entertain the ladies for a bit. Come, fair ladies, your new escorts shall serve you better than the old.'

'Come, ladies,' cried Mr. Richards, who had continued to come near and then ride away, 'exert yourselves, we must away. Heaven knows what these ruffians meditate!'

'Good Heavens,' cried Miss Lawrence, 'Pray go fetch some help, Mr. Richards, for it does no one any good to ride back and forth like that.'

'Never!' cried he, 'Oh, could you think I would abandon two young ladies in need? Push through, I beseech thee!'

Another great laugh rippled through the men, and several of them jumped in front in case either of the two ladies had tried to follow his advice.

At this moment, one of the men placed his arm around Miss Reckert's waist, and in extricating herself, she brought the back of her hand fiercely across his face.

Miss Lawrence screamed to see it and yelled, 'Mr. Richards, fetch help this instant, I implore you!'

In another moment, however, she spotted Mr. Hubert who emerged from the tall crops only a short way away. He was absently swinging a long stick, and at the sound of Miss Lawrence's voice, looked curiously in our direction.

'Uncle!' cried Miss Lawrence, 'Pray help us, for we cannot get free.'

'Good Sir,' cried Mr. Richards, riding up to him directly, 'I beg you to do whatever you can to help the ladies. I am happy to see you wear a sword, for I have no such thing about me, or else I should already have made these ruffians repent their violence.'

While he spoke, Mr. Hubert took no notice of him at all, choosing instead to perform his own appraisal of the scene. When Mr. Richards paused to let him respond, Mr. Hubert turned to him calmly, and without any warning at all, leapt up upon the stirrup and pulled the other from his horse, placing himself in his place.

From the moment of Miss Lawrence's appeal, all eyes had been turned upon Mr. Hubert. There was an audible gasp at this action, which was so swift and sudden, it seemed the work of a second. Once atop the horse, Mr. Hubert drew his sword. Without a word he moved the horse forward in a strange circular pattern, before putting it abruptly to gallop. This suspenseful prelude had raised a fair amount of anxiety among the men, and once he began to bear down upon us, his fierce eyes gleaming, they scattered in all directions.

The sheer thickness of the ripening crops preserved the lives of many of them. Mr. Hubert seemed intent upon overtaking any he could and therefore pursued those who thought to run back along the path which was wide enough for the horse to pass.

Now that the immediate danger seemed to be over, Miss Lawrence cried out to her uncle to stop and return. By then he was out of sight and only distant screams met our ears. At last we had no choice but to return to the house by the quickest route possible.

Mr. Richards had sustained an injury to his arm and he complained loudly the whole way home. He veered between gallantry and complaint, declaring repeatedly that he would have been happy to cede the gentleman his horse 'if he had only asked!'

As soon as they entered the house, Miss Lawrence ordered that Mr. Richards be seen to and a doctor be sent for. Having done so she excused herself to speak to her mother.

Miss Reckert likewise went to her room, where I followed as I was accustomed. The strange sequence of events seemed to almost baffle her powers of speech. Twice she asked me to go down and see if there had been any news, and on the second occasion I encountered Miss Lawrence herself who told me that Mr. Hubert had not yet returned, and that her mother had applied to one of her neighbours for help discovering him. She said also that the physician declared Mr. Richard's arm had been broken in his fall.

A short time later a message was sent up inviting us to come down to tea, and going instantly below, we found Mrs. and Miss Lawrence in the parlour.

Once we had sat down, Mrs. Lawrence said, 'I am happy to find you are unhurt by all the commotion, Miss Reckert, for I could not bear the thought that any harm should come to you while under my roof. My daughter informs me that my brother came to your aid, for which I am truly gratified.'

Despite the cheery demeanour she affected, it was plain that she was very little at ease. Miss Reckert attempted to reply, but the shock of the morning had not yet worn off, and she was unsuccessful. A pause ensued and in the meantime, a neighbour called Mr. Millson, was announced and admitted.

Mrs. Lawrence invited him to join us for tea, and once he had sat down, he said, 'Well, Mrs. Lawrence, I am glad to see that all is well and Mr. Hubert is returned, unharmed.'

'Is he?' cried she, 'Why did you see him, Sir?'

'Clear as day, in the garden. I congratulated him on his heroism, but he did not seem to be in the most communicative mood, so I left him to himself. Did you say he speaks mostly French, madam?'

'Yes; well no. Indeed, I fear he does not say much nowadays. I do hope this whole business won't cause much of a disturbance in the neighbourhood. I am afraid there will be much talk of his eccentricities.'

'Pish,' replied the other, 'if you ask me, a poor man can't be faulted for defending young ladies, especially those related to him, howsoever he does it. And I have said as much to anyone who will listen, Madam.'

'We are quite obliged to you, Sir, but have you had any other news?'

'Why, in truth I rode down there myself and it is a bit of a situation. One lad has lost the use of his arm, but that is the worst of it. I warrant there would not be many arms and legs, nor heads neither, were it not for the corn. A mighty doing there, too, it seems, for when I rode down there were a fair number of people gawking at the sight.'

'How horrible! How distressing! But what were they looking at, Sir?'

'The crops, Madam, all bespeckled with blood and trampled and cut in every which way. Your brother is a most determined kind of man, it seems.'

'Good God!' cried Mrs. Lawrence.

'Nay, there is no cause for concern, for I put things to right on the spot. I reminded those gathered that the French are violent by nature, and it is foolish for any young men to provoke a Frenchman by ill-treatment of women.'

'We are incredibly obliged to you, Sir. This is the most unfortunate thing imaginable! Would to Heaven the girls had not gone out today!'

'The doctors in the area shall appreciate the business, in any case,' observed he, pragmatically.

'But do you think there shall be any other repercussions? I fear Mr. Hubert's behaviour shall be considered unusual at least, and he shall be called before a Magistrate.'

'I see no trouble there, Madam, for you must recall that Mr. Reckert himself is the Magistrate hereabouts, and neither he nor the other gentleman, Mr. Harland, are likely to mind if a few fingers were lopped off in defence of Miss Reckert and your daughter.'

'A few fingers!?' repeated Mrs. Lawrence, growing increasingly pale, 'I thought you said an injured arm was the worst of it, Sir?'

'Oh, yes indeed, and no doubt it is, but it is hard to reckon up directly. The story will come out in several days,' rising to take leave, 'but you may be assured I will be sure to set the matter straight whenever possible. Take heart, dear Madam. Mrs. Millson sends her best, but I fear she shall want me home directly.'

Mrs. Lawrence pressed him to return as soon as he had any further news to give her, and he assured her he would do so.

A short while later, Miss Reckert excused herself to write to her father. I carried the letter to him myself, and found the news had already reached him, and left him in a great state of distress.

Mr. Reckert bid me tell his daughter that he would send the carriage for her at noon the following day, and I was to accompany her. His anxiety was such that everything was ordered and prepared too early the next morning, and I arrived at the Lawrences's a short time before I was expected.

I found Miss Reckert, Mrs. and Miss Lawrence drinking tea with both Mr. and Mrs. Millson, while the latter, a most talkative kind of woman, was purporting to reassure Mrs. Lawrence while effectively alarming her with every second word.

My entrance was hardly noticed by any but Miss Reckert. A few minutes later, as she seemed on the verge of excusing herself, a hush fell upon the room at the unexpected appearance of Mr. Hubert.

Mrs. Lawrence seemed exceedingly ill at ease, knowing that Mrs. Millson was likely to report anything out of the ordinary which occurred. Mr. Hubert stalked to the fireplace and began methodically stirring the ashes, hardly seeming to notice anyone else in the room. After an extremely awkward pause, Mrs. Lawrence addressed her brother with a faint voice, saying, 'Dear brother, won't you take some tea with us?'

Mr. Hubert turned at the sound of her voice, but did not reply, going back to his former occupation. An awkward interval ensued for several moments. Miss Reckert seemed reluctant to excuse herself under such circumstances, and waited for a more opportune moment. Suddenly, Mr. Hubert moved away from the fireplace mantle and began to examine all those present, settling his piercing gaze at last upon Miss Reckert, who sat at the outward position on the sofa, next to Mr. Millson and his wife.

As if to spare Miss Reckert by distracting Mr. Hubert's attention, Mr. Millson declared, 'Ah, Sir, no doubt you will agree, there is nothing more worthy of protection. What would a man not do for a woman!'

Mr. Hubert continued to stare at Miss Reckert and for a long moment I thought he did not intend to reply, but then rather unexpectedly he said, 'Woman,' as if to himself.

'Yes, Sir?' replied the other, prodding him gently to continue. 'Did you say woman, Sir?'

'What of it?' was the reply.

'Why I was just wondering what you meant by it, Sir, if you would be so good as to finish your thought?'

Mr. Hubert was silent again, but finally he turned his eyes away and said to no one in particular, 'Women are designed to cause suffering.'

Mr. Millson laughed heartily at this observation, which he seemed to take as a usual sally of sorts. 'So they are, Sir, I shall not disagree with you there. But certainly we must love them all the same!'

Miss Lawrence evidently wished the conversation at an end, but it was for Mr. Hubert to reply, and he did not seem likely to consult her looks.

'To love is to suffer,' was his laconic remark.

'By my stars,' cried Mr. Millson, 'and so it is! But surely, Sir, to live is to suffer, and women make it all worthwhile?'

He looked to Mr. Hubert again for an answer, apparently enjoying the exchange. Mr. Hubert no longer appeared to be listening to him in the same way, but in a low distracted voice, repeated, 'Stars,' but this time in french.

Mr. Hubert's eyes had fallen upon me by chance as I sat by Miss Reckert, and it seemed to me that he drifted into some distant memory. He seemed to struggle to recall some great source of pain, but if I may guess from his expression, he was not entirely successful.

Mrs. Lawrence now took it upon herself to change the subject. What she said I know not, for Mr. Hubert's expression had a strange effect on me and I could not recall myself from it. While Mrs. Lawrence was addressing some question to her daughter, Mr. Hubert interrupted her with an audible sigh, before saying in french, 'Some stars are merciful, others kill.'

He said something more, softly and to himself, but I could not hear what it was. A moment or two after, he departed abruptly without a word to anyone.

'Please excuse my brother,' said Mrs. Lawrence nervously to Mrs. Millson. 'He has been too long in France and the Lord only knows what has happened while he was there. He is a widower, you know.'

I must skip over any unnecessary details for I fear I have not now the leisure to write them. Suffice to say that the words and expressions of Mr. Hubert struck me and I felt from that point an unremitting uneasiness. I saw something in the soul of that gentleman which frightened me, yet I knew not what it was.

The whole way home that day I tried to decide what was to be done. I was certain that Miss Reckert ought to know what had occurred to delay Mr. Harland's response, yet I lacked the courage to voice it. It seemed increasingly imperative that Miss Reckert should not be exposed to the unpredictability of a man like Mr. Hubert. I knew not how, but I felt his very proximity endangered her.

The next day I set out again for the Lawrences, feeling it was likely Miss Reckert should wish to see me. I thought once or twice the previous day that she was upon the verge of speaking to me regarding her plans for settling me, so I did so with a heavy heart.

On the way I was overtaken by Mr. Harland, who was evidently headed to the same destination. Somewhat unexpectedly, I found he slowed his horse and dismounted, beginning to walk alongside me.

'Do I guess rightly that you are on the way to visit Miss Reckert, Thomas?'

'Yes, Sir.'

'Then I shall walk with you for I am glad of the opportunity to speak with you. The county is wild with rumours of the unusual events of the day before yesterday, and yet if I am not mistaken, you were yourself witness to them?'

I nodded.

'Pray tell me then, what prompted this circumstance in the first place? Can it be possible that Miss Reckert and Miss Lawrence were accosted by a gang of ruffians upon the road, in the broad light of day?'

'Yes, Sir.'

'Pray tell me, what kind of men were they? Peasants, malefactors, young, old?'

'Workers. Mostly young, Sir.'

'And were the young ladies in any danger, Thomas?'

'I think so.'

'And you yourself?'

'I think not.'

'Hmmm,' was the disconcerted reply. Presently he said, 'And this Mr. Hubert, he was walking with you, or nearby?'

'Nearby, I think.'

'And who is Mr. Richards?'

'A shophand.'

'You and two ladies were accompanied by a shophand?'

'Yes.'

'How did that come to pass?'

'He was bringing goods, Sir.'

'What sort of man was he, Thomas?'

I did not answer at first, but he pressed me again and at last I replied, 'He was not sensible.'

'I see. And so the workers attacked him, or perhaps he attacked them, in defence of the ladies?'

'No, Sir.'

'No? But yet I heard he was injured?'

'By Mr. Hubert, Sir.'

'By Mr. Hubert? But did he not come to your assistance?'

'Yes.'

'Then how came it that he injured the shophand?'

'He pulled him from his horse.'

Mr. Harland seemed both surprised and perplexed to hear it, and after another silence, he said, 'I am grateful for this information, Thomas, as it is of the utmost importance. Tell me then, what sort of man is Mr. Hubert?'

'Unusual.'

'I confess I had guessed as much myself. And so the story goes that he chased away this worthless band of workers; is it so?'

'Yes, Sir.'

'And then I presume he came back to assist yourself and the ladies, and fetch help for this Mr. Richards?'

'No, Sir.'

'He did not return immediately?'

'No, Sir.'

'But after a short while then, to ascertain their safety?'

'No, Sir.'

He was silent again. By now we were nearing the house of the Lawrences, and I saw plainly ahead of us Mr. Hubert himself, walking along the side of the road, and carelessly swinging his stick at the tall greenery.

Mr. Harland noticed him shortly thereafter, and said, 'And this gentleman who approaches is Mr. Hubert?'

I nodded. Mr. Harland studied him carefully as we approached, and outpacing me as we drew near I heard him apologize for taking the liberty of introducing himself, but excusing his forwardness by reason of his desire to thank him for his heroism.

Mr. Hubert merely stared at him in response, but just when it seemed he would not reply, he said, 'And what concern is this to you, Sir?'

'I am a friend of Miss Reckert and her father.'

'Well, Sir?'

'I feel entitled to take a near interest in what affects her.'

Mr. Hubert merely gazed off distractedly into the distance as though he was only partly listening. Eventually he turned back to Mr. Harland, and as if from a distant remembrance of what he had said, replied unconcernedly 'I wish you the best with that, Sir,' with which he turned his back to go, beginning to swing his stick again at the verdure as he walked.

Mr. Harland looked after him with some amazement, seeming uncertain whether he behaved thus from a dislike of the unofficial mode of this introduction, or some other motive more incomprehensible.

After this he mounted his horse and continued upon his way. When arrived perhaps a quarter of an hour later, I was seen into the parlour as before, where I found Miss Lawrence and Mr. Harland engaged in conversation.

'Good morning, Thomas,' said Miss Lawrence, 'if you have come to visit Miss Reckert, I fear she sees no one at present, but perhaps you would oblige me and stay somewhat to visit with me.'

I nodded swiftly, then moved to a chair at the far corner of the room, where I took a book from the table and tried my best to stay out of the way.

Mr. Harland sighed in exasperation to understand that Miss Lawrence expected to admit me once he had gone, but said nothing, only paced about a bit, hat still in hand.

'As I was saying, Mr. Harland, despite the unsettling events of the last few days which have affected us all, you may assure Mr. Reckert that Miss Reckert is in perfect health. Every so often she appears to suffer fits of uneasiness, but they preceded the recent drama, and come and go quickly with the occasion.'

Mr. Harland stopped and seated himself, before saying, 'Then it seems I have the unhappiness of timing my visits with these intervals.'

'Indeed, Sir, I have myself thought it quite uncanny.'

Mr. Harland sighed again before saying, 'Forgive me, Miss Lawrence, but I am unsuited to matters requiring concealment and address. If Miss Reckert avoids me, as is my fear and your implication,

I am grieved indeed. I would not disoblige her for the world, but all the same I must speak with her.'

'These two things may be impossible to reconcile. Howsoever that may be, I would not have you conclude from what I have said that I know more than I do in truth. Curiosity and affection are an impertinent combination, and I shall confess to having both.'

Mr. Harland paused for a moment, in thought, but having no other recourse, he said presently, 'I suppose I have only to thank you for your candour, Madam. Good-day.' With that he bowed and took leave.

When he had gone, Miss Lawrence turned to me kindly and said, 'Stay here, dear Thomas and I will try to find out if Miss Reckert is able to receive you now.'

A very short time later I was admitted upstairs. Miss Reckert seemed somewhat out of sorts, but at long last she revived enough to say, 'And so, Thomas, all is decided. You are to go to work for an engraver in Kent, in only three days' time. I am sorry I have not had more time to prepare you, but it seems Mr. Seymour has gone personally to see about the matter himself. He has always been very fond of you. He sent me an express yesterday telling me all the details. He has arranged for you to be an apprentice of sorts to a Mr. Little, with whose family you are to live. He assures me there is not a more gentle, trustworthy fellow alive. If he proves to be mistaken on that count, Thomas, do not fail to write to me and I will send for you immediately. A man can wear a public character very different from his private one, and Mr. Seymour may not always be the most discerning. He has nevertheless sent such anecdotes and examples as would satisfy me. You must read them yourself,' offering me the letter, 'and I am sure you will agree.'

After this she lapsed into silence, gazing sadly out the window. I read the letter as she requested and found everything as she described.

'Three days–' were the words which finally escaped me.

'I feel it, Thomas,' replied she, taking my hand, 'and several times I have been tempted to undo it all. It is a separation of sorts, which neither of us can deny, yet I feel in my heart that no true separation shall ever occur between us. As both your mother and sister in one, I know my duty to you extends beyond keeping you as a mere plaything and companion, when you are destined for more.'

I sobbed like the child I once was, and Miss Reckert made no attempt to hold back her own tears. She had at that time all too many reasons for extreme sensibility, and we remained in that way for some time. When she had regained her composure, she said, 'Mrs. Lawrence had proposed to take us to the coast for a few days. I shall not be sorry to leave the area, but by the time I return on Friday next, you will already be settled. Perhaps that will be for the best, for I do not know how many scenes like this I can withstand.'

This news was rather unexpected. If this was to be our last meeting for some while, there were many things I wished to say. I scrambled for how to broach the subject of Mr. Harland. The difficulty alone could not dissuade me, but unluckily, in my haste to introduce the subject, I blurted out, 'I must speak to you of Mr. Harland, dearest Madam.'

Miss Reckert looked aghast at the very mention of his name, and fell to tears immediately. I tried fruitlessly to say what I meant, but the sight of her distress was too much for me to behold. When she could compel herself to speak again, she said, 'Oh, Thomas, as you love me, do not let me hear that name again; it can only give me pain.'

And so ended my last interview with Miss Reckert.

Three days later I travelled to the home of Mr. Little. He was just as Mr. Seymour had represented him. Mr. Little ran a modest shop in Woolwich, called Little and Sons Engraving. The business had been begun by the current Mr. Little's father, while the present owner had no sons, only two daughters. He specialized in recreating maps or documents, at times transcribing musical scores. I have no time to go into greater detail.

On about the third day of my apprenticeship, I was sent to a nearby town to transcribe a letter for a successful, though illiterate, merchant. As I passed through the town, I saw a man on horseback gathering a little crowd around him. I was surprised to hear him inquire in English whether anyone knew of a man named M. Hubert in these parts. I stopped at the sound of that name, from an instinct of curiosity. There was something about the tone and manner of the inquisitor which made me uneasy, and as the welfare of Miss Reckert was ever foremost in my mind, I paused near the wall of a shop in the hope of hearing more.

In response to his inquiry, no one ventured to say much, and one or two fellows began to barter for a reward for any intelligence they provided. I guessed by their overall demeanours that neither had any information in truth, and so did the inquisitor himself, for he leaned down from his horse and lifted one unlucky fellow in the air. As he did so, my eyes alighted on his hand, where I saw the figure of a star clearly delineated on the back of his hand. At first I thought it was a drawing of sorts, but the longer I looked, the more it seemed like a scar, not so old that was white. As I looked at it, I recalled Mr. Hubert's words. 'Some stars are merciful, and others kill.'

These two circumstances were connected, I felt it in my bones, yet I could not fathom how. As I racked my mind to discover it, I became aware too late that I had attracted the attention of the man himself. Before I knew it, I found he was standing before me, looking down at me with menace. 'So little one, you like my scar, do you?' he said in English, 'You have seen one like it, perhaps?'

I shook my head emphatically in response, but he did not relax his attention, saying after a moment, 'Tell me child, are you from this area?'

I made no answer, but several bystanders took up the question and agreed that they had never seen me before. He smiled mirthlessly and leaned closer, 'Tell me boy, do you know anything of the Marquis de La Croix? Of M. Hubert?'

I shook my head again but my heart was beating and my eyes no doubt betrayed the fear I felt.

'There is no need to be afraid,' said he. 'If you tell me anything of use, there shall certainly be a shilling for you.' He turned from me to his companion, and said in French, 'Take him aside. I will squeeze him and find out what he knows. He has a knowing look, if I am not much mistaken.'

The other man indicated for me to follow him, and as I did so, I heard the inquisitor say in English: 'I need two or three men who can swing a sword, and who will not shrink from the doing so. I have no need of schoolboys or their confessors, but shall reward a stout heart where I find it.'

At these last words my heart beat with the most anxious foreboding. With every ounce of composure I could muster, I said to the man who led me, 'I must deliver this letter, Sir.'

I gestured to the upcoming houses, and seeing they were not far, he said, 'Be quick about it boy, or that shilling shall go to someone else.'

I nodded quickly then ran in haste alongside the first home I saw. Around back there were two horses tied up next-door. As I frantically loosened the rope of one, I said to a child playing nearby, 'I have gone South. South!' and then with all the speed I could muster while staying upon the horse, I did just that.

I knew it would be only a very short time till I was missed and having ridden only infrequently, I had no illusions about being able to out-pace an experienced horseman. When I had gone perhaps a mile or less, I left the road and entered a forest path, leading the horse a fair way in. I tied it to a tree and crept back nearer the road, where I climbed the tallest tree near and waited to see if I was followed. I had hardly been there five minutes when I heard hoofbeats, and shortly after three men rode by at such a furious speed I could hardly discern they were the same I had fled.

Once they had passed, I climbed down and returned to the horse. I shall not attempt to describe the jumble of thoughts and feelings I was pray to at that time. It will suffice to say that my anxiety for Miss Reckert guided all my decisions, but even this, I think is superfluous.

I led the horse further along the path through the forest on foot, till at last I came out the other side. I deliberated very little what to do. It seemed clear to me that I could not return to Mr. Little, having first taken the decision to run. The suspicions which must have been excited by my flight made it all the more imperative I not risk being discovered in any place where I was known, and could be traced back to Miss Reckert and Mr. Hubert.

Without knowing the exact nature of what I feared, I feared it with all my being, and fear it still.

If I was not to return, then I must go in the opposite direction, and so when I reached the road, I continued Southwards myself, though at a fair distance from the road upon which I was pursued.

Night fell and I had no coat, and no money to seek shelter. I spent the night in the woods, and awoke the next morning, chilled to my bones. I climbed atop my horse and clung to it for warmth. The exposure had already taken a toll on me and I fell asleep on its back, letting it go where it would for food and water.

When I next awoke, I was on a cot in a small dwelling. I had a high fever and I drifted in and out of sleep, dimly aware that an older woman tended me from time to time. It was perhaps two or three days later when I awoke more myself...

I must hurry my relation. It is near dawn as I write and M. Tolouse is beginning to stir.

From the old cottager I received new clothes and a bit of money. She had sold the horse at my direction, and I left her with half the proceeds. She was a kind woman, who told me at my departure that I spoke more in my delirium than I ever did otherwise, and that I had talked incessantly of Miss Reckert and Mr. Harland and 'many odd things besides.'

Though I was still weak, it seemed to me that my fever had wrought some change upon me. I was still cautious and retiring, but I felt as if my courage or my will had been somehow emboldened. My identity and my former life, which till then had seemed like a dream, uncertain and obscured, was now clear and undeniable. There is no time to say more.

My horse apparently had continued southwards as I slept. When I bid the cottager adieu, I travelled to the nearest town of Gravesend. From here I meant to form a plan to help Miss Reckert. Although

I had succeeded in leading that strange gentleman southwards for the time being, I guessed that it would allow several weeks time at best. The man who had pursued me did not seem the type to be easily deterred, and no one can be fooled forever. With this in mind I considered writing to Miss Reckert and telling her openly of my fears.

But what could I say? It was my instinct above all which directed me, and neither she nor Mr. Reckert were likely to take action on that basis alone. If I wrote Mr. Harland, the same obstacle existed, and even considering how motivated he might be to protect Miss Reckert, he was hardly in a position to influence her in the direction I wished.

I spent a good deal of time considering the possibilities which were all in some way or other impractical. It was at this same place upon the very next day that I encountered yourself, the young ladies and Mme. Gaspar. Accustomed as I was to reading the thoughts and feelings of others, I was most favourably impressed with yourself. Nevertheless, I will acknowledge that I never meant to stay long with you, but felt to pretend to accept the opportunity you gave me was the 'the path of least resistance.'

This part I write is for your eyes alone.

All this changed that very night when I beheld with astonishment that you bore the same mark on your hand I had seen upon the gentleman I had fled. Again I thought of Mr. Hubert's words, and felt certain you were the counterpoint to the brute I had seen. I decided at once to appeal to you for your assistance, and searched desperately for a way to broach the subject. I thought of mentioning Mr. Hubert, but knew not how I might inspire you to act in relation to Miss Reckert. You alone seemed likely to understand what it was which seemed to threaten her, but the more I considered the matter, the less likely I thought it was that any man should agree to travel any distance and encounter danger and inconvenience for the sake of a complete stranger. I say this not as a reproach but as a general rule. A man may do much to help those in front of him, but is not likely to travel far to locate those who are in need of his help.

All the same I did not lose hope and several times I attempted to begin, but my words escaped me altogether, and I do not think you even perceived the attempt.

Happily, it was at this time that Mlle de Courteline made her request. I realized at once that such a contrivance might enable me to engage your interest and emotions in the fate of one who is dearer to me than life itself. I thought (and I pray it is true) that if once you knew all which concerned and affected her, you would begin to feel for her some part of what I feel, and would not hesitate to do whatever was needed. When I began my story, the voice which emerged in place of my own surprised even myself. It seemed that I could inhabit the place of a narrator in one of the many novels I have read since my arrival in England, and in that character recite the tale which occupied my whole being. That in doing so I was betraying the very object of my solicitude is a truth I shall never come to terms with, but I felt I could not do otherwise. For her sake, I beg you to guard her from the knowledge of how much she has been exposed.

It has been five or six weeks since I last saw Miss Reckert. As I mentioned in the beginning of this letter, I rejoice at Mr. Seymour's arrival, since every week that my tale was still unfinished only added to my desperation.

Dearest Sir, after the last few weeks, my faith in your character and honour has only been heightened. The discovery that you are the Marquis de la Croix, (though I am far from fully understanding the implications) has only increased my certainty that you are the only person to whom I may entrust this charge. Go at once, I beseech you. I fear I have waited too long.

For myself, I mean to leave for France as soon as I may. Adieu, dear Sir. May angels preserve you, and through you, my beloved benefactress.

Thomas (Mouchard)

* * *

I am in haste, but I shall tell you what transpired as well as I am able. Though I copied the letter to you in full, I paused reading aloud where Thomas/Mouchard had indicated, and was amazed at what followed. The name of Hubert caught my interest at first, and the account of Lafont (for who else could it be!) nearly left me in a state of distraction.

Once I had read the remainder to myself, Mlle de Courteline requested, or perhaps I should say demanded, to know what it was Thomas had desired to keep from them.

"It is clear that he means to ask your help, nay, that he has asked for it already. What more must be concealed? Surely he does not fear that Mlle Vallon or I are lacking in discretion, or should betray a confidence? Neither my cousin nor I should ever breathe a word of this to anyone, you may be assured!"

I had no intention of telling them anything of the connections or conclusions Mouchard had drawn regarding myself, but I was too shocked to express myself properly. He had included directions to the region in his postscript, which he described as nearing a town called Crestham, sixty miles southwards along the coast. As soon as I fully appreciated the charge vested in me, I desired nothing but to hasten to fulfil it. Whatever he feared or guessed, Mouchard had no way of understanding what Lafont was capable of, nor of the single-minded dedication with which he pursued M. Hubert's destruction.

Occupied with such a flurry of thoughts, I made the ladies some hasty compliment, only to be recalled by the gentle Mlle Vallon, who said, "Dear M. Gramont, leave us not in such cruel suspense. Tell us at least whether you mean to do what Thomas asks, though I feel sure it is so!"

"Yes, Madam. I go this instant."

"Then we must not delay you. Pray write to us, Monsieur. It is not inappropriate for me to request it, is it cousin?" added she as an after thought.

"Heavens no!" replied Mlle de Courteline, waving her arm impatiently, "for I am sure we shall all go mad if he does not. Adieu, M. Gramont, do not forget us."

From there I fetched M. Tolouse, who scarcely inquired the reason I wished to set out so quickly. Once we were on the way, I told him what Mouchard had written, and he said, "Why I wish I had listened a bit closer to what he was on about. Seemed a good deal about women and the like, so I did not know what to make of it. And this person who Mouchard fears, do you know him?"

"M. Lafont."

"Lafont!" cried he, "Is not he your friend and companion; one of our own, one might say? I have heard he is the bastard son of Marie-Antoinette?"

"He is none of those things, M. Tolouse, but he is everything Mouchard, nay Thomas, fears and more. If he had known what I know, he should not have left it this long."

We rode the entire day and have now stopped at an inn in the town of Kettich, which is reportedly 5 miles from Crestham. Tomorrow I intend to go to Crestham, and I shall write as soon as I can discover the situation there.

Before Mr. Seymour's arrival, I had commenced the beginning of the end of my history and it seems that the two stories are coming together here. I fear sleep shall shun me tonight as I puzzle over what action next to take.

Your servant,
M.C.

Marcel de la Croix to Henri Renault

February 23rd, 1793

Dear Friend,

When I last left off writing my history, I told you of my parting with M. Lafont.

It was dawn again when I returned to the Chateau. Our absence had led to much speculation. Those who had acceded to M. Lafont's plan to deceive me seemed most aware that all was not well between us, and in our absence almost all of them left the Chateau. I know not what has become of them since, or if guilt or conspiracy more prompted their departure. By Philip's account it seems that half a dozen men left together and then several others merely seemed to disappear sometime before or during my return.

I found everyone else assembled in the great hall, perhaps fifteen in total. It was M. Calonne who first addressed me.

'I believe I speak for every man here, Monsieur Marquis, when I say I am glad to see you. What news is there? Where is M. Lafont?'

'It is only what I came here to say,' replied I, 'for I am much fatigued. M. Lafont and I have parted ways, though no blood has been shed.'

'How is that possible?' enjoined M. Mancette. 'Has the fiery Lafont we know become suddenly as meek as a lamb?'

'That, I am sure, is not the case, but I suspect there are others he would rather kill first. Dear gentlemen, dear companions, part we must all do soon, though I trust on better terms. Our time here is done, even the most stubborn among us must acknowledge. I will leave myself as soon as I am rested and perhaps sooner than many of you. You are welcome to my house so long as I can call it mine. Fare ye well, wherever Providence sends you, and I shall remember ye ever as brothers in adversity.'

Having said all I meant to, I retired with no further ado. The crushing weight of my sufferings the last months seemed to overwhelm me, and when I returned to my own chamber, I slept for nearly two days together.

While I slept I dreamt endlessly of the man I had killed. Sometimes I dreamt I was mistaken and he lived still. M. Hubert and M. Lafont were likewise either friends or enemies of mine, and I seemed to grow somewhat delirious. I heard voices, and called to them. I execrated M. Lafont for his crimes but he refused to hear me and my rants were unanswered.

Finally, I started awake at the sound of keys in my door. The main door was bolted from the inside, but there was a second door which connected my chamber to another, and this was only locked with a key. I started up in a frenzy, sword in hand, yelling, 'Villain! Who is it who comes to murder me in my sleep?'

The noise continued and very soon I beheld Philip's placid face. 'It is only I, my dear Monsieur, come with food and drink, and even a physician's advice, if you have not frightened him too much. Come, Sir,' cried he, to a man who stood behind him, 'he is a little delirious but I shall dare swear he shall not kill us.'

A small balding man perhaps five and fifty entered the room behind him.

''Tis my sister's husband, M. Hadre. He came to the gate to give me a message from my sister, who is preparing to leave to France, but as M. Hadre is a physician, I would not let him go till he had looked at you.'

I collapsed once more on the bed, but was brought to sit up presently to be examined. After doing so, the good man declared I was only exhausted, and if once the fever broke, I could be brought to eat and rest more regularly, all would be well. I thanked him and Philip permitted him to depart with many thanks.

'Your speech the other night made quite an impression on the last of the men here,' observed he, as he began to look around and take stock of my belongings. 'Many men have left, though most were reluctant to do so without an additional farewell. Those who remain seek to accompany you, though you have not yet revealed whither you are going.'

'Dear Philip,' cried I, wearily 'you have been like father and mother to me, both nursemaid and Valet de Chambre. The revolution is upon us, and with it comes a new era of equality and emancipation. You need no longer worry about tending to my follies, and I have not the will to tie any living being to my fate. I intend hereafter to bury myself in oblivion and relieve you from any part in my sorrows. As to my fortune, I have scarcely more right to it than you, and you need only name the sum you desire.'

'Your fever causes you to ramble,' said he, making no other acknowledgment of what I said.

'On my soul, it does not,' said I.

'Then for where is it you depart?'

'I know not, I care not.'

'Do you go alone?'

'Most certainly. Fare thee well, my good patient friend. You shall be happier, no doubt, than the person you have had the misfortune to serve.'

'Then by your leave, Sir–.'

'By your own,' interrupted I.

'By your leave, Sir,' repeated he, hardly marking the correction, 'there is still a matter I believe I may be able to assist you with. You asked me to discover what I could of the man you killed in defence of M. Montrond–.'

'I understood you could learn nothing?'

'That was several days ago, for now I can tell you at least that he was called Rublé.'

'And did he have any family?' returned I, attempting to stand in my delirium.

'Be seated, kind master,' said he. 'It is thought he had a sister, but as she is said to be married with family, I have not discovered her name. By your leave, I intend to remain here in the neighbourhood and try to discover it.'

'I do not know how I can accept your offer,' said I, with a sigh, 'for the area is safe for no one. I cannot justify allowing you to remain here unprotected.'

'I do not mean to remain in the Chateau, for no doubt it shall be a most symbolic target for occupation. However, if my sister means to abandon her house, I may live there or some other place. You forget, Monsieur, that I am not a young nobleman. The revolution has no quarrel with poor old men who are neither young enough to serve in its armies or rich enough to attract its attention. I will remain and I am sure in time I will discover what you want to know. Leave me but enough money to make myself agreeable to the friends I will cultivate, and I shall gather whatever I can.'

'You may take it all,' said I, transported with even a small hope of easing my conscience somewhat. 'I have no need of money.'

'I have told you before, young master,' said Philip gravely, 'that I no longer possess your fortune, which has been sent to England. If you fail to posses yourself of it in time, it shall not be my doing. For what has been kept in France,' said he, going to my cabinet and unlocking a small compartment behind outer doors, 'here is all that remains of any value within the Chateau.'

With that he drew forth a collection of money and jewels, which despite his representation, was still of great value.

'These I meant for you to take on your travels, and I have taken the liberty of assembling a great many currencies, in case the gold of Louis XVI is ever viewed with suspicion. By your leave, I shall appropriate a small part of this in order to fulfil your commands, but the rest I consign into your custody now.'

I looked with wonder at the contents of the pouch he presented me, not less marvelling at the care and prudence of the man who had prepared it for me.

'I shall not take it,' declared I, 'though I cannot find words to express my gratitude at the unparalleled care you have always taken of me. If you are able to discover the names of M. Rublé's kinsfolk, I shall be able to value the remainder of my fortune only so much as I will be able to bestow it upon them.'

Philip's eyes narrowed as I spoke. 'Forgive my bluntness, but you are still a child in the world in many respects. You have never yet known the evil caused by a lack of money, except by witnessing the misfortunes of others. Your generous and still impressionable nature imagines it does something noble by sharing in the misfortunes which are the general lot of mankind. Permit me to burden you with the advice of an old man who has seen much in his many years. Neither man nor woman need trouble themselves to create their own misfortune. Leave that to Providence, and be assured that She wants no assistance. Does not your own life tell you that? Though the son of privilege, were you not wanting parental affection and sympathy? Has not your family been annihilated, your country destroyed? With all this, think you still that you are obligated to impose hard conditions on yourself?'

Though I was now somewhat ashamed to do so, I still persisted in my original wish. In time we were brought closer to each other's position by two separate considerations. I was brought to agree to take more than I intended by the thought I might be able to indulge my charitable inclinations somewhat. Philip at last declared that periods of temporary want and deprivation might secure my future good by ensuring I learnt to value money as I ought to.

In the end I returned to my bed and left the arranging of the whole affair to Philip, who diligently outfitted me with everything I needed for my journey. During that time, we agreed to meet in nine months at an inn in Amiens. Philip had often stayed there as a boy. In the event it was no longer there, we agreed to stay at the nearest public house to it, and if that failed, to travel daily between the two towns in the area to find each other. I agreed to stay in France during that time, awaiting the outcome of his researches.

My recovery was not as quick as I had hoped, and during the few days I waited for my strength to return, all of the men who were departing came to call upon me in my chamber and say farewell. Several of them pressed me earnestly to accept their offers to travel with them but I declined. Though these men had been my friends and companions these last months, I felt no great union of thought and mind with any of them.

At last came faithful young Joseph, who told me he intended to set out the next day for the Austrian-Netherlands. He sued for my company rather more as a favour, for he said, 'Since you have become my benefactor, I ask not merely for your company but protection. Though I ought to have more shame in confessing it, the joy I have found in books has given me a newfound fear of perishing at the end of a sword; pleasure in life makes one a coward. I intend to ride as fast as I can to the border, or run there, if my horse tires too soon. I fear a young man of my appearance shall no sooner be seen on the loose than drafted into the army, and then what a sorry end to my existence!'

'If you think my accompanying you should be of any assistance, then I am ready to do so, for it is to your well-timed intelligence that I owe some of the preservation of at least a part of my peace.'

With this being determined, we set out together the following day. Our journey was very uneventful. We kept largely to the fields, changing horses only once and without much difficulty. Several miles before the border, it seemed we could breathe a little easier, for many of the places we passed by then were quite accustomed to our sort. Few seemed to doubt our wish to leave France, and few seemed to judge us for doing so. All the same, I was ill at ease by the thought that I was fleeing my country in its time of need.

We came eventually to a remote Monastery nearing the border, and begging for asylum for one night, we were admitted and treated very kindly.

Ah, but this you know well. My time there I believe you either remember or guess. Joseph continued on his way alone the next day, and I ended up staying for several months. It is here I had the good fortune to make your acquaintance, and cultivate a friendship I expect to endure for my lifetime. I am sorry I could not share my story then, and I hope I have fully atoned for my reticence by now (no doubt you would say I have over-atoned in sheer length and detail, but I confess to have found it cathartic to do so).

I will not dwell too long upon the guilt I struggled with while I remained amongst your brethren, for I know you suffer from a similar affliction.

After we journeyed together from the Monastery, I believe I told you in parting that I meant to meet my former servant, Philip. When at last I received your direction in Switzerland, I fear I had not the means to send you regular letters, and my correspondence was scarcely better than fitful. Despite this, I feel certain you are kind enough to be curious as to what transpired. I have always meant to explain the cause of my long silence, which was nothing less than extreme poverty.

It was still four months from the time I had agreed to meet Philip. The revolution raged on with more force and vigour than ever. I wandered, like Rasselas, searching for the source of happiness on this mortal plain. I did not find it. Under the name I bear now, I ranged around aimlessly. Everywhere I turned I encountered distress and inequity, seemingly not a bit lessened since the start of all the turmoil. Till I left the Monastery, I had not touched the bounty preserved for me, but very soon thereafter I discovered I had run through almost all of it.

Too late I resolved to curtail my expenses; food, shelter and sheer preservation drained my purse. For the first time in my life I experienced hunger and deprivation, the sight of which has always raised my pity. The hunger of those days was unremitting, and it engrossed the attention of my whole mind and soul. I had sold everything about me that I could spare, even the buttons on my coat. For a week I lived on little bits of unripened fruit I found on my way. Sometimes I was chased off by peasants who were understandably protective of their crop. During those days, I never thought of fighting, and lacked probably the strength to do so as well.

A month and a half still remained till the time I was to meet Philip, and I wondered how I would manage to survive till then. My horse I retained, but I felt sure I would need to sell it if I was to live till then, but then how would I travel?

I sat down under a large tree in a field one glorious afternoon, pondering these matters after attempting to eat a most unpalatable pear. I thought of Philip and the many warnings he had given me. I knew that if he could have seen my state, he would have suffered yet more than I did for my folly. Till then I had disdained money and felt that even the possession of it made me accessory to the evil felt by those who lacked it, but in those many days I came all too clearly to appreciate its necessity.

The boots I had worn these long months were by this time hardly fit to wear. I pulled one off as I had done many a time and emptied its contents. What was my surprise when I saw that amidst the rocks which fell out of it was a small green gem. I looked in wonder to see from whence it had come, and I discovered that I had worn away a hole in my sole, from which I could clearly see a small treasure trove of jewels and coin had been stored. An inspection of the other boot revealed that a similar alteration had been made, but that a hole had first appeared in the bottom of the sole, and part of the store had likely fallen on the road as I travelled. There were some still lodged within, and when I tallied it up together, I rejoiced to find I had now almost as much as I had started out with. Having now learnt prudence firsthand, I was now in possession of far more than I would ever need to finish my journey. How did I bless the ingenuity and almost celestial guardianship of my dear Philip! How fondly did I think of him in the first moment thereafter when I tasted food. The value of this lesson shall not be effaced by years.

Now somewhat more reconciled to the burden of money, I continued my journey more pleasantly. As I travelled through regions not too far distant from whence I had come, I heard several interesting tales purporting to involve the League of the Star. It is from such similar unreliable accounts I believe M. Tolouse has whatever information he possesses. The names Lafont and La Croix seem to have been confuted and confused. If you were to give credit to any of these reports, you would believe that one or both of us is the illegitimate son or clandestine lover of Marie Antoinette. Nothing can so forcibly convince a person of the inaccuracy of the general report as having a share in it.

During those last weeks in France, I drifted about witnessing firsthand the upheaval of our country. My habit of travelling on fields rather than roads, joined with my heightened knowledge of the likely impediments faced by travellers, allowed me to travel in relative safety, while all the world seemed to crumble around me. The life of the peasant seemed to change the least, to my eye, for despite the calls for freedom and equality everywhere echoed, they continued to starve as their betters negotiated and ruminated on the finer points of their emancipation.

At last the time arrived when I was to meet Philip. I travelled to the appointed place and found the inn seemingly no worse for the turmoil of the nation. Philip was already there and I was seen immediately to his room.

My heart was cheered to see him once more and even his laconic brow betrayed relief as I entered. We spoke together like long acquaintances, save only that he persisted in using the language and forms of servant and master. He was kind enough to pity the distress I had encountered through my carelessness, and could almost have wept for joy when I described how I had discovered the hidden store he had prepared me.

'I only wished it would be so!' exclaimed he, 'for I knew that your boots could not be sold for any kind of value. From their state, I guessed it would be a few months at least till they began to wear either from the top or the bottom, and at that time you would certainly notice when you inspected the damage. At the very worst, you would never notice, and the bounty would be strewn on the roads as you travelled. Knowing your particular disposition, I felt confident you would be the last to repine if your scattered wealth was picked up by farmers and peasants wherever you went.'

'You were quite justified in thinking so, my dear friend. But come, forgive my impatience, tell me whether you had any success discovering the sister of Monsieur Rublé?'

Philip sighed. 'I see you are as determined as ever to know it,' said he, 'and so I shall tell you at once.'

With a considerable amount of trouble, he had learnt that M. Rublé's sister was called Mme. Dorrel. Mme. Dorrel was a widow with seven children, who had survived these last years partially with the help of her brother's bounty. At his death she had sunk into poverty. Her appeals to his fellow officers and commanders were ineffectual, but it was from the family of one of them that Philip had secured most of his information. Mme. Dorrel had come to request assistance travelling to England, for she said she chose not to expose her children to violence and upheaval while she could not get a bit of bread from those for whom her brother had given his life. She had put by enough to cross over, but has scarcely any more to her name.

'A woman with no money and no connections shall not be difficult to find in England,' said he. 'It seems unlikely she would get far on so little, and there are few ports to dock at. Refugees from our country are likely to flock to the same parts, and so I have little doubt you may be able to find her. But tell me, Sir, has your brush with poverty not dissuaded you from your former intentions?'

'You have taught me a lesson I shall not soon forget, but surely there is another lesson within it I cannot set aside, which is the gift of unexpected bounty to the depressed soul. Although by this action I hope to palliate my guilt, I have no other earthly hope. I have spent a good portion of the last months ruminating upon my plan. I have learnt to be reasonable and I no longer see money as an evil to be avoided. I shall set aside for myself a modest sum from which I shall, with industry and prudence, be able to make up a small living. I will set aside an equal sum for you, for I know better than to recommend independence to you without providing you the means of following my advice. The bulk of my fortune shall go to the family I have robbed of their protection and by this act alone can I hope to know some peace.'

'Consider, dear Master, that you cannot foresee the future. There may come a time when you have children and you will curse the impetuosity which led you to give to strangers all that might have increased their happiness.'

'Here you are wrong,' replied I, 'for if I do not do it, I shall not live at all, for not a day goes by that I do not feel the remorse of a true penitent. As for any children I may have, I assure you it is beyond possibility. I thought at first that I could reverse the sins of my father, and in so doing begin to restore the honour of the name to which I was born. Far from doing so I have only added to its infamy. I have sheltered and abetted a violent unprincipled man, and turned a blind eye to the reports of his misdeeds which reached me, without inquiry into the many I did not hear. I have killed men merely to vent my own rage and satisfy my need for vengeance. However pure my intentions, it is as if the very blood in my veins opposes me. The line of La Croix shall die with its last representative. I have taken a vow never to marry, and intend never to risk the continuance of my family.'

Philip heard me in absolute silence, and so I continued. 'You who have so long been subject to the caprices of both father and son, do you not rejoice at the honourable end of all your obligations? Tell me, dear friend, have you no plans of your own to relate? You are not too old to put into action what you suggest for me. Have you no wish to marry?'

'As I can no longer flatter myself with being able to prevail upon you to abandon your plans, I shall reconcile myself to your will as much as possible.'

Such was the extent of his answer. We parted the next day, and I did not see him again until lately. I hope he means to possess himself of the sum I promised him, and when next I see him, I shall prompt him again.

* * *

I will try to sum up the rest of my adventures as quickly as I may. From Amiens I travelled the straightest path to Calais, hoping and intending to cross to England by the swiftest route. I stopped once to rest at an inn in the town of Merville, where I took my meal in the common room. Several officers of the local militia were there making merry and presently they invited me to join them. Not wishing to seem uncivil, I accepted their invitation, and in their company drank a fair quantity of wine.

Some time during the meal their superior officer, Captain Savoi, entered the room. Instantly all eyes were turned towards him and several toasts raised to him. He bowed to us, seemingly a good-natured man, who had evidently earned the respect and affection of the men who fought beneath him.

I noticed once or twice throughout the evening that he appeared to regard me with special scrutiny, but knowing myself to be the only stranger to him in that party, I accounted for his attention in that way.

When I had finished eating, I bid these merry fellows adieu and left the little inn I had stopped at, which was situated by itself on the road apart from any village or general habitation. I had ridden only a short way when I heard the sound of hoof-beats behind me. I reached instinctively for my sword and turned to see who followed. I had no greater surprise than I am certain you will have when I beheld Captain Savoi.

He signalled for me to pause and then trotted up.

'I could not help but observe, Monsieur, when I saw you making merry with my officers, that your hand bears a mark upon it. May I ask what it depicts?'

I was silent, irresolute, and wondering how I should answer him, cursing my carelessness at the same time.

'It is my duty to inquire,' continued he, 'for all of the commanders in the region have been asked to apprehend any man who bears a star brand on the top of his hand, and thus you see I am obligated to investigate the matter.'

I sighed in sheer frustration. The man before me was of a particular cast, similar in certain respects to M. Rublé. His countenance bore the marks of open-minded generosity and his manner was calm and pleasing.

'I should be sorry if anything would make us enemies to each other,' replied I, 'for the affection of the soldiers who serve beneath you does you nothing but credit.'

'I am myself sorry for the necessity duty places upon me.'

'It is an unfortunate situation indeed where duty and honour places decent men in opposition to each other.'

'You are right, Monsieur, but 'tis not merely circumstances but principles which make men enemies in present times. I have sworn to uphold the cause of liberty and oppose any who fights against it. Must I not keep my word?'

'Truly, but my own case is different. The cause of the revolution is more suited to me than the protection of privilege, but fate intervened and honour has dictated I oppose even myself. I have often told myself I am helpless to do other than what I have done, but my conscience still upbraids me. Several months ago it was my misfortune to kill a man who I would have preferred to befriend, and his image lives with me since. You seem like him an honourable man, and I am loathe to have your blood on my hands.'

He smiled quickly, then said with a sober laugh, 'In any case I should try to spare you the self-reproach if I could. However, your words resonate with me in this case, for I was reluctant to approach you, as you seem to be an honest, temperate sort of man, the kind I should not wish to meddle with if it could be helped.'

He paused for a moment, then sighed. 'And what do you make of these times, Monsieur, if you do not mind me asking? Is France to know peace?'

'I hope so,' replied I, 'but so many things have been turned out of drawers, it may be a long time before they are set straight.'

'I fear you are right. Come, Monsieur, I do not like to act hastily in any matter, and your tale is a cautionary one for a man in my position. I do not think I should sleep well after the sight of your lifeless corpse, and I perceive it would be madness for you to come with me any other way. My house is at the end of this road and my supper is ready. If you will come with me and share my meal, I shall have more time to think upon it.'

I accepted his offer and we walked together to the end of the lane. Mme. Savoi was a pleasant woman, who welcomed me graciously to their home.

'My husband does not often bring home visitors, M. Gramont,' said she, 'and we are very honoured to receive you.'

Between them they had five children, all daughters, ranging in age from three to ten.

'My husband does not despair of someday having a son,' said Mme. Savoi, as she introduced them, 'but for me I am content with what the Lord has given us. He at least knows I do not want for any occupation!'

I hardly knew how to feel worthy of their hospitality, considering that it was yet possible I would be the destroyer of the father and husband so cherished by them all. I consoled myself with the thought that I did not wish it, and wondered if Captain Savoi had taken this method of robbing me of my will to fight him.

After our meal was finished, dishes were cleared and Captain Savoi and I were left to ourselves. I immediately expressed my admiration for his family, and my suspicion as to his motive for bringing me here.

'No, Monsieur, I assure you it was not meditated. Though unintentionally enough, I have taken this method of reminding myself that a man's life is not always his own to sacrifice.'

A moment or two later he stood up and moved to the nearby bureau. He pulled several papers from it and wrote for a short while, then handed them to me.

'These papers shall allow M. Gramont to proceed as far as the coast. Do I anticipate your intentions correctly?'

I nodded, touched by this mark of confidence.

'A man must trust his own judgement,' said he, 'and my judgement tells me it will be no blight to my honour for you to proceed, and no act of virtue to prevent you. If in better times, you return to France, please call upon me and my family. Till then, be sure to cover your hand. Adieu!'

I do not know how much difficulty I might have encountered without these papers, but surely I can say that the ports were watched quite carefully by then. The ship I had hoped to sail upon was delayed for a week, and nearly every day some impudent revolutionary guard accosted me and demanded to see my papers. Were it not for Captain Savoi, I am sure at least there would have been more bloodshed.

And here at last, but for the present, ends the history of Marcel de La Croix. May the fortunes of M. Gramont require less explanation.

I am, dear Sir, your most obedient,
M.C.

Marcel de la Croix to Henri Renault

February 27th, 1793

Dear Friend,

It rained the whole night we stayed at the inn, and in the morning there were still no signs of it stopping. I was loathe to lose any time, but M. Tolouse seemed to expect we would not travel till the weather had cleared up. I asked the innkeeper how long we could expect such a torrent to last in these parts and he merely shrugged and said in English, "On the coast, these storms usually last for days."

"Then we must have a carriage," said I, "or we shall ride by the next post."

"The post don't come this way today, your excellency," replied he, "for there is a better road to the south, and so long as there is no great need to come down here, the weather will send them along the better one, you can be sure."

"Then we shall have to acquire a carriage, or go by horse."

"You can't think of going by horseback in all this, my good gentlemen, for you will be drenched to the bone before you get ten miles from here."

"We need only go a few more. Tell me, do you know of the Lawrence family?"

"Aye, aye, nine or ten miles along this road will get you there, if you head inland. Begging your pardon, but you'll be as wet as rats and twice as muddy by the time you get that far."

"And Mr. Reckert's family lives in the area?" persisted I, ignoring his other observations.

"Aye, so he does. If you are going along the northern road, perhaps six miles along you enter his land, which stretches all the way to Kettich. From Kettich, take the turn into Reckert Village, and the great house will be as clear as your face."

"Then Mr. Reckert is well-known hereabouts?"

"Aye, for he is the richest man for miles around. He comes 'round here now and again and is sociable enough with the quality folk, if you take my meaning. He likes news of the world, and as my guests come from all corners, he drops in sometimes to hear the latest."

"Indeed," said I, hoping for more information, "yet I had heard he rather keeps to himself?"

"All grand folk do, i'reckon. He don't reserve much time for the riffraff, or even an old innkeeper like myself, though I have known him to sit and talk to an ambassador from Spain for nearly four hours. You don't know him yourself, then?"

"It seems we must have a carriage, my good man," said I, seeming not to hear his question. "Be so good as to tell us how best to go about it, or to supply one yourself, if you have one around."

He shook his head, resignedly, "I see you are a determined gentleman, so I shall say no more, else I would advise that the roads shall be unfit to pass by any means. I have an open carriage in the yard, hardly worth your time to look at, and indeed, I should not so much as mention it to you were you not in so great a hurry. Nor is there a horse to be had other than those you ride in upon, as I was telling your man this morning."

"What man?" said I, with surprise.

"Why the older gentleman, Sir, for he said you would need one on account of the weather. I told him much the same as I have told you, but it seems you are both of the same mind, which is just as it should be, I suppose. The nearest beast is not less than a mile's trudge through the field to fetch, and I know of no one who would do it for fifty pounds."

I told him I would be prepared to pay as much if he would find one, and with a look of disbelief, he wandered off with a great many assurances it could not be done.

Once he had gone, M. Tolouse declared, "There is not too much harm in a day or so, I'll warrant. 'Tis a good house, like so many English ones, and if we have fire and food and drink, a day of rest shall do us both good."

I did not reply, but yet was convinced that any delay was a most undesirable thing. A short time later, we heard the sound of a carriage approaching the inn yard. I called the innkeeper again in the hope I might find some way to take advantage of this opportunity, and instructed him to make inquiries about it.

He agreed to do so, though not before assuring me that any carriage we could come by would only be mired in the mud, and then we should certainly be preyed upon by highwaymen. At this last remark, M. Tolouse declared, "If there are highwaymen in the area, that changes things somewhat."

"You need only persuade your friend so, Sir, for I fear he is determined."

"As to that," said he, to me, "you may forget what I said before, for there is nothing I should like better than to kill an English highwayman, and if there are some in these parts, let us go directly; the less reliable the coach the better, I say, for then there shall be no question but that it is warranted."

This strange speech so amazed the innkeeper that he wandered off to do as I had asked without a word of reply.

A minute or two later he returned to us, saying, "Well, I'll be. 'Tis your own carriage you heard coming into the yard. It seems your servant has performed the impossible. I still say you will get bogged down before long, but for the time being I will hold my peace and wish you gentlemen the best, whatever you are about."

With this he departed, and Philip appeared quickly thereafter. He was characteristically dismissive of my gratitude and made shift to pretend as though he had acted on my orders.

"It was not difficult to tell a carriage is needed in poor weather, and as you are almost always in some sort of hurry, I did not see any reason it should be different on this occasion."

After that there was little to do but settle our bill and set out.

A short way from the inn, the rain had lessened, and as we moved inland, the country grew increasingly flat, with only gentle hills on either side. As our intention was to call at the Lawrences directly, we travelled through Kettich with curiosity, but did not stop.

Perhaps two miles from Kettich we encountered another carriage stopped on the road. I inquired of Philip what was the trouble, and a moment later he told me that one of the horses pulling the other carriage was lame, and one of the servants had gone to find a replacement. The carriage was heavy with mud and it seemed more than prudent to do so, but all the same, its occupant was uneasy waiting there. I instructed him to convey the message that we were more than happy to make room for the gentleman. A moment or two later, Philip came back to say, "It seems the gentleman, Mr. Reckert, is the owner of the property hereabouts. He is very grateful to receive your offer, but as he is travelling a short distance in the other direction, he says he would not presume to trouble you to turn around."

However natural it seemed to encounter a gentleman in his own neighbourhood, I could not help but jump to hear his name. When I recovered from my shock, I instructed Philip to inform him we were more than happy to do so, and to prevail upon him to accept if possible. Philip went directly, and M. Tolouse and I dismounted to prepare for him.

A moment or two later, a frail looking man of around sixty emerged from the other carriage with a grateful look. It was still raining hard enough to make an immediate introduction uncomfortable, and therefore one was not performed until we were all in the carriage together.

He apologized for inconveniencing us, to which I replied that we were most delighted to be of service to him.

"Indeed, kind Sir, your offer was the most welcome thing in the world. My constitution is not what it once was, and this cold chills one's bones. Were it not for the cold, I would be content to wait rather than inconvenience travellers like yourselves; it would be quite unfortunate, after all, if one had to fear highwaymen such a short distance from one's house."

M. Tolouse sighed at this, which I prayed he had not understood. Mr. Reckert appeared quite surprised to hear him do so, and as he seemed inclined to believe it was on account of the inconvenience we encountered, I said,

"Forgive my friend, M. Tolouse, Sir, for he has the unusual desire to meet a highwayman in these parts, and shall be distressed if we get too many miles further without meeting one."

Mr. Reckert laughed heartily at this, but said to him, "Pray, Monsieur, what shall you do if you meet one?"

"Why, as to that," replied M. Tolouse, in his most respectful manner, "it is a question I have wrestled with myself, but it seems to me that when the moment arises, I shall know which weapon to use, and so I have tried not to bother my head too much about it beforehand."

Mr. Reckert seemed very well pleased with his answer, and complimented him on his valour. The word was unfamiliar to M. Tolouse but when I conveyed the sentiment in French, he was most delighted, returning him many thanks. I was every moment concerned that he would say something inconvenient, having neglected to caution him beforehand. Happily, he was somewhat awed by Mr. Reckert, and content to allow me to speak for the most part.

After we travelled a short way in silence, he said, "Pardon me, Monsieur, but I believe your servant said you were from France. May I ask how long you have been in England?"

"Several months, I believe," said I, trying to reckon it up.

"Then may I further inquire, if you will forgive my curiosity, if it was the revolution which prompted you to travel here?"

"It was, Sir, in a manner of speaking."

There was another pause, but after a while he resumed the subject, and after some preliminary remarks back and forth, he said thoughtfully, "In considering the revolution, M. Gramont, it seems to me that things have gone beyond what was intended. If you will forgive me for speaking my mind so openly while we are so newly acquainted with each other, many of us here thought that not all of the aims of the revolutionaries were dishonourable, and at first we watched with much interest. The cause of the French peasants had found many a champion on English soil, but now that has all changed. The death of the King, the persecution of the lords, and the sheer violence which has ensued has caused any man who cheered the revolution to blush. But pardon me, gentleman, for my interest in the subject carries me away, and as the recipient of your assistance, I should do better to solicit your own opinion, who have seen much more than I, no doubt."

"The guest who shows he is at ease obliges one the most," replied I, "and I am gratified to discover our opinions coincide so closely on this point, which I mean most sincerely."

Mr. Reckert appeared still more pleased at my answer, and shortly thereafter he said, "May I inquire where you were going when you were so kind as to consent to reverse your progress on my behalf?"

I thought carefully how to reply, before at last saying, "We are hoping to find an old acquaintance of mine in this area, M. Hubert, who I understand is currently living at the home of the Lawrence family."

I could not bear to describe M. Hubert as my friend, but Mr. Reckert took no notice of the appellation, declaring, "The Lawrences, Sir, why I can hardly believe it! Do you know that it was there I was going myself when we were forced to stop? My daughter, Miss Reckert, stays with her friend Miss Lawrence at the moment, and to add to all this, it so happens that M. Hubert has recently done both of us the greatest service. If he is a friend of yours, Sir, you shall not wonder when I tell you that he did so with as much ferocity as bravery, which has caused some problems hereabouts, but nevertheless, we are extremely grateful to him. I do not know him myself, however, but I hope to know him soon. I had thought to see him today, but it seems it was not to be."

I knew not what to say at this revelation, which was not in truth very new to me at all, but I exclaimed my wonder to find it all the same. Such dishonesty was not to be helped under the circumstances.

Mr. Reckert was silent for a short while, pondering our unexpected meeting. "Gentleman," he said presently, "I hope you will do me the honour of taking some refreshment at my house, considering the inconvenience I have occasioned you."

M. Tolouse and I readily agreed. The weather continued to be unpleasant and we were both becoming hungry. I was slightly reluctant to allow any further delay in our journey, but I knew in our particular situation, haste would not answer all. Mr. Reckert seemed inclined to further our acquaintance, which I felt would be more conducive to our purpose than even a hasty arrival near the Lawrences.

Mr. Reckert seemed much as the innkeeper had described, and of a more social disposition than I had expected from Mouchard's story. Prolonged loneliness seemed likely to be the cause, however, for he spoke as one who had been denied his favourite pastime for several days, and wished to fit everything in at once. His expressions and manner were easy, and he passed from English to French with fluidity, when necessary, though most of the time we spoke English. The quickness from which we jumped from one unrelated subject to the next gave me the impression he had stored a great many thoughts and observations for several weeks, and was happy for the opportunity to express them.

I half expected Philip to disappear again when we were inside, but instead he hovered around me tending to imaginary needs and generally raising my consequence in the eyes of our host. A princely stranger is more easily accepted than an impoverished one, I reminded myself, but nevertheless it went much against my grain to be fussed over for such an extended period. At last when Philip had done all there was to do, and left us, Mr. Reckert declared, "Ah, M. Gramont, it seems that the French are as superior to us in their servants as they are in their sauces, their lace, their baking, and I suppose, in their dancing! How would an Englishman prize a servant like yours! Is such a man typical in France?"

"I think not, Sir. He was the servant of my father, and his father was the servant of my grandfather."

"How incredible!" cried he, "I have not been able to keep a cook for longer than six years. Nay, that is not entirely true, for there was Betty, who stayed about ten, yet generally speaking, one must go a-looking for another every year or so, be it maid, valet, coachman, or cook! I am a difficult old man, I suppose and we are tiresome to serve, I make no doubt."

Once we had consumed the bounty prepared for us, it seemed

time for us to depart, though our host seemed reluctant for us to do so. He inquired eventually if we were expected at the Lawrences that evening or would stay at an inn nearby that evening?

I was uncertain how to answer this inquiry, but at last I said, "I fear we have not yet decided where to stop this evening and are not expected at the Lawrences at all, since I have but just learnt M. Hubert is living in the area. For the last few months, we have been living in Sorsten Manor, a ways south of here."

"Then I believe you must know the Etheredge family!" interjected Mr. Reckert.

"Indeed, Sir, very hospitable, as I have found most of the English. Do you know them, Sir?"

"Not personally, I fear, but I know their reputation to be as you say. But pardon me, I interrupted you, M. Gramont."

"I was going to say, Sir, that I fear I am unacquainted with Mrs. Lawrence and her family, and did not realize her family was living in this area till the fortuitous visit of a Mr. Seymour, who came by Sorsten but lately to do some exploring. I believe he said he has lived in these parts for several years?"

"Indeed!" cried Mr. Reckert, with delight. "I have known Mr. Seymour these past fifteen years or so. He is as near to family as one could imagine. I see we have a good deal in common, M. Gramont, and I am more delighted than ever." He paused for a moment. "If you are undecided as to where to go from here, I should not wish to interfere. However I can tell you there are not many inns nearby, save the Red Hen, which is perhaps two more miles in the direction you are going. If you leave here in a short while, with any luck you shall be there by suppertime, or just after. There are other inns near Stearn Manor itself, of course, but you would have a longer way to go, and should get there in time to go to bed." He paused for a moment. "Tomorrow, I intend to try again to visit my daughter. If you do not object, I shall plan to call at the Red Hen on the chance you elect to stay there in the end. If you are there, and it is convenient to you, perhaps we will travel together? You obviously need no introduction to M. Hubert, but perhaps I may have the pleasure of introducing you to Mrs. Lawrence?"

We thanked him very much for the offer, which I was more glad of than I thought it wise to show, yet he said, "Indeed, gentleman, it is the least I can do, but I shall not be offended if you make other plans. Perhaps we shall meet again soon."

With that we took leave of him, on better terms than I could have wished.

"Well," said M. Tolouse, once we had left. "Are you still in a tremendous hurry, or do you wish to do as Mr. Reckert proposes and go to this inn, wherever it may be? Needless to say, I'll do as you see fit."

"We shall go to the inn, I think, for an introduction to the Lawrence family from Mr. Reckert will certainly go a long way to ease our entrance into that society. Let it please God that all be well for another night."

With no further ado, we set out again the way we had gone before we had encountered Mr. Reckert. A few miles past the spot we had met his carriage, we encountered a small village called Wetall, consisting of a church, an inn, a shop and a blacksmith. The Red Hen is perhaps one of the smaller inns I have ever seen, but quite sufficient for our needs. We went to bed almost immediately after supper, in order that we might be up bright and early in case Mr. Reckert came then.

It was after nine the next morning when I finally heard the bell announcing a visitor, and felt quite as delighted to behold Mr. Reckert again as he seemed to behold us.

"I am happy to find you decided to stay here after all, gentlemen, for it was my hope, though I did not like to seem officious. Shall it please you to travel with me, since we have the same destination?"

"We should be happy to, Sir," replied I.

In the carriage, his mood seemed equally cheery, though for a little while, he was silent. At last he said, "I have always marvelled at the mysterious hand of Providence, for I am more and more inclined to bless rather than curse my postponed outing yesterday, as it has been productive of your acquaintance. Indeed, M. Gramont, allow me to say one must feel ever safe in the company of M. Tolouse, ever comfortable in the presence of your dear servant, and well-entertained in your own."

I thanked him for my share of the compliment, but could not help but say, "I hope there is no reason for you to feel unsafe at any other time, Sir?"

"Aye, and so must we all of late, but I fear it is a long story, and perhaps only interesting to inhabitants of this area."

Despite this disclaimer, I found Mr. Reckert quite willing to talk about what he alluded to and after a very little encouragement, he gave me a short history of the neighbourhood and the abeyance of the Earl of C in much the same terms as Mourchard had previously. "Suffice be to say that only lately, the patience of the townspeople has run out and they have taken matters into their own hands. They have begun to build a new town where they feel they are entitled to. At first their work went on undisrupted, for few could truly dispute their claim, and Mr. Harland, who is generally looked on as the authority in this matter, was not inclined to interfere. This was understood as a tacit approval of sorts, and so I believe it was. It so happened shortly afterwards, however, that some young workers were found to have menaced my daughter and Miss Lawrence upon the road. Your friend, Mr. Hubert, valiantly defended them on that occasion, but he did so with such vigour and effectiveness that there were some around who said his actions were unwarranted. For myself, I bear nothing but gratitude to Mr. Hubert, who has protected what is most precious to me. At any rate, for the weeks immediately following, tensions were high hereabouts. Perhaps four weeks after this incident, a gentleman named Mr. Barber sounded the alarm amongst all the families in the neighbourhood when he discovered a large barrel of black powder had been stolen from his cellar–."

"Black powder, Sir," repeated I, with growing concern, "do you mean gunpowder?"

"Indeed, such as is used in arms or explosives. Mr. Barber is accustomed to keeping a few years' supply about him. My gamesman keeps only a fraction of the amount, but Mr. Barber's father was a military man, and that gentleman himself has been involved in production of the stuff, many years since. But as I was saying, a meeting was called whereupon Mr. Barber declared that the amount of explosives lost was enough to level any one of our houses, or supply five hundred men for a fortnight. He advised that we act swiftly to suppress any uprising lest we become like the French (begging your pardon). 'The conditions are right,' he declared, 'for the spirit of the revolution wafts over the ocean. If we continue to do nothing to exert our authority, we shall perhaps lose it entirely.

"His suggestion was that the construction of the town be forcibly halted, and the militia be brought in to ensure it was done. The entire room of people who heard him were equally alarmed and it was my dear friend Mr. Harland alone who kept his head under the circumstances. 'There are none more distressed than myself to hear of this theft of explosives,' said he, 'which came to my ears but yesterday, but from what I have gathered, the townspeople and workers claim complete ignorance of it, and believe instead that it is a ruse engineered to deny them of their rights. I am far from believing so myself, but if we should do as Mr. Barber suggests and summon the militia to halt their work, we must consider how the peace shall be maintained when they withdraw. It may be easy enough to request help to suppress a possible uprising, but how long can we reasonably expect a militia to be stationed here when our nearest neighbouring country declares war with the whole world? Let us instead attempt to discover by whom and for what purpose the black powder was stolen, and leave such extreme measures for when we have no other recourse.

"His argument prevailed," continued Mr. Reckert, "for that moment at least. Mr. Barber did not hide his disapproval, however, and took the unusual step of writing to Sir Edward Clelland of the situation. Sir Edward is thought to be another prominent potential heir of the Earl of C, another of his nephews via one of the Earl's sisters. Sir Edward's brother, Colonel Clelland, is in command of militia which was then stationed in Bury, and at the instigation of his brother, he brought his soldiers to the area as soon as he was able. The effect was disastrous, as Mr. Harland had foreseen. The people gathered to protest their arrival, and by consequence their assembly was deemed unlawful, and by the order of Sir Edward, nephew of the Earl, the site of the new town was hastily barricaded. Mr. Harland intervened in time to prevent any attempt to dismantle it completely, and is credited at least for this in the eyes of the townspeople. His claim to the property of the Earl is at least equal to that of Sir Edward, and so it has always been recognized here, and his objection was easily heeded. Colonel Clelland's militia stayed for eight days, whereupon he was obliged to return them all to their original assignments. Upon their withdrawal, the peasants tore down the wooden barricades swiftly and large bonfires were made in defiance of the interference. I hope you do not tire too much with the detail, M. Gramont."

"Not at all," replied I, having listened with rapt attention, "I am anxious to know what happened."

"Another meeting was called among the families, where it was agreed that the amassing crowds of workers and villagers was a serious threat to all landowners. Mr. Barber proposed small private armies be formed to police the area, and not even Mr. Harland denied the necessity for re-establishing order, once it had been compromised. By vote it was decided that these makeshift forces would keep the worksite closed for the time being. Since then, all of the landed families have sent whatever men we can, some dependants and domestics. I have myself no son to offer, but I have sent the son of my late wife's sister, whose situation is not so as to preclude him seeking advancement in this manner. Mr. Harland, Mr. Barber and three other men take turns maintaining the peace, but the nights are another story, as little can be done, and fear and uncertainty affect us all."

I was very affected by this recitation, of which I believe Tolouse understood only a very little. I was still quite full with various thoughts and consideration when we arrived at the house of the Lawrences.

The home of the Lawrences is called Stearn Manor, and from

the outside it has a rather gothic appearance, being constructed of dark coloured stone, with more points and angles than are normally found in English houses.

I could not help but be somewhat unsettled at the prospect of being introduced to the family, knowing as I did that the reception I received from M. Hubert may well put an end to any connection before it was established.

We were seen directly into the parlour, and in only a very short time, joined by a middle-aged woman, who seemed at once curious, gratified and unsettled by our visit. Mrs. Lawrence welcomed us with a mixture of grace and formality, declaring that any friends of Mr. Reckert were always welcome.

"You do me much honour, Mrs. Lawrence," replied he, 'but I cannot take all the credit for their arrival. M. Gramont is but lately come from France, where it seems he had the honour to know your brother, Mr. Hubert, and so it was that they meant to call here themselves. Forgive me, gentlemen, for no doubt you may speak for yourselves."

"Not as eloquently in English, to be sure," replied I, with a bow.

"A friend of Mr. Hubert?!" exclaimed Mrs. Lawrence, "Sir, you are very welcome." She paused suddenly after saying so, and then with evident caution she added, "I fear, Sir, you will be somewhat shocked by the changes my brother's recent experiences have wrought upon him. He has become withdrawn, uncommunicative and at times unpredictable. However happy we are to see any friend of his, I fear you may repent your trip."

Uncertainty overspread her every feature as she awaited my reply. I pitied her discomfort and could not help but say, "I beg you to be at ease on that score, Madam, for there is no one better than a fellow countryman to understand these matters, and to make any necessary allowances."

"Oh, Sir," cried she, "you are too kind, and I can see, a true friend. I hope only your coming may have a salutary effect on him. For myself, I have less than any idea what misfortunes have befallen him since the death of his wife, for he never speaks of such things.

Indeed, we are so very happy to have you, and of course M. Tolouse. M. Hubert is not at home at present, I fear, and it is sometimes difficult to predict his comings and goings. Tell me, M. Gramont, are you and your friend passing through or is it possible you may stay in the neighbourhood a day or two, that I might have the happiness of seeing my brother reunited with his old friend?"

"Indeed, madam, I hope so."

"You are very good. Where are you staying, if I may inquire?"

"We mean to stay at whichever inn is most convenient."

"The Hogshead is closest to here, Sir, I shall not say if it is the most convenient, for I have never stayed there. The Bluebird is a little further, but it is estimated at least as highly as the first, or so I hear."

"If the Hogshead is closest, Madam, we shall hope to stay there," said I, which she seemed pleased to understand as the compliment it was intended.

After a short silence, Mrs. Lawrence turned to Mr. Reckert and said, "We are happy to see you, my dear Sir. Mr. Harland came by yesterday morning to ask if all was well, but I confess already I am uneasy. Have you seen him lately, Sir?"

"No, but I dine with him tomorrow."

"I hope there is no ill news?"

"Not that I have heard, in any case," replied he.

The interactions between the two tended to be overly polite, and it seemed that neither was very well acquainted with the other, and each more deferential than easy.

Turning to me, Mrs. Lawrence said apologetically, "Perhaps Mr. Reckert has told you some of what has occurred these last few weeks," to which I nodded in reply. "It is most distressing, and we are all uneasy, though very thankful to Mr. Harland, who has been most diligent in his care of us all. I do not know what we would do if he was not. Even so, he cannot be here all the time, and even yesterday, we had a fright when he and his men were away somewhere else. It came to nothing, it seems, or one hardly knows what, or who, indeed, but we are quite on edge."

"Then perhaps you will sleep easier while these gentlemen are nearby," said he, upon which he told the anecdote regarding M. Tolouse's eagerness to meet a highwayman.

Mrs. Lawrence listened to his relation with surprise verging on disbelief, after which she declared, "Most unusual, most uncommon indeed! And would you like to meet a highwayman, truly, Sir? How dreadful!"

I translated briefly for M. Tolouse, who seemed to have got the substance already, "There are few things I should like better, Madam. To own the truth, I saw two or three fellows along the road when we came in who I should like to have a better look at, begging your pardon."

"Out here, Sir?" cried Mrs. Lawrence, alarmed. "Were they nearby?"

"I believe they were pedlars merely stopped down the lane," said I, attempting to calm her growing distress.

"But three together?" said she. "That is unusual! How I wish Mr. Harland was here with his men!"

"Nay, madam," replied M. Tolouse, with a profound bow, "if you feel like that, I beg leave to go have a look myself, and if they can't well account for themselves, I will send them packing."

Mrs. Lawrence highly approved of this plan and M. Tolouse wasted no time executing it; no doubt pleased to have devised a reason to escape the drawing room. Mr. Reckert appeared to have no more concern on the subject than I, having seen how harmless the little group was as we drove in. He took the opportunity of M. Tolouse's departure to inquire whether his daughter was home.

"Oh yes, dear me, what was I thinking? Of course you would see your daughter. I will ring for a servant at once, that Miss Reckert be told of your visit."

While we were waiting for the servant to return, Mrs. Lawrence returned again to the subject of the distress and uneasiness within the neighbourhood, explaining that since the incident upon the road, they were so on edge that every little oddity gave them alarm. She was naturally curious about the situation in France when we left it, and without providing too many specifics, I let her understand that the challenges she faced at the moment were not entirely new to me.

At that moment we were interrupted by a servant who brought word that Miss Reckert wished her father to be sent up, and accordingly he took a kind leave of us both, charging us to return as his guests as soon as may be.

Several minutes later, M. Tolouse returned looking triumphant. He bowed low as we rose to hear his report, saying in French, "Well, Madam, I have despatched them all. They were bickering about something together, as I came up. What it was, I don't pretend to know, but after waiting a while to try to make it out, I thought it best to send them away."

"And they left, Monsieur?" said she, still looking somewhat affrighted.

"They did, Madam, for I insisted they do so."

Mrs. Lawrence breathed in deeply, "Well," said she, "I am very glad you were here just at this time, and I am sorry to have caused you the trouble."

"'Twas no trouble at all," replied he, with an air of self-satisfaction.

Thinking that our visit had been long enough, I stood up to take leave of that lady, inquiring if it would be convenient for us to call the following afternoon after her brother?

"Oh yes, M. Gramont, I would be quite pleased if you should do so; I am only sorry he is not here to receive you, but no doubt he shall be soon."

From there we proceeded directly to the Hogshead. Mr. Reckert had ordered that his carriage be left to our disposal, and we sent it back to the Lawrences once we arrived at the inn. After securing our rooms and ordering dinner, I took a brief walk around our immediate surroundings. I saw little other than farm-workers, chickens and stray children running about. After supper, I set out on horseback in the direction of the Lawrences, but presently reflected that it might seem odd if I were to be seen riding there and back, so

I retraced my steps and threw myself in bed instead.

The next morning I set out before breakfast, intending to have a look around. I went by myself again, riding a little ways beyond Stearn Manor so as not to draw attention to myself. I saw very little on the way there or back, but at least nothing that concerned me. By the time I returned to the inn, I could eat my midday meal with greater peace of mind.

In the early afternoon, M. Tolouse and I travelled once again to Stearn. We were seen in almost immediately to Mrs. Lawrence, who was by herself, wearing an apologetic look.

"Forgive me, M. Gramont," said she, "but I am sorry to say that my brother is nowhere to be found, at present. It is on account of the odd humours he has. I fear you will cease to wish to see him!"

"Not at all, Madam," replied I with a bow.

She relaxed somewhat and asked us to sit. "Again, gentlemen, I am sorry to have caused you the trouble. This morning, I was obliged to repay a visit to a neighbour of mine. I had hoped to speak to my brother before then, but he was not around. I returned only an hour ago to hear I had missed both he and Mr. Harland while I was gone. M. Hubert did not leave word of his whereabouts, and as to the other gentleman, I doubt I will hear from him again till tomorrow. Ah, but these calls must be returned, whether one will or no. Forgive me, M. Gramont, I have neglected to ask how you found the Hogshead?"

"Very well, Madam."

"And do you leave tomorrow, or shall you stay sometime longer?"

"We hope to stay sometime longer, Madam. This is a very beautiful part of the country."

"I am happy you find it so." said she. "But are you at liberty to stay some days and weeks, or must you be gone in a day or two? I confess I find your presence here quite fortuitous for my poor brother, and of course, M. Tolouse as well."

"We are at liberty to stay for a couple weeks, and to own the truth, I am inclined to do so. Were we to stay longer, I fear we would need a more appropriate lodging."

Mrs. Lawrence nodded, "I approve of your consideration, Sir, for a gentleman should never stay very long at an inn, if he can help it. If you will pardon my interference, there are a good many private residences one might find more comfortable for a more extended stay. Courtney Lodge, for example, is but a short way from here and perhaps may be had for less than an inn, if one were to stay at least six weeks."

"I thank you for this information, Madam, and money would be no object, for I should happily pay for six weeks, merely to be more comfortable in three or four."

Mrs. Lawrence seemed pleased to find money was not a concern. "In that case, Sir, I am in the midst of returning a letter to Mr. Reed, the owner of Courtney Lodge, who I have known for many years. If you should like, I could add a few lines on the subject at the end?"

"That would be exceedingly kind of you, Madam."

"Not at all, for in doing so I should hope to oblige my friend by securing him a pleasing tenant, to oblige you if the house is to your liking, and to oblige my brother at the prospect of having an old friend nearby for a longer period. Give me but an hour or so, and you shall have it in hand."

"You are very kind, Madam. If M. Hubert is not at home at the moment, we shall take leave and call back in an hour."

"If you have nothing better to do, Sir, you may ride half a mile down the lane and see the house yourself."

I declared my intention to do so and so took leave. A moment or two, we were overtaken by Mrs. Lawrence's servant, who said, "My mistress bids me invite you gentlemen to dine with her this evening, if you are not engaged. She says she hopes M. Hubert will be there and asks that I return with an answer."

"We should be happy to," replied I, at the same time hearing an audible sigh from M. Tolouse. The prospect of having to endure a formal dinner seemed to dampen his anticipation of any other excitement the meal may bring.

Courtney Lodge was a quaint white house, somewhat more than a cottage, but somewhat less than a manor. There were chickens rambling in lanes and around the side of it, and eight tall windows facing front on the second floor. It was clean in appearance, and though evidently quite old, had been restored in the last few years, showing no obvious signs of wear.

I was quite pleased with it, but to tell the truth, had resolved to be so whatever its appearance. No more was to be done therefore but return to the Lawrences to retrieve the letter. Mrs. Lawrence had not finished it when I arrived and told me by message that I was very welcome to explore the environs, as she would carry it to me momentarily.

I did so with a slight uneasiness, fearing somewhat to encounter M. Hubert while doing so. I dreaded encountering any impediment to the success I had found so far, which was beyond my greatest expectations.

The back gardens were quite well laid out in the English style, and I made a tour of the grounds. On my way back, I was gazing at an odd-looking topiary when through the gaps of a trellis behind it, I espied the figure of a young woman reading. She was seated on a bench under the shade of arbour which bordered the long open patio just outside the inner garden.

The circumstances alone convinced me it was Miss Reckert I was looking at, whom Mouchard had always described as solitary and studious. A strange sort of feeling gripped me to think it, and I was suddenly unsure whether to go forward and solicit her attention, or to go around and attempt to enter the house by another method.

Curiosity at last won out, for I told myself I had gone too far to safely retreat without notice, and I was by no means certain there was another convenient route by which to return. I stepped through the gate, from where it was possible to see her features more clearly. She did not look up immediately, nor seem to imagine anyone else could be nearby.

The young woman before me was tall and well-formed, her figure and movements graceful. Her hair was dark, perhaps black, and as her face turned so that I could see it plainly, I felt a sudden fear for my heart. I had never seen a countenance so designed to appeal; where sense and affability were depicted so harmoniously together.

I was close enough now that my presence was impossible to miss when turned in this direction. As soon as her eyes fell upon me, she started with alarm. I bowed and moved slightly closer, but recollecting the awkwardness of the situation and the lack of acquaintance between us, I paused after I had gone only a few steps.

The young lady herself neither spoke nor moved directly, scrutinizing my person as if to determine whether to retreat or approach.

At long last she did the latter, saying as she did so, "Sir, I have been pondering in what manner to return your salutation, being quite certain I do not know you. One so rarely meets a stranger in the garden, I must confess I am quite at a loss."

My thoughts were such a jumble at that moment, I could think of no appropriate reply in English, and almost as she was upon the verge of quitting me in wonder, I finally said, "Forgive me, Madam, but I would be happy to introduce myself."

"A stranger and a foreigner?" observed she, as if to herself. "An apparition indeed. And does not a man who makes his own introduction, supply his own recommendation?" Although she was evidently surprised by my appearance, her questions were posed with good-humour, lacking any trace of severity.

"I am likely to acquit myself poorly on both counts, I fear, madam."

"I shall not give you the trouble of doing either, Sir, if you cannot first tell me how you have come to be walking in my mother's garden?"

"Ah!' cried I, with a relief which must have been as evident to her as it was inexplicable. "It is Miss Lawrence I have the honour to speak to!" But then quickly after that, recalling that I had made no answer to her question, I said with a bow. "Forgive me, Miss Lawrence, for I ought to have said so at once. Mrs. Lawrence requested I wait here for a letter of recommendation. My name is M. Gramont."

"If you are truly a guest of my mother, then I must beg your pardon. Now that I think of it, however, I do recall she mentioned yesterday a visit from some friends of my uncle, whom I must presume to be yourself, in part. These are uncertain times and the sudden appearance of an armed stranger cannot but be disconcerting."

I had not recollected till then that I still wore my sword, and perhaps in several other ways made an odd sort of figure to the English eye, though by now I had become perfectly accustomed to their general style and mode of appearance.

"And yet, all the same, I assure you I am the only one in any danger, Madam," was my eventual reply, and so I spoke only the truth.

"Indeed," replied she, with surprise, but after a moment or two she said. "I have heard, M. Gramont, that flattery is second nature to the French. Is it not so?"

"I believe so, Madam, but I have had the misfortune of being raised outside of my homeland, and am forced to endure the burden of feeling the sensations I express."

Miss Lawrence could not help but laugh at this curious declaration, but before she made any reply, we saw Mrs. Lawrence coming towards us, letter in hand.

"Forgive me, M. Gramont, for I am long about my letters. Some dash them off without a care, while others labour and labour, only to produce such things as others may exceed in a tenth of the time. Oh well, we must all have our failings and excellencies, and I trust I have my share. I see you have met my daughter, Miss Lawrence. M. Gramont is a friend of your uncle, my dear, and we are in high hopes that he and his friend M. Tolouse shall stay in the area for a little while. Dear Sir," said she, again addressing me, "I fear there is little time to lose, for I have taken so long to write, you have just time to go to Courtney Lodge and see Mr. Reed before you will be wanted back again for dinner. I make a point only to hurry guests away if I do so with the view of having them back again the sooner."

At this revelation, I had hardly time to take a proper leave of them both, as I could see Mrs. Lawrence was becoming quite concerned there was not time for all.

A short way from Stearn Manor, I met Philip, who had been

waiting for me. I told him my errand and proposed we ride together. Many times in the last little while I had meant to speak to him, and discover the reason for his comings and goings. At my eventual inquiry, he replied stoically enough, "It is very simple, my lord: I am married, and married men have not the leisure of single men, so I fear I cannot attend you as well as I should wish."

"Married!" cried I, with nothing short of astonishment. "I give you joy, my dear friend! But how do you find married life, and what possesses you to wait upon me at all, when you may cater to your wife?"

"The married state is a blissful one, my dear Sir, and I should recommend it to all who have it in their power, only I would say that a wife must be chosen carefully, as I have done. I follow you because it is my duty, and a man may have more than one duty. But now permit me to ask a question of my own. Have I not always served you with ability and fidelity?"

"With excessive amounts of both, dear Sir."

"Then how is it you tell me nothing of what goes forth, and I am to discover only indirectly that we are here in search of M. Hubert and not the widow you seek?"

"I did not withhold anything from you intentionally, yet much has happened quickly, and I have been puzzling over things so much myself that I had not thought to mention them to you."

"But if you please, what can have happened in so short a time to reverse the decision you made in France when you let him go? Has he returned to his senses and become somehow eligible for revenge?"

"No, indeed, he is as pitiable as before, and a dependant in the family we just left. But it is not M. Hubert which brings us here, for though he is perhaps dangerous, the Lawrences are aware of his condition, if not its cause. It is his history they seem entirely ignorant of, and little imagine the danger they expose themselves and their guests by harbouring him. Do you see what it is which concerns me?"

Philip stopped his horse for a moment. "If M. Lafont were to discover him," he said thoughtfully, "the effect would quite likely be disastrous. But surely, my dear Sir, was it not you who enabled M. Hubert to wander as he pleased, and begging your pardon, is there anywhere he might be better concealed?"

"You have hit upon the very crux of the matter, for if I had not done so, he would not be where he is. As for his concealment, I am sorry to say it is not to be hoped for, and it is all but certain that Lafont is nearby. I have only to determine whether he has discovered M. Hubert, or looks for him still, and beyond that, to prevent him from any action he might meditate."

"A little task indeed!" cried Philip, shaking his head. "But if you knew he was nearby and you wished to find him, how can it be you did not tell me as much before now? Who might have more success finding him than myself, who knows his every proclivity, and who has spent more tedious hours than even yourself listening to his many schemes and follies?"

I sighed, for he was quite right in saying so, yet replied. "I am loathe to tell you now, my dear Philip, for when you have a wife to dote upon, I do not like to send you over hill and dale searching for such a man. All the same I fear I must, for I cannot do so from the drawing room, nor can I do without an acquaintance among the family I hope to protect."

"Begging your pardon, you may not do so as successfully in any case, for the common folk shall know best what occurs in an area, and they are always wary of fine young men who ask too many questions. You might perhaps lose more than you gain, for your inquisitiveness would be widely published. No one cares for the talk of an old man, conversely," added he with a slight smile.

I was going to say something about accepting his help on the basis of friendship alone, but he prevented me by saying first, "I would feign remind you that this matter is not truly your concern, but I am certain it will do no good. If you do not see me this evening, you may expect me at this house tomorrow."

By this time we had arrived at Courtney Lodge and without another word, he spurred his horse and flew away. At his departure, there was nothing for me to do but call upon Mr. Reed, and I did so at once.

Mr. Reed was a pleasant kind of fellow, of slight build and a sort of over-energetic demeanour. He received Mrs. Lawrence's note on my behalf with greater delight than the occasion seemed to merit, and declared himself most desirous of accommodating us. When I explained my uncertainty as to the length of time we should be wanting it, he avowed himself entirely easy, and that I could have it for two days or two years. Furthermore, he could hardly bring himself to accept payment for it, and wanted no other security. The only thing he seemed desirous of was that his complacency be communicated to Mrs. Lawrence, and through his conduct and hints on the subject, I concluded he was her humble servant, or at least aspired to be.

Eventually it was settled that we would take possession of it the following day, and as matters were settled so easily, I bid him adieu and returned to the Lawrences.

I have written long, and hope my letter does not miscarry. I am happy the others have reached you, and grateful to hear they are prized so highly. I shall continue to address my letters to the monastery as you request, and hope we may cross paths again!

Adieu, dear Sir,

Your friend,
M.C.

Marcel de la Croix to Henri Renault

March 2nd, 1793

Dear Friend,

On my return, I thought almost exclusively about what might take place when I was to meet M. Hubert. My anxiety had not entirely left me, but I had begun to feel increasingly fatalistic on the subject, having inwardly determined that whatever happened, I would see out the task bestowed upon me by Mouchard.

By the time I returned, Tolouse was already present, engaged in conversation with Mrs. Lawrence and her daughter.

"M. Tolouse has been giving us accounts of his doings in battle, M. Gramont," said Mrs. Lawrence. "I find your friend is a soldier through and through."

I bowed in concurrence, upon which he rose and said, "M. Gramont shall know better how to entertain women, I daresay. He knows somewhat of fighting too, though I'll warrant you will never get him to say so."

Just at this time another young lady entered the room. I knew Miss Reckert at first glance. Having once seen her, it was hard to fathom how I could have mistaken Miss Lawrence for her earlier. They are both handsome, but their charms are entirely different. Miss Lawrence is effortlessly good-humoured and agreeable, and her countenance bespeaks a ready engagement with the world. At first blush at least, Miss Reckert is more remote, her beauty more classical. Where Miss Lawrence's eyes are laughing, her friend's are searching and perceptive. My description is inadequate, but this cannot be new to you, dear friend.

I could not help but stare at Miss Reckert from the time she entered, though I attempted to do so without attracting much notice. To me she was like a spectre come alive! After a brief introduction to M. Tolouse and myself, she said nothing at all, and seemed alternatively preoccupied with reading or her own thoughts. I felt something akin to guilt or complicity to think that though I was essentially a stranger to her, I had been privy to her most innermost thoughts and feelings.

Dinner was announced, but scarcely had we risen to adjourn to the dining room than M. Hubert himself entered. The sight of him caused my blood to freeze within me, as it had done before. He did not look at me directly, and I had the chance to recover somewhat while all eyes were upon him. He sauntered over to an unoccupied portion of the room, taking no notice of anyone, till Mrs. Lawrence declared, "Dear brother, come, do you not see you have a visitor?"

Her voice betrayed a great deal of anxiety, which I shared at that particular moment. "Here is your friend, M. Gramont, come all the way from France to wait upon you."

M. Hubert furrowed his brow in perplexity, and lowered his gaze directly upon me. All eyes were turned upon us two, and though I had faced death and danger many times in the last year, nothing seemed comparable to the uncomfortable moments of uncertainty which passed in this interval. M. Hubert seemed to search for some recollection of my person, but at the last he failed to do so.

"M. Gramont?" said he, at last. "I may have known you at one time. Your face is not entirely unfamiliar to me, but whatever the case, the person you see now is a mere shadow of the man you have known. I have no need of friends, or indeed of anything but the quick death which eludes me."

Saying this, he passed directly into the dining room with no apparent thought of doing more. Mrs. Lawrence looked extremely distraught, saying in a low voice, "I fear you did not think it would be as bad as all this, but you may not say I gave you no warning."

"Indeed, madam," replied I, "I am glad to see your brother again, whatever the circumstances, and to confess the truth, I hardly dared hope for better."

And true it was, for I could scarcely conceive of a reception more favourable to my purposes.

Mrs. Lawrence gave me every indication that she was extremely pleased with my answer, and so we all proceeded to dinner. M. Hubert took very little notice of me during the meal, though once or twice I thought he looked at me ponderously when I was engaged in conversation elsewhere.

My own attention was directed mostly upon the two young women, but yet for my own sake I thought it wise to focus upon Miss Reckert, of whom Mouchard had spoken the most, and who I wished to contrast in real life with the picture drawn of her. At first I found this a rather difficult task, for she said very little either to M. Tolouse or myself, and seemed entirely free of any wish to forward our acquaintance. Once or twice, from the corner of my eye, I thought some observation I had made had garnered her approval, but whenever I looked to her to find confirmation of this, I found no sign of it, and was forced to wonder whether it had been my imagination.

M. Tolouse and Miss Reckert had been seated beside each other at the table, and for the first portion of the meal, she neither spoke nor looked at him. Mrs. Lawrence spoke alternately to he and I, but it seemed that the longer the meal, the more uneasy he became.

When Mrs. Lawrence and I had spoken for a little while, she turned again to M. Tolouse and said, "And how do you find the roads in England? Are they as in France?"

However simple such a question seemed, M. Tolouse made several unsuccessful attempts to answer it in English, at last declaring, 'Indeed, Madam, roads are everywhere.'

A pause succeeded this statement, which had elicited several significant looks, but when things seemed most awkward, Miss Reckert looked up and said, "I am quite of M. Tolouse's opinion, for one is so soon acclimated to ones surroundings, distinctions are apparent only in the first few days and then they seem to disappear entirely. How long have you been in England, Monsieur?" though this last question she asked in French.

Her reinterpretation of his response was generous indeed, and from that point onwards, she performed the same service for him, imperceptibly smoothing any interactions he had with others. At times she went so far as to propose subjects he seemed likely to excel at, and by degrees, he was again at ease.

It was from this exchange I began to detect the compassion Mouchard had always described to be part of her character, for it was not until M. Tolouse seemed in some distress that she paid him any attention at all. Furthermore, the speed with which she had detected his discomfort seemed to indicate she was by no means as absent in her attention to what passed as one might guess from her conduct. The reason for her apparent indifference may well be to discourage potential suitors, and on this note, I must confess that Mr. Harland would have no cause for jealousy on my account, for Miss Reckert took no interest in me at all.

Following dinner we retired to the drawing room together. It is the English custom for men and women to retire to different rooms, but as M. Hubert disappeared directly following the meal, there was no thought of doing such a thing.

Some further conversation was had before we left, but it was very much in the common way, and I struggle to recall what was said. Miss Lawrence and Miss Reckert left all topics of conversation to Mrs. Lawrence, and as we had much conversation with her that very morning, our visit came to its natural end shortly thereafter.

"Who can bear talking to ladies so long?" cried M. Tolouse once we had left. "I have never been less at ease in my entire life! Come, M. Gramont, is this fair dealing? Here we are to be fighting, not sipping tea and fumbling for compliments!"

"Then you did not enjoy meeting Miss Reckert, or the Lawrences?"

"Why, I would not go that far. If Miss Reckert is the same as was talked about by Mouchard, then I have no trouble seeing why he was so fond of her, for I have never seen a better woman in my life. A little high, at first, I thought, like Mlle de Courteline, but then the longer we stayed, the more I thought there was no resemblance at all. If it is she we are come to protect, then I would be more than happy to give my life for her, so long as I need not tell her about it over a cup of tea."

We had a good deal of conversation along these lines, where M. Tolouse would declare his admiration, while swearing that another word amongst society would be the death of him.

Halfway to the inn, we spied several gentlemen ahead of us on the road. As they approached, we could plainly see there were five. The first gentleman rode forward to meet us, calling out, "Good evening, gentlemen."

I was preparing to answer him in kind when I was interrupted by the sound of M. Tolouse drawing his sword behind me. I turned in annoyance, as he declared with excitement in French that these were certainly highwaymen.

"Hold, M. Tolouse," cried I, but by then all five gentlemen had drawn their swords and were looking at us with great alarm.

"Please, gentlemen,' said I, struggling to remember basic English under pressure. "Sir," said I to the man who had spoken, "my friend believes you are highwaymen, and while I am certain you are not, perhaps you will be so good as to put away your weapons and confirm as much."

"Indeed, Sir," replied he, "the same may be easily supposed of you, and your friend does not seem inclined to put away his weapon, so I can hardly instruct my men to disarm beforehand. My name is Harland, Sir, and I am no highwayman."

"M. Tolouse," cried I with frustration, "your pleasure must be deferred, for here is Mr. Harland," and then more for the other gentleman's benefit, "of whom Mrs. Lawrence has told us of only today."

M. Tolouse put away his weapon immediately, and so I turned again and said, "Mr. Harland, my name is Gramont, and here is my friend, M. Tolouse."

The other gentlemen put away their weapons as quickly as they had drawn them, and Mr. Harland moved forward to shake my hand.

"I am pleased to know you both," said he. "Did I hear you say you have come from Mrs. Lawrence?"

"Yes, Sir, we were at dinner."

"You are perhaps relations of that lady?"

"No, Sir, my visit was chiefly to M. Hubert, whom I had known in France."

Mr. Harland had not yet smiled, and seemed less likely to with each passing moment.

"And may I ask where you go at present?"

"I am happy to satisfy the inquiries of a friend of Mrs. Lawrence," said I, "but else I must tell you that I do not much take to being questioned on the road by persons I have never seen before. We are going to the Hogshead."

"Forgive me, M. Gramont, I comprehend you," replied he, "and I have not leisure for greater tact or explanation. If you are staying at the Hogshead, by your leave I shall call upon you on my return this evening."

I bowed slightly, but he hardly waited to see it before they were off. Had I no previous knowledge of the gentleman, I would have taken very great exception to being treated so. As it was, I took a great deal more delight in the unexpected encounter than I thought it wise to show, and was by no means opposed to anything which might contribute to the elucidation of his character. Even when I believed it fictional, I had found it to be rather intriguing.

As soon as he had gone, M. Tolouse declared, "Mr. Harland! Who would have thought we should meet him thus, and taken for a highwayman."

"I can heartily agree with you there, for I can scarce think of any man who looked less like a highwayman."

"Why, did he not have a hat and a coat and a sword, and sat upon a horse?"

"We shall meet many indeed by those criteria, but in the future I beg you to have an eye for the newness of boots, the finery of clothes, the gold on the buttons..."

"All this might have been stolen from some unhappy gentleman on the road, so I make a point never to presume. But yet I must confess to liking the appearance of him, for he is not one of those womanish fellows, and if Miss Reckert can fancy him, then there is hope for us all."

"Pray, M. Tolouse, say nothing of this to anyone, for if you should even hint..."

"Nay, nay, threats and cautions shall not be needed, for I am content not to speak to any of them my whole life, and if I am so unfortunate as to come into society again, you shall not hear one word cross my lips but of the weather and how nice the china. But yet I dare-say, Mlle de Courteline and Mlle Vallon will want to know soon enough."

I made no reply and had no intention of writing to them directly, as there were far more serious matters pressing.

When we arrived at the inn, M. Tolouse declared he would stay in the common room for a little while, and I retired to our room to await Mr. Harland. The more time which passed, the more I began to think of the hurried manner of Mr. Harland's departure, and the possible reasons for such haste. I did not much relish the idea that he should encounter M. Lafont, for the gentlemen who accompanied him seemed lacking in any kind of experience, and one or two of them had seemed to tremble at the sight of M. Tolouse on the road.

Perhaps two hours passed before a knock came at the door and Mr. Harland was announced. He bowed at his entrance. "I am sorry for the disturbance at this late hour, M. Gramont, but I did not wish to defer seeking your pardon for what must have seemed like an interrogation of sorts. No doubt it must seem rather unusual."

Mr. Harland's demeanour by no means matched the content of his words, for it was far from contrite. I guessed instead that he had taken the opportunity to satisfy his curiosity.

"On the contrary, Sir," replied I. "I am from France and the situation seemed eerily familiar."

He heard my reply dispassionately, and did not dispute the point. His face rarely betrayed any expression at all, but yet his mind was evidently quite active.

"The English, Sir, are determined not to go in the direction of the French, and so it seems we police the roads to ensure no mobs gather. I myself have always believed that our enlightened property laws and the comparative equality which reigns in our Country, protect us from the chaos and violence which has swept your land. In this neighbourhood, however, other factors have intervened to make this less certain. So it is that you find yourself accosted by inquisitive strangers on the road. I hope you will pardon what has been deemed a necessity."

"I thank you, Sir," was all the reply I could think to make.

"We have, in addition," continued he, "heard several reports of a Frenchman in the area and for that reason your friend in particular caught my attention. I see he is not here at present, but perhaps it is just as well. Will you offer your security for him, Sir?"

"I shall offer no security at all for M. Tolouse. His actions are a perpetual surprise to me. All the same, I am certain he is not the man you speak of, for he has been with me these last few weeks, and we have only just now arrived in the area. Tonight we have been at Mrs. Lawrence's, and last night we stayed at the Red Hen, coming from the home of Mr. Reckert. Before then we were en route to this area from the south."

"Mr. Reckert?" cried he, in amazement. "And do you know that gentleman as well?"

"We had the pleasure of assisting him on the road when his carriage got into some difficulty. I understand his daughter is also at the Lawrence's, and that you were to dine with him this evening?"

"I was unfortunately prevented. But as to M. Tolouse, do you mean to say you believe he presents some kind of danger? Is he not your friend?"

"He presents no danger I know of, and where women are concerned, he is harmless. But as to the rest of it, he is a soldier who has been retired against his will, and I would not put it above him to create his own occupation. Chance has thrown us together in your country, and so we are friends, but in France, it seems unlikely we would have met."

Mr. Harland was silent for a short while, and when he spoke again, he said, "And the purpose of your trip hither is to call upon Mr. Hubert?" I nodded in response, and he said, "I am somewhat surprised to discover that Mr. Hubert has inspired such friendly solicitude. Tell me, Sir, how do you find him?"

"Much as I left him."

"I see. And if I may ask, do you think his behaviour unusual at times?"

"It is a product of his experiences, Sir."

"And as his friend, undoubtedly, you know what these were?"

"Perhaps, but yet I should not feel compelled to reveal them."

He was silent again, but presently he said, "May I ask how long you are staying in the area?"

"A little while."

"Then by your leave, perhaps I will have occasion to call upon you again."

"You will be quite welcome, Sir, but after tomorrow you must look for us at Courtney Lodge."

Mr. Harland seemed hardly pleased to hear it, but merely said, "I see you intend to be here a little while at least. I wish you goodnight, M. Gramont."

When he had gone, I realized it would have been wise to inquire more as to the reason he was looking for a Frenchman, and yet I was too overwhelmed with my own conjectures on the subject to think of it.

Mouchard's description of the gentleman was apt, if incomplete, for his appearance is far from delicate or boyish. I cannot tell by look alone, but I would guess he is not too far from seven and thirty, in either direction. If one would not call him handsome, he is by no means unappealing. The force of his character is stamped upon his features and imbued into his manners in such a way which would make it difficult to doubt his sincerity.

* * *

It was still very early in the morning when I left the Hogshead in the direction of Stearn Manor. I made a point of taking the long route there, and stopping to speak with anyone I met, though in keeping with Philip's advice, I asked only about the area, the crops or the weather. I opened my purse as liberally as seemed wise, and by the close of two hours, purchased as much good will in the area as might still preserve to me a reputation of sanity.

Using Stearn Manor as a starting point, I went a short way in every direction, and by the time decent visiting hours commenced, I felt more certain of the geography of the area. Just before 10 o'clock, I made my way to the Lawrence's.

Mrs. Lawrence and her daughter had just finished breakfast, and they received me in the sitting parlour, where they were visiting with one of their neighbours, Mrs. Alfred. After a brief introduction, Mrs. Lawrence said, "We are very pleased you have called upon us this morning, M. Gramont. Does M. Tolouse not join you?"

"No, madam, he was asleep when I left. I tend to rise early in the morning."

"So it would seem, for we have heard news of you already this morning. Our cook heard from the farmer's wife that you had passed by at half past seven. You must have an excellent constitution, Sir!"

"Many a general might envy so wide a network of informants, Madam. But indeed, I believe I owe my early rising to an overactive mind which will not wait till a decent hour to begin churning again."

"Ah, Sir, this explains my frequent late sleeping, I fear. Why, there is the bell! Quite certainly Mr. Harland. I have a thing or two to tell him immediately, but then no doubt he shall come in thereafter. My dear," Mrs. Lawrence added to her daughter, "Pray entertain Mrs. Alfred and M. Gramont, and I shall return in an instant."

"Have you had opportunity to meet Mr. Harland, M. Gramont?" said Miss Lawrence, when her mother had gone.

"But last night," replied I. "He seems a very impressive sort of man. I see your mother was expecting him this morning, and I hope my presence shall not impede any particular conference between them?"

"You need have no fear of that, for Mr. Harland calls upon us around this time most days."

"Indeed," replied I, but then recollecting that Miss Reckert was not present, I said, "I hope Miss Reckert is in good health this morning?"

"Miss Reckert customarily writes her letters after breakfast, M. Gramont," replied she, "and she is rarely available at this time."

I sighed to hear it, understanding that nothing had changed between Mr. Harland and Miss Reckert since Mouchard had left. When I looked up a moment later, I found both Miss Lawrence and Mrs. Alfred apprising me with varying degrees of knowing expressions.

I realized too late the impression I had given, and before I could think how to correct it, Mr. Harland and Mrs. Lawrence entered.

"I find you have already met Mr. Harland, M. Gramont," said the lady.

"It is a pleasure to see you again, Sir."

"Likewise," said he with a slight bow, but again his expression was at variance with his words.

"I hope we can prevail upon you to take some refreshment for a short time this morning, Mr. Harland?" proceeded Mrs. Lawrence

He thanked her with a slight incline of the head, but seemed generally disinclined to partake in conversation, and positioned himself more as an auditor.

Mrs. Alfred took leave shortly after, and Mrs. Lawrence was beginning to tell a story of some recent happening when M. Hubert suddenly entered the room.

Mr. Harland's eyes were instantly fixed on both of us. Mrs. Lawrence called out to her brother to join us, naming Mr. Harland and myself to him. To my surprise I saw that Mr. Harland made no acknowledgment of M. Hubert whatsoever, most probably in the knowledge that none would be made in return; M. Hubert having long since left off even bowing his head.

M. Hubert turned briefly in our direction, and when called to take particular notice of me, he looked directly at me with curiosity, before stalking out of the room. Mr. Harland regarded me steadily thereafter, as if to remark the lack of contact between us.

In this rather awkward interval, I ventured to take leave, ostensibly to find M. Tolouse and ensure our move to Courtney Lodge was accomplished expeditiously.

"Of course, M. Gramont," said Mrs. Lawrence, as we rose. "I hope you will return very soon."

"You may rely upon it, madam."

Mr. Harland here declared that he too was obliged to take leave, saying to me, "I believe we are going the same direction, M. Gramont, and so I hope you shall not mind if I join you."

I could not help but consent to his company, despite a vague sense of uneasiness as to his motives. All the same, in some respects I found even his suspicions endearing, for they spoke well of his judgement and his heart.

We had gone a short way when he said, "I could not help but notice the interaction between you and M. Hubert, if it may be called that."

I made no answer at all, feeling that a mere observation, however pointed, needed no reply.

Finding this, he said presently, "And were you satisfied by your reception, if I may ask?"

"I shall be satisfied in any case, Mr. Harland. If M. Hubert becomes more expressive, I shall perhaps be more satisfied, but if he remains withdrawn, I will merely content myself with the company of other members of the household."

This response pleased him very little, as I knew it would, but I was piqued by the tone of his questions, and could not help myself.

"It is an understanding friend indeed who does not even require acknowledgment, M. Gramont."

"As I mentioned before, one who knows the cause of his eccentricities shall find his behaviour more forgivable."

As I uttered these words, I felt their very falseness. More forgivable perhaps, but hardly forgivable, in my case. I was angered at the very circumstance which tempted me to stretch the truth in this way.

"Indeed, M. Gramont, but as I recall, you were unwilling to enlighten me accordingly."

I made no reply again, and in time he said, "Perhaps you would consent to satisfy me on one point at least which I have always been curious about, and that is which side of the conflict M. Hubert acted upon?"

"M. Hubert was a revolutionary," I replied, and as the words left my mouth, all the many images associated with him came before my eyes.

At that moment we heard hoofbeats behind us, and turned to see M. Tolouse. I greeted him with surprise, observing that I expected to see him in the other direction.

"I had come this way first," replied he, "but finding you had called at the Lawrences, I decided not to intrude. Let those conversate who may, I say."

He spoke in French and as I found Mr. Harland appeared not to understand everything, I said, "M. Tolouse is not fond of conversation, Sir."

He nodded and I took the opportunity of asking him whether he spoke French.

"Imperfectly. Spoken slowly, I should comprehend most everything, but otherwise I cannot promise much. My speech is still more flawed, and I only do it when absolutely necessary. I have been in France several times for a few months or so, but any improvement gained there seems to dissipate on English soil."

M. Tolouse seemed not to understand much of this, but I did not bother translating it.

"If, as you were saying, M. Gramont," recommenced Mr. Harland, "M. Hubert was a revolutionary and it is thus that you knew him, may one reasonably conclude you were a revolutionary yourself?"

"I fear it is not so clear in my case, but you must excuse me from elaborating."

"And you, M. Tolouse," said he. "Are your allegiances so difficult to characterize?"

This question required translation, but once I had done so, M. Tolouse replied in French, and I translated as follows:

"'Tis no mystery at all, for I was on both sides. I started my career in the King's army, and truth be told there was no other to join at the time. My fellows and I were said to be the hardiest men around, and in all modesty, it was no exaggeration. Time came soon enough for one of us men to be promoted to Captain, and as I still had my leg then, it was an even race between M. Dumiers and myself. Before the word came down, we went out together and over a drink or two we pledged to support the other as heartily as we could if he were chosen. Close as brothers we were. To not be long in the telling, the next day we learnt that neither he nor I had been promoted. Instead of a Captain appointed from within our ranks, we were assigned to lead us a lad scarce old enough in years to grow hair, with a face so dainty you might take him for a woman! Suffice to say our Corps was thrown into chaos and we refused to serve beneath him. By then we had all heard the talk of reform, and we swore we'd not be led by any privileged whelp. We made a valiant stand at first, but then we were disbanded by force. I was one of the first men to enlist under the army of the Estates General, but unluckily, at nearly our first encounter, I lost my leg, or the lower part of it. I spent nearly half a year laid up and after that, no one on either side would have me."

"How did you lose your leg, M. Tolouse, if I may ask?" said Mr. Harland, having listened to his tale with great attention.

"I was thrown from my horse at full gallop, Sir, and when I landed, it was broke in three places. The physician declared it would be of no use to me at all, and said it was best to have it removed. I sometimes wonder whether I ought to have agreed so quickly, as perhaps it would have been better to wait and see how it would heal on its own. But I was in a powerful hurry, Sir, not realizing that a wooden leg itself would disqualify me for battle."

"You were in a hurry to rejoin the army?" inquired he, with a kind of incredulousness.

"Yes, indeed. Would do it now if I could."

"In Britain a man may purchase a commission in the army, but skill and accomplishment alone shall see him promoted."

"And so it ought to be. I would enlist this minute, did I think a crippled Frenchmen would be welcome."

"Would you?" said Mr. Harland with surprise. "Do you wish to defeat the revolutionaries who have taken over your country?"

"They do seem to be making a mess of it, Sir. One or two changes would have done the job. By my way of thinking, the nobles ought not to have had so much, nor be exempt from taxes, and while I am thinking of it, they should not be given the choice positions in the army or church. So far, at least, I agree with the revolutionaries, but as to killing the King, and getting rid of the church altogether, it's taking things too far. And yet, I am not entirely of the mind that a soldier must approve of what he fights for. Soldiers are soldiers and they must fight when fighting's been commenced. A soldier is the tool of the King, or some other body, and it is not for them to decide whether it is right or no to fight. Now if, as often happens, a King gets it into his head to quarrel over some parcel of land, one can't expect the soldiers on either side to bother themselves much about whether their betters have a right to what they claim. A soldier had pledged himself to fight for whoever pays him."

"Will you allow nothing to the patriot, then?"

"Why a patriot is fine by me, and I have known many of them. But if you'll pardon me, it is not a very rational stance. Most men make shift to prefer their country to another's, but what of it? I might prefer France to England, and you the reverse. But in the province where I was born, we had the habit of thinking we were superior to those of our countrymen in the neighbouring province. What's more, the town near my house was said by my neighbours to be superior to the one found five miles down the road. And even in our little village, my mother, God rest her soul, was convinced that my brother and I were the strongest, handsomest, children of any of the families in the area. Now as to the question of strength, I am not one to say she was wrong, for when my brother was ten, he could heave a stone clear over the rock wall around our village from the doorstep of our house, whereas I had been known to throw one over the wall and past the second apple tree when I had reached the same age. But alas, I have forgotten what I was trying to say?"

I was relieved to see Mr. Harland seemed more amused by M. Tolouse's prattle than anything else. Part of what M. Tolouse had said I had translated, and some parts Mr. Harland had understood on his own.

"I believe, M. Tolouse, you were saying that the indiscriminate preference for ones own kind has a tendency to place all men at odds with one another, without providing a better rationale for fighting."

"Why yes, but never so eloquently. At any rate, what I was getting at is that I am a soldier, and so I am content to fight when I can."

Mr. Harland seemed quite thoughtful and we rode a short way in silence. Presently, I said, "May I inquire whether the situation hereabouts has improved since Mr. Reckert described it to us two days ago?"

"I did not realize you were so well-informed,' was his laconic reply. 'At any rate, there can be no harm in telling you that there has been little change since then. A meeting has been called amongst the populace, and it is hoped we may come to some understanding then."

"And what of the Frenchman you told me you were searching for? Have you located him?"

"I have not, and I am not certain he is still in the area. He appears to come and go, and it would not surprise me if he were to leave for good when he hears I mean to speak with him."

"May I ask why you are looking for him?"

"You have a pronounced curiosity on the subject, M. Gramont? Do you know anything which may be useful to me?"

"I fear not, yet I assure you that M. Tolouse and myself are most willing to assist you however we may."

"You are very kind," was his reply, but if I may be permitted to judge, he did not seem very eager to accept the help offered. "My road lies here, gentleman. Till we meet again."

When he had gone, M. Tolouse declared, "I like that gentleman more and more."

"I am in agreement with you, yet I fear the sentiment is hardly reciprocated, on my part at least."

"Nor was it likely to be, if you'll pardon me, for you are younger and well-looking and you visit his mistress, while he is left out in the cold as it were, but as soon as he knows you want nothing from Miss Reckert, which I assume is the case, he'll warm up to you in no time."

By then we had reached Courtney Lodge. Inside we found all laid out and arranged. Mr. Reed had done us the favour of providing us a cook and I discovered that Philip had hired two other servants to attend us. I had expected to see him by then and was just beginning to wonder when this letter was put into my hands:

Dear MC,

I have heard of Lafont. He came to the area five weeks ago, looking for M. Hubert. He stayed at an inn six or seven miles from Stearn Manor. It seems his foreign pronunciation of that gentleman's name caused some confusion, and the landlord told me that it was not until he became quite agitated to hear some of the gossip regarding M. Hubert which circulated at the time, that he understood M. Hubert was the man he sought. At this point he left the inn and by account I have been able to place him in the vicinity of Stearn Manor on several occasions, asking questions about the family. He seems to be as disputative as ever, and is thought to have killed a man in an argument. He made at least one attempt to meddle with one of the Lawrence's servants, who was dismissed thereafter. While the Militia were stationed here, he seems to have left the neighbourhood, for where I have not been able to discover. Two days after they withdrew, approximately four days ago, five men on horseback were seen approaching Stearn Manor after dark. The gamekeeper's dogs alerted him and he loosed seven of them upon them, which was enough to chase them away.

One of the prominent gentlemen in the area, Mr. Harland, has been searching for him as well, but I believe it is on account of the man who was killed. By your leave, I intend to remain as close as possible to Stearn. I have taken the liberty of writing a note to Mrs. Lawrence on your behalf, which I enclose for you to peruse. If you approve, pray copy it directly and send it to me at the Hogshead.

The letter he wrote read as follows:

Dear Mrs. Lawrence,

I happened to hear you are short one servant, and as M. Tolouse and I are quite well-supplied at the moment, I offer my own servant, Philip, the bearer of this note. He has been with my family for years, and I would be honoured if you will accept his services (for a little while at least) as a token of my gratitude and esteem,. I am yours, etc.

As you can see, I mean to stay at Stearn Manor myself if possible. I do not wish to speculate on what M. Lafont intends, but whether it is fire, poison or explosives, I feel confident I should be in a position to prevent him from here. Write your wishes,

Your servant till death,
Philip

I wasted no time copying the letter he had sent me. Once I had sent it to him as he requested, I felt more at ease than I had felt in months, and my head even seemed to lay more soundly on my pillow.

I shall send mine to you now, and hope it finds you in good health.

Your friend,
M.C.

Marcel de la Croix to Henri Renault

March 4th, 1793

Dear Friend,

In the morning I received a short note of thanks from Mrs. Lawrence, who requested I call upon her that day if it was convenient.

I needed no further encouragement to set off just after breakfast. M. Tolouse preferred to remain.

Mrs. Lawrence received me herself, almost in raptures on account of Philip.

"I cannot say what a favour we consider it, Sir! Your servant is so wise, so accommodating, so precise! He anticipates one's needs so completely. My own servants seem disposed to heed his example and if that proves to be the case, it shall be a blessing indeed. We are so obliged to you, you've no notion!"

Shortly thereafter I remembered to inquire after M. Hubert,

whereupon I was told he had yet to be seen that morning. I was glad to hear it, and we went on to a relatively commonplace discussion on domestic matters.

The next day was reserved for exploring, and I roamed as far as seemed advisable to the West and then to the East. On my return to Courtney Lodge, I was surprised to encounter Miss Lawrence walking by herself on the main road between Stearn and Courtney. Considering the very volatile situation thereabouts, after I had greeted her and dismounted, I could not help but say, "I am surprised to find Miss Lawrence walking alone so far from home?"

"You are perhaps disappointed to find me unaccompanied?"

"No indeed, for it gives me an excuse to accompany you. But yet, do you not fear for your safety in doing so?"

"No, Sir. I am not as carefree perhaps as in past years, but I should be ashamed to be afraid to walk in the place I was born."

"And I take it Miss Reckert does not agree?"

"I am uncertain on that point, but if you were in the hopes of meeting her someday, I fear you are likely to be disappointed. Her paths are so varied of late, that I can never discover her myself if I do not accompany her from the start."

This intelligence was not surprising to me, yet I did not welcome the implication my curiosity had again given rise to. I could think of no way to explain my interest, however, so I said nothing.

"Forgive me, M. Gramont, perhaps I am wrong to discourage you."

"There is nothing to encourage or discourage, I assure you."

"Of course, but accept my apology all the same. I mean to turn in this direction," added she, referring to a road that lies about halfway between Stearn Manor and Courtney, and leads in the direction of the site under dispute. "You are welcome to continue with me, but I beg you to feel no obligation. No doubt your way lies elsewhere."

"I am merely exploring, Madam, and so long as you do not object, I mean to follow you. May I ask where you intend to go?"

"This road goes to the site of the town upon which construction has been lately halted; I believe my mother has told you something of it?" I nodded and she said, "I am accustomed to taking a path which runs along it to the South, and so home."

"Do you find it safe to do so at present, madam?"

"I can think of no safer one lately, for there are several men tasked with keeping the site closed, and so they are there at all times."

As we approached I could see a little barrier had been set up and two men stood on either side. From what I could make out, most of the dwellings there were close to finished, many with roofs intact. The cottages had a neat appearance and seemed somewhat larger than was usual. I sighed to look upon them, in the certainty that there could be no peace in the region while the people were being kept from them.

When we neared the barrier, we heard the sound of a horse behind us, and turned to see Mr. Harland approach.

"I hope all is well at Stearn Manor, Miss Lawrence?" said he in greeting.

"It is, Sir."

"M. Gramont," was all he managed in my direction, but his acknowledgement was so cold and apparently forced, it bordered upon incivility. Though he never seemed overly happy to see me, I was unprepared for the coldness of his greeting. He passed by us without another word, greeting the guards then disappearing into the town.

Miss Lawrence and I continued our way via the little path she had described. My surprise at Mr. Harland's curt acknowledgement rendered me temporarily dumb, and as Miss Lawrence could not help but observe my discomfort, she said laughingly, "Mr. Harland seems quite fond of you, M. Gramont."

"I fear it would be of little use for me to pretend so after his greeting, madam. Till now I was not aware of giving him any offence, but it seems I have done so inadvertently."

"I am aware, M. Gramont."

"Are you so, Madam, while I am ignorant?"

"I believe you are possibly the only one who remains so."

"Then I beg you would tell me at once!"

"Readily, though you might not like to hear it, but if I may judge from the conversation we have had till this point, he is justified in his opinion. Mr. Harland, you must understand, is in love with Miss Reckert, though she does not return his affection and avoids him whenever she may. I for one have not seen her in his presence since she had been at Stearn."

"Then I am sorry for it."

"Are you?"

"Most sincerely. Why should you doubt it, and how does this relate to myself, if I dare ask?"

"I shall not pretend to decide the case. If you were to admire Miss Reckert, it would be natural enough in any case, nor would you be the first. But as to your particular question, you will be hard-pressed to find one who does not doubt it. Mr. Harland, you see, treats you as a rival."

"But what can have led him, or indeed anyone, to presume so? Miss Reckert is handsome, to be sure, but I have seen her only one time and have done nothing to give credence to such a report."

Miss Lawrence laughed again and pretended to assent to my argument.

"Please madam," declared I, most seriously, "however amusing my predicament must seem to you, do not decline to help me. Tell me, I beg you, what has prompted so great a misimpression?"

"I fear it might seem unfeeling for me to imply *thou doth protest too much*, or to observe you have been accused of nothing more dire than being an admirer of Miss Reckert's, for which only Mr. Harland would fault you. For this reason, I shall do neither, but as to what has given rise the assumption, it is as follows. On your visit the other day, you inquired after Miss Reckert in the presence of Mrs. Alfred. She went amongst her friends and relayed this observation, with the added detail that you seemed disappointed she was not present. The conclusions of her cohorts strengthened her own opinion, and when my mother visited her on the following day, Mrs. Alfred informed her of this broader consensus. My mother, quite easily swayed by this evidence, must have added a few details of her own, which probably consisted of her observation that you seemed admiring or attentive to Miss Reckert on the evening you mentioned. Nothing more would have been required to decide the matter, which might then be given out fearlessly by any who had heard it, till it was heard by Mr. Harland himself, whose own name had been involved in this tragedy by many well-meaning bodies, on no other grounds than the certainty he would be distressed by the original report. And so it was I heard it myself just this morning, being not less than that M. Gramont is in love with Miss Reckert, and Mr. Harland is distressed to know it. I may add to it myself when I return home, for I might observe how disappointed you appeared to find me alone, and how quickly you inquired where Miss Reckert chose to walk."

I could not help to laugh at this. "I know not how to defend myself, for by this description I see it is hopeless. Where a man is said to love a woman, moreover, he can commit no greater crime than to deny it. Yet all the same, as much as I admire Miss Reckert, for her kindness to M. Tolouse the other night as well as her beauty, I have no other thoughts or pretensions. Mr. Harland would have very little reason to be displeased if he could read my heart, for then he should find that I would like nothing more than for Miss Reckert to favour him."

"For myself I am tempted to believe you, M. Gramont, as you speak with much sincerity, but were I Mr. Harland, I would take no such risk, lest you prove to be a viper in the bosom after all."

"To what do I owe the high opinion you entertain of me, Miss Lawrence?"

"As to that, I am merely in the habit of reserving trust for those I have known for longer periods. I hope you will not be offended."

"By no means, for it is quite wise of you to do so, however it may impact me at present."

The longer I stayed in the company of Miss Lawrence, the less capable I felt of taking offence at anything. Despite her claim of reserve, the frankness of her manner charmed me, and it seemed as though we were old acquaintances. At any rate I was glad to know the answer to what might have otherwise perplexed me, and thanked her accordingly.

At Stearn Manor I stepped in to inquire after Mrs. Lawrence, but as she was from home, I took my leave. On my way back I realized I had neglected to inquire after M. Hubert, from the very truth that I had no wish to see him at all, and I resolved to be more careful of appearing thus.

* * *

March 8th, 1793

The next day when I called upon the Lawrences, I made a particular point of inquiring after M. Hubert. Mrs. Lawrence was preparing to answer when Mr. Harland was announced and admitted, and after the initial greeting was accomplished between us (a cold one on the part of Mr. Harland), Mrs. Lawrence replied,

"Oh yes, M. Gramont, I believe M. Hubert is in the front garden this morning. He often takes his air at this time. Perhaps you would like to join him?"

I had not anticipated this suggestion, but as I felt relatively sure I would not find him if I did not wish to, I declared I would do so at once with all outward appearance of satisfaction. M. Hubert was not in the inner garden, so I wandered around here and there, more in contemplation than anything else.

At last I mounted my horse and began to ride home. Before long Mr. Harland rode up behind me. He was on the verge of riding by, but as he paused before doing so, he glanced along the road and declared, "Is that not M. Hubert in front of us, M. Gramont?"

I observed that it was, and nodded without much enthusiasm, whereupon we proceeded together till we had met him.

With some difficulty, I disguised my reluctance to address him, and as I saw Mr. Harland watched me carefully, I called out, "Greetings, M. Hubert."

He turned around only briefly at the sound of a voice, but neither looked very closely nor showed any concern at all at who was addressing him. I was unsure whether to speak again or take leave, but as I hesitated, M. Harland said, "Perhaps we ought to tie our horses to the tree and follow M. Hubert on foot? It seems he can hardly hear you while we are on horse."

I made no objection, so we both dismounted and very soon were walking several paces behind that gentleman. M. Hubert still took no notice of us, and Mr. Harland was more intent on observing than speaking.

For my own part, I made as little conversation as seemed acceptable; from time to time remarking on something we passed or directing some questions towards him, whereupon he would reply as succinctly as possible. We had gone a fair way in this manner, M. Hubert stalking heedlessly in front, swinging his stick at the weeds, when all of a sudden he came to a stop.

I was in the midst of saying something to Mr. Harland, but could not help but pause to observe M. Hubert. He turned towards us slowly with an unsettling smile on his face, but almost as quickly he turned again and began to walk. He no longer swung his stick and his pace was slow enough for us to come alongside him.

There was no help for it, but my heart misgave me sorely. We walked several paces further without incident, and I began to think there was no cause for concern. M. Hubert began looking around again and his pace quickened so that he was slightly ahead of us once more. He looked towards us a second time, and my heart jumped to see it. He wore the same smile on his face, but his eyes now flashed with recognition and I saw that he knew me.

He did not say anything directly, but after proceeding a few more paces, he said in French, "I know not how, M. le Marquis, but I have thought once or twice that I had seen you. Tell me, how is it you come here?" He stopped and turned towards me. "Do you mean to kill me," he said with a kind of calm deliberation, "or do you reserve this honour for M. Lafont?"

Despite the change in language, I felt certain Mr. Harland had understood this last question and so I replied in French, "I have no intention of killing you, M. Hubert."

"Then perhaps I shall kill you," replied he, drawing his sword.

"What is the meaning of this, M. Hubert?" cried Mr. Harland, drawing his own weapon. "What reason can you have to threaten M. Gramont, whom Mrs. Lawrence has sent to walk with you?"

M. Hubert stared at him with confusion and displeasure, and then at last cried, "Who are you, Sir?" in English.

I took the opportunity of replying before Mr. Harland was able, speaking in English rather than French, "Mr. Harland is a friend of your sister, Mrs. Lawrence."

M. Hubert looked at me again, but his eyes betrayed no sign of remembrance. "Do I know you, Sir?" demanded he.

"My name is Gramont," replied I, inwardly breathing a sigh of relief. Hearing the name, he put away his sword with a kind of hurried distraction, and stalked directly into the field, hopping the fence with animal agility.

Mr. Harland did not move till M. Hubert was almost out of sight, wearing an expression of great uncertainty and dissatisfaction.

"What is the meaning of all that, M. Gramont?" demanded he.

I had already begun to walk in the direction we had come, and as he followed me, he persisted, "Why did M. Hubert address you as he did, for I am all but certain he called you Monsieur le Marquis?"

"M. Hubert does not always know me, Sir."

"That is more than apparent, but why should he draw his sword?"

"He said he believes someone intends to kill him."

"Why should anyone want to kill him, or if they do not, why should he imagine so?"

"These are questions I cannot answer," was my only reply, for I thought it wise to say as little as possible.

Mr. Harland was by no means appeased by my response, and we walked a fair way in silence.

"Do you intend to inform Mrs. Lawrence of M. Hubert's odd behaviour?"

"I had not considered the question, but now that I do, I fear it would only serve to embarrass her if I did."

We walked the remaining distance in silence. Once we had returned to the place we had left our horses, and Mr. Harland had mounted his, he said, "It seems the French have a very different definition of friendship than the English. No doubt we will have occasion to speak of this anon."

This encounter with M. Hubert unsettled me, though I was glad it had proved no worse in the end. I returned to Courtney Lodge to write to you, but after a little while I went out again. I had not heard from Philip when I had expected and I felt increasingly anxious to find Lafont in order that this whole business might be over with. Any species of dishonesty, however well-intentioned, was abhorrent to my nature, and I saw plainly that Mr. Harland would not long remain in ignorance. M. Tolouse was eager to find some kind of action, and when I informed him I meant to look for Lafont in nearby taverns, he seemed very much in favour.

That night we visited three public houses in turn, but I confess that I do not remember as many details of our evening as I ought to. I know only that there was no sign of Lafont, and that nothing we saw or heard was worth the effort.

The next morning I went myself to call upon the Lawrences, though this time a little later than Mr. Harland's usual visit, in the hope of seeing neither he nor M. Hubert. To my surprise, both young ladies were with Mrs. Lawrence in the sitting room. Miss Reckert evidenced no symptom of pleasure, dismay or self-consciousness at the sight of me, whereby I guessed that she had not yet heard of my reputed admiration. Mrs. Lawrence was finishing up a letter of instruction to a tradesmen which her servant waited for, so she bade me speak with the young ladies while she finished, adding that she had full confidence I would not repine at the substitution.

She was perfectly right on that score, for I do not believe there is a man alive who would object to the company of those two women. Neither of them appeared to take much notice of my awkwardness amongst women, affecting not to notice how poorly I acquitted myself. They spoke to each other with ease and affection, and I listened with great interest to all which passed. Every now and then they invited me to give my own opinion, but on the whole they were content to treat me as a privileged bystander of sorts.

After a while Mrs. Lawrence finished her letter and joined us. The conversation which took place thereafter was the most spirited and enjoyable I have ever had in my life, and I was sorry when we were eventually interrupted by the arrival of a messenger.

To my surprise, he handed me a short note. I opened it immediately and read the following.

Dear M. Gramont,

Mlle Vallon and I are in need of your immediate help and protection. Come at once, I beg you,

Mlle de C

"Where did you get this note?" demanded I of the servant, in much perturbation at its contents.

"From two young women in a carriage outside of the house, Sir. They requested I bring a reply."

This new detail only increased my wonder, and looking in the direction of the ladies, I found I was not alone in that regard.

"Forgive me, Mrs. Lawrence," said I, "but it seems I must discover the meaning of all this. By your leave, I shall return in a moment."

It had started to rain since I had arrived, and the carriage he described was at the far end of the lane, as if its occupants had been reluctant to approach the house. I ran towards it with a mixture of concern and annoyance, and on account of the weather, entered immediately.

To my amazement, I found Mlle de Courteline and Mlle Vallon alone inside, without even Mme. Gaspar and with only one servant to accompany them.

"How come you both hither?" cried I, "and without Mme. Gaspar or M. Savard?"

Mlle Vallon looked down, but Mlle de Courteline replied, "Mlle Vallon has taken it upon herself to flee Sorsten yesterday morning. I went after her when I discovered she had gone, but she did not wish to return, and I felt there was no other choice but to try to find you, in the hope we may rely upon your protection. Have we erred in this, Monsieur? Have you forgotten us completely in these two short weeks?"

Before I could reply, Mlle Vallon declared, "Oh no, that is not possible! There is no more generous a man alive, and I am sure he will not desert us, is that not right M. Gramont?"

"Indeed, you may be assured I will do all that is possible to assist you. I am only surprised to find you here. M. Tolouse and I are staying at a house a short way from here called Courtney Lodge, and I will give your driver directions there immediately."

I was going to descend the carriage, but Mlle de Courteline said, "Wait, Monsieur, do you not come yourself?"

"Indeed I do, but I must take leave of Mrs. Lawrence and her daughter."

I chose not to mention Miss Reckert for fear they might detain me with questions, but all the same Mlle de Courteline said, "Pardon me, M. Gramont, but how can Mlle Vallon and I be received with decency into the home of yourself and M. Tolouse?"

"It ought not to surprise you that I have not thought through all the details of a plan which is but the work of a moment," replied I, with some frustration, "but M. Tolouse and I will certainly return to an inn nearby and Mme. Gaspar shall be sent for immediately. I will come as soon as may be." With that I left the carriage and gave the driver directions to Courtney lodge.

Thereafter, I returned indoors and did my best to explain the sudden arrival of my friends. Mrs. Lawrence waved her hand and bid me lose no time helping friends in need, but yet I could not help but guess she meant to imply that when appearances were so unusual, any explanation was presumed to be inadequate and so was therefore unnecessary.

I set out for Courtney Lodge with no further attempt to explain myself, and yet for all my willingness to assist Mlle de Courteline and Mlle Vallon, I could not rid myself of a degree of frustration that their arrival and request seemed so ill-timed.

On the road nearing Courtney Lodge, I encountered M. Tolouse coming from there.

"Well, Gramont, I see we are to be turned out already by the ladies. 'Tis all the same to me, in any case."

"I will join you at the Hogshead presently," said I, "only I want first to know how all this has come about."

When I arrived at Courtney, I could not help but marvel at how quickly it seemed the ladies had always been there. They had but one servant with them, but between the two others supplied by Philip, much had been altered or replaced in mere matter of minutes.

When I entered the sitting room, Mlle de Courteline was in the midst of writing to Mme. Gaspar, which she informed me of immediately. Mlle Vallon had retired.

"We both owe you a tremendous degree of gratitude, M. Gramont. Though we had not heard from you since your departure, Mlle Vallon was certain you would not refuse to assist us. I perceive our arrival was not the most welcome thing imaginable, and no doubt you are very busy with your new friends of late. All the same you have done exactly as Mlle Vallon insisted you would, and therefore I thank you."

The longer she spoke the less certain I became that she was pleased with me at all, and when she finished, I said, "Indeed, Mlle de Courteline, you and Mlle Vallon shall always be welcome to any assistance I can give you. I have, in my absence, become much occupied with the Lawrences, but I am certain this shall not surprise you, since it was the reason I came hither, with your knowledge. If my reception seemed a little hurried earlier, it was only because I was concerned how it might appear for me to have been summoned to a mysterious carriage holding two young ladies. But having said this, in light of your real distress, such considerations are nothing."

"Heaven forbid!" cried she. "I cannot bear to think anything of that sort might have been thought for a moment, by anyone! But how can that be, Monsieur? Does not a woman in need have recourse to honourable assistance in England as in France?"

"No doubt, and I shall explain this as soon as I am able, but in the meantime..."

"In the meantime, Monsieur," interrupted she, "you must leave here directly, for while Mme. Gaspar is not present, it is hardly proper for Mlle Vallon and I to entertain you. Indeed, you may relay my decree to your friends when you speak with them."

"I was going to say that in the meantime I was hoping you would tell me in greater detail how it is you came to be here?"

"I fear I am come to see the perils of our predicament first hand, M. Gramont," cried she, appearing suddenly both grave and alarmed. "Do you refuse to leave, and shall Mlle Vallon and I be obliged to admit you at your will, simply because we have no other refuge or guardian?"

"Calm yourself, Mlle de Courteline. I will leave when you wish, but I cannot help but wonder at this causeless suspicion. What reason have I ever given you to believe I have some design upon you or Mlle Vallon? If I were a villain, no doubt you would have discovered it many times before, having been under my protection almost the whole time you have been in England. If I had any honourable designs, then surely either one of you would only have to refuse me, and all would be at an end. I mean no offence in speaking thus plainly, but I would not have you so frequently concerned without reason. Again, Madam, I leave it entirely to your own discretion whether I go or stay at present, but in the interest of assisting you, I should hope to know sooner rather than later what has occurred?"

Mlle de Courteline sighed deeply and seated herself. "You are very right, and I fear I owe you an apology. I shall tell you what you ask. You may well imagine I have been near frantic these last hours, and so I can hardly feel calm even when I ought to."

"I am sorry to hear that," replied I, softened and surprised by the apology she had made, which was delivered with great sincerity.

"To be brief, Mlle Vallon ran away from Sorsten in the early morning the night before last. Our maid woke me up to tell me but a few hours later. Mlle Vallon had left a short note saying she intended to marry Mr. Etheredge and to do so she had agreed to meet him at an inn a short ways away. When I discovered what she had done, I was extremely alarmed for her. I packed any clothes and money I could conveniently take with me, and taking my maid, I caught the first post out of town at half past six. I left no note for Mme. Gaspar, for there was not time. Before eleven I arrived at the inn Mlle Vallon had named, and without much difficulty, I found her waiting for Mr. Etheredge. I expostulated with her about the danger, the imprudence, the impropriety of the step! She was frightened, but I do not think she would have heeded my warning if Mr. Etheredge had not missed the hour appointed, which was eleven-thirty. At last she declared she would not return to M. Savard, but that she wished to speak to you, as you had always been sympathetic to her fate, and if you advised her to marry M. Savard, she would do so. I made my mind up directly to humour her, for we had certainly been already missed at Sorsten, and it would do no good to return there as if nothing had happened. We could not stay the night so close to home without being found, so I bid the innkeeper make inquires after the Lawrences, the Reckerts or Mr. Harland. Not long after he returned with all the information I desired, as one of his lodgers lived in that area and was just passing through. We hired a carriage and drove directly to the best inn near Kettich. This morning we travelled directly from there to the Lawrences. I hoped from there we may learn of your whereabouts, since you had sent no direction. I must confess that by this point my heroism was on the wane, for I knew not what we might do if we failed to find you."

"Amazing!" cried I, when she was done speaking. "I could never have believed you capable of it."

"Indeed," replied she, with a faint smile, "you may take part of the credit for it if you like, for it was you who told me to begin to think and act independently."

"But yet I hardly had the slightest hope you would follow my advice. What has lead to this change?"

"I shall tell you in a moment, but first tell me what you learnt of Miss Reckert, of the Lawrences? Have you determined whether Mouchard had any reason to fear?"

I told her briefly what I had seen and heard, excepting any mention of Lafont. She was distressed to find there was no better understanding between Miss Reckert and Mr. Harland, though she assured me she by no means faulted Miss Reckert for her rigour, considering the humiliations she had suffered.

Following this, I pressed her again to reveal what had made so great an alteration in her conduct and she said, "You will remember once upon a time you hinted to me that you suspected M. Savard was guilty of deceiving us regarding the fate of my father. At the time, I was incensed and by no means willing to listen to your advice. All the same I could not dismiss the validity of your belief that it was not credible for him to have come from my father and yet bring no word from him. Shortly after you left, this contradiction occurred to me more frequently, and at last I decided to put it to the test. I went to him one morning and inquired after my father, as I often did. He replied as usual that he had heard nothing but did not expect to for some time. I told him that Mlle Vallon had often expressed her reluctance to conclude their marriage while my father was not present, (which was not less than the truth, though by no means her only objection) and he seemed unusually perplexed to hear it. The very next day as Mlle Vallon and I were eating breakfast, he entered the room with a solemn air, holding a paper in his hands. He approached me with such a look of solemnity and solicitude, I both feared and guessed what he would say. He said he had learnt just that morning the most unfortunate news, and that the names of my father and my two uncles had been published in a list of those who had been beheaded in Paris."

She paused for a moment, overcome with emotion.

"I need not tell you how this affected Mlle Vallon and myself. We were both ill for a week. The paper M. Savard gave me had no date upon it, but it seems he had neglected to take note of the date given for the execution, which was even before Mlle Vallon and I had left France, and well before the period M. Savard had claimed to have been with him. I make no doubt that he knew of this all along, and concealed it for his own reasons. In light of this discovery, and upon Mlle Vallon's flight, I could not insist my cousin marry a man of his character, which I must assume my father was not aware of. Even were they better matched in other respects, I could not bear to see it. I do not wish to dwell on this any further, for it a most painful subject. Suffice to say that what you told me at the time was irrefutably true: Mlle Vallon and I are indeed alone in the world, and therefore it has become necessary for me to think and act accordingly."

What a change seemed to have been wrought upon her in two short weeks. I was delighted to find her in a state of mind which seemed more likely to lead to her eventual happiness, however painful it might be in the interim, yet I could not help pity her distress.

"I am most sincerely sorry to hear what you say, though I shall confess it does not come as a surprise to me. As long as I am alive, Madam, neither you nor your cousin shall be alone in the world."

"I thank you again, Monsieur."

As I was preparing to leave, she stopped me once more, adopting her more formal expression as she said, "Before you go, I would wish to tell you that I cannot bear for my character to remain long in doubt, and shall hope to be availed of the opportunity of making myself better known wherever any of my actions have been misconstrued."

"If you mean you desire me to introduce yourself and Mlle Vallon to Mrs. Lawrence, then I shall try my best to do so, but I beg you both to be patient, for these are delicate matters indeed."

She assented to this condition, stipulating that if they were not to meet them directly, I must take every possible means of acquainting them with the dignity of her family, the purity of her conduct and anything else which might enable them to understand her. To this end she gave me an encapsulation of the deeds and ranks of the most important of her ancestors and relations, and assured me they would be of great significance to Mrs. Lawrence.

I pledged to do so and at long last took leave of her. I returned to the Hogshead and before taking any other action, penned a letter to Mr. Reed, explaining that Courtney Lodge would be occupied by the ladies for a short time. Still full of the details of Mlle de Courteline's genealogy, I added one detail to the letter. Partway through I recollected that Mr. Reed was likely to show my letter to Mrs. Lawrence, guessing that he would be eager to gratify her curiosity on the subject. With that in mind, I began the letter anew with the purpose of exonerating myself from any suspicions of improper conduct. I described briefly my connection with the two, the disinterested motive of my conduct and the wealth and respectability of the two ladies, along with a hint of what they had suffered in deprivation of their families. I could not in decency say much about the reason for their abrupt arrival, but I implied it was quite justified.

I read the letter over again once or twice and considered whether I ought to send it or take my chances with Mrs. Lawrence's possible displeasure. At long last I resolved to send it, reflecting that every word in it was strictly true, however designedly included.

When at last I threw myself into bed, I slept as if I were dead, and did not awake till much past ten. I debated whether I should delay waiting upon Mrs. Lawrence till Mr. Reed would have had opportunity to call upon her, but my curiosity to discover her reception got the better of me, for I wished to know whether my precaution had been necessary.

I rode to Stearn shortly thereafter, thinking all the while how regrettably practiced I had become at all manner of subterfuge. For what seemed like the first time, I was told that Mrs. Lawrence was unable to see me. While it was hardly improbable that she would be occupied at some time or other, it was not reassuring news. I returned to Hogshead, and after a while had dinner there with M. Tolouse. Around eight o'clock I received a message from Mrs. Lawrence, who wrote that she was sorry to have missed me when I called earlier, but would be grateful if I would call at eleven the following day. I guessed by now she had conferred with Mr. Reed, and so had appointed this time to allow me further explanation, after which she might be able to determine how to conduct herself.

Nor was I wrong in this respect.

I called the next morning at 11 o'clock, and Mrs. Lawrence was alone to greet me. She invited me kindly to join her in a dish of tea.

"Mr. Harland has but just left, M. Gramont. It seems that nothing good has come of the meeting for which we all had such high hopes, and which took place last night."

"But why so, Madam? I felt certain Mr. Harland would be able to broker some kind of agreement, being that he is so well-regarded on all sides."

"You say true, Monsieur, but there was little even he could do. The workers, that is to say, the people, or however you like, were to be permitted to resume work only if they would return the barrel of black powder taken from Mr. Barber. We were all confident they would accept these terms, and Mr. Harland was only empowered to insist upon it. The representative of the people claimed they have not got it and had nothing to do with its disappearance, if any such thing was truly known to exist. The insistence on its return was believed to be merely a ruse used to deprive them of their natural right. Mr. Harland has at least told them to search among themselves to be sure, and they are to meet again in ten days time. 'Tis a horrible business, and I know not when it shall ever be settled. I for one begin to think they ought to open the site regardless, but as you can guess, that opinion was not shared by the majority of the families when we met."

"I am very sorry to hear it, madam."

"It is not your doing, M. Gramont, heaven knows, and in any case you have done much to ease our suffering by sending your servant to us. But yet, Sir, I have heard here and there that it is no longer only yourself and M. Tolouse that you are to be concerned for, and perhaps you shall have need of him again?"

"You are kind, madam, but I assure you it is not necessary. Mlle de Courteline and Mlle Vallon, the same who sent for me the other day when I was here, have three servants between them at present. I had hoped for the opportunity of explaining to you what might have appeared unusual."

"You owe me no explanation, Sir."

"Indeed, madam, I feel I do, for a woman who has charge of young women is rightly quite concerned for the character of those she introduces to them, and so I would wish to spare you any uncertainty on that score."

"You speak well, M. Gramont, and I shall not refuse to hear an explanation so thoughtfully prefaced."

With no further adieu I told her everything relating to my association with the two ladies; how I first encountered them, the reason for Mlle Vallon's flight, not failing to mention the extreme naivety her secluded upbringing had given her.

Miss Lawrence listened in silence and at times wonder at my relation, remarking at least how grateful she was that her daughter had not endured similar trials.

"But may I ask, M. Gramont, what do you intend to do? Do I understand correctly that these two young ladies are living in Courtney Lodge and that M. Tolouse and yourself will stay at the Hogshead while they are here?"

"Yes, madam, we have been at the Hogshead since they arrived. I hope to find a suitable accommodation for them and Mme. Gaspar. Returning to France is out of the question for any of them and so I believe they must make plans to settle permanently in England, which is what I have suggested."

"Without intending to pry, M. Gramont, have they means enough to do so comfortably?"

"At the moment I suspect they have money and valuables enough about them to keep them for a few years at least, but if they are inclined to take my advice, I shall go to M. Savard on their behalf and insist he restore both dowries to them immediately. If I am as successful as I would hope, they both shall have the means to marry however they like."

"I am delighted to hear it, M. Gramont. I shall not deny I have a great desire to know them, but I hope you will pardon me if I ask you to satisfy me on one additional particular?"

I nodded and she proceeded, "Why then, you must pardon me for inquiring if you believe they are respectable young ladies in all imaginable senses of the word? After all, situated as they have been, one could hardly fault them for a transgression or two. The world is not a friendly place for young women on their own, and so I dare-say there is more than enough reason to fear they would be led to err, however understandably."

"It was to prevent such a misfortune that I first took upon their protection, and I would be sorry indeed had I failed so miserably. Mlle de Courteline is so eloquent on the subject of virtue and propriety, however, she would take great offence were I to take the least credit for maintenance of her honour. Rather I shall say that it is Mlle Vallon who required such particular care, having no experience of the world or the snares it holds. It would be fairly easy for someone to deceive her, and therefore it is fortunate she has been sheltered from contact with most anyone but M. Savard or myself, and of course M. Tolouse. It is my hope she will in time become better able to judge such things for herself, or barring that, that she will marry expeditiously. They are both so devout, I would wager all I am worth that neither of them would ever knowingly be guilty of any immoral action, and it is only Mlle Vallon who might possibly be too ignorant to know if she was led to do so. I fear I may have been overly explicit, but in doing so I hope to assure you that they are both very worthy of your attention, and there is nothing to fear by making their acquaintance. Moreover, I have much reason to rejoice at the prospect for the sake of Mlle Vallon, feeling as I do that she could not but benefit from the society of your daughter and Miss Reckert, who are most worthy of emulation. Lastly, I may assure you that both women are from one of the most prominent families in France, and in that respect as well would only reflect credit upon your house. Forgive me, madam, you see my zeal carries me away."

"However that may be, you have carried your point. I could not refuse to see them both now, for the sake of my curiosity alone. As you have been kind enough to speak openly on the subject, rather than deflect my inquiries, I am more than satisfied for you to bring them here, whenever it is convenient. Only pray do not rush the poor things on my account, for they will likely need some days to recover from their ordeal."

I thanked her sincerely for her condescension and took my leave. Having once received her blessing for an introduction, I was in no rush to accomplish one. It did not escape my consideration that since both of them were handsome, it was not advisable to bring them immediately, for fear it may revive speculation on the subject. I felt it would be impossible to dismiss all doubts completely till they were settled elsewhere.

From Stearn Manor I went directly to Courtney Lodge with the thought that my absence there the day before would not have gone unnoticed. What was my surprise when I arrived there and discovered Mr. Harland himself was present, and engaged in a conversation with Mlle de Courteline while Mlle Vallon looked on in amazement.

Mlle de Courteline was poised gracefully in her seat, exhibiting her most dignified manner, as a queen addressing her subjects.

"M. Gramont may tell you himself what I have said," said she at my entrance, making a slight acknowledgement of her head in my direction. I had never in my life heard her speak a word of English, yet she did so now with an exactness and precision which only heightened the formality of her proceedings.

"Indeed," replied I in kind, "I am more than happy to avow that whatever Mlle de Courteline says is certain to be the truth, but I am far from thinking myself obliged to give assurances or explanations in my own house. How is it that you have come here, Mr. Harland?"

"Why I came merely to call upon you, Sir, but instead Mlle de Courteline admitted me. Is this then still your house, for I thought I had understood from Mlle de Courteline that you do not live here at present?"

"I am happy to lend my home to Mlle de Courteline and Mlle Vallon, so long as they have need of it."

Mr. Harland made no reply, and after a short pause, Mlle de Courteline took it upon herself to speak.

"As with many men accustomed to considering others in terms of their private actions, not merely their public professions, in finding Mlle Vallon and I here, Mr. Harland has no doubt concluded that we are fallen women, and that one of us is the victim of your perfidy."

At this Mr. Harland turned toward her with a look of amazement and attention. I could think of no response myself, and she continued.

"No doubt he fails to reflect that in thinking so he subjects two innocent women, descendants of Baron de Fouré, to the most heinous insults a woman can suffer. Nor does he do justice to the honour of M. Gramont whose family, however humble they may be, can glory in the knowledge that they have produced a man whose character is only matched by his generosity. You may heed me when I say, by the soul of my father, whose body only lately mouldered at the side of the guillotine, M. Gramont has never so much as hinted a dishonourable thought in the direction of Mlle Vallon or myself, though both of us may be said to bear our fair share of the beauty by which the Fouré women have been distinguished for centuries. Rather he has protected, assisted and defended two friendless women, whose fate has deprived them of guardians and country alike. In doing so, rather than being praised for his actions, he has opened his character to the grossest calumnies."

Mr. Harland seemed appropriately stunned by this speech, as I was myself, to a slightly lesser degree. He was silent for a short moment before saying, "If M. Gramont has indeed conducted himself as handsomely by yourself and your cousin as you aver, he is greatly to be commended for it. Moreover, if any of my questions have been understood to imply any aspersion on the character of yourself or your cousin, I apologize most profusely. In my defence, let me say that one does not often meet with a circumstance of this sort, and I am not in the habit of assuming that every man I meet is possessed of the character you ascribe to M. Gramont."

"Do you know anything to his detriment, Sir?"

"No indeed, I hardly know anything of him at all."

"Then you may begin to form your opinion from what I have told you."

"You are very good, madam," replied he complaisantly, before bowing and turning to take leave.

"Forgive me for detaining you, Sir," said she, "but before you depart, allow me to reinforce somewhat of what I have already said regarding myself." At this he turned reluctantly and she indicated for him to be reseated.

"Since it has come into doubt, let it be understood that I believe the basis of my character and even the dignity of my family to be reliant upon the true performance of virtue. Virtue itself is perhaps all the stronger when it has been put though a trial of some sort, and though I have never been tempted to swerve from my duty, I believe that the last few months spent away from my home and country are sufficient to qualify as a trial of sorts. During this time I have experienced no diminution of the strength of my convictions, nor allowed any word, action or thought inconsistent with them. To me, Sir, virtue is not merely comprised of its appearance. There are some who are content to believe that how they behave in private is irrelevant, so long as their public actions sustain the appearance of virtue. I am not one. I could not live in such a degraded state, and would plunge myself into the Seine a million times rather than suffer myself to be guilty of any wrong act. Were I to be faced with the choice of immorality which wore the eternal appearance of virtue, or virtue which wore the eternal appearance of immorality, I would choose the latter."

Mr. Harland appeared still more bewildered by this address, and I do not doubt that he has received very few lectures on virtue from a woman scarcely twenty, whose passion and eloquence on the subject might well be envied by priests all over the country.

"I thank you again, madam," said he, "and I am sorry to have put you to the trouble of this explanation. Let me assure you that I am perfectly convinced of the truth of what you have said, and need no further persuasion."

"My reason for admitting you here," continued she, "though of no prior acquaintance, is I hope now fully understood. I could not bear to think that anyone should hear of two young ladies living in the home of M. Gramont without having the true nature of their character and condition understood. I beg pardon for the theft of your time I have committed."

"No pardon is necessary, Madam, save my own," replied he, and then turning to me. "M. Gramont, I shall not seek to intrude upon your conference with your friends any further, for it is no doubt of a more urgent nature than the matter I wished to speak to you upon. I shall be in the area of the new town for some time today, and therefore if you should chance to go that way, I would appreciate of a small word with you. Adieu Monsieur, Ladies."

With that he disappeared as quickly as if he feared Mlle de Courteline might come up with any further matter to take up with him. As soon as he left, she said, "I ought to have encouraged him to stay during our conversation, so that he might see for himself that there is nothing said between us that anyone might not hear."

"I am certain that after the speech you made him, he shall never be guilty of allowing such a suspicion to enter his mind." As it occurred to me in the context of propriety, I said, "May I ask whether you have heard from Mme. Gaspar?"

We spoke now in French, and she replied, "Yes, and she comes directly, though no doubt M. Savard shall be aware of our situation as well. Yet it matters not. If he comes, I shall require him to answer for how he has deceived us, and that shall be all."

By this time I had recovered from my shock to say, "But come, Mlle de Courteline, tell me how it is that you have exhibited such a grasp of English before Mr. Harland, when I have never known you to speak a word of it before?"

"It seems Mr. Harland does not speak much French, and so it was a necessity of sorts. At any rate, in answer to your question, it is perhaps owing to a failing of mine that I have never done so before. I had English lessons as a girl, and though as I told you long ago, I read Sir Charles Grandison in French, my father refused to order many other translations, and so I have read several other novels in the original English. I was always a very reluctant student, however, and believed that it was beneath my dignity to master the language of such a backward people. Around fifteen, I made a point of forgetting what I knew, and believed I had done so. Necessity has forced me to relearn what I had forgotten and it seems I did not forget as much as I believed myself to have."

"Do you mean we hired a translator because you were bigoted against the language?" cried I, with amazement.

"Not entirely," replied she, calmly. "It would not have been appropriate for me to transact business, so therefore it was you who most needed a translator. Do not judge me too harshly, Sir. You must remember that I am a de Courteline, and a de Courteline cannot tolerate being laughed at for mispronouncing every second word, as I certainly should have done from the start."

I sighed, then said more gently, "From what I have just heard, this need not have been a great concern of yours."

"I thank you for the compliment, M. Gramont, yet I assure you, my knowledge of English was mostly from books, and I had heard it spoken but rarely."

"Why, what did you say to that gentleman, cousin," inquired Mlle Vallon, who had been silent to that point, 'to make his eyes become so large?"

"I told him merely what he ought to know regarding M. Gramont and ourselves."

"Indeed, cousin, you said a great deal. It seems I heard my name half dozen times at least and wondered what it all might mean. And how commanding you seemed, for I should never have dared to speak to him with such authority, being as he is such a great man in the world."

"Virtue endows its possessors with a natural authority, my dear cousin," replied the other, gently. "You may remember it often when you think upon the subject."

I took the opportunity to relay somewhat of what had passed between Mrs. Lawrence and I, and also to propose that the two cousins be settled independently with Mme. Gaspar as soon as may be. Both ladies agreed that such an arrangement would be ideal, and in order to accomplish it, Mlle de Courteline set herself about assembling all the money and valuables they had with them. To my surprise, each of them possessed the equivalent of nearly two thousand pounds or so, and presuming Mme. Gaspar did not arrive empty-handed, they would be handsomely provided for indeed.

"As to that, Monsieur," said Mlle de Courteline, "I empowered Mme. Gaspar to bring with her all my cousin and I are entitled to, save twenty percent of Mlle Vallon's dowry, which we agreed M. Savard may keep to himself to recompense him for any disappointment or inconvenience he believes himself to have suffered."

"I am amazed to see how clear-headed you have shown yourself to be," replied I, "for however dishonest M. Savard has revealed himself to be in other respects, I believe that only a truly abandoned wretch is likely to refuse such an offer."

"I hope you are right. But now, Monsieur, we have discussed all the essential matters and our visit ought not to be extended much further. Mme. Gaspar shall be arriving tomorrow at the latest, and as soon as then we are willing to be relocated, so long as a suitable place has been found. While we remain in your house, I shall be ill at ease and if it is possible, I should prefer to defer being introduced to Mrs. Lawrence till we are established elsewhere. For this reason, I must beg you to look around for a place for us at once, and if it is clean and respectable, upon the level of this house or more fine, then pray take it at once on our behalf. Once you have made these arrangements for us, I am in the hopes it shall be the last time Mlle Vallon and I are forced to inconvenience you."

You may imagine how quickly I agreed to all of this. As soon as I left, I called upon Mr. Reed, in the hope that he might refer me to an agent who would assist me in finding a suitable property for the three ladies, a task I would ordinarily consign to Philip. Mr. Reed assured me it would be the easiest thing in the world to find one, and declared he would be honoured to be permitted to be of some service to a friend of Mrs. Lawrence.

With that accomplished, I returned to the Hogshead to eat. M. Tolouse was there, and he laughed to hear my description of Mlle de Courteline's conversation with Mr. Harland.

"Well, it serves the gentleman rightly to be tormented so. Let the

Lord strike me dead before I am ever tempted to suggest that Mlle de Courteline is capable of doing anything amiss. She carries herself so uprightly on any subject, that one need only look at her to be sure she is in the right. Well, well, I should have liked to have seen it, if only I might have done so from many miles away."

After our meal I went out with the intention of making a very half-hearted attempt to find Mr. Harland. I had not gone very far, however, when I saw him approaching me in the road ahead.

"I am glad to meet you, M. Gramont," said he. "Where do you go at present? I will accompany you, by your leave."

"I came to find you as you requested, Sir, so perhaps we shall take a circuit."

"Thank you, M. Gramont," he paused briefly before beginning, saying. "I feel called upon to make you an apology of sorts. Your sudden arrival in this area and your association with the Lawrences and Reckerts were circumstances guaranteed to secure my interest, and perhaps I have not always treated you with the greatest kindness. I do not mean to say my circumspection is completely at an end, but all the same, if you have behaved as handsomely as Mlle de Courteline asserts, then you are a man of rare character."

"The world should be a sad place indeed if that were true, for my conduct was merely in keeping with what any traveller and fellow countryman might expect from another."

"Mlle de Courteline was quite positive in terms of the exemplary nature of your behaviour, but I shall say no more about it. I cannot help be curious, however, how far your disinterestedness extends, or whether you may have some honourable connection in mind with one of the ladies in the future?"

"I cannot see how such a thing would be a concern of yours, Mr. Harland, but as you have taken the trouble to inquire, I shall not scruple to tell you I do not."

A moment of two later he said, "I am somewhat surprised to hear it, but certainly it is your own affair. I do not know either young lady as well as you do yourself, and perhaps there is an objection I do not see."

"No indeed," said I, "for the objection resides mostly with myself. For reasons I do not care to share, I have no intention of being married."

Mr. Harland tipped his head in slight acknowledgment for this revelation, yet I believe he did not fully credit it.

"Forgive me, Mr. Harland," said I, "but I imagine you did not call upon me today to discover my matrimonial tendencies?"

"No indeed. You may recall that when we first spoke, I mentioned the presence of a Frenchman in the area whom I wished to speak with. After we parted last, I heard another report, and on this occasion a farmer relayed that he had seen the same man several weeks before, when he inquired after M. Hubert, your friend. Now as M. Hubert seemed concerned of something during his little fit of insensibility on the road the other day, I determined to ask you what you knew of the matter, and whether you could guess who it is who seeks M. Hubert?"

I did not answer immediately, trying to decide what I ought to say.

"Have a care," said he after a short time. "I have always observed that one does not need much time to say what is strictly true."

"I have made no secret that I do not feel obliged to tell you all I know of M. Hubert, but this at least I will say: M. Hubert had power and authority enough in France to earn himself enemies, and it is not beyond probability that one of them should trace him here. All too many Frenchmen are in England for other reasons, at any rate."

"Such as yourself, M. Gramont?"

"Such as myself."

Mr. Harland was evidently disturbed and attempted a good many other methods to learn more, but although I was tempted at times to say more, I knew not where to begin. Mr. Harland seemed a sceptical man by nature and I doubted if he would even accredit a part of my story if I told it to him in full.

When we had completed our circle and were returned to the

Hogshead, he took leave of me cordially, although it was apparent he was not in the best humour.

I hardly know how I shall contrive to seal a packet of this size, and so must finish it at this point. Dear Sir, I am ever,

Yours,
M.C

Marcel de la Croix to Henri Renault

March 12th,1793

Dear Friend,

The next morning I received two notes just before breakfast. The first was from Mr. Reed, informing me that he had discovered five potential houses, of which he gave me a brief description. He mentioned that he had taken the liberty of consulting Mrs. Lawrence, who might be a better judge than he on what would appeal to ladies.

The second letter was from Mrs. Lawrence, who requested I call upon her that day. With nothing else to occupy me, I set out to do so just after ten.

When I arrived, Mrs. Lawrence, her daughter and Miss Reckert were all present in the sitting room, and as I had guessed, Mrs. Lawrence was eager to offer her opinion on the houses Mr. Reed had proposed.

"I hope you do not resent my officiousness, M. Gramont, but when Mr. Reed told me what he meant to suggest, I knew two of them at least would be unsuitable. Trenton Park and Dall House are too large, I am certain, and three women would get quite lost. The furnishings are too old in Trenton, in addition, and I am certain it would not do, but after this, I will have done."

"But what of the other three, if I may ask? Grier was one and I do not quite recall the other two..."

"Grier Hall, Liston Cottage and Peldon Manor. If you want my advice, M. Gramont, you should recommend Peldon for the ladies, for it is somewhat larger than Courtney Lodge, and with richer furnishings, though it is a ways away and that may prove a problem. Grier is nice, I believe, but still somewhat too big, and 'twas a bachelor who lived there last, so I shall not presume to recommend it unseen. Liston is neat and would do well, I think, but it is more comfortable than elegant inside, and from what I have heard, Peldon is more in keeping with the taste of your friends."

"I am most obliged to you, madam, for Mlle de Courteline is anxious to be settled elsewhere and I understand Mme. Gaspar is to come today. I shall attempt to secure Peldon immediately."

"Shall you not visit it, Monsieur Gramont?" said Mrs. Lawrence, with surprise.

"You will perhaps think me a poor friend indeed when I confess I do not intend that much involvement in that matter. Your recommendation is more than sufficient for me, and if in time it should prove less than ideal to the three ladies, I trust they shall be able to find another without too much difficulty. Mlle de Courteline especially does not enjoy the sensation of obligation, and for other reasons which must be apparent, instructed me to conclude my search as quickly as may be. She is accustomed to distinguished surroundings and so I am in agreement with you, for Peldon sounds most to her taste. Mlle Vallon will be pleased with anything which pleases her cousin, and so I daresay will Mme. Gaspar."

"Then perhaps you might not object if I offered to arrange the matter myself, Sir?"

"I would be happy indeed, but I fear to accept, for your offer is far too kind."

"Not at all," replied Mrs. Lawrence, "for Peldon is owned by my cousin, Mr. Danbourne, and it would be the work of a moment to take it for them."

Hearing this, I had little to do but accept, and thank Mrs. Lawrence on the ladies' behalf, as well as my own.

"I hope you will pardon my curiosity, Monsieur," began Miss Reckert, after a short interval "but Mrs. Lawrence has given us the most fascinating account of Mlle Vallon's upbringing, and I would be greatly obliged if I might prevail upon you to repeat it for Miss

Lawrence and myself."

I did so readily, and when I had finished, the four of us embarked on a conversation regarding the fallacy of such an unnatural policy of child-rearing, wherein both ladies, most especially Miss Reckert, expressed the wish to be of some assistance to her.

"Oh yes, Monsieur Gramont," interjected Mrs. Lawrence, "you must recommend your friend to Miss Reckert, for she has more experience than any of us with helping poor lost things. It is a shame Thomas has not returned," but seeing that Miss Reckert's expression changed, she said, "Forgive my blundering, Miss Reckert, for I am too apt to say what occurs to me, and my daughter tells me that the loss of the young boy still affects you greatly."

Although she was noticeably affected by the mention of the subject, Miss Reckert shook her head to disclaim that any apology was necessary, then said to me, "Indeed, M. Gramont, though I am by no means endowed with any particular skill or insight on the subject, I am sorry to hear what the two young women have suffered and I would be quite happy to know if I might render them any service. The young boy Mrs. Lawrence mentioned before is a dear friend of mine. Only recently I sent him to be apprenticed and he has disappeared. He sent one letter to say that he is well, but means to make his own way in the world; how or why I cannot guess! I know now I ought not to have sent him, for I fear he was too delicate for even the lightest labour. I am every moment in hope that he will return, but with each day, it seems less likely."

I must have seemed quite sensibly touched by this relation, during which I felt every moment as if I would say something to reassure her, and yet I could not. Nor could I trust myself to say anything at all, so I merely bowed my thanks for her offer regarding Mlle Vallon.

I was spared the necessity of saying more by the sound of the bell. The possibility that Mr. Harland had arrived unexpectedly seemed to pass through every mind. A look of alarm overspread Miss Reckert's face, and Miss Lawrence and her daughter looked at her reflexively. A moment later, Mr. Thomas Etheredge was announced and entered. Miss Reckert seemed to breathe a great sigh of relief, which in itself inclined me to believe she had never yet seen Mr. Harland since Bristol.

Mr. Etheredge did not appear at all surprised to see me and finding that he greeted me by name, Mrs. Lawrence declared with surprise that there was obviously no occasion to introduce us.

"Of course you know my daughter and Miss Reckert, Sir."

"Yes, I am most happy to see them both again," replied he, slightly awkwardly.

"We are delighted you have called upon us, Sir, for I believe it has not been for quite some time. It must be six months now since I have seen your mother."

"Yes, madam, and she regrets it incessantly, but yet we only come in this direction infrequently."

"Of course, I did not mean to put you to explanation, Sir. I was this minute about to persuade M. Gramont to join us for dinner and I hope you yourself might be persuaded?"

"Indeed," replied he, "I meant not to impose upon you..."

Mrs. Lawrence looked to me as Mr. Etheredge fumbled for words and finding I bowed in acceptance, that gentleman said, "I mean, I shall be very happy to, only I did not intend to put you to any trouble."

"It is no trouble but a couple of extra bowls," cried she and ringing the bell, she ordered two extra places be set.

"Now," said she with a smile, "may I inquire how came you to know M. Gramont?"

"My father let Sorsten Manor to he and another gentleman, and of course M. Savard, an older lady and the two gentlewomen."

"Indeed, Sir," replied she, "it must be a rather large place?"

"M. Tolouse and I lived in the Parsonage, Madam," answered I, before Mr. Etheredge could think how to describe it, having appeared to miss the material tendency of the question.

"Then you know Mlle de Courteline and Mlle Vallon, Sir? We were just speaking of the former."

"Yes, indeed," stammered he.

"And how do you find them, Sir? I have heard they are both very handsome women?"

"Why, yes," replied he, "I think so. But yet, I think–, I am hard-pressed to speak of such things when I am quite overwhelmed with beauty, as at the present."

I could not help but raise my eyebrow to hear this, thinking it was no great testament to his regard for Mlle Vallon. He seemed to guess my thoughts, and tried to speak again, but Mrs. Lawrence interrupted, saying, 'Very well then, by all means you may say present company excepted beforehand, but I am very far from thinking that either my daughter or Miss Reckert expect such rigorous devoirs from our guests as to hear no other women praised in their company. Pray, proceed, good Sir."

"In that case," replied he, cautiously, "present company excepted, they are both very well-looking women."

"Well, if that was all you intended to say," declared Mrs. Lawrence with a smile, "then I daresay you need not have taken the trouble to exempt anyone."

All the same, Mr. Etheredge seemed quite sheepish to have done even so much, and I do believe that if I had not been present, he would have made both young ladies many compliments to make up for having said so. A minute or two later we all moved to the dining room.

Mr. Etheredge looked ever as though he meant to communicate something to me, but whenever one of the young ladies spoke, he felt compelled to attend to them with complete attention. I sighed more than once to know that Mlle Vallon's admirer was so fickle, and became generally perturbed as to what to do on that account.

Following the meal we returned to the sitting room. Mr. Etheredge seemed uncertain where to position himself, but as I placed myself near Miss Lawrence, he stood behind Miss Reckert's chair. Presently I noticed that Miss Lawrence was regarding me with her customary laughing expression, and so I bowed and said, 'I am always happy to amuse Miss Lawrence, but yet I fear I do it too often for my credit. Pray tell me how I amuse you at the moment?"

"Why I was only thinking that I intended to apologize to you for my earlier implication regarding my friend, considering you have so many friends of your own. Now, observing how your eyes are so frequently turned, I begin to wonder whether I have any apology to give?"

"You do not indeed, but perhaps not for that reason. And yet I think very soon I shall feel compelled to apologize to you for the disappointment you are to suffer when you discover how truly uninteresting my affairs prove in the end."

I looked again in the direction of Miss Reckert and Mr. Etheredge before saying, "I do indeed have reason to be distressed at Mr. Etheredge's attention to Miss Reckert and yourself, but it is not the reason you suppose."

Miss Lawrence raised her eyebrows with incredulity, then smiled again. "Perhaps then, M. Gramont, if your life continues as uneventfully as you predict, some might accuse you of being the most insensible of men."

"I would like at times to be less sensible and impressionable than I am. Let me merely be thought ineligible to aspire to any of the honours you allude to and that would be nearer the truth."

"Ineligible?" replied she "I do not remember hearing you were married, Monsieur?"

"Nor am I, or ever likely to be. My ineligibility stems from personal inadequacies, I fear."

She laughed again as I said so. "Forgive me, I fear you are in earnest. If you are indeed a determined bachelor, would this not be the result of choice rather than fate?"

"For some perhaps."

"But in your case it is simply ineligibility?"

"I might have hoped to cause Miss Lawrence more disappointment than amusement, yet I ought to be happy in any case."

"But if it is not self-imposed," persisted she, taking no notice of what I said, "must not the cause be investigated?"

"I should have thought part of the cause at least would be obvious, Madam. You know that I am an emigre, a refugee from my homeland. What sort of suitor could a man of this description make?"

"Well, then I perceive you mean to say you are not wealthy but suppose your future wife might be affluent?"

"I have no wish to be so, madam, and who would tolerate that?"

"Who, indeed?" was the reply. "That at least is self-imposed. I shall pry no further."

After this we spoke somewhat of literature and at my request she agreed to prescribe me something to read which might improve my English.

During this time, Mr. Etheredge stayed as well, and I guessed he intended to leave at the same time as myself in order to speak to me. I had no desire to speak with him while I was uncertain as to what I should do, and so I chose instead to wait him out. My device was successful, as a short while later he took leave.

Whilst I prepared to do so myself thereafter, Mrs. Lawrence inquired when I intend to introduce her to the inhabitants of Courtney Lodge. When I told her of Mlle de Courteline's intention of delaying her visit till they were settled elsewhere, she said, "I do not know how we shall be able to wait that long. Pray prevail upon her to come sooner, if it is at all possible."

I promised to do so.

The following day, M. Tolouse and I called at the other house together. Mme. Gaspar was extremely delighted to see us both.

During our visit she recounted M. Savard's displeasure in full, which I hardly think worthy of expending ink or paper upon. Happily, he appears to have conceded to the proposition of Mlle de Courteline, as he has sent a chest of valuables with Mme. Gaspar at her departure. The exact amount had not been calculated, but I was charmed to find that both cousins were disposed to share whatever remained between them, and neither seemed particularly anxious to know what amount was allotted them.

"I am sorry to say it," declared Mlle de Courteline, "but it would be hard to estimate any amount too high to be rid of that gentleman. Mouchard did not seem to like him, and that ought to have been a warning of sorts. I am glad it is over with, at least."

I then conveyed Mrs. Lawrence's wish to see them as soon as possible, and though Mlle de Courteline was reluctant to alter her resolve, Mlle Vallon and Mme. Gaspar soon prevailed upon her, and presently they decided that if they were to do so earlier than planned, they would call upon her that very day. Hearing this, I took the precaution of enjoining them all to avoid saying or implying anything which they had heard from Mouchard, and to be most vigilant in assuring they did not do so inadvertently. Each of them pledged to do so, and so all that remained was for them to change dress. Almost as an afterthought, I informed them of the news regarding Peldon Manor, but now in the prospect of such a visit, it was less momentous than it would have been had I mentioned it at the outset.

After they retired to change, I returned to the Hogshead in the expectation it would be an hour at least. I wrote a short note to Mrs. Lawrence informing her she might expect us, and yet it was a full two and a half hours later that we set out.

The sheer length of time began to cause me to fear they might be outfitted for a ball rather than a casual visit, but to my relief I found that the time seemed to have been employed making it seem as if no time at all had been employed.

Though both of them appeared somehow more charming since the morning, I could not tell how it was, or what had been altered aside from their clothes. Mlle de Courteline wore a fair number of jewels, but arranged in an understated fashion, which I had not thought entirely possible.

The visit was a curious thing in itself. Each of the four young women seemed quite interested in each other, but all were reticent to speak. Mlle de Courteline was again quite full of her own dignity, feeling that a certain amount of reserve was necessary to counter any possible misimpression of her sustained earlier. She spoke only in French, the language that all six seemed to speak easily, though she said but little.

Mrs. Lawrence seemed quite favourably impressed with their

appearance. As a girl, she had lived in Paris with her parents and her brother, and therefore she made several polite inquiries to discover whether they knew any of the families she had known then. She was suitably impressed to discover Mlle de Courteline was the niece of the Marchioness de Scion, who she apparently held in high regard. I do not doubt but that it raised their consequence extremely, for thereafter Mrs. Lawrence observed several times how honoured she was to know the niece of that lady.

Mlle Vallon spoke hardly at all, though she seemed most appreciative of the kind looks and attentions bestowed upon her by Miss Reckert and Miss Lawrence.

The most amusing, and I must say, the most surprising moment came when Mrs. Lawrence made a passing reference to the fact that the two ladies already had occasion to meet Mr. Harland. Mlle de Courteline did not hear her fully at first, but when she repeated the remark upon request, Mlle de Courteline declared, "Mr. Harland is indeed a most exemplary man, and he reflects honour upon the nation which produced him. One cannot speak too favourably of that gentleman."

This commendation, for which you may guess the reason as well as I, wore the most unusual appearance, coming from a woman of her age. Miss Reckert's cheeks flushed red, and she looked at Mlle de Courteline with astonishment, as did Miss Lawrence, though her expression was muted in comparison with her friend's.

Mlle de Courteline remained unconcerned, and Mrs. Lawrence replied presently, "Indeed, you shall not have to look far for agreement. Although I did not know him much till recently, we owe Mr. Harland the most profound gratitude for his care of us in our present need."

She looked hesitantly in the direction of Miss Reckert as if she hoped she had not offended her by the commendation, but Miss Reckert seemed by then too lost in thought to heed what was said.

And so this visit ended like many first visits do; with good impressions all around, as well as with relief that any little awkward moments had been no worse.

The next day I devoted both morning and afternoon to searching for any sign of Lafont. By dusk I was obliged to set out towards the Hogshead no more enlightened that before. As I entered the town, (the *original town* to some, called Gibbons), I noticed a small group of men on horseback across the lane some ways away. As I looked in their direction, I was immediately riveted by the sight of M. Lafont himself, who turned towards me at the same moment. Upon recognition his face contorted into a kind of spasm, and he spurred his horse towards me. He spat on the ground as he approached, and this same moment I became aware that Mr. Harland himself was nearby. Catching sight of this exchange, he began to approach as well.

"Well, Monsieur le Marquis," cried Lafont in French, his voice loud and mocking, "did I not already know I was in the right place, I should certainly be assured of it to find you here. I dare not guess you have come here for the same purpose as I, yet I would be surprised if even you would stoop so low as to seek to protect M. Hubert. Yet it signifies nothing. Neither you nor M. Hubert shall have long to live. I should kill you this moment, but it is better if you first witness justice, and if you have truly come this far to be M. Hubert's nursemaid, then perhaps you shall have the pleasure of dying with him."

With that he turned again and began to depart, "Lafont!" cried I, "You would be a coward to flee me; we must settle this at once!"

Lafont stopped and turned again, "What care I for the notions of a worthless boy as yourself. You are hardly fit to sully my shadow. If you dare pursue me, I shall dispatch you to hell to wait for M. Hubert."

By this time Mr. Harland had reached me. He had stopped in wonder to observe our exchange, but when Lafont began to ride away a second time, he called out for him to return. Lafont paused and looked in his direction.

"Who are you to concern yourself between Marcel de La Croix and myself?" cried Lafont still in French.

"Who do you call the Marquis de La Croix?" repeated Mr. Harland, looking at me.

M. Lafont laughed at this hesitation, and then said to me, still in French, "Well might a man disavow a name he dishonours. Few men would befriend a man who protects the murderer of his family. No doubt this gentleman ought to be more careful of his associations."

With this he returned to his companions, and they began to exit the town together.

"What madness is this, M. Gramont?" cried Mr. Harland, "This man ought not to be permitted to leave. Let us seek to detain him at once."

"We must either kill him or not attempt it, and while there are six men to us two, it would be madness to try. It would be better to assemble your men while I attempt to find M. Tolouse that we might follow them in better numbers."

Mr. Harland agreed, yet he regarded me with surprise and exasperation, "Very well, but should we fail to catch up to him, I expect to receive the explanation which I perceive ought to have been given me already."

We agreed to meet in the same spot in half an hour. I rode to the Hogshead to find out whether M. Tolouse had returned in my absence. He had not been there, according to the innkeeper, and so I immediately rode to Courtney Lodge to discover if he had called there that day. Neither there nor any other place could I locate him, though by the time I had looked everywhere I could think, I was some minutes late for meeting Mr. Harland.

Mr. Harland had arrived early, according to a messenger boy he had left there, and did not wait long. The boy pointed me in the direction he had gone, and though I tried to find him for two hours, there was no sign of either he and his party, M. Tolouse or M. Lafont. I returned to the Hogshead again, but still he did not return. I waited for a short time, but could not bear to be idle for too long, and so went out again.

In desperation where else I should look, I went to Stearn Manor, where Mrs. and Miss Lawrence received me.

"We are happy to see you, M. Gramont," said that lady. "Mr. Harland called here nearly an hour ago to find you, and he seemed quite anxious to speak to you indeed. I hope nothing is amiss?"

"Did he say where I am to find him, Madam?"

"He would say next to nothing, though I asked him any number of questions, and so one cannot help but worry."

"No doubt all is well. I have been looking for him as well, but without success."

Mrs. Lawrence was silent, pensive, then she said, "This is quite distressing! Allow me to say, M. Gramont, that we have all become quite fond of you, and of course Mr. Harland is deservedly held in the highest esteem. It would be dreadful indeed if two men of such merit and understanding were to be involved in a quarrel of some kind."

Till then I had not understood that she feared we meant to fight, and so I said, "For my side, Madam, I can assure you I have no wish to quarrel with the gentleman. I hope I can guess what it is he wishes to speak to me upon, and if he is satisfied with my response, then there will be nothing more to fear. I share your estimation of his worth."

"I am quite relieved to hear it."

"Perhaps it would be wise for me to go in search of him, that this may be resolved as quickly as possible," and without waiting to say more, I took leave.

Whichever way I took I had no better luck discovering him. At the Hogshead, I discovered he had called for me a short time before, so I returned to Stearn Manor in the thought that he might do likewise.

Mrs. Lawrence met me immediately, informing me that Mr. Harland had been there again, and requested that if I were to return again, she desire me to remain. She lamented that she was obliged to go out herself that moment, but earnestly requested that I make use of her home or garden till he might come again.

I thanked her and prepared to do as she suggested. I went out to the garden in order to clear my head. I paced up and down there for several minutes, weighing what I ought to tell Mr. Harland when he arrived. I had no intention of telling him anything of Mouchard / Thomas, but as for the rest, I could not tell how to reveal one thing and not the whole?

As I was contemplating this, I did not observe Miss Reckert enter the garden.

"I am sorry to intrude upon you, M. Gramont," said she, "as I see you are deep in thought."

"I am madam, but I am happy for the interruption."

"I fear you will feel differently when you learn why I wish to speak with you. Though I have no right to do so, I cannot help desire to know if there is any truth to the report of discord between you and Mr. Harland?"

"In truth I cannot say, madam, for I have not yet spoken to him. On my part at least there is little reason to fear."

Miss Reckert was silent for a moment of two, then she said, "But surely if that is the case, nothing could tempt you to risk your life and his, against your own will and inclination?"

"If he should insist upon it, the laws of honour decree that I must, however unwillingly."

She lapsed into thought again, then at last declared with dismay, to no one in particular, "I know not how it can be that duelling is universally abhorred while it is universally practised!"

"Were the matter in my hands alone, madam, no other persuasion would be needed. Though it is hardly my place to say so, I cannot help but feel your influence is slightly misapplied. Would it not be more efficacious for you to speak to Mr. Harland himself? It is in his hands the entire matter rests, and if you will pardon the freedom of my implication, therefore your own."

Miss Reckert appeared grave and defiant at the suggestion, but a moment later the blood seemed to leave her face completely, and turning to see what had fixed her attention, I saw Mr. Harland, who had but recently entered the garden. He too stopped short at the sight of us. He bowed presently to Miss Reckert, at which her faced flushed red and she disappeared through a gate which led to the outer portion of the garden. Judging by the expression of each, it was indeed the first occasion either had seen each other since Bristol. Mr. Harland was more than riveted by her presence, and for a good many moments after she had left, he looked in the same direction.

At last he turned to me and without addressing me by name, he said, "It seems that while I have been chasing first your friend then yourself about the countryside, you have been far more agreeably occupied."

"I can take very little credit for it. Along with Mrs. Lawrence and her daughter, Miss Reckert has become concerned there shall be a contest between us and so it seems she hoped to discourage what she feared by speaking to me."

Mr. Harland stared at me for a long moment. At last he said, "I hardly know where to begin, M. Gramont. When I was in Brussels a short time ago, I remember hearing a ridiculous folk tale about a band of Royalist warriors led by the illegitimate brother of Marie-Antoinette and her lover. I did not recall this until I heard the man we encountered today address you by the name Marcel de La Croix. When M. Hubert called you by a similar name, I was prepared to dismiss it, but yet it seems quite odd for them both to suffer the same delusion. Tell me, M. Gramont, what ought to be made of all of this?"

"I shall tell you what you wish to know, Sir, yet I cannot be answerable for folktales."

"Very well," replied he. "I should be little inclined to believe them in any case. All the same, what is your name?"

"My name is M. Gramont, Sir, but at birth I was called Marcel de La Croix. I am the son of the Marquis and Marchioness de La Croix."

"Many emigres have taken different names in England, Monsieur, and I am not inclined to hold it against you. I do not intend to pry into your affairs at present, as for what I have seen and heard today, there hardly seems time for me to do so. For the time being, I merely wish to know everything you can tell me about the man we met today. Only yesterday you claimed to know very little about this same Frenchman, which I see plainly was not the case. I did not comprehend everything which passed between you earlier, M. Gramont, yet I would swear he declared his intention of killing both M. Hubert, and possibly yourself. Is this correct?"

"It is."

"For what reason does he wish to do so?"

"M. Hubert is responsible for the deaths of his family."

Mr. Harland stared at me with disbelief at this revelation.

"Are you certain, Sir?"

"All too certain."

"Then this is a serious matter indeed. Tell me, if he means to kill M. Hubert, why does he not simply ask him for satisfaction, like a gentleman?"

"Whatever he may once have been, I no longer think M. Lafont has any pretensions to being a gentleman. He is possessed with the idea of revenge, and has no intention of allowing M. Hubert the possibility of prevailing. In a practical sense, M. Hubert is incapable of such a thing, even were Lafont to seek it."

"I have often suspected M. Hubert was devoid of his proper state of mind, M. Gramont, and it seems you are in agreement. And is this M. Lafont aware of it also?"

"He is, Sir, but it matters little to him."

"Then let us speak of the vital matter at hand, M. Gramont. Do you believe this Lafont poses a threat to anyone beyond M. Hubert?"

"It is this very question which concerns me, for I fear he cares not who else may suffer or perish, so long as M. Hubert dies."

"I shall not ask how you have acquired your insight into this man's character, but allow me to hope it enables you to guess what he intends to do now?"

"I fear not, Sir, but yet I would be unwilling to rule out even the most extreme possibility."

"Very well," said he, after a short pause, "I thank you for this information, M. Gramont, however belatedly provided."

Without further word he bowed and prepared to depart. I stayed him to make another offer of assistance, to which he replied, "It may come to that, Sir, but at present there is nothing for you to do."

I remained in the garden a short time thereafter. Though I was relieved he had not asked me for greater explanation than he had, I could not help to be disturbed to see he trusted me very little.

When I returned to the house, Mrs. Lawrence declared she was happy to see we had come to an understanding, as Mr. Harland had informed her that he and I were upon good terms. She invited me to stay for dinner that evening, but I politely declined, feeling quite unfit for conversation. Nor could I imagine sitting down for dinner while I knew Lafont was in the immediate vicinity. I was able to have a brief conversation with Philip before I left the house.

Outside I saw that the gamekeeper and his dogs and two other men were standing watch, which undoubtedly was the work of Mr. Harland. I returned to the Hogshead in the hopes of finding M. Tolouse, but instead I found a letter from him saying he had travelled too far while exploring, and now was staying at an inn rather than returning that evening.

I could not help but consider that if a messenger could make the journey, it was not so far a distance to travel, but upon reflection I concluded that he had probably drunk too much to want to ride any distance whatsoever.

I shall close here, but shall send you the remainder as soon as may be. I flatter myself you may be anxious to receive it.

Your friend,
M.C.

Marcel de la Croix to Henri Renault

March 14th, 1793

Dear Friend,

That evening I slept hardly at all, and woke up quite early. I went immediately to Stearn Manor, taking the longer route to see if there were any signs of activity, but there were not.

When I was shown into the sitting room at Stearn, I discovered Mr. Harland was already there, alone. His mood was rather more intense than usual, yet he seemed neither pleased nor displeased to see me. I inquired whether there had been any news since the previous day, and he merely shook his head.

It was apparent something was preoccupying him, and after only a minute or so of pacing about, he wished me good morning, observing that I was more likely to receive a better reception in his absence.

I was sorry to see him go, yet was conscious he spoke the truth, at least as far as it related to Miss Reckert. Shortly thereafter, Miss Lawrence appeared from the other quarter of the house, seemingly unaware there was anyone in the house.

"Has my mother seen you, Sir?" inquired she, and receiving my answer with surprise, she excused herself to discover what kept her. In a moment or two she returned, saying, "My mother does not rise with the sun, I fear, but she will be here presently."

I apologized for calling so early, but she said with a smile, "It is not very early, as I am sure you know."

Little was said for a few minutes. Miss Lawrence made no allusion to the recent tension between Mr. Harland and myself, and I was somewhat relieved by it. I had made no mention of Mr. Harland's visit, and was deliberating whether I should mention it when Mrs. Lawrence appeared. A short time later Miss Reckert also entered.

The civilities which passed between us were entirely free of any consciousness of the increased activity hereabouts, and in truth, I doubt the ladies were aware of much. After a word or two about the weather, Miss Reckert went in search of a book, and Mrs. Lawrence picked up her work, leaving Miss Lawrence and I mostly to ourselves.

While there was a great deal on my mind, I could think of nothing we might speak of freely, so I waited for Miss Lawrence to begin a subject. She began to speak of books, as we had once or twice before, and I revived my previous request that she recommend something for the improvement of my English.

"I have given a good deal of thought to your request," said she, "and I do not know quite what to make of it, but I confess I have come to think it is slightly mischievous."

"How so, Madam?"

"Why, as everyone knows, women read novels, and if you apply to a woman for a book, you are inviting her to give you a book on love. It is a rather indelicate request, is it not?"

I smiled at this, but told her I believed her library was by no means so limited as to make this a concern.

"Very fine, I see," replied she, "but as it happens, you are right, for there are some truly onerous tomes I think you ought to read."

"But indeed," returned I, with some concern, "when studying a language voluntarily, it is necessary to engage ones interest, to ensure regular study."

"I had anticipated this objection," said she, "which is why I had resolved to inquire what subject is most likely to hold your attention?"

I pondered how to answer this question, for upon reflection I knew that she was perfectly right. I had hoped she would give me some work which had moved her, and would better inform me of the very workings of her heart; a knowledge I had pledged never to have any use for.

I moved in the direction of the bookshelf to bide time while seeming to jog my own memory. Miss Lawrence followed me, but as she passed by the card-table, she said, "Why what is this, M. Gramont? Have you been writing while you waited?"

I turned with surprise to see what had caught her attention. Sitting on a table nearby was a writing tablet on which was written clearly:

"*I did not look till my return. No fool ever suffered more.*"

Only a quick reflection was necessary for me to guess the meaning of it, and then I looked reflexively in the direction of Miss Reckert. Miss Lawrence observed my motion with surprise, prompting me to say, "Not I," rather significantly.

Miss Lawrence seemed to consider the matter for a moment, before turning to Miss Reckert, saying, "Miss Reckert, come and look at this."

Miss Reckert obliged immediately, and as she read it, Miss Lawrence said, "M. Gramont denies writing it. What is one to make of it? Should we believe him?"

That very moment, Miss Reckert seemed to catch her breath and turn slightly to conceal her expression. I have no doubt that Miss Lawrence caught it all, but nevertheless she turned herself as if examining the tablet.

"I know not how to accredit your denial, Sir," resumed she, "for words do not write themselves, and here you were waiting for some while by yourself."

"My own deficiencies shall serve as proof, for however slightly I may be improving, I would not hazard writing in English while I remain such a poor student of the spoken language. Mr. Harland was here when I arrived and perhaps he was making some notes to himself as he waited."

Miss Reckert's eyes had returned to the tablet, where they were fixed as I replied. Hearing the name 'Mr. Harland' she blushed and retired to the other part of the room without a word to either of us.

"Perhaps we have created some mischief, M. Gramont," said Miss Lawrence, looking in the direction of her friend thoughtfully.

"On the contrary, Madam, I am in the hopes we have done a great deal of good."

"How so?" replied Miss Lawrence, "do you know more of all this than others?"

"Why merely that it is plain Mr. Harland wishes to convey some message to Miss Reckert, and she wishes to avoid receiving it. It is my opinion that whatever fault he is guilty of, it cannot be so great that he ought to be permanently denied the opportunity of explanation."

"You amaze me, Sir!" said Miss Lawrence, yet quietly enough that she could not be overheard. "By your description, one would think a misunderstanding alone separates them! Is it not universally believed that Miss Reckert has an unalterable aversion to the author of these words?"

"Whether it is broadly believed is a different question than whether it is true, but you have my assurance that it is at least somewhat short of universally accepted."

A short time later, Miss Reckert slipped out of the room entirely.

"I confess I am always surprised to hear you speak so warmly in favour of Mr. Harland, M. Gramont, and even more so on the heels of the excitement of yesterday. We were all quite relieved to find nothing came of it."

I nodded. Miss Lawrence seemed as if she wished I would say more on the subject, but as I did not, she could not discover any way to press it.

A messenger came for Mrs. Lawrence a short while later, and once she had read the letter, she declared, "Here is some good news for you, M. Gramont. Peldon shall be ready at the end of the week, and your friends are welcome to move there in two days."

"That is wonderful, indeed," replied I, "and I am most grateful for your trouble in this matter."

"'Twas no trouble at all. You must bring them the news as soon as may be."

I ventured to do as she suggested and so took leave. My visit to Courtney Lodge was necessarily hurried. I stopped briefly at the Hogshead thereafter, and left a message for M. Tolouse, lest he should return there, asking he come find me in the vicinity of Stearn.

Again I made shift to explore the area in search of Lafont, but to my surprise I saw nothing of him, Mr. Harland, or anyone at all aside from farm workers. I returned to the Hogshead again perhaps two hours later to take my evening meal.

When dinner was in the midst of being served, the innkeeper slapped his head suddenly and declared, "Bless me, what am I thinking! A message came for you a little over an hour ago now," and with that he went to find it.

When he returned he handed me a hurried letter from Mr. Harland which read simply as follows:

"M. Gramont, I have located Lafont's residence in Warrick, five miles North of Stearn. Come with M. Tolouse if you like, for we go to find him at once. Yours, Harland."

No sooner had I read it than I swallowed a quantity of wine, took whatever food could be eaten in motion and remounted my horse.

I retraced my steps almost immediately to ask the Landlord if he knew the way to Warrick. I ought to have saved myself the trouble, for he gave me only a general indication. A traveller on the road near Stearn gave me better directions, and likewise a farmhand a few miles past confirmed I was on the right path.

By this time it was quite dark. I had neglected to bring torch or lantern with me and was obliged to proceed slowly on account of my horse. At last I saw the light of a small party in the distance, and having no better plan, left the road to get a closer look.

Though I was obliged to go even slower off the road, they were on a path to intersect me, and as they were about to pass me unseen, I heard Mr. Harland's voice and called out to him.

In a moment they surrounded me, but Mr. Harland easily recognized and introduced me to the others.

"Thank you, M. Gramont. M. Tolouse does not come?"

"He has not returned to the inn, but I have told the innkeeper to send him here if he does. But what has happened, what do you intend to do to find M. Lafont?"

"We have already found him," replied one of the men, who had been introduced to me as Mr. Green, a wealthy farmer.

"It seems your former friend is a coward, M. Gramont," said Mr. Harland, signalling for us all to ride again. "Late last night I discovered from an innkeeper hereabouts that he has been keeping company with two brothers called Baird. They are the last representatives of a formerly wealthy and reputable family since come to ruin. It seems the two sons live in the original family home, which is little more than a wreck itself. We were on our way there when we encountered the three together. I called for them to stop immediately but they merely fired upon us and fled."

"Fired upon you?" cried I, with undisguised amazement. "I had thought Lafont would have been beneath such cowardice, but it matters not. Where is he now?"

"If I knew, I would not be wasting time in conversation, M. Gramont."

"Mr. Harland and Mr. Roberts were injured, M. Gramont," observed Mr. Green, interjecting what Mr. Harland apparently did not mean to add.

"Mr. Roberts was shot in the leg," said Mr. Harland, "and a horse was injured. I received a little scratch on my arm hardly worth mentioning."

"Where is Mr. Roberts now?" inquired I, not remembering being introduced to him.

"He has gone home," replied Mr. Harland, "and we have not seen so much as a hair of Lafont and his friends since then. We mean to make another circuit of this area, and then return to the Baird home."

"If you wish, I shall take your place, Mr. Harland, and you may see to your arm." said I, perceiving that some of the other men seemed somewhat uneasy on that score.

"It is unnecessary, M. Gramont, yet you are welcome to accompany us as long as you wish."

For the next two or three hours we rode up and down fields and along roads in the area, yet we neither saw nor heard anything but the sound of startled hounds. From Warrick we rode to the vicinity of Stearn manor. Nothing had been seen there, so we returned Northwards again, going beyond Warrick to a little town called Fern.

By this time we were obliged to stop to refresh the horses, if not the men, and as there were two public houses there, it seemed as good a place as any. I immediately proposed a doctor be found to dress Mr. Harland's wound, to which he laconically replied that one would be hard-pressed to find it, but all the same I ordered one be brought.

When the physician arrived I escorted him to Mr. Harland myself, and made no offer to leave. Mr. Harland did not seem delighted to find it, yet did not suggest that I depart, as if he meant to be above concealment. His wound was in his upper left arm, and had apparently been crudely bandaged by Mr. Green. It was by no means alarming, but yet it was not as slight as he had represented.

"Though 'tis hardly life threatening," observed the doctor who tended him, "it ought to have been tended to immediately. A slight wound may be dangerous when it is infected, and if there had been any metal left in your flesh, it might have become a more serious case. You have a slight fever, Sir, which is natural enough, but if you should rest for a few hours then go home and rest a few more, you shall do quite well."

"I have no intention of resting directly, Sir," replied he, "nor can I conceive how it would be necessary."

"Then I fear you shall understand soon enough," replied he, shrugging his shoulders. "The body does not much like being abused when it wants recruitment, but a doctor may only prescribe, not enforce. Good-day, gentlemen."

When he had left, I said, "Surely it would be folly for you to attempt to do more this evening. In your present condition, you would be very little use if we happened upon Lafont, and as it is you are merely a distraction to the other men, who are plainly already ill at ease on your behalf. I will go out again in your place, and no doubt we shall have greater success when every man has his wits about him."

This argument held considerable weight, and at last with difficulty I prevailed upon him to remain, yet he said, "M. Gramont, though you are perhaps more aware of it than any other, I cannot help stressing to you how vital it is that M. Lafont is apprehended immediately. I have ceded to your argument solely because I fear you are right and that my presence may do more harm than good. I am loathe to leave something of such importance to anyone, yet I would wish you to understand I do not entrust you with it lightly."

I assured him I was quite aware of the seriousness of the matter and would search for M. Lafont till dawn at least.

Leaving Fern we essentially retraced our steps, cutting a rather zig-zag pattern over the land which stretched from Fern through Warrick and in the direction of Stearn again. Rather than return home at that point, an option more than one man was in favour of, I proposed we return to Baird manor.

Although there was some reluctance, all were agreed in the end. Baird manor was truly dilapidated, and a fine roost for pigeons, but little else. The walls and roof were intact and made of stone, but several windows were broken or boarded. There was no light inside, and no answer came to our knocks. I called repeatedly in French for Lafont to come out and face me, saying anything I thought might provoke him sufficiently.

There was no reply at all, and as I had said such things as ought to have made his blood boil, I knew in my heart he was not there.

First light began to break and though I was intent on looking further, Mr. Green said to me, "M. Gramont, I can see you are a good and brave gentleman, and I am most grateful you were able to prevail upon Mr. Harland to take some rest, but now I fear he is not the only one who needs it. We must all go home, but if you mean to return to Mr. Harland, you may tell him that we shall all be ready to go out in a few hours, once we have had sleep and food. Adieu, good Sir."

With a heavy heart I returned by myself to the inn in Fern to relay our lack of success to Mr. Harland.

I found him much as I had left him, and had much reason to doubt whether he had slept at all in our absence. Our ill-success was depicted on my face when I entered, but all the same he requested I describe all we had done in detail.

When I had finished doing so, he said,

"I thank you, M. Gramont. No doubt you did more than many

would, yet it seems M. Lafont has escaped us both. I shall begin to search for him again as soon as it is possible. I have several letters to write in the meantime, and would be obliged if you would request our host fetch me writing materials when you are on your way out."

Seeing that he was far from anxious for me to stay, I went to do so at once. The innkeeper was away from his post, so I asked his man to fetch pen and ink, and in the end returned with them myself.

I had but just closed the door behind me when there was a commotion of sorts in the hall, and when I looked out a moment or two later, I saw a man being carried to the far room. I motioned for the innkeeper to come to speak to us when he had seen to whatever occupied him at that moment, and he came quite quickly, apparently eager to tell us what was afoot.

"'Tis a fine doing, Sir, for the ruckus you observed was one of my rooms being taken up by a dying foreigner. Not that I would be unfeeling, far from it, but the dead rarely pay the tab, and even the living are a little behindhand sometimes."

"A foreigner, Sir," repeated Mr. Harland, immediately alert, "Pray, may we see him?"

"Aye, as you like, though he is not long for the world."

We went together to the room and there before us lay M. Lafont, in the agonies of death. Mr. Harland no sooner looked at him, then glanced at me and left the room.

I stood stunned for a moment or two. The innkeeper himself looked on, shaking his head, and was preparing to leave when I demanded what had been given him for relief.

"'Tis like I said, Sir, the dead do not pay the bill, and liquor must be bought by someone, and what then?"

"Let you only be served the same on your deathbed," cried I, in disgust. "Unless I am much mistaken, you would not have agreed to have him lie here had you not already resolved to rifle his pockets by and by. Fetch something this minute and I shall pay for it myself, but mind that you do not take too long, or I shall see that you pay for it as well, in more ways than one."

He hurried away more meekly and returned in a moment or two with what I requested, and together we made shift to have him drink it.

When at last M. Lafont saw me standing beside him, he laughed bitterly, though the act of doing so itself seemed to cause him much pain.

"So, La Croix, do you nurse me now, though I would have killed you with pleasure? It was always your weakness. I spit on you and your pity."

"Do not give yourself the trouble. Drink and be at peace."

He drank again, but hardly had he done so, than he closed his eyes with a spasm of pain, never to reopen them.

I sat a short while in silence. It seemed but the work of a moment; to find him so unexpectedly, and the next moment he lay dead, having died in the worst way I can think: alone, dishonoured and in pain.

Presently I returned to inform Mr. Harland he had died, but after I had done so, I returned to the innkeeper and inquired how M. Lafont had come there and how he had met his end.

"The fellow who brought him here said he got in an altercation with a man he was drinking with across the way and they crossed swords."

"Where is the victor?" pursued I, feeling a strange desire to know it.

"Being held for the murder of the other, I suppose."

"Where?"

"You may ask at the Magistrate down the lane, your honour, for it was his man who brought the dead man here."

Without further ado I settled the bill and informed Mr. Harland what I meant to do, before going directly to the home of the Magistrate. I was admitted instantly, and after explaining my interest in this matter, I asked to be permitted to see the man in question.

"I have no objection to you seeing him, Sir, though it is a little irregular. He is a great big fellow, like the other one, only the victor has a wooden leg. It is not often that such a man is tried for a crime like this."

"Then surely his name is Tolouse?" cried I, with amazement.

"The very name! And so I see that you know him, Sir. Perhaps you don't need to see him now?"

"In due time, but first let me ask how much is required to secure his release?"

"Fifty pounds, Sir."

I had not that much upon me, but I told him I would return to Mr. Harland and get what remained. At the mention of that gentleman's name, he inquired if I referred to the Mr. Harland who lived near Kettich, and when I replied that I did, he told me that it would not be necessary to do so, and that any friend of Mr. Harland need provide no security at all. I thanked him and went at once to see M. Tolouse.

What irony was to be found in this first encounter with M. Tolouse! Never had I been so pleased with him in my life, yet never had I seen him so sheepish and apologetic. He gave me an account of all that had occurred, which was no more than that he had been drinking and playing cards, and a quarrel had erupted between he and another man, and the quarrel had been transferred to Lafont, who had but lately arrived, in a manner that even M. Tolouse was not fully aware of. M. Tolouse held his ground, the two fought, and he found himself immediately apprehended for possible murder, pending M. Lafont's death.

He was overflowing with gratitude for my unlooked-for intervention, and so eloquent in the act of self-commendation, I could not bring myself to interrupt him.

After we departed together, I stopped at the other inn to take leave of Mr. Harland, only to find he had already departed.

"I see it was not me who brought you both hither," said M. Tolouse, when we set out again. "Nor should it have been, indeed, but I'll wager it was something pretty particular?"

"We were in pursuit of M. Lafont since last evening."

"M. Lafont?" cried he. "So he came at last, when I had all but lost faith he would. It serves me right, to have been locked up at the very time!"

"Perhaps not that very time, but nearly so."

"Well, but what came of it?"

"Mr. Harland encountered him before I came, but was shot in the arm and Lafont fled. We searched the whole night for him in vain."

"And what now?" cried he, "Ought we not to look for him again? I am not tired, and if he is still in the area, I may still have my chance at him."

"You have had your chance at him already, dear friend, for it was he you have killed only hours ago."

At this revelation, M. Tolouse was speechless for several minutes at least, and we rode along in a pleasing silence.

"Indeed, M. Gramont," said he, when I had begun to think he never meant to speak again, "I am not certain this has been fair-dealing on your part, for if I have killed Lafont, who you were all looking for, it seems I have done a very good thing, and in that case you might have saved me the trouble of heaping insults upon myself. But I shan't complain much, for I am not in a bad mood on account of it. No doubt you would have liked to have killed him yourself, and perhaps you are sore on the subject. I suppose that doing so must be thought a very great service to the Lawrences and the Reckerts and the like, and having blamed myself so severely already, I think I may commend myself now, to right the balance. I would not have you think I intend to be vain about it myself, however–."

I can't claim to have listened to every observation he made on the subject, but yet I heard enough to shed doubt on the statement above, and more than enough to cause me to wish I had somehow delayed the revelation till we were more near the end of our journey.

When we neared the Lawrences, I recollected that it was around ten, and from an impulse of curiosity, I resolved to pay a brief visit there while M. Tolouse went on ahead.

As I approached the house I was surprised to see what appeared to be Mr. Harland's horse tied nearby, yet I could scarcely conceive how he could contemplate a visit while he had such great need of rest and possibly more.

Entering the house I was told that Mrs. Lawrence was not at home. I inquired whether Mr. Harland had called there lately, and was told by a servant that he had arrived a few minutes before and was likely in the garden or gone home.

With the intention of expostulating with Mr. Harland on his imprudence, I went to the garden directly. At first I could not see anyone, but after proceeding along a covered walkway, obscured by flowers and greenery, I stopped short all of a sudden at the sight of that gentleman in conversation with Miss Reckert.

I had but just passed by a gap in the foliage through which I had gone undetected. I hesitated whether to retrace my steps and risk being seen on my return, but I was loathe to take the chance of disturbing a conversation so long in the making. I was not entirely inclined to absent myself moreover, for reasons I shall not confess here. The rationale I am less ashamed to own must suffice for all, which is that in addition to what I have already mentioned, my knowledge of Mr. Harland's current delicate condition prompted me to wish to stay nearby and ensure he did not exert himself, if it was at all possible.

These seemingly laboured considerations were but the work of a moment. I decided at last to remain where I was for the time being; concealed by vines, but able to see through the gaps between the leaves.

Miss Reckert was seated somewhat reluctantly, and Mr. Harland was in the midst of saying: "Ah, madam, silence and avoidance are preferable to words such as these! Could a delay receiving your message truly prove so fatal to wishes I only lately learnt to form? Was I only to learn what happiness was possible when it was beyond my grasp?"

Miss Reckert coloured violently at this question, and stood to reclaim the hand he had seized as he spoke.

"Forgive me for speaking so directly," said she, attempting more composure than she managed, "but could I have known it would be twelve weeks before you would acquire the curiosity to look at it, I should never have sent it. I bear more than half the blame for my foolishness in doing so, but the only amends I can make is to prevent the mistake from enduring any longer, which I do now."

"Indeed, Madam," replied he, "however circumstances may seem against me, I assure you it was not a lack of curiosity which caused me to delay looking at what–."

Miss Reckert prevented him from continuing by saying, 'I meant not to give you the trouble of flattery or persuasion, Sir, but rather to explain myself in such a way as to spare you any further effort on my account.'

"I am very far from objecting to your directness, Madam, for the most difficult objection to remove is the one that goes unuttered–."

"Sir–."

"Indeed, I am certain you would tell me it is impossible for it to be removed, but knowing how long I have languished to speak with you, I am persuaded you are too generous to refuse me the opportunity of doing so."

Miss Reckert was silent in irresolution, and when at last she uneasily reseated herself on a bench, he said, "Far from a lack of curiosity, the delay I shall ever curse was the result of a concerted effort not to think of you or your affairs. I felt I had never truly spoken with you till that night, and to ensure you may not suspect me of flattery, I shall confess that until then I was inclined to believe your character was trifling and insubstantial. I thought it likely that vanity had seen so many admirers entertained then dismissed, and I blessed the perceived faults which preserved me from any serious danger while in such close proximity to you. On that evening, I realized fully my mistake! How charming, how sincere, how intelligent you revealed yourself to be! Of coquetry only did I not acquit you, for your looks were so soft and enchanting, I was compelled to arm myself against them. When we parted, I could not help but say to myself, *What unthinking creatures are the best of women; so indiscriminately do they employ their charms, it is a wonder half of mankind is not in misery!* I felt most keenly the plight of your past admirers, and condemned the stupidity of the fool who had unknowingly found your favour. Nothing was further from my thoughts than that any portion of your esteem could have fallen to my share. Now, dearest Miss Reckert, thinking as I did, is it any wonder that I delayed looking at what you had given me? Nor do I believe my curiosity could have been completely repressed had I not believed the item I was entrusted with was the means to unite you with another."

"How wise was I to avoid such conversations with you!" declared Miss Reckert, when he paused, rising again with apparent emotion and speaking as much to herself as to him.

"Whence comes this objection? Surely you do not fear that I would mislead you?"

"Nay, indeed, I do not know what I fear, but yet I beg you will excuse me."

"I am far from wishing to oppose any wish of yours, but I know not how to be content with what you have said? Will you not condescend to tell me whether you doubt what I have said or if there is another obstacle you have not mentioned? I can scarcely conceive of what could be at once so unalterable and indescribable?"

Miss Reckert seated herself again in silence, and after a sigh, and a preface I could not quite hear, she said, "You may well guess I have been unhappy in your perceived indifference, but I have been no less unhappy in myself for what I can scarcely bring myself to pronounce, my own misguided declaration. True affection is not, I fear, to be solicited in this manner. You are generous and devoted to my father; you pity me, and perhaps I may go as far as to say you do not object to what was offered you unlooked for. Your motives are honourable, even laudable, and perhaps I should have expected no less. But to accept your offer would only compound my first mistake and make me still more miserable than I have been."

"Good God!" cried he. "What logic is that which takes passion for cold obligation, and refuses it accordingly? Why must it be that so slight an admission by your sex is forever deemed a blight upon your dignity? Could I have thought possessing you was within the realm of possibility, I should never have ceased striving for it, as I do now, but to my misfortune, I could not have been more convinced the opposite was true. I fear to confess that an admission like that which you made was all too necessary, and without it there would never have been any understanding on my part. Dearest Miss Reckert," added he, "would you give a blind man sight, only to plunge him back into darkness if all was not done following the established mode?"

Miss Reckert did not answer, but sighed again as if she knew not how to respond

"I cannot, help but wonder," began he presently, seeming somewhat more desperate, "if this can truly be the nature of your objection. Can you truly doubt what is nothing less than the natural and undeniable truth? Does not my every action testify to the strength of my attachment; does not my very look announce it? Is it possible I have something more daunting, more pernicious to fear? Was it not only yesterday I found you in conference with M. Gramont, a privilege so steadfastly denied me for months? Tell me, I beg you, openly and without delay, have I no rival to fear? Has this cursed delay allowed another to supplant me in your affections?"

Miss Reckert seemed alarmed at the suggestion, and as if without thinking, she replied "Indeed, Sir, you have no rival–."

As soon as she had uttered the words, she realized her mistake, but Mr. Harland was all too willing to interpret her words as favourably as he could.

"Sweetest Miss Reckert!" cried he, "Can it be possible you can retain even the smallest amount of affection for one who is hardly worthy of it?"

"Indeed," said she, "you have understood more than I have said, or indeed, more than I have meant to say."

This disclaimer only seemed to make the situation worse, and Mr. Harland said "Have you any objection but what you have told me?" to which she hesitantly indicated she had not. "Then if as you have said it is the strength of my devotion alone you doubt, I can hardly refrain from rejoicing to find the only obstacle which exists is that which exists least of all. Truth must be self-evident, and I shall spend however many months or years necessary to convince you of what can hardly be denied. But yet, dearest Miss Reckert, I cannot help but hope to prevail somewhat earlier, for the sake of your father, if you are indifferent to my own sufferings–."

Miss Reckert seemed somewhat overwhelmed by the progression of ideas, but as she was going to reply, Miss Lawrence came through the entry way at the opposite side of the garden from where I was.

At the sight of her, Miss Reckert retrieved her hand, which Mr. Harland had held till that point, and Miss Lawrence looked at them both in astonishment. Miss Lawrence began to apologize for the interruption and turned to leave, but Miss Reckert was too quick and saying something I did not catch, she disappeared in a moment.

When Miss Reckert had departed, there was a short awkward exchange between Mr. Harland and Miss Lawrence before he took leave with a bow. Miss Lawrence stood in amazement for a moment or two, before following him into the house.

Though I have much more to tell, I fear I must leave it for another letter. I am weary and rushed at present. I shall write as soon as I have leisure.

Your faithful friend.
M.C.

Marcel de la Croix to Henri Renault

March 17th, 1793

Dear Friend,

I believe I last left off after the conversation between Mr. Harland and Miss Reckert.

By the time I returned to the house myself to retrieve my hat and gloves, Mr. Harland had already departed, and I caught up with him a short way from Stearn. I exclaimed my surprise to find him visiting before he had even been home, and he declared that Stearn was on his way and there was no reason not to do so. He thanked me for what he called my 'unnecessary concerns,' though was evidently preoccupied. All the same he made a greater effort to be civil than I had ever known him to before.

He asked whether I had found the man who had killed Lafont, and I explained how I had discovered M. Tolouse. He was extremely delighted to hear it, and desired me to thank M. Tolouse on his behalf till be might do so himself, and reassure him that he would intercede to attempt to prevent the matter from going to trial.

"No doubt M. Tolouse is pleased to have been able to do so," added he, "if I may judge from what I know of him."

We spoke somewhat more, but gradually it seemed to become too great an effort for him to do so, and as we approached Courtney Lodge, he said, "I fear you were not entirely wrong, Sir, for I feel suddenly more tired than I expected. It is still three more miles to Kettich and perhaps I would be wiser to go by carriage."

I immediately proposed we stop at Courtney Lodge from where one might be ordered after a short while. He seemed quite unsteady as he dismounted, but declined my help. When we entered the house, he sat at once on a bench by the door, seemingly unable to do more.

At the sound of the bell, Mlle de Courteline came out into the hall, looking at us with surprise. Mr. Harland attempted to rise but I prevented him, telling Mlle de Courteline to inform Mme. Gaspar that Mr. Harland was in need of some rest, whereafter he meant to order a carriage and return to his house.

Mlle de Courteline curtsied graciously and said, "I am certain Mme. Gaspar shall be most honoured to be of service."

A moment of two later she returned with two servants, and informed the gentleman that a room had been made ready for him to rest. This announcement was made with as much firmness as courtesy, so that it seemed hardly possible to refuse.

By the time Mme. Gaspar and Mlle Vallon also appeared, Mlle de Courteline had sent a servant to find a doctor, and then asked me to join them in the parlour.

Once we sat down she said, "How came this to be, M. Gramont? Do you know what ails Mr. Harland?"

In quiet tones and in French I described what had passed the previous night, and that about an hour before I had been surprised to discover Mr. Harland in conversation with Miss Reckert rather than partaking in much needed rest.

Hearing this, Mlle de Courteline appeared largely to acquit me of carelessness in relation to Mr. Harland, and I was somewhat amused to find she regarded me almost as his guardian. She declared that while I could not be blamed for not interrupting any conference between he and Miss Reckert, for obvious reasons, when I first discovered he had been hurt, I ought to have pressed more firmly to take his place.

"No matter, at least he is here now, and my cousin and I, along with Mme. Gaspar, will ensure he is properly attended. There can be no impropriety to his remaining here now that Mme. Gaspar has come, and if possible, we shall not suffer him to leave till he is truly recovered."

I pitied Mr. Harland somewhat, for I knew Mlle de Courteline had a will of iron. In this matter, however, I was inclined to agree with her, for considering that only an hour or so ago Miss Reckert had seemed on the very point of capitulation, I doubted he would permit himself proper time for rest and recovery before attempting to speak to her again.

Being quite tired myself, I prepared to take leave, but Mlle de Courteline pressed me to send another doctor to Mr. Harland as soon as may be. I pledged to do so and when returned to the Hogshead, requested the innkeeper send a physician to Courtney Lodge as soon as may be, before throwing myself on a pillow.

* * *

Many many hours later I awoke to find Philip himself watching over me, having arranged and tidied my belongings as he waited.

"What time is it?" inquired I, presently. "And how do you come here?"

"It is three o'clock. You have two letters, one from Mrs. Lawrence, which she sent last night, and another from Courtney Lodge, which arrived only a short while ago. I have been here about an hour or so, as Mrs. Lawrence sent me herself when she did not hear from you this morning."

I opened her letter as we spoke, and found that already last night she had begun to hear reports of what had occurred, most particularly from her neighbour Mr. Green, and hoped I would come as soon as I might, at any hour at all, and explain all which appeared inexplicable to them at present.

Mlle de Courteline's letter merely informed me that Mr. Harland had developed a high fever overnight, and that two doctors jointly attended him. They disagreed how to treat him so at present nothing at all was being done, and the presence of a third doctor was requested.

As I was not yet in the position to go out, Philip offered to find one for us, and in a very short time he returned to report that it was done. In his absence, I had ordered a meal and only begun to dress myself, and when he arrived I proposed he stay to eat with me that I might tell him the events of the night before.

He listened with great attention to everything I told him, though not everything seemed to be new to him, and he afterwards informed me he made a point of making one or two inquiries the night before. He expressed his joy to find everything had been resolved with seemingly little ill-consequences, apart from the men who had been injured.

After saying so, he grew thoughtful for a long moment, and when I asked what preoccupied him, he said, "As you know, Dear Marquis, I am no longer a single man, and having been away from my home for a short time, I feel somewhat inclined to return home, now that all fear for the family at Stearn Manor appears to be at an end. All the same, you need only say so and I will do what you please."

"Of course your wife shall want to see you after so many days away. I shall inform Mrs. Lawrence as soon as I see her. But dear

Philip, will you not now consent to take the money which is your due? I am sure your wife will be able to make use of it if you will not."

"Do you still intend to divest yourself of all but a small part of your fortune?" inquired he, with a slight smile, not choosing to answer directly the question I had put to him.

"My resolution has not changed," replied I, with a sigh I could not repress.

"I am surprised to find you so steadfast," said he, "despite the multitude of eligible women you see almost every day. But all the same, if you are determined, and I find you are, I shall take what you have often desired to give me, for the sake of my wife and her children."

"Children?" cried I with amazement. "Why, if you have children, I am distressed indeed to have kept you from them for so long."

"No matter, no matter," cried he, with a smile, "they shall have reason enough to bless your name."

"It is a name more than usually in need of blessing," replied I more gravely. "But come, how is it you did not tell me this before?"

"I was afraid you would send me back to them immediately, and I meant to help while I could. One ought not to be surprised," continued he, "for I am an old man, and have no need of a maid for a wife. It is better to have a partner closer to own age. But if you would have me take the amount you generously intend me, do you wish to take the rest of your fortune into your possession now?"

"No indeed," replied I, "I am quite happy for you to keep possession of it. I shall leave here for a short while, but you may write to me at Peldon manor, where I shall send my direction to Mlle de Courteline, and the others. If you write your direction, I shall send to you when I have been able to find M. Rublé's sister."

He merely bowed low to hear it and took leave thereafter. I know not when I shall see him again.

It took me somewhat longer than usual to ready myself to visit Stearn, but at long last I mounted my horse. It was six o'clock when I finally arrived, though they did not customarily dine till seven or eight, and I was shown into the sitting parlour to await Mrs. Lawrence.

In a very short time all three of the ladies appeared at once, seating themselves expectantly.

"M. Gramont," cried Mrs. Lawrence, as she did so, "you cannot conceive how happy we are to see you! We have heard such strange things since yesterday and when we heard nothing from Mr. Harland or yourself, when both of you have been so accustomed to call so regularly, we became quite concerned indeed!"

"Forgive me, Madam, I am ashamed to confess I have been sleeping almost without stop today, having had very little rest the night before."

"So we have heard, Monsieur! How astonishing! But pray tell us, how is Mr. Harland? We have all been quite alarmed since Mr. Green swears he was shot in the arm while pursuing some unknown fellow. We know not how this can be, for my daughter and Miss Reckert saw him that very morning when nothing seemed to be amiss. Since then, we have heard nothing from him!"

"Mr. Green is right to assert that Mr. Harland was injured, for so he was, and I was surprised to encounter him here afterwards, when I thought he would be resting. I accompanied him on my return to the inn, but on the way we were forced to stop at Courtney Lodge as his heroics caught up with him there. Mme. Gaspar and the two young ladies are ensuring he gets every attention at present, and three doctors have been called to attend him, so I am optimistic he will recover presently."

"Three doctors!" exclaimed Miss Reckert.

"The number of physicians ought not to be thought an indication of the seriousness of his condition, but rather a sign of how well he is being cared for. At present, I believe he merely has a fever." I then further explained how so many had been called.

"I do not understand how this can be," declared Miss Reckert, "for I spoke to Mr. Harland for several minutes myself and saw no sign at all that he was ill, or even discomforted!"

"Yes, madam, he must have had a particular reason to wish to conceal any sign of it, and I hope he shall not suffer any grave consequence for doing so."

There was a profound silence thereafter.

"Let us all hope so!" said Mrs. Lawrence eventually

"I mean to call at Courtney Lodge next." said I. "Perhaps you would prefer that I do so directly and send you tidings of that gentleman?"

"You are very kind, Sir," said Mrs. Lawrence.

I was myself somewhat apprehensive when I approached Courtney Lodge. Judging by Miss Reckert's concern, and her behaviour the previous day, when she had seemed almost on the verge of giving way to Mr. Harland's argument, I felt it would be nothing short of a tragedy for him to fall ill at this juncture.

Inside Mlle de Courteline informed me that Mr. Harland continued to have a fever, but that the third doctor, Dr. Palmer, had recommended that nothing but rest be prescribed, and he would visit the gentleman the next morning.

He was resting at that moment, so I did not attempt to see him myself. I told Mlle de Courteline that I intended to return to the Hogshead to write to Stearn Manor, whereupon she told me that she was in the process of writing a letter herself.

My note was much shorter on this account, merely revealing that he had a fever, more would be known on the following day, adding that Mlle de Courteline intended to send her a more in-depth account of his condition

My visit to Courtney Lodge was short, as I did not want to prevent Mlle de Courteline from finishing her letter.

M. Tolouse was at the Hogshead and still in high spirits from his triumph the night before. When I told him how Mr. Harland had pledged to interfere on his behalf to prevent a trial, he was merrier still.

Despite how pleased I was that everything seemed on the verge of being resolved, I was not truly in a celebratory mood.

Lafont was dead. The condition of M. Hubert's mind was more broadly known. Barring any complication from illness, Miss Reckert and Mr. Harland seemed to be near some sort of understanding. Mlle de Courteline and Mlle Vallon were positioned to establish themselves more favourably than I had thought possible, and in truth, every possible reason for delaying my search for Mme. Dorrel no longer existed.

Without going into any detail, I hinted to M. Tolouse that it likely would not be long till I departed, and asked him if he had any plans of his own. He shrugged, but said that if I had no need for him, he would find his own way easily enough.

After this I retired to my room and left him to make merry with the other patrons of the inn, as the preponderance of my thoughts were of another character.

The next day I went directly to Courtney Lodge to inquire after Mr. Harland, only to discover from Mlle de Courteline that he had taken upon himself to return home that very morning before anyone else was awake and before even the doctor had called to see him.

Hearing this, I deliberated somewhat as to whether to ride in the direction of Kettich or go to Stearn Manor. When I considered the reception I would likely receive if I called upon Mr. Harland, I thought it would be better to go to Stearn and merely relay the sheer lack of information.

It was slightly earlier than ten o'clock when I arrived there, and I was seen into the sitting room where only Miss Reckert was present.

She informed me immediately that Mrs. Lawrence had not yet come down. She appeared pensive and expectant, and in but another moment, she said,

"May I ask whether you bring any further news of Mr. Harland, M. Gramont?"

"As I wrote in my letter to Mrs. Lawrence, when I arrived at Courtney last night, I learnt only that his fever continued. I called there this morning before coming here in the hope of bringing some better news, but Mlle de Courteline informed me that when she woke up this morning, Mr. Harland was no longer there. It is understood he has gone home, but beyond that I know nothing at all, I am sorry to say."

"Gone home, Sir?" cried she, "I do not understand how that can be?"

"I wish I could bring you better tidings, Madam."

Miss Reckert attempted to appear unconcerned and we sat down together. I waited to find if she would begin any subject and though she attempted to do so once or twice, her mind was evidently distracted.

In time the bell sounded again, and to our mutual surprise, Mr. Harland himself was announced shortly afterwards.

Miss Reckert had risen in expectation and seemed almost dumbfounded at his entrance. He seemed far from delighted to find us together, and as he paused to determine how to begin, I bowed and congratulated him on his apparent recovery.

He returned my greeting then bowed to Miss Reckert, who merely stared at him in wonder.

Eventually she said, "Indeed, Mr. Harland, I am very surprised to see you, for we understood just yesterday that you were gravely ill?"

"Slightly ill, perhaps, Miss Reckert," replied he. "I hope you are not disappointed to find otherwise?"

"Nay," said she, "yet I certainly did not expect to see you so soon. No doubt you must wish to speak to Mrs. Lawrence and I will attempt to fetch her," moving to the door as she said so.

"There is no need, Madam, for her servant went to inform her I am here. Forgive me for saying what I hope is obvious, but as much as I respect Mrs. Lawrence, my visits here have always been predominantly to you."

Miss Reckert had paused midway, but in light of this simple avowal, she had little choice but to stay. With unavoidable uncertainty, she seated herself on the sofa.

Rather than interrupt, I had slowly begun to move to a table where several books had been arranged and pretended to take little notice of what passed.

Mr. Harland remained standing at first, but after a minute or so,

Miss Reckert asked him rather incredulously if he meant to stand. I suspect she intended for him to take the chair nearest the fire, having positioned herself so that it was the most likely place, but he chose instead to sit on the same sofa as herself, which I could not help but smile to see from the corner of my eye.

"Again, Sir," began she, attempting to take no notice of this. "Since we understood that only yesterday you had an alarming fever, I hardly know what to make of seeing you now."

At this moment, Mrs. Lawrence and her daughter entered, and Miss Reckert and Mr. Harland rose to greet them.

Both women were evidently surprised at the uncommon sight of the two together, and Mrs. Lawrence said, "Pray do not disturb yourselves on our account, Mr. Harland least of all. Dear Sir," continued she, after they reseated themselves, "I must confess I am surprised to find you here, in light of what we have heard the last two days!"

"I was on the verge of telling Miss Reckert there was no cause at all for concern, as circumstances often seem worse in the re-telling."

"I would happily believe it, Sir," answered Mrs. Lawrence, "yet I fear Miss Reckert has great reason to doubt such assurances, for no one was more shocked to hear you had been injured. It seems you spoke to her that very day, without even dropping a hint of it. It is a wonder to see you up and about already, when you were said to have a high fever just last night!"

"How could I be expected to heed such trivial considerations in the company of Miss Reckert?" answered he. "I feel perfectly cool, but if my credit is so low, perhaps it would be advisable for Miss Reckert to verify my claim," and with this he held out his hand for her to take.

More than one laugh was raised at this suggestion, and after an embarrassed hesitation, Miss Reckert took his hand in hers, releasing it a moment or two later without a word.

Mr. Harland smiled, but then without taking his eyes from her, he said, "You may all be called to witness that Miss Reckert has accepted my hand."

There was a general laugh at this contrivance, and Miss Reckert herself could not withhold a smile.

"Well, at least it must be said that your wit is not affected," declared Mrs. Lawrence.

"But will you not attest to my health, Miss Reckert?" persisted he. "I dare not offer my pulse."

Miss Reckert blushed and after a moment or two she said, "I assure you I do not mean to take it, Sir. I fear you intend me for your physician."

"No, truly," replied he quickly, "I have a far different title in mind."

"Good gracious!" cried Mrs. Lawrence. "Why, to be sure you must have some kind of distemper, to tease Miss Reckert this way. It is fortunate for you we have all been so concerned on your behalf, or no doubt she would have run away by now."

"Indeed," declared Miss Reckert, seizing the opportunity to extricate herself, "as Mr. Harland would make us believe our company inspires him to be reckless with his health, I would not wish to be complicit in remaining. I have not called upon my father in several days, and no doubt he would be happy to hear encouraging news."

Saying so she arose to depart. Mr. Harland began to offer to see her home, but before she had replied, the bell was sounded and Mr. Reckert himself was announced.

"Ah, Mr. Reckert," declared Mrs. Lawrence at his entrance, "you have saved your daughter the trouble of coming to find you!"

"I am glad I have not been completely forgotten," replied he, "and yet I cannot but confess my amazement to finding Mr. Harland here. But for your note last night, Sir, I would have been fearful for you indeed."

Mr. Harland merely bowed and Mrs. Lawrence said, 'We have all said so, Sir, to little purpose.'

We all sat down together. Miss Reckert seemed anxious for her father to sit near Mr. Harland, but when he learnt with surprise that it was her own seat, he would not hear of it, and sat on the other side of her.

"Well, a good deal of strange reports have been circulating about," declared he, immediately. "I have made a little tour of my closest neighbours, and everywhere I hear a new version of what has happened. I meant to have the actual version from my friend here this morning, but it seems he felt it was vital to call at Stearn beforehand, and so I was left to guess whether he lived or died."

"Pure hyperbole, my dear Sir," replied Mr. Harland.

"Not entirely," declared the other, "for I had heard some accounts of you dying of fever at Courtney Lodge, and another bleeding for hours in a field. But perhaps such things ought not to be discussed now."

"Nor ever," declared the gentleman, "lest they begin to bear greater resemblance to truth!"

"Indeed," ventured Mrs. Lawrence, "although some things are better left unsaid at present, I have a strong curiosity to know how all this came about, most particularly the reason you Mr. Green, M. Gramont, and whoever else, were racing around in search of an emigre no one had ever heard of before?"

"Nor am I the best person to satisfy you on that point," declared Mr. Harland, looking momentarily in my direction.

I began to dread some explanation would be required of me, having lately determined to avoid any species of dishonesty now that it was no longer necessary.

In the interval caused by my hesitation, Miss Reckert addressed her father to say, "M. Gramont has been so kind as to bring us news these last two days, but from what we have already heard, one cannot but be concerned that Mr. Harland risks his health merely to assure us of it."

"No doubt you are right, my dear," replied he, raising his eyebrows somewhat to understand her intent. Addressing Mr. Harland, he said "I am sure you cannot be unmoved by the universal concern for your well-being, Sir, therefore I beg you will consent to join me in my carriage, and that way we shall be able to visit upon our return to Kettich. As my daughter has suggested it, I feel certain she will consent to accompany us and so make the offer seem more appealing. Mrs. Lawrence must forgive me for trying to lure away her company!"

"You are right to attempt to do so," replied she, "for as much as we enjoy that gentleman's company, we shall enjoy it all that much more in perpetuity."

Mr. Harland seemed very far from making any objection at all, and seeing it was a good opportunity to do so, I likewise rose and took leave.

* * *

March 19th, 1793

Having witnessed the scene between Miss Reckert and Mr. Harland, I felt increasingly confident that all would be well between them, and returned to the Hogshead in good spirits. I found there a note from Mme. Gaspar informing me that they were now removed to Peldon, and whenever M. Tolouse and I should wish, we could return to Courtney Lodge.

I prepared at once to do so, having determined to keep the place for several more months at least, whether I lived there or not, and so communicated as much to M. Tolouse.

That day was almost entirely engrossed with preparations for the move and then my eventual departure. I did not see too much of M. Tolouse, who pursued his own way as he often does.

The next morning I resolved to call at Peldon, a fair ways away from Courtney Lodge. It is quite a handsome house, much as Mrs. Lawrence described, and I was happy to find its new inhabitants were quite delighted with it. I mentioned in passing the possibility that I would leave the area for several weeks at least. It was impossible not to perceive the general alarm to hear it, but I tried to assure them I did not mean to be gone forever, however uncertain I felt on the subject myself.

I took leave shortly thereafter to avoid the necessity of deferring any inquiries I could not satisfy. Upon my return I rode through Gibbons, descrying Miss Lawrence ahead of me as I did so. As it seemed likely to be one of my last opportunities to speak to her alone, I hailed her and offered to accompany her a short way.

She did not object, and soon enough the subject of Miss Reckert and Mr. Harland was raised.

"I do not know how, M. Gramont, but it seems you were quite justified in your opinion of Miss Reckert and Mr. Harland, and considering how well you bear your disappointment, you may possibly be acquitted of excessive partiality towards my dear friend."

"Indeed!" cried I with delight, upon which she regarded me with amusement, and I said, "But is my disappointment so very certain, Miss Lawrence, for I have heard no announcement?"

"Your disappointment, M. Gramont, has never been less certain, but as to an announcement, I have heard none myself, yet I know enough of Miss Reckert to guess that the mere act of allowing that gentleman in her presence speaks favourably enough for his suit, since no one need doubt her ability to avoid him if she should wish it."

"Indeed, Madam, no doubt you are envious of this skill, seeing as you are forced to bear my company so frequently."

"The analogy may not be permitted to stand, M. Gramont, for you are hardly an admirer of mine, and so I need take no trouble on your account at all."

"Though I can easily believe you take no trouble about me, yet I hardly know how one may know Miss Lawrence without being her admirer."

"Very well," replied she with unconcern, "but a woman has little cause for vanity on account of a suitor who provides his own excuses."

"I suppose I ought not to expect compassion, for compassion often necessitates a sympathy of feeling."

At this she laughed again, "Such a thing cannot be looked for, when one considers the very number of apparent ineligibilities of the would-be suitor, but now that we are on the subject of your various inadequacies, after our conversation the other day, I could not help wonder why you have abandoned the idea of marriage entirely, in light of how much you claim to regret it? Ought you not to go in search of a partner in life whose moderate aspirations resemble your own?"

"And would Miss Lawrence persuade me that such women exist?" replied I, incredulously.

"All kinds of people exist, M. Gramont, and since there are specimens of your own kind, I see no reason to believe your counterpart does not exist, if you would but take the time to look."

"And what are your own feelings on the subject?"

"I have just expressed them, surely."

"I am sure you have not misunderstood me, Madam, therefore I must believe you will not understand me."

"As to that, if you are attempting to discover which women should find you acceptable were you to deign to offer, you may certainly strike me from the list," said she laughingly. "From the beginning, I was struck by the very number of inadequacies, ineligibilities, and various other shortcomings, which are apparent at first glance. Moreover, since my mother brought my father five-thousand pounds, which I am destined to bring my husband, I have determined that there is hardly a man alive who would meet my requirements."

Finding I could not compel her to be serious on the subject I pressed her to tell me more of these requirements.

"As to that," said she with mock gravity. "My christian name is Eleanor, and with so fine a name, I should like something to adorn the front of it, as well as the back."

I could not help but laugh myself at her comical mode of expressing herself, but she stared me into better form, so I said "Such a sad subject for me, but with such a beautiful name, I fancy you would like to hear it more. Have you any other personal requirements for a spouse, other than the ability to transform you into 'Lady Eleanor?'"

"None so far as character, personal accomplishments or appearance are concerned, but it goes without saying that I should like to own a vast stretch of land and have money enough to buy whatever my fancy dictates."

"Such as?"

She hesitated somewhat, then said, "I confess I am not yet aware of what objects shall be required to complete my happiness, but I am convinced that a certain amount of time and study shall inform me. No doubt my husband will take me to London, where my new fashionable friends may school me."

"Heaven forbid!" cried I. "But as you are presently in ignorance of the happiness provided by such trinkets, is there not hope you may be happy without them?"

"Happiness itself is quite out of fashion," replied she, "and I believe there is a consistency there not often found in hats and gowns. Let us leave this subject, however, M. Gramont, for I am persuaded there is nothing further to say."

I did not dare oppose her, for she seemed more earnest than was her custom.

"We saw M. Tolouse, yesterday," said she, presently.

"Did you?" replied I with surprise.

"He gives a strange character of you which is not entirely in keeping with what I have seen."

'How is that?'

"I know not how to express it exactly," and for the first time I believe she almost appeared awkward, "but to me you seem to have a truly feeling disposition–."

She paused, but though I waited for her to go on she did not. Eventually I said, "But M. Tolouse has described me as an unfeeling sort of person?"

"Not exactly. My mother, however, was telling M. Tolouse how happy she was it was him who had met M. Lafont, for she would fear for any other. M. Tolouse declared that you would have had as fair a chance of prevailing with Lafont as he. You may imagine how strange a debate took place between them; my mother protested your gentle character, but M. Tolouse swears otherwise, each of them meaning to defend your reputation, though in different respects."

I was completely at a loss as to what reply to make, and as Miss

Lawrence had asked me no particular question, we walked on a short ways in silence.

"No doubt I have made you uncomfortable, M. Gramont," said she, "and indeed, I blame myself for raising the subject. I hardly know why I felt compelled to do so!"

"I do not fault you for doing so," replied I, "but I confess I know not what to say at all. I should be distressed to erode my character in your estimation."

"Do you mean to say M. Tolouse is correct? Can a man whose outward appearance is all gentleness and consideration truly be practised in shedding the blood of others?"

I shuddered at this description. "I hope not, Miss Lawrence, but perhaps you will better credit my words when I tell you of my inadequacies. But for the revolution, I would be exactly the man you described, with a clear conscience and good prospects. My initiation into the monumental conflict was not gentle, nor was it according to my will. I know not what more I can say."

"I thank you, M. Gramont. I am grateful to have this incongruence at least partially explained." She was thoughtful for a moment, before saying, "M. Tolouse also mentioned that he believes you mean to leave the area in the next few days."

I could not help but be annoyed at not being permitted to reveal this news myself, and said with a sigh, "I suppose I should be grateful he goes into company infrequently."

"My mother, of course, shall be sorry to lose you."

"I am most obliged to her. I am sorry to go, but I fear the longer I stay, the less able I shall be to go at last."

Miss Lawrence took no notice at all of my musings, and when we neared Stearn manor, she said, "I have at last selected a book to recommend to you, and though my mother is not at home, I hope I may persuade you to step in for a moment that I may fetch it for you. You need not think of returning it."

In a few moments she returned with a small book.

"I am relieved at least to see it is not as onerous as once threatened."

"Nor does it treat of love," added she, and with that she gave me Rasselas, Prince of Absynnia. "Have you read it in French, Sir?"

"No, madam, I confess I have not."

"Then I hope your opinion of it conforms to mine."

With this we parted. I was far from happy with the outcome of this conversation, though I have thought of little else. I have found fault with M. Tolouse for talking too much, and he has taken to sulking.

Mlle de Courteline, Mlle Vallon, and Mme. Gaspar have moved to Peldon manor, and they seem quite happy and comfortable there. I have not yet spoken to Mlle Vallon of Mr. Etheredge, but it does not seem entirely pressing at the moment.

I feel the longer I stay here the more miserable I will become. I mean to leave in a day or two, and tomorrow I shall call at Stearn again.

Dear Sir, I shall end here, noting only that I am,

Your Faithful friend,
M.C.

Marcel de la Croix to Henri Renault

March 21st, 1793

Dear Friend,

My last visit to Stearn Manor did not go as I hoped. I was hesitant to call, lest I be requested to describe what I knew of M. Lafont's connection to M. Hubert, yet I could not resist the temptation to see Miss Lawrence once more before I departed.

Oh, misleading impulse!

Mr. Harland was also present, evidently calling upon Miss Reckert, and I observed with some relief that Mrs. Lawrence was preoccupied *appearing not to observe them*, and had little attention to spare me. I was quite happy to see it, and so approached Miss Lawrence.

"So I find you are not yet gone, M. Gramont?"

"To my folly, I fear."

"Why so?"

"Why because every moment increases my reluctance to go, Miss Lawrence."

She merely laughed at this, but shortly afterwards, adopting a look of mock seriousness, she said, 'Indeed, I had forgotten your sufferings.'

"'Twould be a happy day for me could I persuade you to take me in earnest!"

"And unhappy one for me, Monsieur Gramont!"

"Why so, Madam? Do I dare to hope I could arouse your pity?"

"I hope not!" declared she. "It has ever been my experience that there is a certain species of gentleman who travels around attempting to inspire soft sighs and regrets wherever he wanders. It is shameful behaviour, do you not agree?"

"Most heartily, with which I fear you would confute me!"

Our conversation continued much in this way for a few more minutes, till suddenly the general mood of the room was altered by the unexpected entrance of M. Hubert. He did not seem as distant or distracted as usual, though evidenced none of the intensity which seemed to mark his more lucid moments.

Mrs. Lawrence called out to him with less timidity than usual, naming Mr. Harland to him, and making special mention of "his friend, M. Gramont."

"I know no M. Gramont," replied he, cooly, looking in my direction, "yet I am always happy to see Marcel de la Croix."

"Indeed," replied his sister, with some surprise, "I fear I do not understand you, brother?"

M. Hubert ignored her and wandered over to the card table where Miss Lawrence and I were sitting in conversation, "I am more hesitant than my sister to describe us as friends, Monsieur le Marquis, but as you are the only one who knows my history, I am almost tempted to think so. It is ironic, is it not, for such a connection to exist? I am half-tempted to like you myself, for your very decency seems to prove the brilliance of my original design, does it not?"

He smiled mirthlessly, then began to laugh, "Do you disagree, Monsieur? Perhaps you are unwilling to commend a plan which led to the deaths of your family?"

I said nothing, at a loss for how to conduct myself, but my blood boiled within me at the sound of his words.

"Good God, brother!" cried Mrs. Lawrence, "What is it that you say? I fear you must be unwell to talk so unaccountably!"

M. Hubert took no notice of her at all, but continued his address to me as if we were the only people in the room. "In some respects I suppose I may take as much credit for making you a Marquis as an orphan, and am almost deserving of your gratitude. But yet I fear it is not so, as you seem to take little joy in the title and instead have begun to style yourself Gramont. Perhaps you loathe your name as much as others?"

"Dear brother, you cannot know what you say, and I must beg you to take some rest. You are not yourself, I am sure!"

"Monsieur La Croix is of your opinion, sister, and scorns to revenge himself upon a madman. It is more pleasant to sit by the window and take tea with my charming niece, and so I would hardly blame him. But yet, Sir," added he, his voice changing so that he addressed me in the most clear, cutting tones, "perhaps you would be interested to know that for the last two days, I have been perfectly cognizant, and were you to desire satisfaction for the loss you have sustained, I am prepared to accompany you at once."

This announcement struck me like a thunderbolt. I had so long become accustomed to thinking of M. Hubert as beyond any honourable revenge, that to hear him speak as if he were completely possessed of his senses was more than I could bear.

Everything else seemed to fade away in the face of this revelation, and I neither thought nor cared for any other consideration. It seemed in that moment that I had mistakenly allowed him to live, and that ambivalence, or an improper sense of honour had led me astray.

I stood up with the intention of accompanying him immediately, but before I could speak, Mr. Harland intervened to say, "M.

Gramont, do not refuse me a word or two outside," hardly giving me a moment to consider before leaving the room.

I followed him to the foyer, not looking at anyone else as I left the room.

"I understand your intent, M. Gramont," said he, "but if M. Hubert is indeed sane, he shall be so in a moment. Have patience and I will join you outside in a moment or two."

What a miserable being was I in that interval! I walked up and down in front of the house, feeling I was culpable for the delay seeking justice and preparing to face M. Hubert.

It seemed the length of an eternity before Mr. Harland returned, but it was likely no more than ten minutes.

"The family is in great disarray, as you may imagine," said he. "I requested that Mrs. Lawrence allow me to speak to M. Hubert alone, but she insisted on remaining. I asked him a series of questions regarding yourself, M. Lafont, and even the revolution, or anything else I thought might test him. At first he would say nothing at all, but then he began to hum to himself and repeat a french couplet of some kind in which I heard your name, and something about a rose. Mrs. Lawrence attempted to reach him, and asked him to explain what he was speaking of, but she was near frantic herself, and he looked as if he did not know her. I believe it was a great exertion of will for him to speak to you as he did, for while we were interrogating him he broke out into a cold sweat of sorts, and Mrs. Lawrence called the servants to take him to bed. Before coming to you, I attempted to determine how he has seemed these last days, and have gathered enough anecdotal information in these short minutes to assure you that his claim of cognizance is not to be relied upon. Two of the servants and Miss Lawrence have related observations from that time period which accord with the disorder of his senses both you and I have observed. He desires death, M. Gramont, and for a short time was lucid enough to seek it."

I listened with attention, alternating between anger and relief. I thanked Mr. Harland rather incoherently for his help, then merely bowed and readied to leave, hardly knowing what to do with myself.

"M. Gramont," cried he, as I prepared to mount my horse. "It seems your affairs are far more complicated than one might guess. You once expressed your willingness to relate the particulars of your life, and now more than ever, I would be most grateful to know them. I understand you do not mean to stay much longer in the area, but I hope you will not fail to call upon me at home before you depart. It may perhaps fall to me to explain what part of your conduct must seem mysterious, and I should hope thereby to be enabled to do the greatest justice to your character, in which I have great faith."

I thanked him again and pledged to do so before I left, but did not hazard any more than was necessary, before riding away as one pursued.

* * *

March 26th, 1793

The very next day I proposed to leave the neighbourhood as soon as may be, and attempted to regard the revelations which must stem from M. Hubert's actions as a blessing of sorts, in that no other course seemed so advisable at present.

I decided I would call and take leave of Mr. Reckert, Mr. Harland, and the ladies at Peldon that day, and depart on the one following.

I travelled to Kettich first to call upon Mr. Reckert, yet I could not help but be somewhat apprehensive in doing so, for I knew not whether he had heard of what had transpired, and might possibly decline to see me. I waited a good many minutes and just when I began to be certain that Mr. Reckert did not intend to see me, I was instructed to go to the breakfast parlour.

To my surprise, Mr. Seymour was also there, and it was clear from his expression that he remembered me.

"Forgive the wait, M. Gramont," said Mr. Reckert, "if it is any consolation, I treat old and new friends alike, for here is my dear friend Mr. Seymour, left to wonder if I meant to come down today or tomorrow. Pray, join us for breakfast, I beg you."

I did not refuse and Mr. Seymour said, "Having come unannounced, I am more than happy to be fed. Your servant, M. Gramont, I believe we met at Sorsten Manor, did we not?"

I returned his greeting and Mr. Reckert exclaimed, "Truly, I had forgotten that circumstance, but I believe you told me, M. Gramont, when we first met. Come, let us eat, before the meal gets too cold."

After a few general remarks, Mr. Reckert asked Mr. Seymour if he had seen Mr. Harland yet.

"I thought I had better call upon you first," replied he, "seeing how he and I were somewhat at odds when I left. When I received your letter the other day, I thought it might be a favourable time to return. Pray tell me, Sir, what news is there?"

Mr. Reckert smiled, "As to my letter, Sir, you must forget every word of it, save the signature. I fear there is no hope of reviving the match you have invested so much time in."

Mr. Seymour was evidently much distressed to hear it, which he acknowledged openly. "But pray, Sir, may I ask if it is certain indeed? What prevents it?"

"The strangest thing in the world, in all truth," answered the other. "Mr. Harland is engaged to be married."

"Engaged?!" repeated he, with astonishment, "It cannot be! Surely you are mistaken. He had, as far as I am aware, no decent prospect of his own. I have often wished he would take the trouble of speaking to a woman now and then, but to no avail."

"It would seem he has done so, Sir, and to good effect."

"I can scarcely believe it! But who is she, and if I can be pardoned for inquiring, how shall this effect the abeyance? Is his future wife titled, wealthy? I dare not hope her family has some connection to the King?"

Mr. Reckert smiled at this question, then turned to me and apologized for talking of things I could have no idea of, whereupon I assured him I was completely happy for him to do so.

"As to such matters," said Mr. Reckert, again to Mr. Seymour, "I am by no means certain the match helps at all. There is no title, and no additional influence at court may be expected. Wealth at least may be thought adequate, for you know Miss Reckert is my only heir."

"Forgive me, Sir," replied Mr. Seymour, "but that seems neither here nor there–." He paused once he had said it, and after a moment or two, his expression changed to one of astonishment and disbelief.

"You do not mean to say–." began he. "No, it is impossible!"

"I am of your opinion, Sir, or at least I was."

"Mr. Harland is to marry your daughter?"

"No other," replied he, he eyes sparkling with delight.

Mr. Seymour sat completely still, and I took the opportunity of giving Mr. Reckert joy on that account, being nothing less than a sincere expression of the true joy I felt to hear it.

"Forgive me, dear Sir," said Mr. Seymour. "I ought to have said so at once, but my senses have all but left me. No one could be happier than myself to know it, but I scarce know how to believe it. Pardon me for saying, but if there was any person I thought less likely to enter the married state than Mr. Harland, it was Miss Reckert, and now to think they are to be married to each other! I should have no more expected lightning to strike a man on his way to town, and then again on the way back."

"I could not agree more, Sir, but it seems that those who are difficult in marital matters ought to be paired with each other, and so I shall ever recommend if I hear of another case."

"But yet, Sir, I fear if I am to truly believe it, I must certainly hear how it all came about?"

"I should be more than happy to gratify your request," replied he, "if M. Gramont can pardon a fond foolish father for wanting to dwell on the subject?"

I assured him I would be equally pleased if he would do so, and he said, "A few days ago there was another unfortunate disturbance in the neighbourhood, which I shall not go into now, but it had the unfortunate consequence of injuring our dear friend, Mr. Harland. I say 'unfortunate,' but I have reason to think he would not characterize it as such himself. As I have mentioned to you in my letters, my daughter has made a point of avoiding that gentleman since ever she knew of his admiration. I could not even prevail upon her to speak to him, even to officially refuse his offer; she would hear of nothing like it! On his part, he insisted he would listen to no refusal which she did not give him herself. I thought several times that I ought to compel her to grant him an interview, but I am reluctant to compel her to do anything, and Mr. Harland was likewise opposed to such a measure. Time passed on without resolution, till the incident I mentioned, as a consequence of which he became slightly ill. From that time I noticed that she had softened somewhat in that regard, at least so far as to allow herself in the same place with him, which I had never known her to do before. I took this favourable opportunity to exert my parental authority, to tell her that however she felt, decency demanded the gentleman be permitted to speak with her and state his case, whereupon she would be free to decide as she wished, as always. To my surprise she assented readily. I rejoiced at having so successful gained my point, and commended myself for having finally mastered the exact balance of reasoning and authority to move her. Naturally, I had no doubt that she would refuse him and began to muse upon the possibility that we might begin to recommence our communal efforts (pardon me, M. Gramont, if this is not entirely understandable to you) considering that the abiding circumstance in this area seems more and more to necessitate some change. It was for this reason I wrote to you as I did, making such hints as I thought might make you consider returning in the next little while. I then wrote to the gentleman himself and told him that Miss Reckert had agreed to an interview, and if he still desired such, she would travel here from Stearn Manor the following day. He replied instantly that he meant to come at ten o'clock in the morning and intended to wait her arrival. Truth be told I was somewhat uneasy on his account when considering the disappointment he was to suffer, but I reasoned that he knew as well as I what could be expected, and it was better for the matter to be concluded immediately, rather than drawn on indefinitely. My daughter arrived before ten, and the gentleman only a few moments later. After what seemed like a very short period of time, my daughter emerged and excused herself. Anticipating Mr. Harland would be rather subdued, I was surprised to see that his face wore every sign of euphoria. My surprise only increased when he told me my daughter had accepted his offer. I was so far from believing it possible, I first doubted my hearing, then his understanding. 'I little thought that would be the case, Sir,' replied I gravely, attempting to cause him to reflect on how unlikely it was, 'when I saw my daughter emerge so soon.' He merely bowed and confessed that she objected to the enthusiasm of his acknowledgments, and had requested he speak to me immediately. I merely blinked at his reply, unable to make heads or tails of what he said. I believe he pitied my predicament, as he declared he was certain I wished to speak to my daughter immediately, and so would call upon me again in a few hours. At first I was too stunned to do anything, but presently went in search of her. To my utter astonishment, she merely affirmed what he had said, and hoped I was not distressed for any other reason. Oh, you may imagine my sensations were far otherwise at that moment! My daughter had the kindness to allow me to think that her decision was in part in deference to my wishes, but since then I have thought better of it. Though I do not truly understand how all this has come about, I have been able to confirm that the regard between them is mutual."

"Most astonishing, Sir!" declared Mr. Seymour, "Most astonishing. I would dearly like to confirm it with my own eyes. Does Miss Reckert remain at Stearn?"

"She is expected to return home tomorrow, and the marriage is to take place just under a month from now."

"'Tis nearly inconceivable! But pray tell me, what sort of admirer does your future son-in-law make?"

"A most impatient one, Sir. Only two days ago, I happened to see them from my window, and was surprised to find he kissed her as if they were already married! My daughter objected to this freedom, and he attempted to make amends, but from what I can tell, there is little to stop such things from occurring ten times a day. I hardly know how I will manage matters when she is living here again, but

Mr. Harland seems ill at ease while she remains under the same roof as M. Hubert, and I am certainly unwilling to place her at any risk."

We had a good deal more conversation, but I have transcribed all which I thought would interest you the most. At length I took leave of them both to call upon Mr. Harland across the park, and Mr. Reckert most cordially wished me well in my travels, assuring me of a welcome reception whenever I should return.

Mr. Harland was at home, and welcomed me most sincerely. I wished him joy at his betrothal, and he thanked me with such complaisance that I was convinced his happiness was in need of no augmentation.

I told him that I meant to leave the area on the following day, and so called upon him to take my leave and to satisfy the request he had made. I could not help but inquire after the inhabitants of Stearn manor, and he told me that they were all in good health, but great confusion reigned still from the events of the day before.

"Mrs. Lawrence especially is beset by confusion and anxiety. She asked me today to tell her what I knew of the matter and I begged leave to delay any discussion till I had spoken with you."

"I thank you, Sir. I am prepared to tell you all you wish, but I feel I should warn you that a full account of my history, which is what I feel to be necessary, shall take several hours at least."

He made no objection at all, and so I began to recount my life in much the same terms as I have done to you, though generally omitting the many details regarding my internal struggles which you have been kind enough to tolerate.

Mr. Harland listened with polite interest, gradually becoming amazement, offering hardly any interruption at all in the space of two hours. When at last I had finished, he said,

"Indeed, M. Gramont, I was prepared to hear an unusual tale, but you have far exceeded my expectations!"

"By which perhaps you mean I have exceeded the limits of credulity, Sir?"

"One might say so, but yet I fear that in doing so I would be paying a compliment to your powers of invention which is in itself unlikely. Nor has anything you have said conflicted with events as they have unfolded. Should you take offence were I to ask to see the mark you say M. Hubert gave you?"

I showed him at once, and when he examined it briefly, he said, "I thank you, M. Gramont. I fear it would be foolish for me to doubt a story which every circumstance affirms."

"I dare not hope to be pardoned for seeking admittance into the home of the Lawrences under false premises, but I hope that my reasons for doing so shall at least palliate my offence."

"Indeed, M. Gramont," replied he, "I believe it is fair to say that your dilemma was by no means a common one, and when I speak to Mrs. Lawrence, you may be assured I will advocate on your behalf. I am persuaded you have acted in the interest of assuring the safety of Mrs. Lawrence and her family, not to mention my beloved Miss Reckert."

I thanked him most sincerely for his kind intention. He told me he had made further inquiries after the Baird brothers and had learnt that barrel of black powder was found in their home once he had ordered their arrest.

"I shudder to think what your former friend intended," said he, "needless to say you may tell M. Tolouse that the magistrate who detained him in Fern, Mr. Appleton, has assured me he no longer means to make any charge against him for what he describes as an 'accidental service to the neighbourhood.'"

I told him I would relay the message, and shortly after that I took leave, wishing him joy once more in parting.

I did not dare to attempt to visit Stearn Manor before I left. I called at Peldon Manor, but as luck would have it, the two young ladies were on a walk, and I saw only Mme. Gaspar before departing.

Since leaving the area several days ago I have had little inclination to write. I made inquires for Mme. Dorrel in several places without luck, and begin to think I should have requested Philip's help in doing so, to save me from searching in vain for weeks.

* * *

I have heard my first report of Mme. Dorrel in the town of Ashford. It seems her health necessitated she stop here a short time and accept the charity of the proprietor of a local boarding house. She and her children were housed there for several weeks after she had recovered, in order that Mme. Dorrel might work off her debt. The owner of the house, also French, confessed to me that any work Mme. Dorrel could do was always more than out-weighed by the trouble and expense of housing so many children. Though Mme. Dorrel had only accounted for a part of her debt, it was all forgiven in the understanding that they would go elsewhere.

From Ashford, I was pointed westwards in the understanding that Mme. Dorrel meant to travel to a town called Rocksend. This place has proven slightly elusive and I have been forced to remain for a short while in a town called Barnham, to recover from a slight illness. I have been able to determine at least that when I recover, I will only need to go a few miles northeast, where I am told I am sure to find it.

* * *

April 1st, 1793

From Barnham I travelled directly to Rocksend. The route was not as straightforward as I had hoped, but nevertheless, I arrived there in the afternoon. I immediately made inquires after Mme. Dorrel, but found to my despair that no one knew of her. At last I was told there was a town called Lochsend, forty odd miles to the north, which was sometimes mistaken for this.

Not being able to find out what I wished in Rocksend, I had no choice but to set out for Lochsend, though my hopes were not high. By the following evening, I arrived there. Taking a room at the first inn I saw, I inquired after Mme. Dorrel. The landlord remembered the lady immediately, and told me he had agreed to house her and her family for one night only, as he had few other customers and they had little money. He had given them the name of a draper who sometimes employed seamstresses in her little shop. He gave me her information when I asked for it, and although it was too late for me to think of going there instantly, I went to sleep with every expectation of being able to find her soon.

The following morning I went directly to the house of the woman she had mentioned, and after a fair wait, I was able to speak to Mrs. Fenton. In response to my inquires, she said, "Why I know just who you mean, Sir, but it has been nearly three months since she left."

"Left?" cried I, with some frustration. "Do you know where, Madam?"

"I believe the entire family lives in the country now, and from what I have heard, they are very comfortable there."

She offered to find the exact direction and send it to me at the inn, and I thanked her for her trouble.

To spare you exhaustive detail, the next day I travelled out of town to the location given me, which proved to be a very pleasing home, perhaps the size of Courtney Lodge.

I hesitated before going within, having expected to find a family in abject poverty, not a family who bore every appearance of sufficiency. Nevertheless, I had come too far to do anything else, so I went inside and inquired for Mme. Dorrel.

The house was arranged more for convenience then formality, with only one servant visible, who was so incommoded by the children running here and there that she scarcely had time to speak a word to me. She bid me merely to wait in the parlour while she sent to see if her mistress could see me, and in her absence, the children elected to follow me. I have only occasionally had the opportunity to see children in almost any setting at all, so I was quite pleased to find they did so. I felt I could trace some resemblance of their uncle in one or two of them, but I suspect it was mere fancy for me to think so. As I had often done, I began to think how much good my fortune could do them, but as their rosy faces danced and played before me, I could scarce conceive that anything was required. I know not exactly how much time passed before Mme. Dorrel herself entered, for I felt almost hypnotized by the exuberance of her children, for the few children I had seen over the last two years had been restrained by careful parents.

I rose immediately to greet her, being a pleasant looking woman slightly over forty. Her face was careworn, but for the present at least, I saw no sign of anything but contentment.

"Monsieur Gramont," said she, "I am all but sure I do not know thee, but all the same you are quite welcome. To what may I ascribe the honour of your visit?"

I bowed and said, "Forgive me for coming upon you thus all of a sudden, Madam. I knew your brother, M. Rublé, when I was still in France, though only slightly."

We sat down together and she replied, "Then you are still more welcome. If you knew him but slightly, Monsieur, 'twould be enough to know he was a good man, and so must you be, for he befriended no other kind."

I was unprepared for this commendation, and my guilt rose up within me and nearly overpowered me, rendering me incapable of uttering even a syllable.

She looked at me kindly for a short while, waiting for me to state my purpose, but finding me mute, she said, "Pardon me if I am prone to be too frank, M. Gramont, but I have myself only lately been obliged to track down even the most distant connections in the hope of finding the help I sorely needed. Providence has sent a blessing to me and so I say to you, though you hardly seem in want, if there is something I may do for you, do not hesitate to ask for it, as I am more than willing to assist you."

"Madam," said I, almost panting for breath, "I am obliged to you for your offer, but indeed I came here to try to be of some use to you!"

"Indeed!" cried she, "Then you are kind indeed, and had I met you three months ago, I would be only too happy to hear it. But forgive me if I ask what can have prompted you to come all this way to try to find the sister of a man you barely knew?"

"To own the truth, Madam, I fear I wronged your brother when I knew him, and it weighs heavily upon me to this day."

"If you feel you have wronged M. Ruble," said she gravely, "then it is probable you have. My brother had a forgiving temperament, and I am in the habit of thinking that regrets of that sort ought to be buried with the remains of the deceased. As to your intentions, as kindly meant as may be, you may easily see I have no need of anything. You will scarcely find a happier soul alive! You may come upon those who are equally well provided for, that is sure, but only those who have felt the lack of the bare necessities shall estimate their blessings truly as they ought to, and such a one am I."

To hear this I felt entirely at a loss. I congratulated her on her rare good fortune, and without any prompting, she proceeded to tell me how she had come to it.

While working in Mme. Fenton's shop to support her children who lived with her above stairs, she had become acquainted with a fellow emigre from France. He paid her a fair amount of attention, coming daily to the shop seemingly to speak with her. In a very short time he declared himself, and moved herself and her children to this house, which Mme. Dorrel considered a veritable palace.

I congratulated her again at the end of her relation, observing as I did so that her husband was one of the more fortunate emigrés.

"Oh, he is not a nobleman, Monsieur Gramont, he has always told me that. All you see here is merely owing to the generosity of the man he serves, the Marquis de la Croix."

One may only guess how I must have looked at this pronouncement; I have never been more shocked in my life. For a moment or so she waited for me to reply, but presently one of her children fell over and began to cry, and in all the noise and confusion, I could think of doing nothing but taking leave.

I paused when I had nearly gone as far as the door, and begged to know if her husband was away from home. When I could make her understand me, she told me he was expected in a few hours, and so I made a point of telling her where I was staying.

I can hardly describe the jumble of my thoughts at the time. Any conjectures were useless till I had spoken to Philip, and so I resolved to wait for him, nearly wearing a hole in my floor as I did so. It was nearly four hours later that he arrived at the inn, and appeared in my room as the supper dishes were being cleared away.

He looked his customarily inexpressive self, and while I grappled somewhat for how to begin, "I find you have met my wife, dear Sir. You will see I have chosen quite carefully, as I said."

"Carefully indeed!" cried I, "Dear Philip, what is the meaning of all this?"

"I should have thought it would be evident. When we parted in France so many months ago, I thought I might be of service to you by finding Mme. Dorrel, to save you the trouble later. I reasoned that if I found her in want, I may be able to help her in your stead, and so it proved, for there have been many other claims on your assistance since then."

He paused, I gazed, and so he proceeded.

"Mme. Dorrel was indeed in a rather pitiable state, and I felt called upon to do all I could to assist her. When you and I parted, you gave me two commands; one to accept a sum from you, and the other, to look about for a wife. 'Twas natural enough for me to consider that if I married Mme. Dorrel, it would accomplish three of your wishes in one, and as I found her goodnatured and agreeable, I did so at once."

When he had finished, I paced around ruminating on all he had said, and at last I replied, 'This is all very well, but what about my other avowed intention, which you have not mentioned, that of leaving my fortune to Mme. Dorrel and her children?'

"If you will pardon me for saying, dear Monsieur, there seems to be no need for such a thing, for my family is quite well provided for as it is, thanks to your generosity. Were you to do so now, Mme. Dorrel's property would merely come to me as her husband, and I would have no use for it but to preserve it for you as I do now, and in the event you were to find a need for it, or come to your senses and marry, it would be available to your family and your heirs."

To hear this, I was completely deprived of speech, whereupon he added, "I hope you will not be too displeased with me, for though I have acted rather high-handedly, I have only done so in your interest. M. Rublé, whatever kind of man he may have been, is dead.

It was he who sought to confront you; he did his duty, and you did yours. No further amends need be made to anyone. No doubt it is not my place to say so, but I cannot help but implore you to live your life and be at peace."

As he spoke I was occupied considering all he had done for my sake. Such devotion was as unparalleled as it was to me inexplicable. To tie himself to a woman and her children merely that I may be unable to do the penance I wished; I could hardly begin to understand it!

"Dearest Philip," said I, after a while, experiencing equal parts awe, frustration and gratitude, "What compels you to such a sacrifice for my sake?"

"It is hardly a sacrifice, Monsieur, for my wife is a good companion and I have become quite fond of her children."

"I am glad to hear it, and I hope you would not have done so otherwise, though I am hardly convinced of it. But all the same, I cannot help but wonder what can compel you to serve so faithfully a man like myself? No one would be worthy of such devoted service, least of all the last unfortunate representative of an accursed race."

As I spoke I saw a little glint of the hardness I had seen but a few times before. Though my question was somewhat rhetorical, he said, 'For two-hundred and fifty years, the family of Renard has been in the service of the Marquis de La Croix.' I was going to interrupt him but he prevented me. "For two and a half centuries, my ancestors have faithfully served and died for yours. Your father, like his father before him, was a cold, callous man, and since I was a boy of ten, I have carried out his wishes. It was the last wish of my father, and perhaps it had been for his. For forty years I helped your father take from those around him, deny those in need, defraud those he ought to have obliged, punish those he ought to have relieved. My life was in the service of his, as had been my father's and my grandfathers's to his father. I do not mean to repeat myself–."

"I am grieved to hear it," said I, unable to contain myself longer, "but you have merely enforced my point!"

"And you have missed mine," said he, gravely. "Forgive me for speaking this strongly, but could you think that after two and a half centuries of serving the Marquis de La Croix, howsoever he may behave, a descendant of a Renard could be guilty of deserting the first noble-hearted bearer of the name?"

I stood still in astonishment. Having never considered the matter in this light, I could think of no reply to make, no point to counterbalance the one he had made.

For several minutes we remained together in silence. At last, finding that time passed bringing me no form of utterance, Philip bowed, saying only, "If you have no further commands for me, dearest Monsieur, I shall return to my wife and children."

As I still made no reply he merely bowed once more and left.

I shall write more soon. Write if you can. I am ever,

Yours faithfully,
M.C.

Marcel de la Croix to Henri Renault

April 11th, 1793

Dear Friend,

In the hours and days which passed, I considered all of these matters anew. I left the area and wandered aimlessly for several days.

As I travelled I read the book Miss Lawrence had given me. Despite my growing proficiency with English and the comparatively modest size of the book, it took me above a week to complete it.

As the quest for happiness is the subject of Rasselas, I reflected how unworthy I found myself of such, even were it possible to achieve it. And yet the sight of the happiness of Mme. Dorrel, nay, Mme. Renard, had a soothing effect on my conscience. Even before leaving Suffolk, time has lessened the force of my guilt, whereas admiration for Miss Lawrence had quite shamefully weakened my resolve.

For several days I refused to consider availing myself of the freedom Philip's marriage had given me. I say 'refused to consider' yet that did not prevent the idea from occurring to me several times a day.

I shall spare you a minute description of my soul-searching, and only tell you the end result. At last I concluded that making myself miserable in no way atoned for the faults I had committed, and were I to persist in doing so, I would only squander the sacrifice Philip had made on my behalf. Moreover, I reasoned that the events which had taken place before I departed the area made it all the more unlikely that Miss Lawrence would accept me, thus somehow authorizing the attempt.

I know not how you shall view such self-serving logic, but I have decided to return to that area, and shall know presently if my pessimism is as justified as I fear.

* * *

April 15th, 1793

I returned to Courtney Lodge late last night. M. Tolouse was still there, and quite pleased to see me. This morning I slept longer than I intended, and he was gone out by the time I woke up.

I determined at once to call upon the ladies at Peldon Manor, considering I had not been able to see them before my hasty departure several weeks before. Though I had written a short letter since my departure, I had left no return address, and was eager to see and hear how they had been since then. Peldon is not less than four miles from Courtney Lodge in a southerly direction, and therefore it took me more than an hour by horse. When I arrived there, I discovered that the ladies had only recently departed in the direction of Kettich to attend the wedding of Mr. Harland and Miss Reckert.

Having somewhat lost track of time over the last days and weeks, I was quite unprepared for this news. It was with some regret that I retraced my steps to Courtney lodge. As I neared Courtney again, I espied M. Tolouse a short way along the road, heading east in the direction of Kettich. I guessed at once he was on his way to attend the wedding as well, and so caught up to him as quickly as I could.

He was outfitted in his best clothes, and when I inquired as to the obvious, he informed me there was hardly a person in the area who was not going, as Mr. Reckert had issued a general invitation, complete with the promise of entertainment.

He appeared to assume I meant to attend as well, and so told me he would be happy to tell me the latest news after I had returned home to dress, etc.

I could hardly make up my mind about the matter, having a great desire to attend, while an almost equally powerful reluctance to doing so uninvited, and still worse, without having first had the opportunity to renew any of my recent acquaintances thereabouts.

Nevertheless, in the end I returned home almost compulsively, remounting my horse some while later with the vague intent of deciding what I ought to do once I had arrived nearby.

I had not gone very far before I saw ample evidence of what M. Tolouse had declared, for people of every description could be seen making their way by foot or carriage. Music and merriment could be heard from afar and in light of this, I saw no reason to exempt myself. The wedding party was being held outdoors, so I tied my horse and joined the gathering of merrymakers who awaited the new couple.

Distinguished guests were to be seated in the inner garden, which was delineated by the defence walls which remained in most places at half height, while the rest of the grounds slope gently downhill till about half way.

Being as I was uninvited, I had no intention of entering the inner courtyard, but was content to station myself under a tree from which I could observe the scene.

In the many faces who passed by singing and drinking, I saw no sign at all of the rancour which had gripped the area. Unlike in France years before, the peasants and farmers of this area tended to be broader in cheek and middle. With the abundance of food and entertainment Mr. Reckert had arranged, every person present seemed ready to bless their host and the new couple. Many spontaneous toasts were offered in the crowd, where the general public had accommodated themselves on tables, which were somewhat limited, stumps or benches, but most upon the universal green bounty provided by Mother Nature.

It was dusk when the noise of the crowd announced the approach of the happy couple. They were truly an inspiring sight, seeming in that moment to represent at once all the happiness, beauty and hope at the height of mortal aspiration. Amongst the onlookers it was declared there never had been a more beautiful woman than Miss Reckert, a more honourable man than Mr. Harland, and not a person could be found to dispute that Mr. Reckert was the most generous, good-natured fellow alive.

I was closer to the path of the procession than I had expected and as the tree I stood by was on a tiny hill, I came in full view of them both. Miss Reckert smiled to see me, but yet it must be said that she smiled frequently beforehand as well. Mr. Harland seemed pleased to see me, and motioned for me to follow, but as I guessed it was mere politeness, I did not attempt to do so. Several minutes later, however, as I was looking around, a servant came to inform me that Mr. and Mrs. Harland begged the pleasure of my company.

I was quite moved by this gesture and followed immediately. Mr. Harland rose from his place to greet me, and I congratulated him again, complimenting him on the very scope of the celebration.

"The credit for it must be reserved for Mr. Reckert, for left to myself, I am unlikely to plan such a lavish celebration, if only to avoid drawing out the evening. Howsoever that may be, we are all very pleased to see you, and I beg you will consent to join us in celebration," with which he indicated for me to be seated at the main table, a short distance away from he and his bride.

Doing so at once I found myself situated near the end of the table, between Mr. Seymour and Mrs. Churling, whose name I recalled from Mouchard's story. Mr. Churling sat beside his wife, and across from him was Mrs. Lawrence, whose daughter likewise faced his wife.

You will have little difficulty believing my acknowledgments were clumsy indeed. I did not know most of the other occupants of the table, yet I guessed the lady seated near Mr. Harland was his sister. Mr. Green and his wife were on the far corner from myself. Glancing at the next table, I saw at once M. Tolouse, Mme. Gaspar, Mlle de Courteline and Mlle Vallon, the last two regarding me with astonishment. As always, Mlle Vallon seemed more pleased than surprised, and her cousin seemed more surprised than pleased.

During our meal, Mrs. Churling gave me to understand that my place had been initially reserved for Mr. Harland's nephew, Mr. Whinston, who had sent word at the last moment that he was prevented from attending. Seeing as I did not seem likely to appreciate the full reasons for him doing so, she dropped half a dozen hints on the subject of his disappointment. Mr. Reckert was seated on the other side of Mr. Seymour, (rather than at the head of the table, where places had not been set at all) and the two spoke happily throughout the meal. Many toasts of joy were raised, throughout which a theme of astonishment was consistent. Presently, after a certain amount of wine had been consumed all around, Mr. Reckert prevailed upon Mr. Seymour to retell what he had told him in private as to his theory of how this 'whole improbable business' had come about, having claimed to have understood it himself at last.

"Begging the pardon of the groom in advance," began Mr. Seymour, upon which Mr. Harland accorded him a nod of the head, "who if he objects, ought to find fault with his new father, who knows exactly what I shall say. Quite simply, after a fair amount of deliberation, I have satisfied myself that it is vanity itself on the part of the gentleman which has brought this match about!"

Mr. Harland smiled with surprise to hear it, while the new Mrs. Harland blushed with confusion. Mr. Seymour continued, emboldened by the laugh he had raised.

"Why then, as I told Mr. Reckert, like many of you I was surprised at first to hear of this match–."

Here someone had cried out 'all' in place of 'many,' and so Mr. Seymour took up his sentence again, saying with mock gravity, "Like all of you, I was surprised to hear of this match, having been convinced anything was more likely. This being the case I wracked my memory to think what might have brought it about, and in doing so recalled a time the gentleman and I had been together in Bristol. Along with the other revered persons present, I had not been accustomed to thinking Mr. Harland a vain man, and so was surprised one night to interrupt him occupied examining himself in a little pocket mirror. I say 'interrupt' yet perhaps it is not the proper word, for I am not entirely sure he was aware of my presence. I explained that I had left some papers behind earlier, but he hardly looked up at the sound of my voice. I retrieved my papers so as not to disturb him, and then waited a moment to take leave. I soon found it was no purpose to do so, for the gentleman continued to look in the mirror as if he had never seen his own reflection before. Consulting this remembrance only lately, I became convinced that it was this very day when the trouble began, or so I once thought it. Accordingly, I have deduced the following: that as a result of this examination, Mr. Harland apparently concluded that nothing should prevent him from aspiring to the most beautiful, and one might also add, the most discerning woman in the county. At first, it shall be fair to say, Miss Reckert was not entirely of his opinion, but gradually it seems that the self-approbation of the gentleman, who continued his suit without encouragement, must have been apparent to her. However it came about, Mr. Harland was at last able to assure the lady he was her equal, and whether as a result of pity or persuasion, it is evident that he prevailed in the end."

Broad laughter followed his speech, and a loud toast was raised to 'Vanity!' in which Mr. Harland joined as heartily as any, confessing that he feared his happiness was owing more to pity than anything else. Mrs. Harland had blushed through the telling and seemed quite relieved when Mr. Seymour had done, and grateful for Mr. Harland's interposition.

Lively conversations resumed after this as nearly everyone was in high spirits.

You shall not be surprised when I confess to looking frequently in the direction of Miss Lawrence throughout the meal, but while she returned my look without displeasure, her expression wore little sign of the light-hearted character of our former interactions. Her mother likewise seemed ill-at-ease in my company, though as civil as ever.

Nearing the end of our meal, I was somewhat consternated to find a letter placed in my hand by a servant. I assumed at first it was a mistake, seeing that no one could possibility know to find me here, but upon seeing the name 'M. Gramont' written clearly upon, I excused myself to read it.

When I broke open the seal, I was amazed to see Mouchard's neat hand, and read the following:

Dear M. Gramont,

I write to you from a carriage nearby. What joyous sounds reach my ears, even from here! Since we parted, I travelled to London in the hope of hearing some news of my mother, the Viscountess de Vitteaux. To my great joy, I discovered not only that she was alive and in good health, but had been living in London these last five years. It seems she left France several months after she sent me to England, and after searching in vain for any trace of myself or Mr. Grey, had at last settled in London in despair. There is no time for me to describe the joy of our reunion, so I must trust you can imagine it.

Presently, we travel together to Austria and by my request, my mother has been kind enough to direct our route through this area. Arriving nearby several days ago, we heard of the blessed event to take place, and I begged her to remain till this night at least. I cannot write more at present, but you may imagine my mother is as grateful to Miss Reckert as I am myself.

Such happiness! Such merriment tonight! It is perceptible even from the carriage where I write. Miss Reckert is happy, I am sure of it. I only wish I might see it for myself. It is not possible, I know, and it is enough to feel assured it is so.

I cannot bear to think that any uncertainty on my account might diminish Miss Reckert's happiness. Though I long to throw myself at her feet and receive her blessing from her lips, I fear my guilt and self-consciousness shall ever forbid it. Instead, my mother intends to write a long letter of explanation to her from Austria.

I cannot resist the urge to thank you, while I may, for what you have done, of which the whole area speaks. You have my eternal gratitude.

Dear Sir, may blessings rain down upon you for your life,

Your ever most obliged and faithful servant,
Mouchard (Viscount de Vitteaux)

You may imagine that such a letter was beyond my expectation. I returned to the table hardly recovered from reading it.

When dessert had been eaten, Mr. Reckert announced that there would be a small display of fireworks for his guests, and so we all made ready to follow the new couple to where they were to take place. A multitude of children preceded them, while the rest of us followed behind, and still more came behind us, amidst much cheering and throwing of flowers.

Our procession wound its way through the garden till at last we stopped where seats had been set out for the married pair to observe the display.

Miss Reckert, nay, Mrs. Harland, seemed discomforted at being the centre of attention, but soon enough our eyes were turned towards the heavens to observe the fireworks. I had never had opportunity to see such a thing before, and watched with great delight. Once they were finished, the procession started again, and this time proceeded in the direction of Mr. Harland's residence.

Mr. and Mrs. Churling walked together, and I as prepared to keep company of the Lawrences, Mrs. Lawrence declared she could not think of walking that far, and commended her daughter to my care, seeming somewhat relieved of the necessity of speaking to me.

Miss Lawrence and I set out together alone, but as she did not venture to speak directly, I could not think exactly how to do so myself. At last I said, "I was going to observe my dismay to find Mrs. Lawrence does not seem entirely delighted to see me, yet I fear the same may be said for her daughter."

"Indeed, Monsieur, in light of the distressing revelations we have heard since your departure, I am sure you cannot wonder much to encounter some discomfort."

Her manner was reserved and subdued, in stark contrast to the gaiety I had ever known her to exhibit. I sighed to see it, and after a brief hesitation, said, 'I confess I hardly know how to acquit myself, yet I had hoped somehow I might not have forfeited your friendship.'

"Though I do not claim to understand all which has occurred, yet I realize my family owes you great obligation for your care of us, though we were but strangers to you. For this you have my greatest gratitude. Nor can it be doubted that over the last several months, we have enjoyed the company of M. Gramont. All the same, you must forgive me for saying that till several weeks ago, all I felt certain I knew of you was that your name was Gramont, you were a friend of M. Hubert, and your circumstances were avowedly modest. Will you be surprised to discover some reluctance to forwarding a friendship the entire basis of which may no longer be relied upon, and is by all appearance the very opposite of what it seemed?"

All the while we spoke, our processional continued over the hills in the direction of Mr. Harland's home. For some while I was completely at a loss to reply, and as Miss Lawrence somewhat quickened her pace, I saw she meant to discourage it.

Presently, we reached a narrow woodland path quite overgrown with thick greenery, along which we were obliged to walk in single-file. When we emerged into a clearing, the other house became visible across the lawn and Mr. and Mrs. Harland paused to take leave of the crowd of well-wishers. Amidst further cheers and fanfare, they were at last permitted to proceed alone to the house.

Miss Lawrence and I watched them disappear longer than most, and when at last we turned to walk, we were some of the last.

There was very little light by which to see our way back and we were obliged to keep pace with the party ahead of us, so as to not lose the light provided by their torches and lanterns. Presently I acquired one of the torches which had been lit along the path, that we might walk somewhat slower.

"Indeed, Miss Lawrence," began I, at long last, "whatever my name once was, it has been Gramont since I arrived in England, and I have no intention for it to be otherwise. The modesty of my situation–."

"Pardon me, M. Gramont," began she, preventing me from going further, "I had no idea of putting you to any explanation, but only wished to account for the distance you complain of, by which I was far from wishing to offend you."

With a sensation of desperation, I realized she meant this to be the last conference between us, and as I reflected it was no longer appropriate for me to call at Stearn Manor, I felt it was imperative to say more.

I closed the distance between us again and said, "You will wonder I continue to persecute you when it is clear you want nothing more to do with me, and yet I cannot help it. It was to provide the very explanation you claim unnecessary that I have returned, and so must beg you most earnestly to hear me."

Miss Lawrence paused in apparent surprise and irresolution, then said, "I fear I do not understand you, Sir. Permit me to hope you have not truly taken such trouble on my account?"

"Rather on my own account, Madam, for I know not how to do otherwise. I am sure you will not profess surprise when I say that I adore you, for it is what I have hardly concealed. When I left several weeks ago, I believed an insurmountable obstacle prevented me from aspiring to your favour. My surprise was great to discover this obstacle had been unexpectedly removed, and so I resolved to return here at once and make the attempt, however hopeless. Yet even to do so would require a long and painful explanation I fear you will hardly have the patience to hear, and yet I beg you most earnestly to permit it!"

Miss Lawrence regarded me with astonishment, but after a moment or two, her demeanour uncharacteristically grave, she said, "I would not wish to appear ungrateful to one it would seem we owe so much, yet I am reluctant to give you the trouble of such an explanation in the context of a suit I fear has very little chance of success. Forgive my directness, M. Gramont, but I feel it would be a greater form of cruelty to encourage you."

"You need not fear doing so, Madam, and I am certain I shall not know peace till I account for myself as well as I am able."

By now we had reached the crowd again. As we attempted to pass through the multitudes, we heard a band of fiddlers begin to play to our left, and scarcely a moment later, throngs of lively men and women began to make their way to the dancing green. Miss Lawrence was slightly ahead of me as we began to climb a slight hill, and we were unavoidably separated by the streams of would-be dancers who flocked to where we were.

When I looked up to find where she was, I saw with dismay that she had returned to the party of her mother, where I was reluctant to follow her. After a short while it began to rain and the many parties arranged on the grass began to gather their belongings and depart. What began as a light shower soon turned into a heavy one, and a general cry was raised to procure carriages and umbrellas.

Observing Mlle de Courteline, Mlle Vallon and Mme. Gaspar some ways away, I excused myself to assist them. They had already sent a servant for the carriage, but I pledged to see that it was brought as soon as possible, and so went to the front court in an attempt to do so.

The line of carriages and those waiting for them was very long. There was little hope of doing anything until the crowd had thinned somewhat, but as I waited I espied the Lawrences waiting for their own carriage, which was the third in line. As they only had one umbrella between mother and daughter, I moved nearby to offer the use of mine.

Mrs. Lawrence civilly acknowledged my attempt, but her daughter merely seemed discomforted and begged me not to take any trouble on her account, observing that I was likely to get wet myself. You may well imagine I did not heed this request, and after a short wait, the carriage moved forward.

I handed Mrs. Lawrence into the carriage first, but as I prepared to assist her daughter, I could not help but say, "Will Miss Lawrence refuse to hear me then?"

She hesitated somewhat before saying, "If you are intent upon doing so, despite what I have said, I shall not attempt to prevent you. My walking habits have not changed since you have been gone."

Though it was a small concession indeed, I could not help but be elated. There was no time for acknowledgments, however, for I was obliged to hand her into the carriage, whereupon they were soon out of sight.

I waited there some while longer in order to find the other ladies' carriage. When at last I saw it begin to approach, I went to fetch them directly.

"Have you come by carriage yourself?" inquired Mme. Gaspar, "for if you have come by horse, 'tis sure you ought to accompany us home in the carriage. There is plenty of room."

I accepted the offer at once.

"We were very surprised to see you, Monsieur," continued she, once we were in the carriage, "for we had no idea you meant to come back directly."

"Nor did I, in truth. I called at Peldon just this afternoon, where I discovered you had already left here. I am glad to find you are all in good health?"

Mlle de Courteline had not yet spoken a word to me, and at last I felt obliged to ask if I had been so unhappy as to displease her?

"No indeed," replied she, "and yet since your departure, I must say we have heard the most remarkable, the most unaccountable things!"

"I cannot guess what they may be," replied I, still somewhat distracted, and little thinking what she alluded to.

"Can you not?"

I begged her to tell me what it was she meant, but guessed in the moment she declared it.

"Why it is merely that these last few weeks you are everywhere reported to be the Marquis de la Croix!"

I had neglected entirely to consider how such news would impact her, and unable to think how to respond immediately, I was cross with myself for not anticipating the question.

Mlle de Courteline looked at me all the while, at last saying, "You do not mean to reply, Monsieur? Surely you do not mean to say it is true?"

"It is a question of some delicacy," replied I, faltering somewhat. "You will perhaps recall that I told you myself on one occasion that the name I have adopted here is not the one I was born to."

"And yet, the Marquis de la Croix! It is impossible, surely!"

"If you wish it so."

"I beg you to be explicit."

"I mean to be so, but I fear you are not inclined to hear me."

"If you assert it, of course I should not contradict it, but pray tell us at once."

"My name is M. Gramont, yet there was a time I was known as Marcel de la Croix, when my late father, the Marquis de la Croix, was still alive."

"Astonishing!" was the response. Presently she added, "But come, how is it you did not ever mention this before, even when you knew how uncomfortable I was to accept the help of a man I did not know!"

"As you did not know me by any name, I fail to see what difference that would have made."

"But truly it would have made a world of difference in my view."

"I fear we are not destined to see eye-to-eye on this subject."

"Forgive me," persisted she, "but it was always my opinion that your humble origins alone had prejudiced you so!"

"Indeed, yet it is often observed that familiarity breeds contempt."

"'Tis nearly unaccountable! But how shall we address you?"

"The same as you have done. I have no intention of setting up as a Marquis in England. French nobility shall be of little significance here while they are no longer acknowledged in France."

To this Mlle de Courteline made no reply, and after a moment or two, Mlle Vallon declared, "Indeed, M. Gramont, I began to fear we should never see you, whatever you might be called! How happy I was to see you tonight. To think, Mr. Harland and Miss Reckert are married! What a pretty couple they make; I could have looked at them for hours."

Mlle Vallon and I maintained the conversation for much of the way home. I had neglected to bring up the subject of Mr. Etheredge with her before my departure, and so could not help inquire whether he had called at Peldon. She replied ingenuously that he had done so once or twice, but that on the second occasion, Miss Lawrence was also visiting. After his departure, Miss Lawrence had observed her uneasiness, and invited her to confide the cause of her disturbance. Once she had done so, she told me that Miss Lawrence did not wholly approve of the gentleman's conduct, and advised Mlle Vallon to proceed cautiously and make no sudden decisions.

Mlle Vallon followed her advice to the letter, and gradually Mr. Etheredge has discontinued his visits.

I could not help but be charmed to find that Miss Lawrence continued to visit them since my departure, and even seen fit to guide them when necessary.

I would not be so foolish as to draw any favourable conclusions regarding myself, however, yet I could not help but be happy to hear it.

Tomorrow I shall go in search of Miss Lawrence. I know you will be almost as anxious on my behalf as I am myself.

* * *

April 20th, 1793

The day after the wedding I hastened to the area between Gibbons and the construction, where I had often encountered Miss Lawrence, with the hope of meeting her there. To confess the truth, I was upon my third round of the area when I finally encountered her.

Her demeanour was still grave and I could see she was far from at ease to see me. I acknowledged my gratitude that she was willing to hear me but at every moment she seemed on the verge of retracting her consent, I began an account of my history which might best be described as clumsy and incomplete.

At first, Miss Lawrence listened with a polite silence as I described my upbringing and the conditions in France. When I came to a description of the night which had altered my fate, I attempted to pass over all mention of M. Hubert as quickly as may be, but to my surprise Miss Lawrence requested clarification on several points in connection with this, by which I saw she guessed much of what I did not reveal.

When I mentioned that Mr. Harland might have already informed her of these particulars, she revealed that while Mr. Harland had spent a lengthy time in conversation with her mother, she knew very little of the matter herself. She told me that shortly thereafter, Mrs. Lawrence had arranged for M. Hubert to live with another relative of theirs, a single man and a priest, which I could not but rejoice to hear.

At last we approached Stearn Manor and I prepared to take my leave of her, daring to ask if she might allow me to seek her the following day. "Indeed, Monsieur, you may rely upon what I have already said. And yet, hearing how you have suffered at the hands of my uncle, I cannot forebear expressing my astonishment that you have had patience for his relations? How is it possible you have always been so calm and amiable to myself and my mother, considering all you have told me?"

"Since I discovered the state of your uncle's senses, (a time I have not yet arrived at in my relation), I have thought of him as little as possible. My reasons for seeking admittance into your house were curiosity and concern, but the very moment I knew you, I felt only admiration and the desire to serve you. M. Hubert's presence was at times difficult to bear, but for the most part, his apparent instability merely strengthened my determination to remain nearby in the hope of averting any danger you might unknowingly have been exposed too."

Miss Lawrence said nothing and presently I was obliged to take leave. The following day I came across Miss Lawrence on merely my second round, and it seemed she was less uneasy to see me. Possibly for this reason, I was able to tell my story with greater coherence, managing to describe my partnership with Lafont and the many regrets I had on that front, ending with the death of M. Rublé.

Once we reached Stearn Manor, Miss Lawrence regarded me with a strange kind of earnestness I had not seen before, but merely thanked me for my relation.

The following day, I encountered her at approximately the same spot as before. Though she listened to me with the same attentiveness she had previously, I was pleasantly surprised to see some small signs of her former carefree demeanour had resurfaced.

On this day, I described how I had encountered M. Hubert, and from there how I had travelled to England in search of Mme. Dorrel. I made no mention of Mouchard, but told her I had chanced to hear that M. Hubert was settled with a family hereabouts, and so was curious enough to see for myself. As soon as I had done so, I told her I felt compelled to remain till I could be certain regarding Lafont.

To my surprise, she had heard very little of what had transpired on the night he had died, and compelled me to describe it in full. I described the result of my attempt to locate Mme. Dorrel, at last ending with the discovery I made having done so.

"Dearest Miss Lawrence," said I thereafter, "I hesitate to inquire what you have made of my tale, and fear that you will think me the most presumptuous of men to sue for your hand in spite of all I have told you."

I was hardly encouraged to find she wore a look of some perplexity, and after some little hesitation, she said: "Forgive me, M. Gramont, for I confess that although you have been so good as to give me so complete an account of your life, I am tempted to inquire into something you have not mentioned, but which I had anticipated might be included in your recital."

I assured her I was perfectly willing to tell her anything she would condescend to ask, acknowledging at the same time that I had no idea what it could pertain to.

"You will recall," began she, "that on the night of the wedding between Mr. Harland and Miss Reckert, you received a letter during dinner. I could not help but notice that it had an impact upon you. Though I am ashamed of my own curiosity, in the context of your story, I have been unable to account for it, and although you have made no mention of it, I cannot entirely rid myself of the sense it is nonetheless significant."

"You are justified in think so, my dear Miss Lawrence, and you may be assured I would have done so were I at liberty to. The letter was from the Viscount of Vitteaux, who wrote under the cover of his mother, who I have not the happiness to know. Although I am not at liberty to reveal the subject of his letter, I can assure you it does not pertain directly to me, nor would reflect any discredit upon me were it known. Were it otherwise, I would have discovered a way to confess it without betraying the trust vested in me. In any case, I have reason to believe that the matter shall be at least partially brought to light in a short time by the Viscount himself or his mother. In that case, I trust I shall hear about it no earlier than yourself or any other."

"Your words are nothing short of incomprehensible to me, M. Gramont," replied she, "but after all you have said, it would be perverse of me to believe you capable of concealing any shortcomings you believed yourself to have."

"Permit me to ask in turn what it was you suspected?"

Miss Lawrence blushed and did not reply immediately, "I am sure I ought to emulate your candour, M. Gramont, but it does not come so naturally for me to find fault with myself, and still worse, am more inclined to conceal my weaknesses than declare them!"

"Your very acknowledgement belies your claim," replied I.

"In that case I shall confess that your emotion at receiving the letter the other evening convinced me one that of the things you meant to confess was a prior attachment, and as I felt completely incapable of accepting a man who has betrayed the smallest promise to one of my own sex, I hardly know how to understand you have done nothing of the sort. As to your story in general, it is indeed a sobering one in many respects, and I have been most sincerely affected to hear it. My opinions coincide almost entirely with those you have formed in hindsight, but in other respects, I am inclined to agree with your dear Philip's assessment of your culpability. In unusual circumstances, often one's actions will not withstand scrutiny. Though you are inclined to find fault with yourself, it is certain your intention was ever to do what was right, however difficult that may have been to determine. Far from damaging my opinion of you, I must acknowledge that your tale has only increased the respect and esteem I bear you. More than anything else, it strikes me that the severity with which you appraise your own failings gives one the best understanding of the nobleness of your character. Few women, I fear, may boast such knowledge of their suitors."

"Dearest Miss Lawrence, it would be cruel indeed for you to treat my faults so gently did you intend to refuse me in the end!" cried I, with delight I made no effort to disguise. "And what do you make of my backwardness in regard to wealth, and indeed, my unwillingness to make use of a fortune I feel little right to? Indeed, I shall not scruple to own it is the point on which I feel the greatest uncertainty, and so I beg you will tell me without reserve."

"Of all you have told me, it is what has concerned me least, or perhaps I ought to say where we are most alike. Yet I cannot help wonder if you have fully considered what you do in attempting to connect yourself for life to a woman whose uncle has– nay, I shall not say more. You may easily imagine it is the part of your story which gave me the most pain."

"It would be unpardonable indeed to confound Miss Lawrence with the crimes of her uncle. Yet I beg you, do not delay any further giving me your decision, for my hope outstrips my patience."

"In that case," said she, with a smile of infinite sweetness, "I must tell you I accept your offer wholeheartedly."

I hardly remember what was said thereafter.

After we had talked some while longer, I ventured to inquire if she would be content to be known as Mrs. Gramont. She assured me at once she would accept no other title, save from Philip alone, who may call her how he wished.

"I fear it would be useless to try to prevail upon him to do otherwise. But yet, did you not once tell me you desired a title?"

She laughed at this recollection, but said, "I meant merely to punish you for the impertinence of your question, though I confess I little imagined at the time that you were perfectly able to answer my imaginary requirements!"

"Indeed," replied I. "I felt certain I had a very small chance at least when you said you had no requirements in terms of 'appearance, character or accomplishments.'"

"Were I to strongly contradict you in such matters," replied she, "I fear you would become used to a diet of flattery, and that would not do for a precedent."

My dear Sir, in the days which have passed since then, I have only discovered greater perfections in my dear Miss Lawrence, and further similarities in our ways of looking at the world.

I shall send this letter to you now. If you are still inclined to visit England, do so now, I beg you, for I am as settled as I ever intend to be. Dear Sir,

I am your servant,
Marcel Gramont

The Right Honourable Mr. Kerns, Minister to his Majesty King George III to Mr. Seymour

September 24th, 1793

Dear Sir,

I have but a moment to convey to you the encouraging result of the conference with his Majesty on the subject of the longstanding abeyance respecting the properties of the distinguished late Earl of C.

His Majesty instructed me to assure interested parties that he is by no means insensitive to the inconvenience the unavoidable delay resolving this matter has occasioned. I showed him the letter you were pleased to send me on the subject, and he empowered me to tell you that his opinion does not contradict your own.

His Majesty is obliged to take a short trip out of London, but intends to give the matter his full attention as soon as he returns. You will be happy to learn that at present he is convinced that no descendant of the Earl of C is more suited to succeed him than Mr. Harland.

It is my understanding that his Majesty means to congratulate that gentleman on the occasion of his nuptials, and no doubt he shall write more particularly to that point.

Dear Sir, I have the honour to be,

Your most obliged,
R. Kerns